"We thought somebody was being mugged," Sestius said in a low voice. "We knocked the door open and then . . . sir, what *is* this?"

The creature's torso was segmented like one fashion of body armor. There was a collar of tiny tentacles, only inches long, where a human's shoulders would have been. At approximately the midpoint of the body was a girdle of three larger arms spaced evenly around the circumference. The limbs were hardened, like the body itself, but the thin hoops of chitin with which they were covered made them as flexible as a cat's tail.

"Yeah, Calvus," Aulus Perennius whispered. "that's a good question. What is it?"

"An adult," said the bald man, "a Guardian. There should be five more of them. They are your opponents."

BIRDS OF PREY

Tor Books by David Drake

DAVID DRAKE
BIRDS OF PREY

A TOM DOHERTY ASSOCIATES BOOK

BIRDS OF PREY

Copyright © 1984 by David Drake

A Tor Book
Published by Tom Doherty Associates, Inc.
49 West 24th Street
New York, N.Y. 10010

Cover art by Michael Whelan

ISBN: 0-812-51356-8

First Tor edition: August 1985

Printed in the United States of America

0 9 8 7 6 5 4 3

For Glenn Knight, with whom I have spent the past several years proving that a few thousand miles' separation need not affect a friendship.

ACKNOWLEDGMENTS

A lot of people helped me in the writing of this novel. Among the most significant helpers were Glenn and Helen Knight, who gave me a guided tour of Cilicia and points east; Jim Baen, who was in at the beginning and provided great help and support of various kinds along the way; and my wife, Jo, whose calm support helped me out of a lot of the pits I dug for myself.

CHAPTER ONE

The leader of the mob carried the head of a lion with six-inch fangs. It was on a stake just long enough for him to wave it as a standard while he bawled a slogan back to his followers.

Aulus Perennius, a block and a half down the street, could not make out the words. It was only reflex, anyway, that made him want to jot down the slogan in his mind, to freeze the faces of the mob's first rank for a later report. Beside Perennius, Gaius reached under his cloak. "Rome isn't our assignment," Perennius said to the younger man. "What we do now is get out of the way. It'd peeve Navigatus no end if I got trampled to death a couple blocks from Headquarters after he went to all this effort to call me back to Rome."

Perennius had spoken lightly, but he was muttering a curse that was more general than the immediate situation as he stepped into an alcove. A barred door there served one of the larger units of the apartment block. The common stairways to the third through sixth floors were open, but they were already disgorging a rabble which would join the mob for entertainment. Gaius, Perennius' protégé from his home village of Doklea, slid into the doorway beside him.

Aulus Perennius was five feet nine inches tall, a touch above the median. He was a blocky, powerful man with hands hard enough to be a stone mason's and a face as weathered as a field slave's. His tunic and dark blue cloak were both of better quality than a laborer could have afforded, however. It did not require the angular shape of a short sword beneath his cloak to give him a military appearance. Perennius looked to be a forty-year-old soldier of Illyrian descent. That was what he would in fact have been, had he not become an agent of the Bureau of Imperial Affairs ten years before.

Gaius was half the agent's age; taller, slimmer—a cheerful-looking youth, and that not only by contrast to his dour companion. He too wore a sword, a cavalry spatha long enough to project beneath the hem of his cloak.

Perennius stared at the mob. He knew that it was not the cause of the collapse of everything he had spent his life trying to preserve. It was no more than a symptom of that collapse. The agent's expression was nonetheless that of a man who had lived so closely with anger and death that they might now be his only friends.

The bow shock of the mob was clearing the street ahead of it. Rain earlier that afternoon had left a slick shimmer of mud and filth on the paving stones, since the sewer beneath was blocked. A sedan chair came to grief as it tried to turn around. One of the bearers lost his footing and the whole rig came down on him with a crash and a scream. The woman inside tumbled through the curtains and fouled her silk tunics in the muck. "Dressed like a whore!" Perennius whispered savagely, but she was too old to owe her success to that. No doubt she was an official's wife, tarted up just as his mistresses were.

Gaius started to go to her aid. The agent's hand stopped him. The woman stood on her own hefty legs and screamed at her chairmen. An onlooker scooped up a handful of mud from the gutter and flung it at her with a taunt in Aramaic. The woman cursed back in the same language, but there were more hands dipping toward the gutter and the mob itself was closing fast. The woman gathered her skirts and darted for the relatively dry surface of the covered sidewalk to make her escape.

Her servants followed her. Three of them snatched up their poles and strutted off with the chair. They were in trouble enough for falling. Loss of the vehicle besides would invite a level of punishment worse than anything

they could expect at the hands of the mob. The fourth
bearer limped along behind his fellows. He squeezed his
right thigh with both hands as if to force out the pain of
the bruise it had received between a brace and the stone
pavement.

Shops were closing abruptly. Like the upper-class
woman, they were obvious targets for the mob that would
at other times comprise their clientele. The manager of
the wineshop in the alcove next to Perennius slammed
down his shutter without even delaying long enough to
tug in the cups chained to the counter. His three patrons
kept an eye on the approaching tumult as they slurped
their mixtures of water and powerful African wine. In a
bread shop on the ground floor of the building across the
street, a lounger tried to snitch a roll. He squawked as the
counterman caught his wrist and pinned his forearm to
the limestone counter with the iron-edged shutter. The
hasp of the padlock within must have had enough reach
to close despite the impediment, because the loafer continued to scream even as the mob boiled past him.

The counterman was almost certainly a slave, perhaps
not even the person responsible to the absentee owner for
management of the shop. He had acted not from necessity
or even from personal involvement. In frustration and an
anger more general than the immediate impetus, he had
lashed out against the closest permissible target.

Perennius felt a rush of fellowship for the counterman
as he watched the thief screaming. His palm sweated on
the worn bone hilt of his sword.

The mob streamed past with the ragged implacability
of the tide on a strand. The front ranks were of husky men
who probably had a purpose. They were shouting, "Down
with Baebrio!" The slogan meant little to Perennius and
perhaps less to the jeering multitude following those
leaders. This was simply entertainment for most of the
crowd, the landless and jobless, the helpless and hopeless.
They would pour on, shouting and smashing, until a company of the Watch was mustered to block them. Perhaps
by that time, their numbers would have grown so that it
was the Watch instead that scattered in a hail of bricks
and roof tiles. If the riot went that far, it would last a day

or more before squadrons of imperial cavalry arrived
from Milan to wash the streets clear with blood.

Thugs with cudgels were running down the sidewalks
like outriders, banging on doors and shutters. Gaius and
the agent were hidden by their dark cloaks and the shade
of the pillar-supported sidewalk covering. A thug who
had just bellowed something back at his companions recoiled in surprise from the alcove. He was young and
burly, with a touch of Germanic pallor to his face. The
cudgel that had halted in surprise he now cocked back
with a snarl and a curse. He did not know the pair of
them or care about them as men, but license faced control and reacted to it like acid on lime.

As the cudgel rose, Perennius grinned and spread his
cloak with his left hand. His sword had been slung
centurion-fashion from the left side of his equipment belt.
It was that sword rather than the ball-pommeled dagger
in the other scabbard that poised to respond to the club.
But it was the grin that froze the thug, not the twenty
inches of bare steel in Perennius' hand. The fellow dropped
his weapon and rushed on.

"Let him go," Perennius ordered as Gaius lunged to
catch the man. He was nothing but flotsam on a dirty
stream. Perennius, a cloaked figure in the shadows, would
be forgotten by nightfall. The death the agent had been so
willing to offer would be forgotten also, until it came
calling again in a tavern brawl or a drunken misstep. The
thug did not matter to the world, and to Perennius he was
only the latest of the hundreds who, for one reason or
none, had considered killing him.

More interesting than that exchange was the head of
the cat which was both banner and probable occasion for
the mob. The great canines winked like spear-points from
the upper jaw. Perennius had seen cats as big, but he had
never seen one similarly armed. The folk surging down
the street past the agent were inured to strangeness by
the beast shows of the Circus, but this was to them also a
unique marvel, an omen like a cow which spoke or thun-
der from a clear sky. It was reason enough for riot; it, and
the barren wasteland of their lives.

Perennius felt the cat grin at him as it was swept past; but the feeling, of course, was nonsense.

Ten minutes after the head of the mob had passed, the street was empty enough that Gaius and Perennius could walk against what had been the flow. The agent was weary from a journey of over a thousand straight-line miles—and he had not traversed them in a straight line. He was used to being weary. He was used to being delayed as well. Throughout the past six months, Perennius had been delayed repeatedly because the draft transferring funds to his account in Antioch had not arrived.

The agent had made do because he was the sort of person who did make do. Perennius had never learned patience, but he knew the value of restraint and the power of necessity. The banker in Antioch had advanced some money and more information when he understood precisely what alternatives the stocky Imperial agent was setting before him. The sum Perennius had set as the bottom line for both of them to walk out of the room alive would not bankrupt the other, even if the "mistake" in Rome were never cleared up.

The banker never seriously considered the possibility that Perennius was bluffing.

The mob had not done a great deal of damage, since its racket was warning enough for most potential victims to drop their shutters or scamper out of the way. Half a dozen shopkeepers had dared a police fine by spreading their merchandise out on the sidewalks in front of their alcoves. Anarchy had punished them more condignly and suddenly than anything the law might have meted out. One old man moaned in the remains of his trampled, looted woolen goods. His wife was chattering in Egyptian as she dabbed blood from the pressure-cut in the fellow's scalp.

Perennius picked his way past them with more anger than sympathy. The Empire would work if everyone obeyed its rules. No one knew better than the agent how great was the Empire's potential if it would cling together, if its millions would accept what the Empire offered them in the knowledge that it was more than they would get from chaos if each went his own way.

But no, Britain and Gaul separated, as if they could deal with the Franks better alone than if they waited for the central army to handle the irruptions across the Rhine after it had blunted more pressing threats. Generals and governors repeatedly tried to parlay their commands into the Imperial regalia. The attempts guaranteed death for the usurpers, death for their rivals, and almost certainly death for the system over which they squabbled and slew. On a lower level, the rabble, dissatisfied with unproductive sloth, rioted in the streets in an apparent desire to smash the mechanism that fed it.

And shopkeepers defied ordinances aimed at keeping open the thoroughfares on which their business depended. Well, let them lie in the street and moan. They'd made their choice.

Somewhere in the building toward which Aulus Perennius walked was a clerk who had made a similarly bad decision. The clerk had siphoned off funds meant for secret intelligence of the Autarch of Palmyra; intelligence that Perennius was risking his life to supply.

The Headquarters of the Bureau of Imperial Affairs, Western Division, was a converted town-house on the edge of the Caelian Hill. It was a two-story structure, lowered over by the six-floor apartment blocks more prevalent in the district. There was little to distinguish Headquarters from private houses elsewhere in Rome. Its façade was bleak and completely windowless on the stuccoed lower story. The upper floor, beyond the threat of graffiti and rubbing shoulders, had been sheathed in marble. The veneering was not in particularly good repair. Missing chips revealed the tufa core. The windows were narrow and barred horizontally. Most of the glazed sashes were swung open for ventilation despite the nip of a breeze to which spring was coming late.

Originally, the lower story had been flanked on all sides by shops just as the neighboring apartment blocks were. The shop doorways had been bricked up when the building was converted to its present use almost eighty years before, during the reign of Commodus. Even at that dis-

tance in time, the windows and doors could be deduced
from shadows on the stucco caused by a moisture content
in the bricks differing from that of the surrounding stone.

The main entrance was off a closed court, not the street
Perennius had been following. He paused on the corner,
sighed and cinched up his equipment belt. The agent was
used to palaces, to great houses, to headquarters of many
sorts; but he had never felt comfortable in this one. It
occurred to him that it was because he had no real business there. There were Imperial agents and informers
throughout Rome, and no doubt the Emperor had as
much need for them here as he did for them anywhere
else in the Empire.

That was not a duty Perennius thought he could live
with, however. On the borders or across them, the agent
could convince himself that he was working to preserve
the Empire. When he was at the core of that Empire, he
saw that the rot, the waste and treachery and peculation,
was as advanced as any nightmare on the borders. What
the dour agent was about to do to a finance clerk was a
personal thing. If Perennius permitted himself to know
that a similar tale could be told of a thousand, a myriad,
highly-placed bureaucrats in the capital, he would also
have had to know that nothing whatever Aulus Perennius
did would have any significant effect.

A pair of armed guards stood in the entrance alcove of
the building. Their round shields, stacked against javelins
in opposite corners of the short passage, were marked
with the blazons of a battalion of the Palatine Foot. The
Palatines were one of the elite formations the Emperor
was forming as a central field army. All the Empire's
borders were so porous that there was no longer a prayer
of dealing with hostile thrusts before they penetrated to
the cities and farmland of the interior. Because the Palatines were an elite, it was all the more frustrating to
Perennius that the younger of the guards had not bothered to wear his body armor.

Both of the uniformed men straightened when they saw
that Perennius and Gaius were not sauntering toward the
apartment block at the end of the court. The lower floors
of that building seemed, from the advertisements painted

on the stucco, to have been converted into an inn and brothel. The guard who called out to Perennius was the older of the pair, a man not far short of the agent's own forty years. "All right, sir," the guard announced with no more than adequate politeness, "if you've got business here, you'll have to state it to us."

"Get up on the wrong side of the bed this morning, straight-leg?" snapped Gaius in reaction to the tone. The young man flopped back the edge of his cloak to display his chest insignia, medallions of silvered bronze. Gaius had been an aide in the Bodyguard Horse before Perennius arranged his secondment to the Bureau as a courier. The morning before, when they had reached Italy—and very nearly the limits of friendly territory—the younger man had unpacked and donned his uniform trappings. That was harmless enough in itself, a boastfulness understandable in an orphan from an Illyrian village no one had ever heard of. What had sent a chill down Perennius' spine was the realization that Gaius had been carrying the gear when he arrived in Palmyra to deliver an urgent message to Perennius.

The situation between Gallienus, who styled himself Emperor of Rome, and Odenathus, who claimed less but perhaps controlled more, was uncertain. The two were not friends ... nor, at the moment, were they clearly at swords' points. Perennius travelled as a spice trader, but that was only a veneer over his claim to be a secret envoy from Postumus, Emperor of the Gauls. Given what the agent had learned in those paired personae, there was very little doubt as to what the Palmyrenes would have done if Gaius' vanity had unmasked the pair of them as agents of the central government.

Of what liked to think of itself as the central government, at any rate.

The older guard reacted about the way Perennius would have reacted had he been on entrance duty. "Don't worry about how I slept, sonny," he said. "Let's just see your pass." The guard wore a shirt of iron ring mail over his tunic. The metal had been browned, but the linen beneath his armpits bore smudges of rust nonetheless. It was that problem of maintenance which led many men to prefer bronze armor or even leather despite the greater strength of the iron.

Of course, a lot of them now were like the younger guard who wore no armor at all. Blazes! See how comfortable they'd be the first time a Frank's spear slipped past the edge of their shields.

The agent reached into his wallet and brought out one of the flat tablets there. It was of four leaves of thin board. The outer two acted as covers for the inner pair. "These are my orders," Perennius said, holding out the diploma. "If they're forgeries, then I've made a hell of a long trip for nothing."

The older guard took the tablet. The wax seal had been broken. He held the document at an angle to the light to see the impression more clearly. The guard's helmet quivered as his high forehead wrinkled beneath it.

"You know," said the younger man as his partner opened the tablet, "just having a pass won't get you farther than the hall. Now, it happens that the receiving clerk is a friend of ours. You understand that everything's open and above-board inside, what with so many, let's say hands, around. But if I were to tip him the wink as I sent you through, then it might save you, hell, maybe a day warming a bench in—"

"Maximus," the older guard said. He looked from the diploma to his companion. Perennius was smiling at the corner of his eye.

"—a bench in the hall," Maximus continued, his conspirator's smile seguing into a quick frown at the partner who was interrupting his spiel.

"Maximus, shut the *fuck* up!" the older man snarled. He thrust the open tablet toward his companion.

What was written on the enclosure was simple and standard. It named Perennius, described him in detail which included his four major scars, and directed him to report to Headquarters—not further identified—with all dispatch. As such, the document served both for orders and for a pass. There was nothing in the written portion to frighten anyone who knew as little about Aulus Perennius as either of the guards could be expected to know.

The tablet had been sealed with the general Bureau signet, a seated woman holding a small sheaf of wheat. It was a hold-over from the days a century before when the organization had officially been the Bureau of Grain Supply. The seal within, at the close of the brusk orders, was a personal one. It impressed in the wax a low relief of a man gripping the steering oar of a ship. Though the guards might never have seen the seal in use before, they knew it for that of Marcus Optatius Navigatus. Navigatus was head of the Bureau, formally the equal of a provincial fiscal officer in authority and informally more powerful than most governors . . . because he directed men like Aulus Perennius.

Maximus got the point. The helmsman signet smothered his snarl into an engaging grin as he turned from his partner back to the agent. "Hey, just a joke, sir," he said. "There's just about no traffic through here anyway, except the morning levee and from the courier's entrance." He gestured with a quick flick of his head. It was more of a nervous mannerism than a direction toward whichever other entrance to the building he meant. "No harm done, hey?"

"There could have been," said Perennius.

The older guard closed the tablet carefully and offered it back to the agent. "Thank you, sir. Now, if—"

Perennius ignored him. His eyes forced Maximus back a step. The agent's hard voice continued. "It still *could* be, son, couldn't it? *Look* at me, damn you!"

Gaius cleared his throat and laid a hand lightly on his superior's shoulder. He had seen the reaction before, always in rear areas, always in response to someone's attempt to parlay petty authority into injustice. The younger Illyrian knew that it would be to the advantage of everyone if he could calm his protector before matters proceeded further.

For the moment, Perennius noticed Gaius as little as he did the older guard. Maximus squirmed as he met the eyes of the shorter, older man. "Listen, you slimy little thief," the agent went on in a fierce whisper, "If I ever again hear of you shaking down people on the business of this Bureau, I'll come for you. Do you understand?"

Maximus nodded his head upward in affirmation.

"*Do you understand?*" Perennius shouted.

Gaius stepped between the two men. "Say yessir, you damned fool!" he snapped to the guard. "And you better mean it, because *he* does. Aulus," he added, turning to Perennius, "you back off, he's not worth it."

"The gods know *that's* true," Perennius muttered. He gripped Gaius' shoulder for support and took a shuddering breath.

"Yessir," said the guard. He could not believe what was happening. He had just enough intellectual control to suppress the desire to grasp his sword hilt. This *couldn't* be happening!

Still touching Gaius, though the support needed was no longer physical, Perennius retrieved his orders from the other guard. "Sorry," he said to the mail-clad man, "but if I don't cure him, who in blazes will?" He thrust the diploma into his wallet and began to unbuckle his equipment belt. Gaius stepped back and wiped his forehead with the inner hem of his cloak.

"Ah, that's right, sir," said the older guard as Perennius loosed his shoulder strap, then the waist buckle itself. "We'll return your weapons to you when you leave."

"Sure, couldn't have me going berserk in Bureau Headquarters, could we?" said the agent with the only smile among the four men. His wallet and purse were hung from a separate, much lighter belt. That saved him the problem of unfastening the hook-mounted scabbards when he disarmed, or handing the sword and dagger over bare to be dulled when somebody inevitably dropped them.

"Ah, sir," the guard added tentatively, "the pass is for you alone."

Everyone paused. Perennius laughed abruptly. Maximus flinched away from the sound.

The agent was amused, however. He was not just going through some prelude to the murderous frenzy about which he had joked. Perennius had intended to carry his protégé in to see Navigatus. It would be good for Gaius' career, especially if the emergency summons meant the Director might need Perennius' gratitude. Under normal circumstances, the agent could have squared the guards easily enough and taken Gaius into the building. He did not see any practical way of doing that now that he had thrown a wholly unnecessary scene. The guards might be willing to compromise—Maximus looked both confused and terrified—but Perennius' own sense of propriety would not permit him to openly proclaim himself an idiot.

"You know," the agent said as he gave his sword and dagger to the younger guard, "there's times that even I think I've been on the job too long. The only problem is that when I go on leave, I get wound up even tighter." He grinned and added, "Don't know what the cure is." But he did know, they all knew that death was the cure for men in whom frustration and violence mounted higher and higher.

"Well, I'll wait out here," Gaius said. He was a good kid, prideful but not ambitious enough for his own good. It had probably not occurred to him that he was missing the chance of a real career boost. "Or look, there's a tavern right there—" he thumbed toward the end of the court. "Look me up when you're done with your interview."

Perennius glanced first at the westering sun, then back to the younger man. Everybody in a cathouse this close to Headquarters was probably an informer or a spy in addition to their other duties. Gaius was the friendly sort who tended to be loose-lipped when he had a cup or two in him or was dipping his wick. Perennius could not imagine that such talk would do any intrinsic harm, but it would get back to the Bureau for sure and Internal Security would drop on the kid like an obelisk. "Look," the veteran agent said, "why don't you head straight to the Transient Barracks and make sure they've assigned us decent accommodations. There's a nice bath attached to the barracks. I'll meet you there, soon as I can—and there's shops in the bathhouse, better wine than they'll serve around here."

Gaius shrugged. "Sure," he agreed. "I'll catch you there." The glance he cast over his shoulder as he walked off was from concern over Perennius, not because the older man was manipulating him.

The agent took a deep breath. "Look," he said to

Maximus in a calm, even friendly, tone, "if you wear your body armor, you'll live longer. Whether or not that's a benefit to the Empire sort of depends on whether you have sense enough to take good advice."

Maximus nodded stiffly, but there was no belief in his eyes—only fear of the result of giving the wrong answer to a test that he did not begin to understand.

Perennius sighed. He looked at the older guard, the one with the mail shirt and the scar snaking up his right arm to where the sleeve of his tunic hid it. The infantryman smiled back at the agent. The expression was forced but perhaps it was the more notable for that. "Quintus Sestius Cotyla," he volunteered. "Third Centurion of the Fourth Battalion, Palatine Foot."

"Tell him about it," Perennius said with a nod toward the younger guard. "When the shit comes down, habits'll either save you or get your ass killed. For a soldier, walking around on duty without armor is a damned bad habit. But blazes, I've got work to do, I guess."

Sestius nodded. He rapped sharply on the door with a swagger stick. "Pass one," he called through the triangular communication grate.

"The tribune doesn't object so long as our brightwork's polished," said Maximus unexpectedly. He held a rigid brace with his eyes on the opposite building instead of on the man he was addressing.

The door groaned and began to swing inward. Perennius looked at the guard without anger. "Your tribune," he said "may not have seen as many feet of intestine spilled as I have, sonny. But, like I say, it's a problem that'll cure itself sooner or later." He stepped between the men into the short passageway that led to the shabby elegance of the entrance hall.

The interior of the building was very dark by contrast to the sunlit street. Perennius nodded to the functionary who had opened the door, but he did not notice that the fellow had raised a hand for attention. "A moment, sir," the man said in a sharp voice as Perennius almost walked into the bar separating the passage from the hall proper.

The hall was a pool of light which spilled through the large roof vent twenty feet above. The agent's eyes adapted well enough to see by the scattered reflection that the man who spoke was too well dressed to be simply a slave used as a doorkeeper. There was a shimmer of silk woven into the linen of his tunic. "Your pass, sir," he said with his hand out. Beside him stirred the heavy-set man with a cudgel, the civilian equivalent of the two uniformed men outside. Since the last time Perennius had been here, the Bureau had added its own credentials check to duplicate that of the army. Clerks seated at desks filling the hall glanced up at the diversion.

Perennius fingered out his diploma again and handed it to the doorman. "First," he said, "I need to see a fellow named Zopyrion, Claudius Zopyrion, in one of the finance sections."

The doorman ignored what the agent was saying. He closed the document with a snap and a smile. "Very good, Legate Perennius," he said in a bright voice. "The Director has requested that you be passed through to him at once. His office is—"

"I know where the Director's office is," Perennius said quietly. He could feel muscles knotting together, but he managed not to let his fists clench as they wanted to do. Rome always did this to him; it wasn't *fair*. "First I need to see—"

"You can take care of your travel vouchers later, I'm sure, Legate," the functionary interrupted. His smile was a caricature, now, warping itself into a sneer. "The Director says—"

"*Read my lips!*" the agent hissed. His voice did not carry to the assembled clerks, but the bruiser in the passage straightened abruptly. "I said, I'll see Navigatus when I've finished my business with Zopyrion. Now, if you want to tell me where to find the bastard, fine. Otherwise—" and his eyes measured the bruiser with cool detachment before flicking back to the doorman—"I guess I'll go look for myself." Unconquered Sun, Father of Life! He should never have come back.

"Upstairs," the doorman said. He slid aside a curtain behind him. There was a doorway, punched through a frescoed wall when the house was converted. The plain wooden staircase might have been original. "He's the head of Finance Two. Follow the corridor to the left."

"Thank you," Perennius said with a nod. He strode to the staircase.

"I'll inform the Director that you're here, Legate," the doorman said in a distant voice. "No doubt he'll be amused by your priorities."

"Wish to blazes his priorities amused me, buddy," the agent flung over his shoulder as he stamped upward. He had replaced his orders in the wallet. Now he was taking out another, similar tablet.

CHAPTER TWO

When the building was a residence, its upper floor had been divided into small cubicles—slave quarters, storage, and ladder-served additions to the shops and rental housing on the exterior of the lower floor. The open peristyle court and the garden provided light wells for the rooms to the rear. The entrance hall, though double height, was roofed except for the vent which served as a skylight and fed the pool beneath it. The area at the top of the stairs was lighted and ventilated only by the outside windows.

Most of the partition walls had been knocked down during conversion. The windows were opened out from their frames like vertical louvers to catch what breeze wandered through the maze of higher buildings and surrounding hills. Even so, the atmosphere within was warm and stuffy. Perennius unpinned his cloak and gripped it with his left hand. Even in the street, he had worn the garment mostly to keep his weapons from being too obtrusive. The sword and dagger were legal for him but he preferred to avoid the hassle of explanations.

A unit of forty or so clerks occupied the area to the left of the staircase. They sat on low stools in front of desks which were boards slanted from pedestals with holes for ink pots. There was an aisle between the desks and the enclosed main hall. Perennius followed the aisle in accordance with the doorkeeper's instructions. The room was alive with noise. Most of the clerks read aloud the reports which they copied or epitomized. Baskets of scrolls and tablets sat on the floor beside each desk. The din seemed to bother neither the men who were working nor those who were talking with others at neighboring desks. Some of the clerks worked and chatted simultaneously. Their fingers and pens followed lines of manuscript while their tongues discussed the chariot races of the day before.

A supervisor almost walked into Perennius at the corner. "Yes sir?" the man said, startled into Greek.

"I need Claudius Zopyrion," the agent replied. He flashed the document in his hand so that the other man could see the name of the addressee. Battle in closed ranks had made Perennius as facile at separating information from noise as any of the gobbling clerks around him.

The supervisor gestured down the aisle in the direction from which he had come. Perennius edged around the corner so that he could follow the pointing finger. A dozen cubicles remained along the outside wall, though the partitions of most of the rooms which had faced the light wells had been removed to seat more clerks. "Third office on the left," the supervisor said.

"Thanks," replied the agent. "And who's his boss? Zopyrion's?"

"Gnaeus Calgurrio," the other man said. He had begun to frown, but he did not ask the agent's business. "Head of Finance. First office."

Perennius smiled his gratitude and walked off in the indicated direction. He could feel the bureaucrat's eyes follow him past the ranks of clerks.

The first office was double the width of the others in the row. As Perennius stepped past, he caught a glimpse through the doorway of a plump, balding man reclining on a brocaded couch. Seated upright between the couch and the door was a younger man with hard eyes and a face as ruthless in repose as Perennius' own. Perfect, the agent thought. He had no immediate need for the department head and his aide, however. Not until he had prepared things in the second office over.

Perennius slipped in the door and closed it before the cubicle's inhabitant could more than glance up from the scroll in his hand. "Zopyrion?" the agent asked in a husky whisper.

"Herakles! Who are you?" the other demanded. Zopyrion

was a short man with the cylindrical softness that marked
him as a eunuch more clearly than his smooth chin. Like
his department head, Zopyrion had a couch and window;
but only one window and a couch with a frame of turned
wood instead of the filigree of his superior's.

The section head spoke Latin with a pronounced Carian
accent. Perennius answered in that dialect, though he was
not fully fluent in it. The partitions separating the offices
were thin, and the agent wanted only Zopyrion to understand him at the moment. "I've got a letter from Simonides," the agent said, proferring the sealed tablet in his
hand. "He said for me to take back an answer."

There was a one-legged tablet near the head of the couch.
It held writing instruments. "Simonides?" the bureaucrat
repeated as he took the document. He picked up a stylus
with which to break the thread which held the tablet
closed. Concern had replaced the initial anger in his voice.

"Simonides of Antioch, the banker," Perennius said as
he stepped closer. "You know, the one you used to wash
the—"

"Silence, by Herakles!" Zopyrion gasped. He too had
slipped into his native Carian. That was a result of confusion rather than a conscious desire for secrecy, however.
He looked down at the document in his hand.

It was a tablet of three waxed wooden leaves, hollowed
to keep the writing from being flattened to illegibility
when they were closed. Zopyrion began to read the first
page in a low sing-song, holding the page by habit at a
flat angle to the light so that shadows brought the wax
impressions into relief. " 'Simonides, son of Eustachios,
greets Sextus Claudius Zopyrion. I return herewith the
draft by which you ordered me to transfer two hundred
gold solidi from Imperial accounts to your brother-in-
law, Nelius Juturnus. . . .' " The clerk looked up again in
utter, abject terror at Perennius, who now stood beside
him. The agent's left hand rested on the table, covering
the alabaster ink pot there. "Why in the name of Fortune
did he write this?" Zopyrion demanded.

The agent laughed. "Oh," he said, "maybe it was when
I asked him which orifice he wanted to swallow my sword
through, hey? But take a look at the draft—" he tapped

with his right forefinger the pair of pages which were still closed. "You know, it seems to me your department head's seal is a bit fuzzy, like somebody used a plaster copy instead of the original."

Zopyrion's eyes followed the tapping finger. As his head bent slightly, Perennius hit him behind the ear with the base of the ink pot. It was an awkward, left-handed blow, but there was enough muscle behind it to spill the clerk flaccidly onto the floor. The table went over on top of him with a crash.

Perennius set the stone pot down on its side carefully, so that there would be no additional noise. There was a neat circle of ink on the palm of his left hand. He did not wipe it off, because the smear might be harder to hide than the ink where it now was. Working fast, the agent unhooked a skin of powerful wine from the inner hem of his cloak where it had been hidden. He tilted up Zopyrion's face and squirted a jet of wine into the corner of the unconscious man's mouth. The liquid drooled back down his chin. The air of the office filled with the wine's thick, sweet odor. Perennius laid the skin, still uncorked, beside the eunuch's outflung hand. Its contents leaked and pooled across the terrazzo, drawing whorls of ink into them.

The agent straightened. In a voice that even he could barely hear, he said to the fallen man, "Next time you leave somebody hanging in hostile territory, make damn sure that he doesn't make it back."

He threw open the office door. "Sir! Sir!" he cried as he ran toward the double office at the head of the row. "Sir, you've got to come here!"

Calgurrio's sharp-eyed aide was on his feet before Perennius completed the two strides to his door. The department head himself was far slower to react, though he did swing his heavy thighs over the edge of his couch. Startled clerks leaped from stools in the aisle to crowd around the door of Zopyrion's office. "Get back!" snapped the aide. The group dissolved in a flurry fearfully righting the stools they had knocked over in their haste.

Speaking rapidly, Perennius followed the aide back to the unconscious eunuch. "A banker in Antioch wouldn't fund my mission like he was supposed to," the agent said, "but he gave me a letter for this Claudius Zopyrion when I got to Rome. The guy was drinking when I got here—"

The aide knelt down by Zopyrion, keeping the hem of his tunic clear of the pooled ink and wine. He picked up the open tablet and skimmed it, keeping the wax side turned away from Perennius at his elbow.

"Ah, I looked at it after he fainted," the agent said softly. "I was horrified. What sort of punishment could be sufficient for an embezzler like that?"

"What happened, Anguilus?" demanded Calgurrio as he waddled into the room. The department head stared at Zopyrion in amazement. The eunuch was beginning to moan. "Isis and the Child, what *is* this?"

Anguilus swung the door closed and handed the tablet to his superior. "I think we have a problem with Zopyrion, sir," the aide said. Calgurrio began to read the document to himself with increasing astonishment. To Perennius, Anguilus whispered, "And just who are you, good sir?" The words were polite, but there was no deference in the aide's tone. His face was as blank as a sheet of marble and as hard.

The agent handed over the diploma with his orders. The clerks had returned to noisy confusion as soon as the door had closed them from Calgurrio's sight—or more probably, from Anguilus'. Using the hubbub to mask his words from everyone but the aide, Perennius said, "If he were transferred to a garrison unit in the sticks—one of the little posts in Africa out on the fringe of the desert where the Moors raid every few months. He wouldn't be able to lie about how he split the money with his department head then."

Anguilus closed and returned the diploma. His eyes were as chill as steel in the winter.

"Mother Isis!" Calgurrio blurted. "Anguilus, did you read this? It says—"

The aide put a hand on his superior's shoulder. "Yes, sir," he said with his eyes still watching Perennius, "but I think we can deal with the problem without it having to go beyond these walls." He nodded toward the closed door and the commotion beyond it before he added, "This gentleman is Aulus Perennius, one of the Bureau's top field agents, you may remember. We're very fortunate that the situation was uncovered by someone of his proven discretion." Anguilus flashed a tight rictus, not really a smile, toward the agent.

Zopyrion moaned again. His eyes opened, though without any intellect behind them. The right pupil was fully dilated: the left was not. Anguilus glanced down at the eunuch. When he looked back at Perennius, his sour grin showed that the evidence of concussion only supported what the aide had known all along.

"Sure, I trust you to clean house yourselves," Perennius said. "Maybe the next time I'm here at Headquarters, I'll check just how it did come out." He nodded toward Zopyrion. "Until then, be well." The agent turned and reached for the door's lever handle.

"It won't happen to you again, fellow-soldier," said Cagurrio's aide. The Bureau's field staff was recruited from the Army, but Perennius would not have guessed that Anguilus had the right to use that particular honorific. "Don't worry."

Perennius turned again to look at the aide with his silk and his smooth hands and his eyes like a wolf's. They came from different backgrounds but the two of them recognized each other. "I don't worry," the agent said. "I leave that to other people."

As Perennius left the office, thrusting his broad shoulders through the press of clerks, he heard Calgurrio saying plaintively, "But why did he put something like this in writing?"

CHAPTER THREE

One of the troopers muttered in disbelief. The decurion, Ursinus, hushed the man, but Ursinus' face showed some doubt also.

"You don't mean here, Mother?" asked Sacrovir. He glanced toward the building they were passing on the way to what must be a brothel. The corner building had military guards, showing it had official status of some kind. That seemed a more likely resort of the "source of power" they sought than did a whorehouse, even a whorehouse in Rome.

Julia nodded to her son like a bird bobbing its head. She wore an enveloping gray cloak, hooded and pinned shut in front. The garment was not for warmth but to hide from view the costume she wore beneath it. The seeress' breeches and long-sleeved shirt were a patchwork of skins from over a hundred species of animals and birds. Alone, the outfit was that of a tattered scarecrow. Those who saw Julia wearing the costume, moving in it, could not doubt that the garb had purposes beyond those of mere clothing. "I know where I am being led," the seeress said. Her voice, though distinct, had the unworldly quality of a distant echo. The soldiers, all but Julius Sacrovir, her son, stirred uneasily.

"Let's go, then," Sacrovir ordered. He was slightly the youngest of the five-man escort, but he had been born to authority. Further, Sacrovir had a familiarity with his mother's work so that it did not make him uneasy as it did the others.

Sacrovir himself had sung the prelude to the rites in Trier from which this mission had sprung. The youth's clear falsetto had rung from the stone arches as dignitaries waited tensely and the Emperor Postumus shivered in the armor he wore as a public reminder of his military valor. On the feather-cushioned throne, Julia had begun to speak in a voice like the piping of birds. . . .

Now the little woman followed as if drawn by the wake of her tall, powerful son. The other troopers marched to either side of the seeress, pair and pair. They kept step by habit, unremarkable in this city of soldiers and troop-guarded administrators. If the entourage was unusual, it was for the fact that it surrounded a woman afoot.

It was too early in the afternoon for the brothel to be busy, though there was probably a back entrance and a latchbell for emergency service even during the hours the front doors were barred. Those doors were open now, however, and the madam was in her barred kiosk just within them. She looked startled by the size and ordered bearing of the party. A slave who had been mopping the gray and green terrazzo floor scampered off, perhaps to wake the bouncer. Alcoves led off the entrance hall. An open staircase led up to the rooms on the second story.

"How can I help you, gentlemen?" the madam asked brightly as her fingers clicked shut the cash box. Cartoons frescoed over the arch of each alcove suggested a variety of possibilities. In some cases, these official displays had been supplemented by notes and still cruder drawings added by customers waiting on a full night.

"There's someone here we need to see," said Sacrovir, wishing he had more details.

"Why of course, honey," the madam began with her false smile.

Julia reached out from beneath her cloak. "Up there," she said to her son. She pointed with a hand wearing a cat-skin mitten. The fur side was inward, but it spilled out in purest white where the mitten was drawn over the seeress' wrist. Sacrovir obeyed the direction, striding to the stairs without another glance at the woman in the kiosk. The young man was wired into another universe, though by no means as thoroughly as was his mother.

The madam paused with one hand on the door of her cage. Her mouth was open to cry out. Ursinus rang a coin on the travertine counter, silencing the alarm before it was uttered. "Won't be any trouble," the soldier said in his Gallic accent. He waved the other troopers by with his left hand. "Kid's a little strange, you know, but it won't be any trouble." Ursinus followed the rest of the group up the stairs, his hand close by the hilt of his cloak-covered sword. In the kiosk, the madam was looking with surprise at the face on the coin she had just been given.

Two girls were arguing over a bracelet in the upper hall. Their shrill voices softened quickly into overtures as the men and Julia pushed by. One of the troopers paused a half-step when the blond prostitute caught his eye and stroked her bare breast. A snapped command from Ursinus moved him on again.

"Here," said Julia. She reached out and tapped a door. The usual price marker had been removed from its peg, leaving a lighter square on the door panel.

"Hey, you can't go in there," called the blond girl who had tried to accost them. "That's a special rental, sort of."

Sacrovir knocked louder.

The latch snicked, allowing the door to open a crack. It would have closed again if one of the troopers had not blocked it with his foot. "Go away," rasped an indescribable voice. "I am not to be disturbed."

"We offer you help for help," said the seeress. She shrugged and her cape dropped away. The different sheens and patterns of the costume beneath blended into an odd unity. Perhaps that was a trick of the uncertain light. "The power of our Emperor, for the—power you control."

The bouncer, naked except for breeches and a three-foot cudgel, pounded up the stairs. The oil with which he had been being massaged shone on his bunched shoulders. Ursinus motioned one of his men to his side, though neither Gaul drew a weapon for the moment.

The door opened fully. The figure within the room was short, caped and cowled as the seeress herself had been. It wore a veil. The features beneath the shadowing veil were so still as to belie their appearance of flesh. "Come," said the figure in its harsh voice that did not move its lips. Something bright as jewelry, too bright for a weapon, winked from a fold in its garment. "What is it that your Emperor thinks he allies himself with?"

Julia moved like a sleepwalker. She followed the figure back into the chamber. On the other side of the room was a door open onto a balcony. Daylight blurred and haloed the other figure. Sacrovir paused on the threshold and looked back to the other men of the escort.

Ursinus clenched his fist with the thumb displayed in a gesture from the amphitheatre. "We'll keep our friend company out here," the decurion said. He nodded toward the bouncer. "Convince him that there's nothing going down that he needs to worry about."

Sacrovir jerked his head in assent. He slipped into the private room after his mother. The door latched behind him.

"With your help," Julia was whispering, "there can be an Empire united again on Trier. I have seen it, seen armies melting away before Postumus like trees struck by summer lightning. . . . What do you wish of Postumus, then? We are sent to make it yours."

Sacrovir backed without noticing his own motion until his shoulders pressed against the door panel. His eyes jumped around the room like sparrows in a bush. The youth did not let them light too long on either his mother or on the sunlight-shimmering figure his mother had journeyed so far to meet.

"You know nothing," the figure said in wonder. The object it held was no longer so clearly not a weapon.

"We know you have the power to destroy armies," the seeress replied without emotion.

"These others are fighters?" the figure asked abruptly. Its gesture rumpled but did not pass the enveloping cloak.

"My son, yes, and soldiers," Julia said. "There are thousands more soldiers for the Emperor Postumus to lead at your bidding—and with your aid. There are infinite futures, but I have seen . . ."

"No," the figure said, the word alone without the gesture of negation to be expected with it. "Not thousands. I have hired certain fighters here . . . but yours might serve

me yet tonight. Then later, there is a—treasure—to guard.
For a year."

"You pledge your support to the Emperor, if we help
you tonight and guard a treasure?" Sacrovir demanded.
He spoke to release the tension which the figure's grating
voice raised in him.

"The treasure is in Cilicia," Julia said, neither a question nor a demand. "We would have gone there, but you
in Rome were closer." In her present state, the seeress
had little connection with the immediate world. She did
not note the way the glittering object shifted toward her
when she spoke. Her son noticed. His general tension
focused on a tighter grip on his sword.

"That is correct," the figure said. "How did you know?"

"I have seen," Julia replied simply.

"For one year?" repeated Sacrovir. He knew that the
tension must break in one fashion or the other.

"In Cilicia," the figure said. "For one of your years.
After that, there will be no need of guards."

"We agree," said Julia in her dreamy, half human voice.

"Then," said the figure, "we need only to determine the
details." A rippling of its cloak offered them seats on the
broad, low couch. "I will have food and drink brought if
you require it while we plan. . . ."

CHAPTER FOUR

The peristyle court in the center of Headquarters had been converted into a clerical pool like most of the areas which had been open when the building was a residence. As Perennius returned to the ground floor by a rear staircase, he was amused to see that the back garden was just that again. Flowers and several fruit trees including a cherry were now growing where more ranks of file clerks had squatted two years ago, the last time Perennius had been at Headquarters. Navigatus had been complaining then that he missed the sight and smells of the garden he had had when he was a District Superintendent in Trier. Apparently he had done something about the lack, though Perennius could not imagine where the displaced clerks had gone. The agent had for years believed that the Bureau could accomplish its tasks better with only half the Headquarters personnel; but he knew the system too well to doubt that if half of the clerks were eliminated, it would be the incompetent ones who somehow were retained.

The Director's office was what had been the large drawing room between the peristyle court and the back garden. Eight men of the Palatine Foot lounged in the side passage where the door was placed. Several of them were dicing without enthusiasm. Clerks and a pair of bored-looking ushers in civilian dress mingled with the guards in the passage and spilled back into the court. There they jostled the seated copyists. The large windows in either end of the drawing room were pivoted open to encourage a cross draft from the garden to the court. Through the window from the latter, Perennius could see Navigatus on his couch. Standing with him in the room were a dozen other men: functionaries, personal attendants, and suppliants for the attention of the Director. Navigatus looked very much like a private magnate holding his levee.

Marcus Optatius Navigatus was a plump man of sixty whose primary affectation was the black, curly wig he wore even to the baths. Perennius had known him for almost twenty years, from the days when Navigatus had commanded the battalion of the Rhine Army to which Perennius had been assigned. They were both Illyrians. The younger man had an intelligence and drive which brought him early to Navigatus' attention. Far more rare in a man of his caliber, Perennius had none of the personal ambition that would have made him as potentially dangerous to his superior as he was immediately useful.

Perennius had followed Navigatus to three more line commands, jumping in rank each time. When the older man had transferred to the Bureau of Imperial Affairs, itself a part of the military rather than the civil establishment, Perennius had accompanied him again. Oddly enough, it was then that their paths had begun to diverge again. Perennius' trustworthiness, his intelligence, and his ruthless determination to accomplish a task at whatever cost, would have made him even more valuable to his superior than he had been while in uniform. Four months of staff duty in Trier had driven Perennius to insist on either a field assignment or a return to uniform.

The pettiness, the dishonesty ineradicable in a system built on secrecy, the filth he must know about the Empire which it was his life to protect . . . all of those factors had put the Illyrian on the edge of eruption. The eight following years in the field were at least seven more than he could have survived in a Headquarters billet. By now, however, Perennius had come to the gloomy conclusion that nothing would save him from himself much longer.

There was a guard at the window on the peristyle court. He was there to make sure that no one slipped in that way in a desperate attempt to get the Director's approval of a plan or document. Perennius nodded to the soldier.

The man laid a brawny arm across the opening as the agent stepped toward it. "Keep clear, buddy," the guard snapped. "Go see them if you need to get in." He nodded toward the ushers in the passage. They were already hedged about by men who felt they had to talk to Navigatus.

"Calm down," Perennius said. He felt unusually calm himself, now that he had taken care of his business with Zopyrion. It was a state almost like that following orgasm, the relaxation which follows the draining of all the self's resources into a single triumphant moment. It took the edge off the sword of his temper, though the iron baton which remained could be nasty enough in all truth. Perennius reached out to the stone frame, holding his orders closed in his hand.

Navigatus reclined on the other side of the drawing room. He faced three-quarters away from the agent. Unexpectedly, one of the other heads within was turned toward Perennius rather than toward the Director. The man staring at the agent was six feet four inches tall, but much thinner-framed than the norm of protein-fed barbarians of that height. He was starkly bald with only a hint of eyebrows like those which regrow after facial burns. The eye contact surprised Perennius. Its intensity shocked him, stiffening the agent with a gasp which convinced the guard to get involved again.

"*Hey* there," the soldier said. He set his left palm at the lower end of the agent's breastbone. "Get the hell *back*, I—"

Perennius gripped the other's wrist with his own left hand and squeezed. There was no emotion in his response. That part of the agent's body was working on instinct. His right hand slapped the wooden tablet three times against the sill. The sharp rattle of sound cut through the buzz of concurrent conversations. It drew all eyes toward Perennius, as it had been intended to do. That was no longer an intellectual act either. The agent's conscious mind was focused on the bald, spare man who looked at him and looked away, just as Navigatus shouted, "Aulus! By Pollux, everybody make way for my friend here!" The Director rose to his feet with a touch of awkwardness because in reclining he had slowed the circulation to his left leg.

Perennius laughed. "Say, I'll come through the window," he called, "if it won't earn me a foot of steel up the ass." He released the guard, looking at the man with interest for the first time. Perennius' grip on the soldier's wrist had paralyzed the man as small bones, already in contact, had grated closer. "Christ the *Savior*, you bastard!" the soldier hissed as he massaged the injured limb with his good hand. Perennius had been distracted or he would not have squeezed so hard. Still, no permanent harm done, the agent thought as he swung himself over the waist-high sill to meet his superior.

The two men clasped and kissed, to the amazement of most of the others in the room. Navigatus was not, all things considered, a particularly arrogant man, but he had a strong sense of formality. He wore his toga on all public occasions. His subordinates and those outsiders seeking audiences with him had learned early that if they wished to be recognized, they too had best don the uncomfortable woolen garment. Even then the Director tended to keep his distance; though so far as Perennius knew, Marcus had never gotten to the point of greeting everyone through his usher as if direct verbal contact would somehow soil him. Seeing Navigatus embracing the agent and his travel stains was more of a surprise than word of another attempted coup would have been.

Much more of a surprise than that.

Navigatus continued to hold the agent by one hand as he turned to his head usher. "Delius," he said, "clear this—no, Aulus and I will go out in the garden, that's what we'll do. Close that—" he pointed at the window opening into the garden—"and see that we're not disturbed."

"Just *one* moment, your Respectability," begged an intense young man with the broad stripe of Senate membership along the hem of his tunic. The Senate itself was a debating club rather than the governing council of the Empire, but those who debated there tended to be rich and powerful men in their own right. The young Senator reached out with a scrolled petition in his right hand, while his left hand tried to clutch at the Director's sleeve.

The usher thrust out his ivory baton. The broad stripe saved the man who wore it from rapped knuckles, but it did not bring him any nearer to the response he sought. "Later, Felix, later," Navigatus grumbled over his shoulder. "My goodness, Aulus, you're looking so fit that it makes a used-up old man like me jealous. And how's that boy of yours, Docleus? Pleased with his appointment, I trust? You know, we sent him to bring you the recall orders because we weren't sure you'd accept them from anybody else."

Perennius looked sharply at his superior. The guards in the passage were pushing the civilians among them back into the peristyle court. Navigatus had a bland expression as he stepped out of the drawing room and led the agent away from the confusion. "Gaius is well, thank you," Perennius said cautiously. "He does indeed appreciate the favor you've shown him; and of course, I appreciate it as well. His father was a friend of mine until I enlisted. When he drowned, I sort of—tried to look after the boy, you know."

"Of course I know," agreed Navigatus as he stepped out into the sunbright garden. "No children of your own— just like me. Though of course I married, at least. Would you like some wine, Aulus? I'll admit we didn't expect you for another several days at best."

Perennius ran an index finger down the side of a young fig tree. The bark was as gray and dry as the skin of the lizard that scuttled around the trunk to where it could no longer see him. "Why did you recall me, Marcus?" the agent asked softly. "I was perfectly placed, *perfectly*." He looked up at the older man. "Marcus, I was helping *plan* the attack. Personal representative of the Emperor Postumus of Gaul—oh, they were very pleased, they'd been planning an embassage themselves but it had been let slip in the press of other business."

The Director sighed as he bent over a bed of russet gladiolas. "It's come to that, then?" he said. He clipped a stalk beneath its spray of blooms, parting the pithy stem with his long thumbnail. "The Autarch of Palmyra is disloyal to the Emperor after all?" He lifted the regal blooms to his nose and sniffed.

"Marcus," Perennius pleaded, "Odenath was never loyal. He's a jumped-up princeling who fought the Persians because they wouldn't accept his surrender. He won because he knew his deserts and because he's a sharp bastard, a really sharp one, I give him that. But he didn't save the Empire; he saved his *ass* . . . and now he figures that fits him to rule the whole business in place of his Majesty, the Emperor."

"Well, we can use him, I'm sure," said Navigatus. "Such lovely flowers as these, you'd expect them to have a marvelous odor also." He laid the spray against the hem of his toga. The russet blossoms were almost identical to the pair of narrow stripes that marked the Director as a Knight. "But instead there's nothing, only the color."

"Damn it, Marcus!" the agent cried. He slammed the heel of his hand against the fig. The lizard catapulted through the air, twisting madly until it hit the ground and scurried off. "Can we use Postumus too? Is it to the Empire's benefit that Gaul, Britain, Spain all claim they're independent now? Can we make clever policy out of the fact that every field commander with a thousand men thinks he ought to be on the throne instead of Gallienus?"

A large carpenter bee with a black abdomen lighted on the gladiola spray in Navigatus' hand. The Director's attention appeared to be concentrated on the bee as he said, "Aulus, we can't worry about every little thing that goes wrong. We have to carry out our assigned duties as best we can, and we have to trust that other people do the same." He sighed again. "Now if all my personnel were like you . . . are you sure I can't convince you to join me here in Rome? There's so many things . . ."

"We're not talking about little things, Marcus," the agent said with dispassionate certainty. "We're talking about Franks raiding from the Rhine to the Pillars of Hercules, while Goths and Herulians spill through the Bosphorus into the Aegean."

"Well, I know that, of course, but—"

"Do you know that we were damned near caught by those German pirates when we sailed from Sidon? That

they were *this* close—" Perennius snapped his fingers—
"before a little storm blew up and separated us?"

"I've said how much I appreciated your haste in
returning, haven't I?" the Director said. The spray in his
hands was trembling so much that the bee retreated from
its flower cup and hung an inch or two away in the air,
buzzing querulously.

"Marcus, *sir*," the agent went on, "everywhere I go, I
see the big landowners shutting off their estates. They
grow for themselves, they manufacture whatever they
need in house, they've got their own armies . . . and the
good *gods* help the tax gatherer who dares to set a foot on
their lands."

"Aulus, there are agents assigned to that duty—" the
Director began.

"Then they're doing a piss-poor job!" his subordinate
shouted. "*Piss* poor. And the coinage!" Perennius reached
into his purse. "Have you tried to get someone to take a
recent denarius, Marcus? Without feeding it to him at the
point of your sword, I mean?" He found the coin he
wanted, a freshly-minted piece with the bearded visage of
Gallienus on the obverse. The stocky agent strode to the
fountain in the center of the garden. A marble boy held a
marble goose on his shoulder. Water spurted from the
beak of the goose and the penis of the boy. Gesturing with
the coin like a conjuror introducing a sleight, Perennius
then rang it leadenly on the stone curb.

"No difference but shape between this and a sling bullet,"
he asserted with bitter accuracy. "Even the goddam *wash*
on it—" his thumb kneaded the shiny surface—"is tin, not
silver."

Navigatus said nothing. Perennius took a deep breath.
In a voice much quieter than that of his last diatribe, and
without meeting the Director's eyes, he said, "Marcus,
you say 'trust other people to do their duty.' Nobody does
their duty but you and me, and the Emperor. And when I
see this—" he spun the coin expertly off his thumb. It
made a glittering arc over his head, then splashed down
in the fountain where the two jets merged—"I swear if I
don't think I'm giving his Majesty too much credit."

"You don't want to say that," Navigatus murmured,

correct in a number of ways. The bee had left him, but the spray of blossoms was still again in his hand. "You know, Aulus," he said to the flower, "I've never meant to be other than a friend to you—"

The agent paced quickly to the older man's side. "I know that, Marcus," he said. "I didn't mean—"

"—but I sometimes regret what I've done," the Director continued, quelling the interruption by raising his eyes. "If I hadn't—pushed you, you might be much happier now, one of Postumus' battalion commanders and married to that little girl of yours."

"Nobody makes another person into something he wasn't before," said the younger man quietly.

"I often tell myself that, my friend," said Navigatus. He let the gladiolas fall and took Perennius by the hand again.

The agent stared at something far distant from the clasped hands on which his eyes were focused. "Besides," he said, "Julia ended it herself. Her—emotional state was causing conflict with her duties as a priestess." As old as the phrase was in his memory, it still had edges that could tear. "That's why I accepted the transfer to Numidia with you, Marcus. Not because of the promotion." He smiled at their linked hands.

"Ah," said Navigatus. "I, ah. . . . Well, of course, there's still the matter that forced me to recall you from Palmyra, isn't there?"

"Indeed there is," agreed the agent as he led the other man to one of the stone benches against the back wall of the garden. "When all else fails, there's always duty."

"You see," said Navigatus as he fished a slim scroll from the wallet beneath his toga, "he came with this, which isn't something that I see every day. Even here." He slipped off the vellum cover and handed the document to Perennius.

The agent read the brief Latin inscription carefully. "Can't say it's not to the point," he remarked as he rolled the document again. It had read, "The Emperor Caesar Publius Licinius Gallienus Pius Augustus to Marcus Navigatus. The bearer of this rescript, Lucius Cloelius Calvus, is to be afforded the full support of your Bureau.

All his requests are to be executed as if from my lips. When it is necessary to accomplish the tasks thus imposed, you may apply for assistance from my Director of Administration, Aurelius Quirinius."

The damned thing was in vermilion ink, Perennius noted, and it didn't look to be in the handwriting of a professional scribe either. Blazes! "All right," he said as he handed back the imperial rescript, "what *does* he request?"

"You, Aulus," said the Director, meeting Perennius' gaze steadily. "He wants you."

"Blazes," the agent repeated aloud. He had an urge to wrap his cloak around him again, even in the sunlit garden. "He's the tall one in there, isn't he?" Perennius added in sudden certainty.

Both men glanced toward the drawing room. The window was lined with the faces of men waiting with an impatience which bid fair to master their senses of decorum. In the center was the bald man with whom Perennius had locked eyes earlier. He was the tallest of those watching and the only one who looked calm. His face was as still as a statue's as he watched the men in the garden.

"Why yes," said Navigatus in surprise. "You know him, then? Frankly, I haven't been able to find anybody who did."

Perennius grinned at his Director. He wondered briefly whether an appearance of omniscience might not be worth cultivation. Not with Marcus, though; not with family. "Don't know a thing but what I can tell by looking at him," the agent admitted. "Must just have been his name." But the cognomen Calvus, Baldie, could have come from generations before. There was something in his easy identification that bothered Perennius in a way that hunches generally did not.

"Umm," said his superior. "He told me nothing at all, Marcus, except that he needed my best agent for a dangerous mission. And then he named you." Navigatus smiled. "Not that there was any question in my mind, of course, but I'm not sure I would have withdrawn you from Palmyra if he hadn't been so specific. And while the fellow was polite enough, well . . . he knew what the rescript he brought said, didn't he?"

Perennius turned his head so that the other man would not see his expression and grimaced ruefully. Another startled lizard ran spraddle-legged a dozen feet along the vertical surface of the wall. "I've been doing you an injustice, Marcus," the agent said. "I thought you'd jerked me because you were getting nervous again."

"I didn't want the Palmyra mission assigned to you, that's correct," the older man said carefully. "You've paid your dues, and I think it's time you left some of the risk to others. But I've never scrubbed you from a mission which you wanted and for which you were qualified. Which is anything short of a bed-chamber attendant for the Empress, as I well know."

Perennius laughed. He slapped his would-be protector on the shoulder and said, "Hell, what good did my balls ever do me, Marcus? But if the well-connected gentleman has been roosting in your chamber since Gaius was sent for me, you'll probably be glad to be shut of him. Let's bring him out here, learn what he needs and then the two of us'll get out of your hair." He stood up.

Navigatus rose also. "That's an odd thing, Aulus," the Director said. "He brought the rescript eighteen days ago today. I said I'd send for him as soon as you arrived—he has an apartment in the palace, but nobody there seems to know him. Except his Majesty, I suppose. . . . But he returned today without being summoned. I was rather concerned because we didn't expect you, you know, not for a week at least."

The two men looked back toward the building proper. To their mutual surprise, the door was open and the chief usher was ceremoniously bowing out the tall, marble-bald subject of their conversation.

"Blazing Noon," muttered Navigatus in the Dalmatian dialect of his childhood. "If he can get around Delius that way . . ." And then both of them put on false smiles to greet the man whom Gallienus had sent to them.

CHAPTER FIVE

On closer examination, Lucius Cloelius Calvus was a stage more unusual than Perennius' initial glance had suggested. Calvus' skin had the yellowish pallor of old ivory, but it was as smooth as a young child's. The skin's gloss suggested someone much younger than the black eyes did. Perennius had heard that the Chinese, on the far end of the route by which silk arrived at government warehouses in Alexandria, had honey-gold complexions. He wondered if the stranger could have come from that far away. Like his skin, Calvus' features were flawlessly regular; but their proportions, their symmetrical angularity, were not those of anyone Perennius had met before. Also, there was something in the slim neck that nagged him. . . .

"Interesting that your usher reads lips," said Calvus in accentless Latin as he approached, "but I suppose it's a valuable ability for someone in his position." He shifted his eyes to Perennius. "Or yours, sir."

"Delius reads *lips?*" sputtered Navigatus.

Only a facet of Perennius' conscious mind listened for content. Calvus blandly expressed surprise that Navigatus had not known that his attendant could follow conversations out of earshot. The agent did not care about that—Delius, in his position, could be expected to know enough to get his superior hung whether or not he was a lip-reader. What interested Perennius more was the chance to determine Calvus' homeland from the patterns within the Latin he was now speaking.

47

With two languages, Latin and Greek, a traveller could wander the length and breadth of the Empire without ever being unable to order a meal or ask directions. From the British Wall, to Elephantine on the Nile where a garrison watched the Nubians south of the Cataract; and from the Pillars of Hercules to Amida across the Tigris, those tongues were in themselves entrée to almost the smallest village. The addition of Aramaic would add textures to the East and to areas of Eastern immigration like Rome itself; but even there, the Greek was sufficient.

But Latin and Greek were not always, even not generally, first languages. There were still farms within a hundred miles of the capital in which nurses crooned to infants in Oscan, for instance. Childhood backgrounds gave a distinctness that went beyond mere dialects to versions of the common tongues. Languages were as much Perennius' present stock in trade as swords had been when he served in uniform. He was very good with both.

But the stranger had no accent whatever. He spoke with the mechanical fluency of water trembling over rocks. Calvus' voice had no more character than that of a professional declaiming a rich man's poem for pay. He gave the words only the qualities required by grammar and syntax.

"If we sit here with our backs to the building," Calvus was saying with a nod toward one of the benches around the fountain, "we can have our privacy. I should explain, Director—" he nodded in an aside to Navigatus—"that the reason I have not taken you into my confidence before now is that I felt Aulus Perennius should be informed by me directly. This way he will make up his own mind. There are risks involved, and I understand your relationship goes beyond bare professionalism." The tall man seated himself on the curved berth, gesturing the others to places to either side of him as if he were host.

Perennius grinned as he sat down. He wondered if Calvus had been told that the agent was Marcus' chicken. Perennius had been a number of things over the years, but not that. Only the Empire had screwed him.

Navigatus frowned. "I've read the letter," he said, tapping the wallet into which he had returned the rescript, "and I understand my duty."

"Ah," said Calvus, "but one owes duty to more than the State, surely. There is one's—" He paused, his tongue groping for a word that was not there—"there are friends, that is; and there is humanity as a whole, don't you agree?"

"Sir, I'm not a philosopher," Navigatus said. His uncertainty as to the other man's position made him more uncomfortable than he might have been in the presence of the Emperor himself. "The Bureau is to give you full support, and it will—if you'll tell us what you require."

Calvus nodded his head upward in agreement. The agent was watching him out of the corner of his eye, keeping his face turned toward the fountain. The pool curb of porous tufa was very old, like the statue itself. The fountain could have been original to the house. Perennius knew that only two years ago, the garden had been smoothly gravelled with no features but the battery of clerks who filled it. On drizzly days, tarpaulins overhead had permitted work if not comfort. By choosing the furnishings he had, Navigatus was trying to turn the garden into a time capsule. It was not merely an enclave of color and beauty on which the Director could rest his eyes: it was a way of returning to an age long before his birth, when the Empire could be embarrassed by foreign disaster but never threatened.

"I have made the Emperor aware of a conspiracy," Calvus said, "and he has empowered me to put it down."

The Director started to say something, but a flick of Perennius' hand kept him from interrupting. The agent's open attention had been focused by the word "conspiracy." He wanted to hear the story in the informant's own words, with as little as possible imported to it by cross-examination. There would be time for that later.

"There would be some advantages to using military force directly," Calvus continued, "but I believe that would draw a response that itself would be a terrible risk. It seems better to deal with the matter through a few individuals."

Perennius did not nod, but his mind flashed agreement. Slip in, bribe a bedroom attendant to suffocate the leader, and slip the hell out again while his lieutenants cut each others' throats. Finesse had ended revolts that a battalion couldn't have touched.

"The right man," Calvus said with a gesture of his eyes toward Perennius, "can put me in a position to destroy this, this—" and again the lips tried to form a word which did not exist in the language Calvus had been speaking flawlessly. "Unspeakable thing," the tall man chose at last. He loaded the term with the first genuine emotion the agent had heard from him.

Calvus swallowed, then added, "The site is in Cilicia, not far from Tarsus."

"*Blazes!*" Navigatus spat out.

Calvus looked surprised. That surprise might become anger when the disgust of the Director's outburst sank in. The agent said, "Ah, sir, as my superior and I are well aware, Cilicia has always been a—difficult area, even in less, ah, troubled times." Perennius sought eye contact with the taller man to give the impression of utter candor. As before, the black eyes jolted him. Out of sheer discipline, the agent stumbled onward, "At the—this particular time, the province is one of those under the con—ah . . ."

"The direction of the Autarch Odenathus, who has recently recovered it—most of it—from the Prefect Callistus," Navigatus supplied helpfully. He had gotten his irritation under control during the breather Perennius had offered him. Now the Director continued smoothly, "Your dedication to his Majesty is beyond question, Lucius Calvus; but if I may suggest something from my, ah, peculiar perspective, a threat in Odenath's back garden, so to speak, is not necessarily a threat to his Majesty at the moment. And an outbreak of banditry in Cilicia would be more conspicuous by its absence." He smiled affably. There were crackpots less harmless, the Almighty Sun knew; and this one had at least the ear of the Emperor.

Calvus smiled. It was a gesture, not an expression. He continued to look toward Perennius rather than toward the Director who was seated on the other side of him. "Not bandits, your Respectability," the tall man said. His quiet formality was as daunting as a more direct reference to the rescript. The formal relationship of the two Bureau personnel to Calvus was that they were under his absolute control. The stranger continued, "You may think of them as a sect, if you like. Yes, a religious sect, very like that. Small at the moment, but going to grow in the future."

"How long were you a member of this sect?" the agent asked. He deliberately begged the question of Calvus' participation in what appeared to have been an illegal organization.

The reaction surprised him. "Don't *ever* say that!" shouted the tall man in an access of loathing. "I and— *those*?" His face smoothed itself with difficulty. The virulence of the stranger's emotion was the more shocking for its contrast with the nearly flat personality he had displayed until that moment. "Yes, of course," he said, aloud but not particularly to the men beside him. "You wonder how I came to know about the situation."

Calvus attempted his smile again. He glanced toward Navigatus before continuing, "I'm afraid that for the moment, you will simply have to take it on faith that I'm correct. I'll try to find an acceptable mechanism to explain my knowledge, but I don't suppose that will affect your plans. That is—" he turned up his right palm—"the worst case is that I will be proven correct. If you plan for that, then the event of my being proven wrong and a madman—" he flipped up his left palm—"will not increase your risk or difficulties. Since the effort must be made in either event."

If you think, Perennius mused, that I can't find a way to grease you between here and Cilicia, and a tragic story of your end that'll satisfy Gallienus or any damn body, then you're wrong. But aloud he said to the placid face, "I used to—live with a woman who saw visions. She insisted I listen the same way I would if it were something she'd seen with her eyes. I didn't much like it then, but I took it from Julia; and I'll take it now, I suppose."

Navigatus relaxed slightly on the other side of the tall man. He knew as well as the agent did that Gallienus' writ ruled little beyond Italy and parts of Africa, at the moment . . . and that nothing but a sense of duty could be truly said to rule Aulus Perennius. Perennius had accepted the assignment now. That meant there was the best chance possible of satisfying this seeming confidant of the Emperor.

A small butterfly landed on the web of Calvus' right hand. He watched it palpate him with its proboscis as he continued: "You will want to know the strength of our opponents. There are only six of them, we believe. Six— true devotees. But they may have any number of hirelings. And they are almost certain to have very powerful weapons, weapons that you could compare only to natural catastrophes, thunderbolts and volcanoes."

Perennius smiled and said, "Yes, well . . . I told you, I have experience accepting the remarkable." But the fact that he joked instead of nodding gravely implied that there was a level of belief in the expressed skepticism. As Calvus had said, it was cheaper to believe him and be wrong than it would be to be surprised the other way.

The shadows of the hills had cut off the sun. Now Navigatus glanced over his shoulder at the Headquarters building and saw the windows of the upper story were being swung shut by the cleaning crews against the threat of rain. The lamps hanging from the drawing-room ceiling silhouetted against the panes the figures of men whose need to see the Director outweighed their dignity.

Navigatus stood, scowling. "Here," he said, "this is foolish. We'll go to my house, bathe there, and discuss this over dinner." He looked anxiously toward the bald man. "If you don't mind something simple, Lucius Calvus? I work here so late that I almost never have time to attend a proper dinner party, much less give one."

Perennius and the stranger rose also. "Marcus, I appreciate it, but your household servants already know as much about my affairs as I intend to let them," the agent said. "Besides, if you don't clear those out of your office properly—" he nodded toward the lamps and those waiting beneath them—"it'll eat at you till you don't sleep tonight. Even though there isn't one of them who's worth a gray hair to either of us."

The Director touched his wig unconsciously. "Well, if you wouldn't feel offended, Aulus," he said apologetically. "I probably would feel better if I dealt with them." He eyed the lighted window again. "Not that you're wrong about the . . . lack of consequence," he added morosely. "I sometimes fear that I've concentrated too much on minutiae in the past few years because the major problems are . . ." His voice trailed off.

"No problem is insoluble," said Calvus. His flat calm made the statement an article of faith. He must have been surprised at how he sounded, because his body at once gave a tiny shudder as if to settle its contents. "Aulus Perennius," the tall man went on, "I will accompany you, then."

"No," said the agent, dipping his head in negation, "that won't be necessary, sir. I'll call for you at the palace in the morning." He smiled. "We're in a transit barracks, my companion and I. I doubt you'd find the accommodations much to your taste." The three of them were drifting back toward the door, now. The social circumstances were too unclear for either of the Bureau employees to act as decisively as they would have preferred to do.

"I'll have to get used to worse accommodations and to none at all," Calvus said simply. He stepped briskly ahead of the others, knowing that the discussion would end when an attendant opened the door for them. "And you'll have to get used to me, I'm afraid, because it is quite necessary for me to reach the site."

The agent laughed. It was Navigatus who actually found words to comment. "In school," he said, "I read Homer's accounts of ships that sailed themselves and gods trading spear-thrusts with mortals. . . ." He gestured his companions onward, through the doorway and into the corridor with the men eagerly awaiting their pointless audiences with him.

"I couldn't imagine how anyone ever had believed such nonsense," the Director went on. "But I see now that I just needed exercise to increase my capacity for faith."

CHAPTER SIX

Perennius swore as his iron-cleated boots skidded on a greasy stone. "Slow up, damn you," he snarled to the linkman. "I hired you to light our way, not run a damned race with us!"

It embarrassed the agent that Calvus seemed to walk the dark streets with less trouble than he did. Anyone lodging in the palace should have done all his night rambling on the legs of litter bearers.

Tall buildings made Rome a hard place for Perennius to find his way around in the dark. He supposed that he used the stars more or less without thinking about it in cities where the apartment blocks did not rear sixty feet over narrow streets as they did in the capital. Even though the barracks were nearby, he had hired a man with a horn-lensed lantern to guide them. The fellow was a surly brute, but he had been the only one in the stand at the whorehouse who was not already attending someone inside.

The raised lantern added a dimension to the linkman's scowl. "Through here," he muttered in a Greek that owed little to Homer. "Me go first." As he spoke, he scrambled into a passage less than three feet wide. The narrow slit of sky was webbed with beams cross-connecting the upper floors of the apartment buildings to either side. Poles draped with laundry slanted from windows, though it was doubtful there was ever a breeze there to be caught.

"Hold the damned light where it does some good!" Perennius said. He turned to his companion. "Here, sir, you go first. It won't hurt this—" he gave his travelling cloak a flick—"to get dropped in the slops again."

"This is safe, then?" Calvus asked as he stepped past the agent. There was curiosity but no apparent concern in his voice.

"Slow *down*," Perennius shouted. In normal tones he continued, "Safe for us. I wouldn't advise you to wander around here without your own attendants, but—we're sober, and even a boyo like the one ahead of us knows the pay-out wouldn't be worth the trouble of trying to bounce the pair of us."

"I wondered," said the tall man, "because this—" he rapped the right-hand wall. He had been tracing his fingers along it as if he needed support—"is the back of the building where we hired this guide. The brothel."

"Well, that doesn't—" Perennius started to say. Metal rang behind them, at or near the entrance to the passage. Darkness and the curve of the walls hid the cause. The agent's sword whined against the mouth of its scabbard as he cleared the blade hastily. "Come on, quick," he hissed to Calvus. His arm gestured the tall man forward, around a blind angle after the linkman.

The right-hand wall angled back abruptly, widening the passage into a court ten feet broad at the far end. There, another wall sharply closed the reentrant. The court was large enough for a second-floor balcony above the brothel's rear entrance. There were figures on the balcony, and there were at least half a dozen men in the court beneath.

"Take the dagger!" Perennius said. He thrust the ball pommel against his companion's hand. Calvus was as still as a birch tree. His fingers did not close on the knife. The agent saw sweat glittering on the tall man's face and scalp as the guide lifted his lantern higher.

"Yes," rasped one of the figures on the balcony. The voice was indescribably harsh. Only the word itself was human. "Kill them."

"Aulus!" cried the other figure, a woman, but twenty years smothered Perennius' recognition of the speaker.

As the agent lunged forward, he pivoted his sword arm to slash rather than to stab. His blade was Basque steel, forged in the Bilbao Armory before it slipped away with Postumus. It had a sharp edge and held it while Perennius sliced through the lantern, the hand holding the lantern, and into the pelvis of the guide who had betrayed them. The bravos waiting in the court surged forward in the darkness.

Perennius was on the stones and rolling, now. He would have called to Calvus, but there was nothing useful to say. Their retreat was surely blocked. It would be a miracle if even confusion allowed either victim to escape through the other end of the court. Besides, the tall man had funked too badly to move, much less to fight or run.

The guide spun off screaming. The sword that was killing him had bitten so deeply in the bone that Perennius had let it go. There was a crash and double screams as the wounded man collided with his friends and another blade. Someone stumbled on Perennius' torso. The agent thrust upward with the dagger Calvus had refused, ripping one of the ambushers from thigh to sternum.

"Gaius, go back!" the woman was crying in Allobrogian. The passage the agent had followed to this killing ground was alive with voices and the ring of blades too long for the surrounding walls. A club or a boot numbed Perennius' right arm. His legs were tangled with the thrashing body of the man he had just disemboweled. The agent slashed his dagger in a brutal arc a hand's breadth above the pavement. Boot-webbing and tendons parted. Someone screamed like a hog being gelded. A club swished toward the sound. The weapon must have been a section of water pipe, because it crunched against a skull with none of the sharpness of wood on something solid.

"Hold up! Hold up!" a male voice bawled from the passage.

The door serving the balcony from within opened.

To the men who had been fighting below in total darkness, the rectangle of light was dazzling. The two figures on the balcony were struggling with one another. Calvus stood as white and frozen as an unpainted statue. He had not moved since the lantern shattered. Now one of the bravos hit him in the face with the lead-studded glove of a professional boxer.

"Hey!" cried someone from the open doorway. Perennius was raising his dagger for a left-handed throw at the man who had just struck Calvus. He thought he recognized the speaker—Maximus, the guard from Headquarters—just as the first of the lightning bolts struck.

One of the figures locked together on the balcony fell in on itself in a blue glare. There was a hissing roar like that of a wave on the rocks. The flash was momentary, but the roar echoed hellishly in the angled court.

The two thugs still on their feet ran for the door in the other building. The men who had followed Perennius down the passage did not exit into the court. Their accoutrements clattered as they ran back the way they had come. Calvus' knees had buckled. The tall man had slid down. His back and sagging head were supported by the wall behind him while his legs splayed out on the stones. All this Perennius could see clearly in the strobe of the second world-shattering flash.

The balcony had a wicker guard-wall. The figure pressed back against it was short and dressed in cape and cowl. Those details were clear because the actinic glare flooded through every interstice as its fury exploded in the balcony doorway. The roar and the screams merged in a sound that could have come from fiery Phlegethon.

Options were clicking through Perennius' mind, overprinted with the retinal memory of the flash. Better to act and bear the consequences than to freeze and become the pawn of others' actions. He gave his dagger a half-flip, caught it by the blade, and threw it with all his strength toward the figure which had been silhouetted above him.

The balcony door was still open, and a lamp burned beyond. The doorway was only a yellow dimness, however. It was no longer able to illuminate the court to eyes which the lightning had blinded. The air stank with burning wool and burning flesh, with wastes voided in terror and wastes spilled from disemboweled victims.

The bravo who had died across Perennius' legs held a meat cleaver. It was an awkward, foolish weapon, but it was the closest one now to hand. The agent appropriated it as he slid from beneath the corpse. His own right shoulder felt swollen to twice its normal size, but he had the use of that hand again, after a fashion. He stepped carefully to where Calvus had fallen. There were moans and even movements from the ambushers who had not run, but none of them was likely to be a threat. They were all fools. In the darkness, they had been worse enemies to each other than Perennius had been to them.

A white form lifted jerkily against the wall. "Did you kill it?" asked Calvus. His voice was weak but unmistakable for its near lack of emotion. The tall man touched the agent's forehead. That minute contact seemed to give Calvus the strength to pull himself fully erect.

"We've got to get the hell out of here before the clean-up squad comes in," Perennius whispered. "I'll go first and we'll try the door to the left there." He gestured with the cleaver. His sight was returning, though he still saw dancing purple flashes every time he closed his eyes.

"No," said Calvus, "we'll go up. None of the fighters were on the balcony. And we have to see that it is dead."

Anger at being contradicted rolled almost at once into an awareness that this time the panicky civilian was right. But though the floor of the balcony was only some eight feet above the pavement, Perennius' own injury—

"Here," said Calvus, lacing his fingers into a stirrup. "If it still moves, kill it. But draw me up quickly if it is dead."

The agent started to protest, but the bald man appeared to know what he was about. He was in a half squat, with his buttocks braced against the wall as a fulcrum. Lean as Calvus looked, there had been nothing of softness in his lines; and anyone who could shrug off a blow like Calvus had received had to be in good physical condition.

Besides, the first one over the wicker railing might need an aptitude for slaughter. There was no doubt as to which of the pair of them that called for.

Perennius measured the distance, measured the chances. He shifted the cleaver to his right hand, hoping his fingers could grip the weapon while he jerked himself up with the other arm. He socketed his foot in the stirrup, touched the balcony with his free hand, and said, "Go!"

The tall man shot Perennius upward as abruptly as a

catapult. Instead of having to catch himself on the railing and pull his body over, Perennius soared. He scarcely brushed the wicker. The agent tried to swing his legs under him, but he hit the floor in an awkward sprawl anyway. Something crunched beneath him like under-fired terra cotta. Remembering the violence that was always his companion, Perennius switched the cleaver to his better hand even as he twisted to see who shared the balcony with him.

The agent had landed on a body that powdered under his weight. The second figure lay face down with half the length of Perennius' dagger pinning its cape to its shoulders. The doorway into the building proper was shattered. The door itself was in splinters, and the stucco over the stone and brick core of the wall was crazed away in a six-foot circle. On the floor of the room within lay two men. One of them was shrunken to scarcely the bulk of a child. A triple ceiling lamp, suspended from bronze phalluses, lighted the room. Other faces peered around the jamb of the door on the other side, where the room opened into a hallway. "Imperial Affairs!" the agent croaked to the frightened onlookers. "Get the Watch here fast!"

One of the sprawled men groaned and lifted to one elbow. It was Sestius, the centurion, and that meant the shrunken thing beside him must be Maximus. What in *blazes* had hap—

"Perennius!" Calvus called from the alley. "Get me up!"

"Stand clear," the agent ordered. He glanced down to make sure that Calvus was not gripping the balcony floor. Then he split the woven guard-wall with a single blow of the heavy knife he had appropriated. Perennius left the blade an inch deep in the balcony framework. He reached through the slit to give the other man the lift he requested. Calvus' legs flexed as Perennius jerked upward. The tall man thumped to the floor, then squirmed upright.

"Herakles!" the injured centurion muttered. "What was that?"

There were more questions than that to be answered, Perennius thought as he tugged his dagger clear. A hand's breadth of the blade was greasily discolored in the lampglow. A lighter blade might have disconcerted the man it struck, but not even the power of the agent's arm could have guaranteed it would sink deep enough to be fatal.

"Yes, turn it over," Calvus said as Perennius reached toward the cowl that still shrouded his victim. The cloth was cheap homespun. It slipped back from the head it had covered.

"Unconquered Sun," Perennius whispered. Sestius, who had crawled forward, gave a shout compounded of fear and loathing when he saw what the agent had uncovered.

The head was not featureless, as shock had insisted in the first instant; but the features resembled those of an elbow joint more than they did a human face. Death had relaxed an iris of bone around what had to be a mouth, though it was at the point of the skull. A thin fluid, not blood and not necessarily the equivalent of blood, drooled between the bony plates of the iris. There were no eyes, no nose . . . no skin, even, as the agent learned by prodding the head gingerly. The surface was chitinous and slick as waxed bone. There appeared to be smudges of pigment shadowing the generally pale surface. Perennius ran a fingertip over them. Sestius watched in horror, Calvus with the detached calm of a woman carding wool. The large blotch where a human's mouth or nose might have been was made up of pores pitting the surface of the chitin in whorls. Higher on the conical head was a circumferential ring like a diadem. The tissue there was brown and flaccid, unlike the surface that supported it. It felt like fresh liver or the eye of a week-dead corpse.

Perennius swore. He jerked the cape completely away from the thing he had killed. His other hand kept the dagger pointed so that if the corpse reared up, it would impale itself. The pose was unconscious and an indication of how great was the fear that the agent controlled when he touched the creature. Sestius continued to stare with the fascination of someone watching a tapeworm thrashing from a friend's anus. None of those peering from the hallway could have seen past the centurion's torso. Perennius had cleared most of the gawkers by naming the Bureau. The madam might possibly summon the Watch;

but no one cared to display too much interest in the secrets of the Bureau of Imperial Affairs.

"We thought somebody was being mugged," Sestius said in a low voice. "We'd stopped in for a drink when we got relieved. Maximus was shook, you know, you . . . We knocked the door open and then . . . sir, what *is* this?"

The creature's torso was segmented like one fashion of body armor. Its surface was of the same glaucous chitin as that of the head. There was a collar of tiny tentacles, only inches long, where a human's shoulders would have been. At approximately the midpoint of the body was a girdle of three larger arms spaced evenly around the circumference. Two of them held objects in the triple fingers with which they terminated. The limbs were hardened, like the body itself, but the thin hoops of chitin with which they were covered made them as flexible as a cat's tail.

The body beneath the trio of arms was a pliable sac on three stumpy legs. The creature vaguely reminded Perennius of a lobster or a spider; but those familiar animals were oriented on a horizontal axis, while this one was as upright as a man.

"Yeah, Calvus," the agent whispered. "That's a good question. What is it?"

"An adult," said the bald man, "a Guardian. There should be five more of them. They are your opponents."

"A religious cult, you said," Perennius snarled. His control was crumbling in reaction to what he had just done and seen. "Six *cultists!*" he said even louder. The point of his dagger wove intricate patterns in the air as the agent's right arm trembled.

"I said you could think of them that way," the tall man said. As the agent rose, Calvus straightened also to tower over the shorter Illyrian. Greatly to the agent's surprise, Calvus's eyes and the icy will behind them remained steady despite the volcanic fury they faced. Perennius had met those who could match his rage with rage, but he had never before known a man who could meet his savage bloodlust and remain calm. "And I said I would find some way to explain it to you," Calvus continued. "I did not expect to be attacked here in Rome, but it seems to have done a better job of explaining what you face than any method I had considered using." His eyes jerked down. "No, don't touch that," he said to Sestius.

Perennius looked down as the centurion snatched back his hand. Sestius had reached out toward not the dead creature itself but rather toward one of the metallic objects in its hands. Now he stared up in surprise at the two men standing above him. "The, the whatever it was that hit me." Sestius explained. "I thought it came from . . ." He gestured at an object that looked like a bell-mouthed perfume flask.

Calvus dipped his head in agreement. "Very likely it did," he said. "But if anyone but one of *them*—" again the disgust loaded one word of an otherwise neutral sentence— "handles the weapon, all its energy will be liberated against the person holding it." The tall man turned up his palm. "And those nearby," he added.

The Watch was not coming, that was clear. Someone burly enough to be the bouncer looked through the doorway to the hall, then leaped back as if struck when his eyes met Perennius's angry glare. "Probably just as well," the agent said aloud. "Marcus has the clout to get us clear, whatever the City Prefect thinks about it . . . but I guess we're going to have enough problems without a story like this one chasing us to Cilicia." He shook his head. "It would, too, sure as sunrise."

"Do we just leave it, then?" Calvus asked. He was curious rather than concerned, much the way he had been when he allowed Perennius to send him down the passage toward waiting murder.

"Quintus, can you stand?" the agent asked. He offered a hand as the centurion struggled to obey. Sestius's limbs seemed whole, but they were not entirely willing to accept his mind's direction. "We'll dump it down there with the other meat," Perennius said with a nod to the court below. "I don't care what the folks who come to strip them think, I just don't want our names on it. If the gear's that dangerous, we'll wrap it in the cloak and deep-six it in the Tiber. Quintus, I hope for your sake you know how to keep your mouth shut, because if you start blabbing, I swear I'll strangle you with your own—hey, what in blazes happened here?" Perennius touched the soldier's vest of iron rings.

"Their weapons are two-stage," Calvus said. He did not coin new words, but his use of familiar ones was disconcerting. It was rather like hearing a priest using his sacerdotal vocabulary to describe hog farming. "An ionizing beam, polarized in three dimensions, that provides the carrier in any liquid or gas. Then—"

Sestius's armor had been of wire links, bent to interlock each with four other rings. It was not an expensive vest. The individual links had not been riveted into shape. Now the front of the vest was no longer a flexible mesh but something as stiff as a sintered plate. There was a hard weld at every point where metal touched metal. Close up, Perennius could separate the odor of burned leather from the avalanche of stenches with which the varied butchery had filled the night. The mail vest was backed with leather to spread the weight of the links and of blows upon them. As the metal flowed and fused, the leather had charred beneath it.

"—the secondary beam, a high-current discharge, travels down the carrier precisely like a thunderbolt," Calvus was saying. "It destroys the controls of sophisticated equipment. And, of course, it destroys life forms . . . but their own body casing, though natural, appears to be totally proof to current, at least at the frequencies their weapons discharge it."

"Blazes," the agent muttered. He understood nothing of the tall man's explanation. The reality was clear enough, though, the flash and bodies seared to powder in the instant. He did not think Sestius had been alert enough when he awakened to really look at his companion. Maximus had nothing recognizable as a chest or face. His linen tunic was yellowed below the waist, completely missing above it. A chain and gold medallion shimmered on the blackened husk. It had been so hot that the minted features had lost definition.

Calvus had already acted on the agent's plan. He was prodding the creature's instruments onto the cloak of the figure incinerated on the balcony with it. The second body was human, probably female from the breadth of pelvis exposed when a point-blank discharge fried away flesh. The torso pulverized when Perennius leaped onto it. The bare skull was shrunken to the size of his two fists clenched together. The agent wondered vaguely what they had been struggling about, the woman and the creature, the Guardian. Blazes, though, there were more more important questions than that to answer.

Perennius sheathed his dagger and gripped one of the creature's limbs. It was hard-surfaced but pliant, like a length of chain. The agent's back crawled. He kept his face impassive as he reached under the slick, conical head with his other hand. He heaved the carcass over the railing. "Somebody's going to get a good sword in the morning," he muttered, "but they're going to get a surprise along with it. Let's get out of here."

The three men stepped out of the room by the hall door Maximus had forced to intervene. Calvus was supporting the centurion with an arm around his shoulders. A fold of the tall man's toga shielded Sestius's face from the remains of his companion.

Under his breath, Perennius muttered, "Told the bastard to wear his armor." But nothing could erase his awareness that the young guard had saved the life of Aulus Perennius in a situation the agent's boastful assurance had gotten him into.

CHAPTER SEVEN

The water began to sizzle and hiss almost as soon as the cloak hit it. Perennius levered the stone sewer grating back with a grunt.

The tall civilian touched him with the arm that did not support Sestius. "I think we'd better step back," he said calmly. He suited his own action to the words.

The agent moved aside at once, though the request had surprised him. He had chosen to ditch the alien paraphernalia in a street grate a few hundred feet from the barracks. Steam-blurred light was flooding through the cuts in the stone trough. The hissing built into a roar, then a scream. "Let's move on," Perennius shouted, afraid that the noise would attract the official attention that he thought they had avoided when they left the brothel unchallenged.

The roar dropped abruptly to the echo of itself reverberating down the sewer pipe. Simultaneously, the grating crackled and several chunks of it fell in. Unperturbed, Calvus resumed walking Sestius toward the barracks.

Perennius swore as he followed the other men. "Do you have weapons like that?" he asked.

"Not here," Calvus said. "We could not send any . . . object. Besides, I was not raised to fight."

"Blazes," the agent said. He had thought the tall man was a coward when he froze during the ambush. Nothing Perennius had seen since supported that assessment, however. He did not understand Calvus any better than he did the other aspects of this situation in which monstrous insects flashed thunderbolts in the darkness.

"This one will die of shock if he isn't kept warm," Calvus said. Unexpectedly, he spoke in Illyrian. The stranger's intonations were as mechanically perfect as those of his Latin had been. "Do you want that?"

"What?" the agent blurted. He was sure at first that he was being chided for not showing more concern for the injured centurion. It struck him then like a death sentence that the question had been asked in all seriousness: would he prefer that Sestius die? "Blazes, no, I don't want him to die!" Perennius said angrily. "Whatever gave you that idea?"

Calvus shrugged. "You wanted secrecy," he said simply.

The transient barracks stood on a middle slope of the Caelian Hill. Externally they were built like a four-story apartment block with a central courtyard. Inside, each wing and floor was divided like a pair of ordinary barracks blocks. There were ten squad-rooms along each face, inner and outer, backed by an equipment storage space attached to each squad-room. In each corner were larger units designed as officers' quarters.

The assignment desk was served by a swarthy civilian, probably the slave or hireling of the watch stander properly assigned to the task. The clerk seemed bright and willing, but he was not fluent enough in either Latin or Greek to understand what Perennius was asking. He kept trying to assign the three of them to a room instead of directing them to the room Gaius would already have taken. Soldiers tramped through the lobby at one stage or another of their search for an evening's entertainment. Their babble made more difficult a task which already seemed impossible.

Perennius was unpleasantly aware of Sestius's state. He had seen men die of shock before. Its insidious peace frightened him more than blood or a sucking hole in the chest. Wounds you could at least see to treat. In Aramaic, the agent began, "*I* am not Gaius Docleus, I want the *room* Gaius Docleus is—"

Calvus broke in. The bald man spoke in an Eastern language, one which the agent could not precisely identify. Calvus's free arm flared in broad gestures as he spoke.

The clerk's face blossomed in amazement and understanding. Perennius had not been on the verge of losing his temper. To the agent, rage was as much a tool as his sword itself was, and he used it only where some good might result therefrom. Here, the clerk was being as helpful as he could be—though it would not have been a fortunate time for the soldier properly responsible to return to the desk. The anger building behind the agent's hard eyes was evident enough, though; and the clerk was at least as happy to achieve understanding as the others were.

Calvus turned back to the agent. "The Senior Centurion's chamber," he said in Latin, "on the fourth floor, north-west corner."

"Three flights to lug him," Perennius muttered with a moue at Sestius. Surprisingly, the comatose man seemed to be getting a little of his color back.

"That won't be a problem," said the tall civilian as he led the way to the outside staircase.

Calvus's words were no more than the truth. Though the injured soldier was a solid man with the weight of his equipment besides, Calvus mounted the stairs at a brisk pace without suggesting the agent help him with his burden. It should not have surprised Perennius after the way the stranger had launched him onto the balcony. Intellectual awareness differed sharply from his instinctive reaction to Calvus's apparent frailty, however.

"We'll want the first—" the agent had begun to say, when the door to which he was about to direct Calvus opened.

"Hey," called Gaius, natty in a fresh tunic and polished brass, "I'd about given up on—" He paused when he realized that the men ahead of his friend were actually accompanying him. "Blazes, Aulus," he said as he stepped back, "you started the party without me?"

"It was a party I'd have liked to have you at, buddy," Perennius said grimly as he shut the door behind him. "See if we've got any field rations in there, will you . . . ? Because I'm starved, and we're not going anywhere until Lucius Calvus here has explained a few things."

The tall man arranged Sestius carefully on one of the beds. "Give me your cloaks," he said, stripping off the

woolen formality of his own toga. Calvus's skin was the
same old-ivory shade wherever it was visible, legs, arms,
and face. In the same matter of fact tone, he continued,
"The creature you killed is from another world. There are
very few adults on Earth at present—six, only five now,
we are quite sure. There are millions of eggs, and the
creatures can breed in their larval forms. They dissolve
rock and crawl through it. When they all become adults
simultaneously, there will be more billions by a factor of
ten then the Earth ever held of humans. They will sweep
us into oblivion unless we stop them now." With neither
haste nor waste motion, Calvus tucked his own garment
around the shivering centurion. He reached for the cloak
of the dumbfounded Gaius.

"Aulus, what on earth—" the younger man blurted.

Perennius stopped him with a raised hand and a frown
of concentration. He was trying to blank his mind of
preconceptions so that he could really *hear* what the tall
stranger was saying. The words did, after all, make internal sense. It was the way they fit—failed to fit—into the
world that made them absurd.

And a tripedal creature four feet tall, with tools and a
voice that could have come from a millstone . . . that did
not fit Perennius's world either. He was professional enough
to believe that it might be his world that was wrong.

"Who are you, Lucius Calvus?" the agent asked softly.

The tall man sat on the edge of the bed. His fingers
massaged Sestius's forehead. The contact seemed to re-
duce the centurion's spasmodic trembling far more than
it should have done. "I'm a traveller," Calvus said, his
calm eyes on the older Illyrian. "An agent like yourself,
Aulus Perennius."

Perennius slammed the heel of his hand against the
closed door. It crashed like a catapult releasing. "Do you
think I don't see that?" he shouted. "*Whose* agent, damn
you?"

"Mankind's," said the man who called himself by a
Latin name. "But I came from another sort of distance,
Aulus Perennius. I come from a place fifteen thousand
years into the time that has yet to come."

Gaius threw up his hands. "Blazes," he cried to the

ceiling. "Aulus, are you all drunk? Him babbling non-sense and you sitting there serious as an owl like you were listening!"

"How are you going to stop them if you didn't bring any weapons?" asked the agent. He did not raise his voice again, but the taut malevolence in it sent a shiver up Gaius's back. Perennius had not liked the world that Fate had shown him, but it drove him to helpless fury to feel all the certainties draining away from even that. There were few things that Aulus Perennius would surrender without a fight. Reality was not one of those things.

"We knew we could find a weapon here, Aulus Perennius," said the calm, seated figure. His hands continued to stroke the injured centurion. "We knew that I could find someone like you."

Gaius seized Calvus by the shoulder. The young courier was a good-sized man, but his attempt to shake the seated figure was as vain as if he had tried to shake an oak. "My friend isn't a weapon!" Gaius shouted. "He's a *man*, and men aren't just things!"

"Let him go, Gaius," the agent said quietly. He was not really watching the scene. He had a task to perform, five *creatures* to kill in Cilicia if they did not come to meet him earlier. Perennius was considering ways and means of accomplishing that task.

CHAPTER EIGHT

When the sunlight through the clerestory windows touched his left eye, Perennius blinked. On the bed next to him, Gaius said in a chiding voice, "You didn't sleep all night, did you?"

Perennius turned sharply toward his protégé. "Sure I did," he lied.."Ah—didn't keep you awake, did I?"

Gaius chuckled as he got up. "Oh, not a bit," he said. "Like with my brothers. You share a bunk as often as you and I have, you don't notice how the other fellow tosses and turns any more than you do yourself. But I also know you well enough to know you weren't sleeping."

There were two beds in the room, because a centurion was expected to travel with at least one personal servant. The two Illyrians had dossed down in one of the bunks, leaving the other to Sestius and the traveller. Calvus had said the body contact as well as the warmth would be good for the injured man. The centurion could not well be moved, and the agent would not have allowed Calvus out of his immediate reach even if the tall man had shown a desire to leave.

"Oh, well, you know how it is," Perennius said as he got out of bed. "I need a while to think about things before I go off and do something. A mess like this, blazes—it's better than a week at the sea-side." He stepped to his baggage and began searching for clean clothes. Nude, the agent's body was ridged with muscles and scar tissue—puckers, the thin lines of cuts, and the knotted, squirming

73

lumps from the time he had been beaten with a studded whip.

"Do you like the sea, Aulus Perennius?" asked Calvus as he also stood up. The traveller was still dressed in the wool tunic he had worn under his toga. The centurion was stirring and grumbling on the bed beside him.

Professionally bland, the agent looked at Calvus and said, "No, as a matter of fact, I never had much use for the sea. Except as something to get over. Which I figure we'll do this time, little as I care for the idea."

"Blazes!" Gaius protested. He peered from the folds of the tunic he was shrugging into. "After what happened on our way back? Look, it's a *lot* safer to hoof it, even the way roads're likely to be in Cilicia."

"Maybe true if we were alone, the three of us," Perennius said. "But we're going to need a couple squads at least for the job. Archers, slingers . . . and I don't give much of a chance of Odenath or Balista, whichever's boys we run across, letting a body of troops march through Asia. Even a *small* body of troops." He smiled grimly at Calvus. "A better chance than that your rescript from Gallienus would get us anything but a quick chop. Maybe you could come up with something by the Autarch instead?"

"Odenathus, you mean?" said the tall man. He was as serious as Perennius had been sardonic. "Yes, if that's necessary. It will delay us considerably, though; and I think delay is to our disadvantage, now that we know the Guardians are aware of me."

Gaius laughed. Perennius did not. "No," the older man said uncomfortably, "we'll enter at Tarsus on forged orders from Palmyra, some song and dance. By the time somebody checks back with headquarters, we'll be long gone." He barked a laugh of his own. "Or long dead, of course."

"Let me come with you," said Quintus Sestius.

The three others looked at the centurion. Sestius was poking fixedly at his welded mail. The night before, he had not really been aware of what had happened to him. "Look," he said, "I come from near Tarsus. I can help you a lot. It's not a province that outsiders get along in real well." In the same defensive tone he added, "Maximus is dead, isn't he? I remember him being right in front of me, and then . . . that was him on the floor, I guess. It was his cloak, so it had to be."

Sestius had thrown off the wrappings that had kept him alive until his capillaries contracted and brought him out of shock. Calvus now bent and retrieved his toga without speaking. He had set the objective, but it appeared that he was going to allow Perennius full responsibility for the means of achieving that objective.

"Ah," the agent said. Except for Gaius himself, the troops for the operation were an anonymous rank in his mind. He was not opposed to Sestius being one of them but . . . "Look," Perennius said, "Maximus likely wasn't the last to take early retirement because of this thing, Sestius. It's going to be dangerous."

"Herakles!" the centurion spat. "And what isn't now?" He stood abruptly so that the unwelded back of his vest rustled on the leather. "Listen, sir—I joined the Army because it'd be secure. Nothing's secure now, nothing . . . but if I could be home again, with my kin around me, then at least there'd be *somebody* to trust, somebody. . . . Sir, take me along. I'm as good a man as you'll find, and I know the territory. And when you've done what you need done, just . . . turn your head. But I'll stay with you until then, I swear I will."

Perennius listened without expression. An Imperial soldier was planning desertion aloud and proposing to make the agent himself an accomplice in the plan. But Perennius had a task now on which he could focus. He could use that task as a set of blinders by which to shut out every other flaw and cancer in the Empire . . . and if the centurion's proposal was as sincere as it sounded, there was nothing in it to intrude on the present mission.

"All right," said the agent. Gaius, prepared for violence, sighed out a tiny breath in relief. Perennius found a scriber and one of the blank tablets he kept in his wallet. He sat on the corner of the bed and began writing in firm, rapid strokes as he continued, "Gaius, I'm giving you this note and the orders recalling me. Between them, they ought to get you to Marcus. If you can get through the mob inside without acting like me, fine. But remember, we're in a hurry, however much fuss you have to make."

"I couldn't act like you, Aulus," the younger man said with a grin. He was lacing his right boot, braced on the footboard. The tips of its iron nails winked where the rust had been polished clean.

"Sure, anybody can act like me," Perennius said. He began to work the signet ring off his left little finger. "Just remember that everybody you meet in a place like Headquarters is more afraid of a scene than you are. Blazes, boy, *you've* got the right—this is all on his Majesty's orders." He tossed Gaius the tablet, signed and sealed. "Or are you going to let some jumped-up pretty boy in silk make you cool your heels because you're afraid to raise hell?"

"Here, take this too," the agent added more gently. He handed his pass to the courier as he had said he would. Gaius waited uncertainly, ready to lace his other boot as soon as he was sure that nothing else was going to be flipped to him. "I won't bother to write down what we need, you *tell* Marcus personally and he'll dictate the orders. First—"

"Sir," Sestius interrupted, "I should be on duty now myself, and—"

"If you'll hold your damned water," Perennius snapped, "you'd hear that you're going along with Gaius. I'll get the Director to release you from your duties as of last night." He frowned. "Your buddy too, Maximus. Might save inquiries that wouldn't do us any good, damned paper-pushers. But first—" he continued, turning back to the courier who jumped up from his boot laces—"I want letters to the Prefect of the Fleet at Misneum and whoever the hell his lieutenant is at Ostia. Full cooperation, he'll understand. Make sure they're countersigned by Respectabilities in the right offices so that we don't get a lot of crap when we're ready to move. While you get the paperwork going, Lucius Calvus and I—" he nodded to the tall man—"are going to see whether we can find what we'll need in Ostia."

The agent rose from the bed and began to buckle on his

equipment belt. "That's the first thing we do when we leave this room," he said as he fingered the empty slot of his sword scabbard. "*After* I replace some hardware I figure we'll need."

CHAPTER NINE

"Just a moment, gentlemen," said the usher. "I'll see if the Tribune is free."

Perennius had been quite honest in saying he did not care for the sea. Ostia was no beach resort like Baiae, either. It was a working port, and it stank like one. The breeze drifting through the colonnades of the old Customs Station was ripe with spoiled goods dumped into the harbor along with the burden of the town's sewer system. Still, the agent was feeling unexpectedly cheerful. "You know," he said in a low voice to his companion. "I wasn't counting on being able to see anybody officially until Marcus got some orders cut. All I figured we'd be able to do was look around and probably buy some information for a cup or wine or two."

The reception room in which they waited was dingy. It seemed to be used to store old Customs records, judging from the seals on the dusty document cases stacked along one wall. The naval contingent at Ostia was under the Naval Prefect at Misenum, one hundred miles south on the Bay of Naples. The vessels here were attached to the Customs Service, and their command staff was housed in a corner of the Customs Station. Ill-housed, not surprisingly, and furnished with cast-offs from their senior partner.

Calvus looked around the room. Monochrome stucco was flaking from the walls which were not covered by boxes, and some of the marble bits of the mosaic flooring had worked loose from their concrete bed. "I mention this because it may be necessary for you to know it, Aulus Perennius," the tall man said. "I can sometimes influence persons to fall in with a course of action. Especially when the emotional temperature is low, or when the other person is very excited and considering the desired course of action himself. The course I desire."

It did not occur to Perennius to doubt what the other man was saying. The agent's skin flashed cold and his right hand curved over the grip of the sword he had been issued only hours before. "Now, tell me what that had to do with me being here," the agent said softly.

The hands that had lifted Perennius without effort remained crossed in Calvus' lap. His eyes were alert but fearless as they met the agent's. "That ability had nothing to do with you," the tall man said simply. "I don't want—could not use—anyone who needed prodding to act. I told you, Aulus Perennius: I was not raised to handle weapons." Calvus grin was brief and unreal. "My weapons have to handle themselves."

Shoes slapping down the hall and a burst of voices discussing insect netting drew the attention of the waiting men to the doorway. A plump man in his mid-twenties stepped into the reception room, calling one last objection over his shoulder to someone unseen. The newcomer had a curly beard, well-trimmed, and wore a tunic with the two thin stripes of equestrian rank. He nodded to Calvus and Perennius before seating himself on the wood-framed couch facing them. A layer of dust lifted from the couch pad, provoking first a curse, then a sneeze. When he had recovered himself, he said, "All right, gentlemen, Terentius Niger at your service. Nine chances in ten, what you need isn't in my department. This is the *Naval* contingent, not Customs. If you're the lucky tenth, I probably can't do a thing for you either—you know that those bastards won't issue gauze curtains for my office? *You* try and work there some night when you can't read a document for the gnats in your eyes!"

"I'm Aulus Perennius from Imperial Affairs," the agent said, watching the young tribune stiffen. The agent saw no reason to hide his identity or that of his office. "I realize you won't have received the orders yet, but it would help us a great deal if you could tell us what major naval units are available here—and of course at Portus." The administrative offices had remained at Ostia when Portus, the artificial harbor for heavier vessels, was constructed adjacent to Ostia some two centuries before, Perennius had learned not to be over-specific when trying to learn something from a bureaucrat.

"Major naval units available," Niger repeated. He grinned bitterly. The tribune was young enough to hope that by being frank, he might be able to get word back up the line to where it might help correct the situation which he deplored. "How about jack shit?" he said bluntly. He leaned forward in his couch. "You know how quick Rome'll start to starve if the grain supply from Africa is cut off? Weeks if we're lucky! And *that's* if nothing happens to the warehouses here." He waved his hand in a dramatic, ring-glittering circuit in the air. "The only things to stop pirates from sailing right into the harbor and burning it down around our *ears* are the gods, may they continue to preserve us, and my twelve customs scows. There's half a dozen light galleys laid up in Portus, but they haven't been in the water since Commodus died—and I couldn't crew them anyway." Niger grimaced and added, "Besides which, my Marine contingent just got drafted into a Field Force legion. Now you two tell me—is that a safe state for the capital of the Empire?"

Hell, no; but it's the state that everything else's in, Perennius thought. Aloud he said, "I'd like to take a look at those galleys you mentioned. I'm sure something could be arranged about crews . . . and we wouldn't need all of the ships, of course."

Niger stood up. "You think I'm joking?" he asked. "They haven't touched keel to water in seventy years—and Neptune alone knows when the damned things were built! But come along, you can see for yourself." He stepped to the doorway by which he had entered. "Rufio!" he called. "Rufio!"

The attendant who had greeted Perennius initially appeared in the hallway. "Sir?" he said.

"I'm taking these gentlemen to Shed Twelve," the tribune explained. "They want to see what passes for naval power in this wretched excuse for an age."

As Perennius and Calvus followed him to the stand of government litters and bearers, the agent thought of how many times he had performed this basic task: checking garrisons, fortifications, or supply dumps so that Rome could better estimate the war-making capacity of an enemy. Normally, however, the agent would have been equipped with a packet of documents—forged, of course, but convincing even to a skeptic. It did not strike Perennius as particularly humorous that he was being shown Rome's own defenses without any of the preliminaries he would have thought necessary as a spy.

"Well, here they are," Niger said. His voice whispered back and forth between the brick walls and high roof timbers of the dry dock. "Go on, tell me it's not as bad as you expected."

The shed was a single building with six separate roof peaks. The troughs were supported by columns rather than by walls. From where the three men stood on the raised entrance platform, they could see all six of the docked galleys. The murky water of the harbor lapped just beyond the open front of the building, but the hulls were on dry ground. Timber baulks held each upright.

Niger had opened the shed door using a key with two large prongs to turn the wards. Now he stepped to the nearest of the stored vessels and pressed the prongs against the railing without result. Patiently, he tried a few feet further, then further yet. On the third attempt, the iron prongs sank in as easily as if they had encountered a cheese. "There," said the tribune in gloomy satisfaction, "dry rot. What did I tell you?"

The rear platform of the shed was nearly of a height with the galley's stern rail. The bowsprit and stern posts of the vessels curved up sharply above either end. The poop itself was raised a full deck above the planking that covered the waist of the ships. Perennius stepped aboard the nearest ship. His hob-nails echoed like rats scurrying along the roof of the shed. Though one whole side of the building was open, its interior was hot and dry and smelled of pine tar.

"All right, these look like what we need," the agent said. He swung himself down to the main deck with a thump, disregarding the ladder pegged to the bulkhead. "What sort of complement do they carry?"

The agent began to walk toward the bow. The hull, shrunken by years in storage, quivered enough in the baulks to give itself a queasy sort of liveliness. Two long ventilator slots before and abaft the mast step ran most of the length of the deck. The ventilator gratings had been removed and were leaning against their low coaming, giving Perennius a view of the interior as his eyes adapted. In the ovals of gray light through the oar locks, he could see four axial columns of benches. The outboard pair, nearer the hull strakes, were low and barely wide enough for one man and the oar he had to swing. The interior benches were separated by a storage well three feet wide which ran the length of the lower deck, directly above the keel.

"For oarsmen, thirty-six men on the lower bank, seventy-two on the upper," Niger said. There was a slight pique in his tone at the agent's refusal to be horrified at the ship's condition. Perennius had seen border posts whose garrisons were equipped primarily with the farm implements they needed to raise their own supplies. The tribune might think that dry-rotted hulls were a disgrace, but that was because of his youth and the parochialism of a central-government official. "You can use fewer oarsmen, of course, the ship just doesn't move as fast. If you depend on what *I've* got available, you use a *lot* fewer oarsmen."

"It's a bireme, then?" the agent asked. The main deck was almost flush with the hull. It was capped with a coaming a hand's breadth high rather than a railing or bulkhead. Outboard of and a step down from the deck proper was a covered outrigger whose frame supported a bank of oars. In a battle the catwalk would permit a rank of Marines to fight with locked shields while archers on the main deck fired over their heads.

"If you want to be technical, it's a liburnian and a sort of trireme," Niger said, "but I never noticed that putting a name to something made it sail faster. Or found a crew for it. You need a couple dozen seamen, too, you know, unless you expect to row all the way—which you can't. And I told you what happened to my Marines, didn't I?"

An animal miasma still drifted up from the rowing chamber, despite its decades of standing empty. Normally the oarsmen would have voided their wastes over the side, like the Marines and the deck crew. That would not have been possible while the vessel was under oars, however. Beyond that was the effluvium of over a hundred men straining in the rowing chamber while the sun baked the deck above them and glanced from the oar-foamed surface of the water. The whole blended in an amalgam sweeter than the vegetable odors of the ship herself, and as permanent as the pine timbers which it had impregnated.

"She'd carry fifty soldiers comfortably?" Perennius estimated aloud. He had reached the bow and was peering over it, past the upcurved bowsprit.

"Eighty on war service," Niger called, "if she didn't break up under their weight as she probably would now. You see the bronze sheathing's gone from the ram, the gods know how long ago. Stolen or turned to coinage, it doesn't matter. Ram anything with the hull this rotten and the bronze'd be the only thing that didn't powder."

Perennius turned and looked back the way he had come. Calvus stood just inside the open street door, spare and silent. Distance and the lighting hid the stranger's face, but Perennius had enough experience now to imagine its expression of preternatural calm. A damned strange man, but at least Calvus did not complicate with instructions the task he had set for the agent.

The tribune was poised on the platform with one hand on the stern rail. He was shifting his weight from one foot to the other, but he had not quite decided to jump onto the deck as the agent had done. Not a bad kid. Like Gaius, one of those there would have been some hope for, if there were any hope for the Empire they served. "All right," Perennius said. He began to stride back along the hundred feet of deck separating him from the other men. "How long would it take you to put one of these in shape for a long voyage? If you had the men and stores turned over to you, whatever you said you needed and could be found in the port."

For the space of six measured strides, the only sound in the drydock was that of the agent's boots on the planking. When Niger spoke, it was with caution and none of the bitter wise-cracking of his earlier remarks. "Not less than three days," he said. "Maybe as much as seven. She'll have to be caulked and repitched. . . . For that matter, we'll have to survey all six and see which is most likely to hold the water out. Mast and spar, fighting towers, oars . . ."

The tribune's musing aloud paused when Perennius fell below his line of sight past the poop deck. When the agent had climbed the ladder, their eyes met again. Niger looked troubled. "I'd appreciate it if you'd start the list of men and materials required," Perennius said to the younger man. "Figure out where you could get them if you had a blanket authorization. In an hour or two, that's just what you'll have."

Niger dipped his oiled beard in assent. "Yes, sir," he said. The animation, the sharpness of tone, was gone as he contemplated the situation. "Sir . . ." he went on diffidently. "I'll see to it that she's put in order to the extent possible. But she'll still be an over-age, under-maintained disaster waiting to happen. If she's really being fitted out for a long voyage . . . I don't envy the men aboard her."

"Don't envy anybody, my friend," said Aulus Perennius. He braced his left hand on the stern rail, then swung himself back to the platform with a clash and sparkling of boot studs and concrete. By the blazing Sun, he could still eat men half his age for breakfast, he thought in a surge of pride springing from the exertion. He grinned at the surprised tribune like a wolf confronting a lamb. "No," he repeated, "don't envy anybody."

The single, unsprung axle of the carriage found a harmonic with the courses of paving stones. The sympathetic vibration escalated what had been a burr into a series of hammering jolts. Perennius, at the reins, had been lost in thought before the jouncing lifted him back to present realities. He clucked to the pair of mules, urging them into the extra half-stride per second that broke the rhythm.

The agent looked over at his companion. Calvus had braced himself firmly with one hand on the seat and the other locked on the frame holding the carriage top. They had taken the vehicle from Rome to Ostia because Calvus had said he had never ridden a horse. Perennius had the feeling that the tall man had never ridden a carriage, either, now that he had watched him in one. Calvus seemed to have no subconscious awareness of where the next bump would come from and how he should shift to receive it. He was using his surprising strength to keep from being literally bounced out of the vehicle, but the battering that earned him must have been equivalent to all-in wrestling with a champion. Calvus never complained, though.

"How did you get that imperial rescript?" Perennius asked without preliminaries.

"The way I told you," the other man said. "I can't force a decision, but I can influence one. Like the wheels just now."

"Eh?" The agent glanced back from the road, but only for an instant. They were overtaking an official carriage. Common sense and the quartet of tough-looking outriders enjoined caution.

"Normally the vibrations of the wheels cancel themselves," Calvus explained. "There for a moment, the bumps and the period of oscillation of the carriage were perfectly in tune. Instead of a constant tingle, each bounce was higher and higher—until you changed the rate at which we encountered the bumps."

He paused. The agent continued to watch the road as they swept by the larger vehicle. Nothing in Perennius' face betrayed emotion. He was gathering information. From past experience with Calvus, it would make sense eventually.

The bald man went on, "I can advance an idea. Nothing complex, nothing like—what the ability was meant for. Pure communication with my siblings. But 'Help this man' or 'Believe this' . . . or simply, 'Run!' A little prodding of the recipient's mind at a level of which he isn't aware, so it becomes his thought. And it keeps returning, a little stronger each time, until he acts on it. Nothing that he might not have done anyway, of course, but there are so many actions that are within the capacity of an imperial usher, for instance, that it isn't hard to find one that prepares for the next stage of action. And at last, the Emperor comes to believe something which is in fact true but which he would probably not have acted on if approached in any other fashion."

The rumble of their iron wheels on the road made Perennius' bowels quiver and his head nod toward the sleep it had not gotten the night before. Everything was going smoothly now. He had conceived his plan and put it into operation. The agent's mind was ready to relax, now, until the next of the inevitable disasters lurched into its path to be dealt with. "Calvus," the Illyrian said.

"Yes, Aulus Perennius," the other replied.

"Don't screw with my mind. I know myself pretty well. If I ever find myself acting . . . some way I don't, I'll come after you. It . . . This world doesn't always seem to have a lot for me in it, but *that's* always been my own."

"Would you file the edge of a good sword?" asked the tall man.

Perennius had been avoiding Calvus' eyes. Now he glanced back at the tall man. "Hell no," he said.

"Neither would I, Aulus Perennius," Calvus said.

They were nearing the formal boundaries of the city. Both sides of the road were lined with tombs and funerary steles. In recent years, many of those who could afford it were being buried whole instead of being cremated as their ancestors had been. Instead of a single stone plate with a prayer for their spirits and a base on which a wine and food offering could be left by relatives, they wanted to be embalmed to await resurrection. Fools and their mystery religions, their Isis and Attis and Christos. But when there was increasingly little hope or security in the world, how could anyone blame people who looked for hope elsewhere?

Perennius muttered a curse. Easily. If the damned cowards would buckle down and *do* something about the present, they wouldn't need to despair about it. Miniature pyramids, polished granite sarcophagi with peaks on the corners in Syrian style ... Those were the fancy ones. For the poor, there were boxes of tufa, so strait that even short men must have their legs folded at the knees or separated by a bone saw.

The agent's face stayed blank, but his hands were gripping the reins so tightly that the skin striped white and red over his knuckles. Calvus watched him closely. With the care of a scout trying to disarm a deadfall, the tall man said, "I couldn't have affected the gang which waylaid us last night, even if I hadn't been immobilizing the Guardian's weapon. There were too many of them, too hopped-up, and it was too sudden. But I did encourage the group behind us to run, after you killed the Guardian."

"What?" Perennius said. Curiosity dissolved from his mind the anger directed at his whole world. The agent's muscles relaxed to the normal tautness of a man driving a pair of spirited mules. "What were you doing to the thunderbolt thing? That is what you mean?"

The bald man nodded. "For the weapon to work, two small metal parts had to touch each other inside it. While I could, I kept them from touching by keeping a layer of—" he risked a gesture with his left hand—"part of the air between them. Until I was hit on the head, that is." He smiled.

Perennius had the impression that the smile was real, not a gesture trotted out for a suitable occasion. That lightened the agent's mood as much as did the interesting problem which the statement posed. The stable from which they had rented the carriage was in sight. Wheeled vehicles were unlawful in the city during daylight, and only goods wagons were permitted on the streets even after dark. They would walk to Headquarters. Perennius had a dislike for sedan chairs, a fear of being closely surrounded by four strong men who had every reason to dislike him as a burden. No doubt chairmen who really did hate the folk who hired them soon enough found another line of work, but the feeling persisted.

"Then you can make things move without touching them," Perennius asked in a neutral voice. Calvus' abilities interested him, but he was able to discuss them without concern except for when they involved meddling in his own head.

"Nerve impulses, very easily." the bald man said with what was only the semblance of agreement. He buffed his thumb against the two fingers as if there were something in between. "Tiny bits of the air, not so easily . . . but that too. If you mean move a sword or a key, no. No more than you could lift those mules and throw them." He nodded toward the team. The mules, familiar by years of experience with the route, had left the road without command and were turning into the stable to be unharnessed. Calvus held onto the frame with both hands again as the wheels rang over the curb. "It's important that you know my limitations, you see."

"Whoa," called Perennius to the mules. They had already stopped, and he drew back on their reins needlessly. The ostler was walking toward them, turning a sharp eye on the condition of his animals. Habit, habit. The agent jumped down to the stable yard and walked around the back of the vehicle to help Calvus dismount. "Just remember," Perennius said as he reached a hand up to his awkward companion, "I have limitations too. I'm only human."

"Actually, Aulus Perennius," said the tall man as he stepped down, "you aren't even that, not entirely . . . not at least as we would define the term, my people." He released the callused, muscular hand that had just braced him. "That's what makes you so valuable, you see," Calvus concluded with a smile.

CHAPTER TEN

The crew was marching aboard the forward gangplank of the liburnian *Eagle* under the eyes of a squadron of Household Cavalry. Working over the stern gangplank was a gang of a dozen slaves with their tunics knotted up around their waists. The slaves were singing cheerfully as they brought aboard the last of the provisions, grain and wine in sealed pottery jars. Their light-heartedness was in stark contrast to the attitude of the free crewmen.

"Blazes," Gaius complained as he squinted against the sunlight, "what prison do you suppose they rounded the crew up from?"

Perennius was on the *Eagle*'s poop with Gaius, Calvus, and a pair of preoccupied ship's officers. The agent watched the shuffling column with an interest equal to his protégé's and with far greater experience to draw from. The number of sailors was right or close to it. The men were more or less of working age, with the swarthy complexions and muscles of men used to labor outdoors. For that matter, they seemed to be in good health when one made allowance for the sores, scars, missing limbs and eyes, and the other similar blemishes to be expected in any group of sailors. "No," the agent said, "they were probably all free men until last night or so when the Army swept some fishing village." He frowned as he considered. "Or maybe some boarding houses here in Ostia. Bad in the long run. Bad for taxes, bad for trade ... bad for the Empire, I guess, for an imperial decree to affect its citizens like—"

he gestured to the glum file of seamen—"this. But in the short run, it had to be done."

Gaius snorted. "You're convinced of that?" he gibed.

Perennius looked from his friend to Calvus, standing beside the young courier and showing no concern at the conversation. "I'm always convinced that what I'm told to do is necessary," the agent said. He laughed. "I only get into trouble when I come up with ideas myself."

Gaius started to laugh with the older man, but the question on the surface of his mind made the laughter thinner than he had intended.

"Who are these, then?" asked Calvus. He pointed to a separate contingent marching down the quay toward the *Eagle.* There were scarcely twenty of them. They carried arms—spears and belt gear, with helmets and plain shields slung on their field packs—but they showed no more capacity to keep step than the sailors had. The section leader was at the left front of the short column of fours. He gave a sharp salute to the officer in charge of the detachmen of Household Cavalry. That worthy ignored the salute after a disdainful look at the newcomers.

Perennius swore with a bitter fury. He leaped to the main deck with the lithe twist of a cat charging. Officers were trying to organize the milling seamen, sending rowers below to their benches to clear the vessel for casting off. The agent slipped through the mass behind the point of his left shoulder, making as little contact with the other frustrated men as was consistent with the swiftest possible progress through them to the stern gangway. Gaius followed, using his greater size to make up for his lack of finesse. His chest and shouted threats cleared a path for Calvus, behind him, as well. By the time they caught up with Perennius, however, the agent was already reading the diploma handed him by the leader of the section of troops.

"By the icy shades of *Hell!*" Perennius shouted. He slapped the wooden tablet closed against a palm no less hard and handed the document to Gaius. "Read *that,*" he snapped. "How in the . . ." The Illyrian's voice trailed off as he glared at the contingent of troops. The tight-lipped leader of the unit had made two attempts to defend himself against the agent's fury. Now he was staring straight ahead. His men were describing a series of variations on "At ease."

Aloud, Gaius read, " 'Master of Soldiers, West, Bureau of Assignment, to Commanding Officer, Liburnian *Eagle*. April 14. This order transmits Draft 737, twenty effectives under a watch-stander, as Marine complement of said vessel. In accordance with instructions 12th instant, Director of Administration.' " The courier looked up from the document to the troops. "But Aulus," he said, "you said there'd be a full eighty men including the ones that'd be getting off with us. And none of these are missile infantry."

"None of them are goddam infantry at all!" the agent snapped.

The troops were an assortment more varied than the sailors had been. One in the front rank was a Nubian from well below Elephantine. His head had been shaven, but the hair was beginning to grow out again in tight ringlets against his sepia skin. By contrast, several of the others were Germans—tall and blond and sunburned to the point of blistering. The remainder of the draft fell between those extremes with a certain bias toward eastern physiognomies, Syrians and Cappadocians predominating. The closest thing to a common denominator among the troops was the prevalence of shackle-scars on their ankles. In some cases, the marks were fresh enough to be bleeding.

"You," said Perennius to a blond man. "How long have you been a soldier?"

The fellow turned to the man beside him and whispered a question. Without waiting for the other to translate, Perennius switched from Latin to Border German and repeated, "How long have you been a soldier?"

The blond man drew himself up proudly. His exposed skin was pocked with sores, and a sunburn gave him the complexion of an over-rouged corpse. "All his life, Hermann has been a warrior," the man said. He spoke in heavy Schwabish, the dialect of the tribe which had grown to the point of calling itself the 'All-Men,' Alemanni. He gripped the pommel of his standard-issue sword. It looked absurdly small beneath his huge, bony hand.

"But Hermann's leg irons got struck off some time this

morning, didn't they?" Perennius said bitterly. He turned to Calvus. "Our so-called Marines are a draft of freed slaves," he said. "The orders were clear, so somebody's playing games in the Ministry of Soldiers. Well, we'll send these back and start looking for the whoreson who's getting in my way!"

"How long will that take?" the tall man asked.

Perennius had not really expected a response to his diatribe. He paused in mid-stride and looked back at Calvus. His mind was assimilating the implications of the question. "Two, maybe three days," he said carefully. "Do we have a deadline you haven't told me about?"

Calvus glanced down the section of Marines. The agent made the same calculation simultaneously. He walked along the quay toward a lighter unloading hyenas destined for the amphitheatre. Gaius frowned, but this time he did not follow the other men without being summoned. Perennius had a useful vocabulary in a score of languages, and the traveller had proven his fluency in still others. Neither of them were willing to bet that they had a language in common which was not shared with at least one of the newly-conscripted Marines, however.

"I haven't made a point of this," said Calvus against the backdrop of growling beasts, "because I knew you were acting as quickly as possible. But the—" he swallowed—"Guardians located me once. By now it seems evident that the one you killed was here by himself and that there will not be another attempt until another can arrive from Cilicia. . . . But even if they must rely on—locally-available transportation, every day makes the second attempt more probable."

Perennius sucked his lower lip between his teeth. He turned. "Longidienus!" he shouted down the quay. "Watch-stander!"

The leader of the Marines braced to attention. He at least was a trained soldier. "Sir?" he replied.

"Get your men aboard. We'll be sailing as soon as the captain tells me he's ready," Perennius ordered. In a low voice, he went on to the traveller, "I suppose you know how the bug found you?"

Calvus lifted his forehead in negation. "We hadn't expected anything of the sort," he said. "They—you see, we're used to dealing with th-them in a different aspect. It's easy to underestimate them, because the individuals are treated as so many blood cells, so many flakes of skin. But the gestalt . . ." He turned his palms upward. "My arrival here would have caused an enormous shift of energies. We didn't think they would be able to detect it. Obviously, they detected something. Perhaps it was that."

The hyenas stank with a feline musk which made the agent's stomach turn even in the general reek of the harbor. He stared at the spotted, scabby beasts while his hands rested lightly on the weapons beneath his cloak. There were a dozen of the hyenas, each of them a man's size or larger; and Perennius thought he understood the frustrated rage with which they glared out of their crates. "How are chances that they can keep right on tracking you?" the agent asked. He spoke toward the beasts.

"If they simply located my—point of arrival," Calvus said, "then they have no more way of following us when we leave the vicinity that anyone else in this age would have. They will be waiting, of course, but you will still determine how and when to strike." He paused as if to take a deep breath; though in fact, Calvus' breathing was, as always, mechanically regular.

"That's one possibility," said Perennius to the hyenas.

"Yes," Calvus agreed. "And yes, they may be able to locate me at all times, wherever I am, whatever I do. In that case, I see very little possibility that our mission will succeed."

"Yeah, that was how it looked to me, too," the agent said. He met the tall man's eyes again. Neither of their faces held any particular expression. "Let's get aboard," Perennius said. "We'll assume that they'll lose us as soon as we get under way."

The three and a half hours of unexpected delay which followed would have grated on Perennius even if Calvus had not given him a specific reason to fear delay. He tried to react as he would have done if he were simply waiting for a Bay of Naples ferry to cast off to take him back to base from a brothel. The stocky Illyrian stood in a curve of the poop rail, letting his senses absorb the confusion around him while his mind saw only the dance of sunlight on the murky waters.

The problem was the oars. Perennius was not familiar with the process of fitting out a large warship—nor, for that matter, were many of the crewmen and dockworkers involved. Because the liburnian was decked, there was no practical way that the twenty-two foot long upper-bank oars could be inserted from inside the seventeen-foot wide rowing chamber. Instead, each oar handle had to be thrust through its port by men on the quay, then grasped and drawn in by the oarsmen inside the vessel. The oarsmen were experienced sailors and generally used to the shattering drudgery of rowing, but the *Eagle*'s cramped rowing chamber was new to them and thus chaotic. Most merchant ships—all but the monstrously largest ones—carried a few pairs of sweeps to maneuver them in harbor or to make landfall when the inshore breeze failed at evening. Such work, and that of trawling with a dingy, were just as hard as anything the liburnian demanded. The *Eagle* ranked over a hundred men in blocks of six, with four feet separating oars horizontally and only one vertical foot between the ports of the upper row and the lower.

Upon consideration, it was not surprising that it took so long to position the port-side oars, then to warp the starboard side to the quay and repeat the awkward process. It was not something Perennius had considered ahead of time, though, and only by excising his consciousness from the events could the agent restrain his fury. Under certain circumstances, he could wait with the patience of a leopard. Now, however, there was no kill in prospect.

"Cast off bow!" a ship's officer called, and the halves of Perennius' mind segued into alignment again.

A pair of sailors in the bow were thrusting at the quay with boathooks, while someone on the dock loosed a hawser from the bollard holding it. The cavalry squadron had remounted. It was forming in column of twos, while wagons and stevedores bustled on other quays. The face of one of the onlookers was unexpectedly familiar: Terentius Niger, the tribune who had handled the arrangements with verve and skill. Perennius saluted him. Those virtues made up for any lack of security-consciousness the younger man had shown.

"Where the hell is Sestius?" the agent asked suddenly. He had been ambivalent about the Cilician initially. Now, given the size and quality of the Marine complement, Perennius did not care to miss even a single trained soldier—whether or not the soldier knew the ground where the operation would climax.

"He and his friend boarded just as they were about to raise the gangplanks," Gaius said. He stood near Perennius, but he knew the agent too well to intrude on his brown study until called to do so. "I thought they'd come back here, but they've stayed up in the bow." He nodded. Perennius, following the motion, caught sight of the centurion in a group of Marines. "I didn't think you'd want to be disturbed, so I didn't say anything."

"Cast off aft!" cried the officer. The shaft of a boathook missed Calvus' gleaming pate by inches as a sailor swung the tool over the rail.

"Let's go see him," Perennius said. He wondered with a certain humor what would happen if Calvus were brained in a boating accident. He had a gut feeling that the whole fantastic nightmare would melt back to the reality of a few weeks before.

Though that reality was nightmare enough, the Sun knew.

"Hope to blazes his friend's a soldier," the agent muttered as he stepped down the ladder. "That's the least of the help we need."

A drum thudded in the rowing chamber, thudded again, and then the coxswain began screaming curses forward as oarblades clattered together. The officer responsible below decks was trying to ease the vessel out of harbor with a few oars, leaving the rest shipped until the *Eagle* gained sea room. Even that conservative plan had not proven an immediate success.

"I thought of using a merchant ship," Perennius said to the tall man. Calvus had not asked for an explanation, but the obvious chaos seemed to Perennius to demand one. "Might've been faster, and for sure it was simpler.

But I just came from those waters. I don't see us making Tarsus without having to run or to fight at least once."

The ship lurched forward as a dozen oars bit the water simultaneously. A Marine stumbled against Perennius and caromed off as if from a stone post. The soldier's tunic hung over his bones as if from a rack, and he cringed away from the agent as if he expected a boot to follow the contact. "Right now," Perennius added gloomily, "I'm praying that it's run."

The fighting towers were wooden and six feet in each dimension. At one time they had been painted to look like stone. In combat they gave both vantage and a little extra wallop to missiles flung at an enemy from them. For carriage, the towers were knocked down and laid flat on the decking where they would be erected at need. The forward tower thus made a slightly raised table. A number of enterprising Marines had already started a dice game on it. Sestius and others looked on. As he approached the centurion, Perennius' face began to go blank. Gaius knew him well enough to know the expression was more threatening than another man's open rage.

"I haven't met your friend, yet, Quintus," the agent said in a tone that only a ferret might have thought was friendly and bantering.

The centurion had watched them approach, at first out of the corner of his eye but at last with a stiff smile of greeting. Sestius moved a step toward the unrailed edge of the deck, drawing his companion along with a gesture. "This is my friend, Sabellius," he said nervously. He converted the summons into an introductory gesture. "He'll be a lot of help to us." Froth scudded off in the breeze as the oars feathered. It spattered Sestius' high-laced boots and the Gallic trousers of his companion.

Perennius paced toward his quarry, past the oblivious Marines and a pair of sailors checking the forestays of the mast. Calvus and Gaius followed him like the limbs of a V. The courier's face showed a concern which the tall man never seemed to feel. The agent was staring at Sabellius. Shorter than Sestius, Sabellius wore a waist-length cloak over tunic and trousers. The hood of the cloak was raised over reddish, rough-cut hair. The garment's throat-pin was arranged so that the cloak hung closed.

"Sir, pleased to meet you—" Sabellius began, extending a hand toward the agent.

Perennius reached past the proferred hand and gripped the throat of Sabellius' drab brown tunic. Sabellius screamed. The centurion shouted in anger and tried to seize Perennius' wrist with both hands. The agent used Sestius' weight and his own strength to jerk the tunic down. The blend of wool and linen tore as Sabellius' knees banged against the deck. The breasts displayed behind the cloak and torn tunic were large-nippled—flat for a woman, but a woman's beyond any question.

Perennius released his prey. "All right, soldier," he demanded grimly as he turned to Sestius, "what the *fuck* do you think you're playing at?"

The dice game had broken up with a cry of interest. The shooter had raised his eyes from the board to call on Fortune and had caught a glimpse of tit instead. Gaius shifted between the agent and the Marines. His instinct was to give Perennius room to handle the situation whichever way he chose. Help against one man, even an armed soldier like Sestius, was not something the agent would need or want.

"Look, buddy," the centurion blustered, "we agreed that I'd bring a friend, and Sabellia's—"

Sestius still held Perennius' right wrist and forearm, though his grip was loosening as the soldier drew back in embarrassment. Perennius locked the other's elbow with his right hand. He cracked Sestius across the face with the callus-ridged fingers of his left hand. The shock would have put Sestius among the threshing oars had not the agent held him simultaneously. "Don't *give* me that shit!" Perennius shouted. "You were *hiding* her, weren't you? Do you think I'm stupid? Do you think everybody aboard's *blind* so they won't notice the first time she takes a shit over the side? There's a hundred and fifty of us on this tub. That's pretty close quarters for a bit of nookie, don't you think?"

"Sir," the centurion said. All the hectoring arrogance was gone from his voice. "It's not that, it was for after—"

Perennius released him. The man slid a heel back for balance. His boot thudded on the coaming. "And you thought if I didn't catch on before we left port that I wouldn't put her ashore at the first landfall, is that it?" the agent demanded in a quiet, poisonous tone. Voice rising again, he added, "That I wouldn't dump her over the side?"

"Sir," repeated Sestius, grimacing.

Perennius turned his back on the other man. What he saw behind him was a chilling surprise. Not the raucous Marines, not the back of tall, capable Gaius as he acted as a buffer. Calvus was frozen in the concentration which the agent had mistaken for fear that night in the alley. Sabellia was quiet also. She knelt where Perennius had thrown her down in ripping her tunic. The knife in her hand was short-bladed, but it looked sharp enough to have severed ribs on its way to the agent's heart.

"I don't think that's necessary any more," Perennius said very softly. He did not reach for the knife or the woman, though the weight came off his right boot minusculy.

"Bella," Sestius said in a strangled voice. "Put that away!"

The sheath was inside the waistband of her trousers, where the fall of the tunic hid the hilt. Sabellia looked at Perennius, not the centurion, as she slipped the weapon away again. "I should have put it in you," she said. Her throaty contralto was actually deeper than the masculine tone she had tried to counterfeit in greeting. "Then we'd see how tough you were." She rose to her feet with a sway of cloth and flesh. Calvus relaxed visibly.

One of the Marines had enough Latin to call, "Hey Legate—save me sloppy seconds!"

Perennius looked at the soldiers. His smile sent the speaker flinching back while the others quieted. "Tell you what, boys," the agent said in Greek, as being the closest thing to a common language for the unit, "why don't you all go back to your game? We're short-staffed for the work anyhow, and I'd hate to lose some of you."

The hint was too clear and too obviously serious for the troops to ignore it. The dice rattled in the palm of a short

man with a beard like the point of a knife. The other
Marines looked at him, then hunkered down on the fore-
castle again with only a glance or two back toward
Perennius and his companions.

Gaius turned. "Look, Aulus," he said, "we don't even
have to turn around. We can put her aboard one of the
Customs—"

Perennius laid a hand on the younger man's elbow to
silence him. The agent looked from Sestius to the woman,
then back. The centurion had struck a brace. His face was
as still as dicipline could make it. The *Eagle* was leaving
the inner harbor now. The constriction between the
column-headed moles caused the swell to dash itself into
whitecaps. Sestius appeared queasy, but he did not move
forward from the edge of the deck.

Now that she had been exposed, literally and figuratively,
Sabellias looked obviously to be a woman in dumpy clothes.
Her hair had been cut short. Her face was broad and her
small nose turned up, giving her almost a Scythian look
which her Gallic accent belied. She glared eye to eye at
Perennius. One hand clasped her cape across the torn
front of her tunic, while the other hand was still obviously on the hilt of her knife.

"Sestius," the agent said, "you acted like a fool, and it
could have gotten you killed." The agent's tone was flat,
his words neutral enough to leave doubt whether the
implied slayer was an enemy or Perennius himself in an
access of rage. Perennius' hand was on the courier's arm,
as if the older man were drawing some support from the
contact.

"Yes, sir," the centurion said. His eyes stared across at
the shore. He had sense enough not to add anything to the
minimum required. Sestius had seen men like the agent
before, and it was only need that had put him in the
Illyrian's path.

"You told me what you planned to do after the operation," Perennius continued in the same flat voice, "and
that was all right; I could plan for it. But I can't plan for
what I don't know, can I, soldier?"

"No sir." Sestius' cheek was red and swelling with the
print of the agent's fingers. Sabellia glanced at her com-

panion and sucked in her breath. The slap had been lost
to her in the wave of her own confusion.

"And would you like to guess how I feel about people
who think they've fooled me, soldier?" the agent went on.
His fingers tensed, only momentarily but hard enough
that Gaius winced.

"Sir," said Sestius to the air, "I didn't think we'd fool
you, but I was desperate. Having Bella with me was the
only way I was willing to, to settle. I'm sorry."

Perennius looked at the woman. She was younger by a
decade than Sestius, but that was normal for a soldier
with some rank on him. She edged closer to her man. The
agent remembered another Gallic girl who had not been
willing—or able, but it was all the same to love's victim—to
stand by a soldier. "All right, Quintus," Perennius said
softly, "she can stay until I hear some reason why she
shouldn't. But don't ever try to play me for a fool again."

He turned abruptly. "I'll show you our cabin," he threw
over his shoulder. "You can get your gear stowed properly."

Calvus was with him, a half step toward the stern
before even Gaius realized what was happening. To the
tall man, Perennius muttered, "Thanks. I was so mad
about what the fool had done that I forgot it wasn't a
thing he'd tried to smuggle aboard, it was a person. Spunky
bitch."

They were striding between the ventilator grating and
the starboard edge of the deck. Though the span of deck
was as wide as any sidewalk in Rome, Calvus stumbled
badly enough to make the agent nervous. Perennius crossed
behind the taller man to walk outboard of him, just in
case. The coxswain had shifted stroke to the lower bank
of oars, endeavoring to exercise the raw company by
thirds before trusting them to keep time in synchrony.
The principle was all well enough, but it did not wholly
prevent clattering and lurches of the hull as rowers caught
crabs. "You noticed immediately that the companion was
female," Calvus remarked. His hand brushed the agent's
shoulder to save his balance. Gaius was directly behind
them, with the couple a pace further back. Though it did
not appear to matter, the traveller spoke no louder than
Perennius alone could hear.

The agent shrugged. "Sestius was hiding something," he said. "Something he didn't want noticed. I thought he'd brought his chicken aboard. Then I saw her move, the way her throat looked—and knowing there was *something* going to be wrong with her . . . Well, it wasn't chicken, it was coney." He looked sharply at Calvus. "You knew before I did, didn't you?"

The tall man nodded. "I didn't realize it would matter to you. It can be difficult to know what information you want—or when I ought to give it to you."

The liburnian was anything but luxurious. Still, the five passengers had as much privacy as one of the pair of stern cabins could give their number. Perennius opened the hatch and pegged it back to the bulkhead. Amidships, a party of sailors was preparing to hoist the mainsail under directions shouted from the poop. "She earned a berth when she pulled the knife on me," the agent said quietly. Louder and with a gesture toward the diffident centurion, he called, "Stow your duffle, but remember this is all the shelter we'll have if the weather turns sour, Quintus."

Sestius stepped into the cabin between Calvus and the agent. He swung his stuffed field pack off his shoulder to clear the low lintel. Sabellia followed him with a burden scarcely smaller. Her eyes watched Perennius with wary acceptance.

"But I really don't like to be played for a fool," the agent repeated to the figure across the hatch from him.

CHAPTER ELEVEN

"Dolphins ahead!" cried the lookout at the masthead, but Perennius in the prow could see that the monster approaching them was no line of dolphins. Presumably the sailor from his better vantage knew that too and had spoken in the same hopeful euphemism that caused the Furies to be referred to as the 'Kindly-minded Ones.' The friendly, man-aiding dolphins were traditionally bearers of good luck, while the creature now rippling toward the *Eagle* looked to be none of those things.

Gaius and Sestius were all, giving the Marines their third day of weapons drill. When they broke up for individual fencing practice, the agent would join them. At the moment it was as least as important to teach the contingent the meaning of basic commands in Latin. The *Eagle* was west of Corcyra, the landfall intended for that evening. The liburnian was proceeding with a fair wind and a slow stroke—practice for the rowers, while the Marines drilled above them.

Sabellia, at the agent's left in the bow, squinted and said, "*That's* what a dolphin looks like?"

"No," said Calvus, "not a dolphin. Not anything at all that should be on Earth at this time."

"Blazes, that's the truth!" Perennius said. He glanced around quickly to see what weapons there were that might be more useful than his sword.

The creature's head was broader than a horse's and was more than twice as long. Because the thing was approaching and Perennius was low enough that spray wetted him

105

even in a calm sea, the agent could not be sure of the beast's length. It appeared to be an appreciable fraction of the ship's own hundred-plus feet. The yellow teeth in its jaws were large enough to be seen clearly as the distance closed. Porpoises undulate vertically. The mottled fin along this creature's spine did rise and fall, but the body itself rippled sideways in a multiple sculling motion. It looked like nothing Perennius had ever seen in his life, and it looked as dangerous as the agent himself was.

"Stand to!" Perennius roared in a barrack's-square voice which even the open horizon did not wholly swallow.

It was incredible that this ragged-toothed monster could have thrashed within a ship's length of them and attract so little attention. The lookout was paralyzed at his post now that proximity gave the absolute lie to his optimism. The deck crew had its tasks or its leisure, neither category worth interruption for a pod of dolphins. Sabellia was willing enough to act in a crisis, but the sea and its creatures were all so new to her that she did not even realize there *was* a crisis at the moment.

As for Calvus, Calvus was—as always—calmly interested. While Perennius shouted and ran for one of the boat-pikes racked against the mast, the tall man watched the dark, serpentine creature until it sounded and disappeared beneath the liburnian's keel.

The Marines had exploded out of formation at Perennius' cry. They gripped their spears for use as they stumbled forward to join the agent. The crew, seamen and officers alike, jumped up alertly as well. Like the Marines—and Perennius himself—they were looking toward the bow. The waves continued to foam around the stem and the barely-submerged stump of the ram. The sea held no tracks, and there was no sign of the creature remaining.

"It won't be back, I think," Calvus said before Perennius could ask his question or the mob of men on deck could ask theirs of him. "Calm them. It won't do any good to have them wondering."

"Easy for *you* to say," Perennius snarled. He knew full well that anything he could say to calm the men around him would make him look a fool. Well, any attempt to convince them that he had really seen a monster with daggers for teeth would have the same effect—if he were lucky. If his luck was out, he'd have a mutiny no threats could quell.

"I guess it was a log," the agent said aloud, giving the onlookers a weak smile. Sestius had stepped quickly to Sabellia's side. She took his arm. The woman walked the ship with a hand on her knife, but she was never far from the centurion or Perennius either. Any dangers the agent posed went beyond a bout of unwanted slap and tickle. "Or maybe it was—" Perennius wet his lips—"some dolphins, yes." He glanced up at the lookout involuntarily. The sailor stared back at him in frozen agreement.

By the unconquered Sun, thought the agent, maybe it *was* all a dream, a mirage. They were alone on the sea with no more than the waves and a single high-flying seabird as company.

"All right, fall in again," Gaius ordered harshly. He liked the authority he got from drilling the Marines; but after he spoke, he looked back carefully to Perennius. As the sailors returned to their own duties, one of the mates said, "His Highness is seeing mermaids. Maybe one of you lads ought to offer to haul his ashes for him before he hurts himself on a knothole." There was general laughter.

Perennius appeared not to be listening. He walked back to the bow. The fourteen-foot long pike was still in his right hand. He carried it just ahead of the balance so that its butt brushed the deck and its point winked in the air ahead of him at the height of a man's throat. The only sign the agent made to show he was not simply bemused at making a foolish mistake was his peremptory gesture to Calvus to join him by the bowsprit. It was unnecessary. The tall man had already turned in unison with the agent. Sabellia followed also, unasked but expected as Sestius went back to his training duties.

"Now, what in *blazes* was that?" the agent asked. His voice held the fury of Father Sun, reswallowing the life that was his creation in tendrils of inexorable flame. "And don't give me any crap about dolphins!" Even to himself, Perennius would not admit how fearful he was that what he had "seen" was only a construct of his diseased mind.

"It was less like a dolphin than you are," said the

traveller calmly, always calmly. "It appears to have been a—" he looked at the agent, his lips pursing around the choice of a word—"marine reptile, a tylosaurus. It eats fish, though it would probably make short enough work of a man in the water. The ship itself is far too large to be potential prey, so I was not concerned."

The fact of identification has its own power over the thing identified. Perennius looked from Calvus to the pike in his hand. "Oh," he said in chagrin, conscious of the woman's eyes as well. He *had* made a fool of himself in his panic. "I hadn't seen one before."

"No, you certainly hadn't," the traveller agreed. "The last of them disappeared from Earth sixty-five million years ago. I don't think it will be able to stay alive very long in this age. The seas must be far too salty, so that it will dehydrate and die."

In a society that valued rhetoric over communication, mathematics were a slave's work—or a spy's. Numbers—of men, of wealth, of distances—were a part of Perennius' job, so he had learned to use them as effectively as he did the lies and weapons which he also needed. But even in a day when inflation was rampant and the word for a small coin had originally meant 'a bag of money,' the figure Calvus had thrown out gave the agent pause. While Perennius struggled with the concept, the Gallic woman sidestepped the figures and went to the heart of the problem. "You say they're all dead," she said in her own smooth dialect of Latin, "and you say we just saw one. Where did it come from?"

The traveller was looking astern, toward the empty waves past the rope-brailed canvas of the mainsail. Perhaps he was looking much farther away than that. "Either there is something completely separate working," he said "or that was a side-effect of the way I came here. I can't be sure. I was raised to know and to find—certain things. And to act in certain ways. This isn't something that I would need to understand, perhaps . . . but I rather think it was not expected."

The tall man shrugged. He looked at Sabellia, at the agent, with his stark black eyes again. "This was not tested, you see. It was not in question that the technique would work, but the ramifications could be as various as the universe itself. That's why they sent all six of us together . . . and I am here."

"Calvus, I don't understand," Perennius said. He watched his hands squeeze pointlessly against the weathered gray surface of the pike staff. "But if you say that it's all right, I'll accept that."

"Aulus Perennius, I don't know whether or not it is all right," the tall man said. "We didn't have time to test the procedure that sent us here." The smooth-skinned, angular face formed itself—relaxed would have been the wrong word—into a smile. "We did not have time," Calvus repeated wonderingly. "Yes, I've made a joke. I wonder how my siblings would react to me now?" He smiled again, but less broadly. "Contact with you has changed me more than could have been expected before we were sent off."

Sabellia began to laugh. Perennius looked at the woman. "You too?" he said sourly.

Sabellia's hair was beginning to bleach to red-blond after days of sea-reflected sunlight. "It's the idea of anyone getting a sense of humor by associating with you, Lord Perennius," she said. Her giggle made the sarcasm of "Lord" less cutting, though abundantly clear.

"That wasn't quite what I meant," said Calvus. He looked from one of his companions to the other.

But as the agent strode toward the mast to rack the pike again, he too began to laugh.

CHAPTER TWELVE

The sails were to windward of them. That was bad enough. What was worse was the fact that their attitude shifted even as Perennius watched them. If he was correct, the vessels were turning toward the *Eagle*, not away. In this age, in these waters west of Cyprus, no honest seaman wanted to meet another ship.

"Those two ships are turning toward us," said Calvus, as if to put paid to the hopeful doubt in the agent's mind. Perennius glanced sidelong at the tall man, wondering just how sharp his eyesight really was. "Why are they doing that?"

"Herakles, Captain!" cried the lookout who had given the initial alarm a minute before. "They're making for us! Pirates!"

"That seems to me to cover it, too," said Perennius. He struggled to keep from vomiting. Disaster, disaster . . . not unexpected in the abstract, but its precise nature had been unhinted only minutes before. The voyage had been going well. The oarsmen and the Marines were both shaking down in adequate fashion—

Across the surface of the agent's mind flashed a picture of his chief, Marcus Optatius Navigatus, burying himself in trivia as the Empire went smash. It was easier to think about the way a rank of Marines dressed than it was to consider chitinous things that spat lightning—or the near certainty that he would have to battle pirates with a quarter of the troops he had thought marginally necessary to the task.

Screw'em all. Aulus Perennius had been given a job, and he was going to do it. Not "or die trying"; that was for losers.

There were men shouting on deck and below it. The captain was giving orders to the coxswain through a wooden speaking tube. The agent turned his eyes toward the putative pirates again. They were still distant. Though interception might be inevitable, it would not be soon. With genuine calm rather than the feigned one of a moment before, Perennius said, "It could be that these aren't simply pirates, Calvus. Like the bravos we met in Rome weren't just robbers. Can you protect us against thunderbolts here like you did then?"

"No," Calvus said as he too continued to watch the other sails. The upper hull of the nearer of the vessels was barely visible. It was a sailing ship, and that was at least some hope. "Their weapons—and I can only assume that what you face here is identical to what we knew—their weapons will strike at a distance of—" a pause for conversion. The agent would have given a great deal to know the original measurement—"two hundred double paces, a thousand feet. My capacity to affect anything physical, or even—" a near smile—"mental, falls off exponentially with distance. At ten feet, perhaps, I could affect their weapons. No further."

"All right, we'll keep you out of the way," Perennius said. His mind was ticking like the fingers of an accountant. "Put you on an oar, you're strong, or maybe the cabin's the best idea, just in case we do get close enough you can—"

"Aulus Perennius," the traveller said, interrupting for the first time, "I said that if there are Guardians on those ships, they can tear this craft apart from a thousand feet."

"And if it's just pirates, they can't!" the agent snapped back. "Think I didn't goddam listen to you?" He pointed toward the cabin into which Gaius and Sestius had disappeared at a run. Their armor was there. "I'll have hell's own time finishing this job if you've caught a stray arrow on the way. And if it's your lobster buddies after all, well ... I just might be able to arrange a surprise for them even at two hundred paces. For now, get to blazes out of my way so that I can get on with what I need to do!"

Which was to kill people, the agent thought as he strode to the forward fighting tower. "You two!" he shouted to a pair of nervous-looking seamen. "Give me a hand with these cables!"

It was nice to have a skill that was in demand.

Perennius and his scratch team had three sides of the tower cleated together and were raising the fourth when Sestius and a pair of the Marines staggered forward. The soldiers were in armor and were carrying the ballista. With its base and a bundle of iron darts, it was a load for all of them.

"Drive home that peg!" the agent ordered. He thudded one warped timber against another with the point of his shoulder. Sestius dropped his burden obediently and rapped at the peg with his helmet, the closest equivalent to a hammer. Perennius grunted and lunged at the wall again. Sestius struck in unison, and the pieces of the tower locked in place. The sailors were already completing the task by dogging the bottom edges of the tower into the bronze hasps sunk permanently in the deck for the purpose.

"You pair, lift the roof in place," Perennius wheezed to the Marines. "There's a horizontal stud on the inside of the walls to peg it to."

The men looked at one another blankly for an instant. Then the centurion repeated the order in Greek. With a willingness that at least mitigated their ignorance of *every* goddam thing, the men dropped the ballista and began lifting the remaining square of planking.

"Do you want me to raise the aft tower while you arm yourself?" Sestius asked. Perennius had stripped off his cloak and equipment belt for the exertion of erecting the tower. Sweat glittered on his eyebrows and blackened the breast of his tunic in splotches. The Centurion looked fully the military professional by contrast. His oval plywood shield was strapped to his back in carrying position. His chest glittered with armor of bronze scales sewn directly to a leather backing. The mail shirt was newly-issued, replacing the one whose iron rings were welded to uselessness during the ambush in Rome.

"No goddam point," the agent said. "We don't have enough men to need this one," he added, levering himself away from the tower which supported him after he no longer needed to support it. It wasn't that he was getting old, not him. Even as a youth Perennius had paced himself for the task, not the ultimate goal. Here his strength and determination had gotten the heavy fighting tower up in a rush that a dozen men could have equalled only with difficulty. It didn't leave him much at the moment, but the pirates weren't aboard yet either. He could run on his nerves when they were. "Get the ballista set up and pick a crew for it—"

"Me?" Sestius blurted. "*I* don't know how to work one of these things." He stared at the dismantled weapon as if Perennius had just ordered it to bite him. "Sir, I thought you . . . I mean, these Marines, what would they . . . ?"

"Good work, Centurion," Gaius called brightly as he strode to the fighting tower. He wore his cavalry uniform complete to the medallions of rank. They bounced and jingled against the bronze hoops of his back-and-breast armor. The armor was hinged on his left side and latched on the right. The individual hoops were pinned to one another in slots so that the wearer could bend forward and sideways to an extent. That was fine for a horseman who needed the protection of the thick metal because he could not carry a shield and guide his mount with his left hand. It should serve Gaius well here, also, in a melee without proper ranks and the support of a shield wall.

Perennius had a set of armor just like it back in the cabin, and he would not be able to wear it—blast the Fates for their mockery!

"I'll take over with this now," the younger Illyrian was saying cheerfully. He lifted the heavy ballista base. "You, sailor—scramble up there and take this! And I'll need both of you to crew the beast."

The seamen Perennius had commandeered looked doubtful, but it was toward the agent and not toward their own officers that they glanced for confirmation. Perennius nodded briefly to them. "Right," he said. "I'll be back myself in a moment."

"Marines to me!" Sestius was calling in Latin, then Greek, as he trotted amidships. He obviously feared that if he stayed nearby, Perennius would assign him to the ballista after all. The centurion was more immediately fearful of the hash he would make trying to use a weapon of which he was wholly ignorant than he was of the fight at odds which loomed.

Perennius slapped Gaius on the shoulder and ran back toward his cabin. Men and gear made an obstacle course of the eighty-foot journey. The deck was strewn with the personal gear of the Marines. They were rummaging for the shields and ill-fitting cuirasses which might keep them alive over the next few hours. There was neither room nor permission for them to store their belongings below as did the deck crew and oarsmen. The seamen resented the relative leisure of men so recently slaves. Now, the rush to packs lashed to the deck cleats had created more incidental disruption than one would have guessed a mere score of men could achieve.

It occurred to the agent that this might well be Gaius' first real action. That at least explained the youth's enthusiasm. The boy had been given all the considerable benefits of training and preferment which Perennius could arrange for him. Gaius had thrown himself into each position with ability, though without the driving ambition that might have gained him a provincial governorship before he reached retirement age.

Or a stage above that, whispered a part of the agent's mind. Perennius hurtled a Marine an instant before the fellow straightened up the spear he had drawn through the lashings of his pack. How many provincial governors had become emperors during Perennius' own lifetime?

But Gaius, for all his skills and willingness, had never been closer to the front lines of a battle than the day he stood with the troop of personal bodyguards around the Emperor at Arlate. Accidents could occur—as they had to Gallienus' own father and co-emperor, captured two years before by the Persians. But as a general rule, the safest place to be during a battle is with a commander. It had proven so that day, despite the vicious struggle of the Alemanni. The boy's first front-line experience was going to be in this shipboard chaos without real lines.

As accommodations on the small warship went, the poop cabins were the height of luxury. Each had a glazed window in the rear bulkhead. The stocky agent still had to pause to let his eyes expand for the dimmer interior. Time was at a premium, and he knew consciously that no one inside was waiting to brain him; but it was a survival reflex of more value than the seconds he might have saved by over-riding it.

Sabellia edged aside to let Perennius by. The centurion had presumably ordered her under cover, but she had taken station in the hatchway. Perennius did not need the glint of steel to know what the Gallic woman held in her hand. Calvus stood silently at the inner bulkhead which separated the passengers' cabin from that retained by the ship's officers. Calvus was clear, by chance or intention, of the agent's gear stored against the curving outer hull of the ship.

The tall man *could* not be as calm as he looked, Perennius thought as he thrust aside his own heavy body armor to get at the pack beneath it. He had seen Calvus' face work when the tall man discussed the Guardians and the threat he was sure they posed to the Empire. And while Calvus had a level of unworldliness as surprising as his linguistic knowledge, he was not a fool. It required no particular experience to understand how dangerous a threat to their mission was posed by the two raw-looking pirate vessels bearing down on the *Eagle*.

Perennius found the weapon and ammunition in their leather pouch. "If you want to curse me for the chance I took going by sea, you can," he said angrily to Calvus. He slung the strap of the pouch over his shoulder and reached for his helmet. "But it was still the better chance, Hell take it!"

"Aulus Perennius," the traveller replied, "you will do what can be done by man." Calvus' smile looked thin, but again—as a rarity—it looked real. "I was not raised to be concerned about tasks that are the domain of others."

The agent swore and slid past Sabellia to the deck again. He felt a sick fury at what he saw. The pirate ships had been at the limit of sight on the horizon. They had now halved the distance separating themselves from the liburnian, even though they were beating to windward. A major reason that the pirates were closing so fast was that the liburnian had sheered slightly to starboard but had not turned directly away from the hostile ships.

Before the sighting, the *Eagle* had been proceeding toward her next landfall on the fair wind and a reduced stroke by all her rowers. The oars had added perhaps two knots to the three that sail alone would have offered her. Now the sea was frothing to either side under the full power of the oars, increasing the ship's speed by at least a half despite the state of the hull and the rowers' inexperience. In consequence, the *Eagle* was nearing the pirates—or the one of the pair which lay half a mile to the other's port—that much the faster.

A seaman was scrambling down the ladder from the poop. Instead of waiting for him, Perennius gripped the poop coaming with both hands and swung himself up—waist high, then legs slicing sideways in an arc. His sword and dagger still lay on the main deck where he had been working, but the pouch he had snatched from the cabin slammed him leadenly in the ribs.

The captain was a Tarantine named Leonidas whose experience had been entirely on the smaller Customs vessels. Now he was screaming toward the mainmast. The Marine detachment was becoming entangled with the bosun and a party of seamen who were attempting some activity with the sail. Sestius was already sorting out the confusion. The centurion was leading half the small unit sternward, while the remainder stumbled toward the bow with Longidienus, their original commander.

Ignoring the tangle as a problem solved, Perennius rose to his feet in front of the captain. "Why are we sailing toward the pirates instead of away?" the agent demanded. The short question ended loudly enough to be heard all over the ship, because Leonidas had started to turn away while the agent addressed him.

The Greek seaman spun back around with a look of

fury. "Do you want to take over?" he screamed in the agent's face. "Aren't you quite sure your orders have gotten us killed already? Hermes and Fortune, *I'm* sure!"

Sick despair threatened to double Perennius up. There was no unified command on the *Eagle*. That was his fault. It was perhaps inevitable as well, because Perennius had neither the talent nor the training for organizing other people. He could carry out a task himself or lead others if they cared to follow him; but he had never cared enough about command to try to learn why men who were not self-starters as he was seemed willing to take suicidal risks for some officers.

So the agent had command of the *Eagle* only by virtue of orders on a scrap of papyrus. That had increasingly little effect as death reached for the liburnian against the wind. Perennius had shown no interest in Leonidas and his deck crew, so long as they provided the transportation he required; and if the efforts of the oarsmen below were meshed effectively with those of the seamen proper, then that was nothing for which Perennius could take credit either. Now the ship was in danger, and there was no plan for how it could fight or run as a unit.

Swallowing an anger that was now directed at himself and not the captain, Perennius said, "Leonidas, I'll do what I can to save us now, but you'll have to tell me what to expect."

Behind Leonidas there were four sailors instead of the usual one, leaning their weight on the tiller which controlled the paired steering oars. The liburnian was heeling enough to the right that Perennius suspected the blade on the port side must barely be clipping the waves. The starboard oar would be providing full turning force. Leonidas gestured toward his straining men and said, "If the gods grant the wind freshens, we'll pass to port of both of those bastards and be able to make land safely if the oarsmen hold out—as they will not." He spat over the railing with an angry intensity which he seemed to be trying to direct away from the agent. He looked back again sharply. "No way we can keep them from stripping and burning the ship, but we can maybe get our own bums clear."

The agent's mouth was dry. He wished he had his sword hilt for his hand to squeeze. "All right," he said, looking past the windward edge of the sail toward the pirate who was already more nearly ahead of them than on their port quarter. Even if a fresher breeze did add a knot or two to the *Eagle's* speed, it was too late to hope that would get them clear. "Can we ram?" Perennius went on with as little emotion as possible. As if he did not know the bronze beak had not been replaced, as if he had not heard Niger's sneering certainty that any of the laid-up vessels would crumble to dust if they struck another ship.

"Buggering Zeus!" screamed the Tarantine captain as panic and frustration overcame his momentary control, "don't you see the fucking mast's still stepped? We're not in fighting trim, we're *cruising*. If we hit anything now, the whole thing, spar, cordage, and sail, comes down across our deck and the oars! Wouldn't you rather we just lay to and surrendered without all that fuss?"

The bosun shrieked a question to Leonidas from amidships. It was unintelligible to Perennius not for language—the vessel worked on Common Greek—but for vocabulary. The captain pushed past Perennius to answer, and this time the agent let him go. Leonidas would do his best in conditions which were likely impossible. For his own part, the agent now had an idea that might at least offer more than prayer seemed likely to do.

Perennius leaped to the main deck again with a crash of boots which the confusion swallowed. He landed near the aft hatchway, which he ignored. If he went below that way, he would have to struggle the length of the rowing chamber while it was filled with fear and flailing oar-handles. Despite the chaos on deck, the agent could get to the small galley forward better by dodging the sailors and humming ropes above.

One of the pirates was close enough to be seen clearly, now. As the agent had feared, the vessel was not of Mediterranean design at all. The sail was the pale yellow of raw wool, criss-crossed diagonally by leather strips sewn across the stretchy fabric. The wool bellied noticeably in the squares within those reinforcements, but even a landsman like Perennius could see that the pirates' sail met the wind at a flatter angle than did that of the *Eagle*.

Half a dozen years before, the Goths and Borani had begun raiding the Black Sea coasts in ships crewed by Greeks from the old settlements at the mouth of the Danube. In the past year, however, another tribe, the Herulians, had made the long trek to the Black Sea. The Herulians had begun building craft of the same type as their ancestors had used to sail the Baltic. If the *Eagle*'s opponents had depended on Greeks, either hirelings or slaves, there would have been a slender hope of confusion or mutiny within the pirate ranks. There was no hope of that now.

The liburnian was so much bigger than her opponents— heavier, in all likelihood, than both together—that she looked to overmatch them entirely. Perennius kept thinking of a cow pursued by wolves. From the expressions on the faces of the seamen he passed, most of them took an even less optimistic view of the *Eagle*'s chances than he did himself. The nearer of the pirates was in plain view. The ship was as broad as the liburnian, but it had only a single open deck over the ribs which joined together the hull planks. It was shorter than the liburnian, seventy-five or eighty feet long in comparison to the *Eagle*'s hundred and ten feet at the water line. As such, the Germans should have sailed poorly against the wind. That they did not was a result of three developments, visible as the ships bore down on their prey.

First, there were flat cutwaters fore and aft. These increased the effective length of the hulls and greatly aided the vessels' resistance to slipping sideways under the pressure of breezes from ahead or alongside. Second, when the prow of the nearer pirate lifted from a wave with a geyser of foam and a cheer from her complement, Perennius could see that the cutwaters were extended below the shallow hull by a true keel. Though the pirate vessels still drew far less water than the *Eagle*, the sheer-sided keel was clearly an advantage against stresses in which the liburnian's rounded bottom allowed her to wallow. The final development was the one which gave the Germans' bulging sails the effectiveness of the tighter, civilized Roman weave. A long pole was socketed in the lee gunwale of each ship. The pole reached across at a diagonal to the forward edge of the sail, half-way up, where it was clamped. The pole kept the edge of the sail from fluttering and halving its effect as it met the wind at a flat angle.

Skipping like melonseeds, the pirate vessels closed on the fat liburnian. They sailed at an angle the *Eagle* could not have matched except when she was driven solely by her oars. It was obvious now to the agent why Leonidas had been unwilling to try to flee into the wind.

Perennius would have cheerfully granted sailing excellence to the Northerners if the *Eagle* had aboard the eighty trained soldiers whom he had requested. Physical danger frightened the Illyrian less than other aspects of life did; but even so, the threat they faced—he and Calvus and the mission—with twenty ex-slaves chilled him. The pirate ships were not being rowed, though they surely had some provision for sweeps. One of the reasons the oars were not in use was the fact that both ships were packed to the gunwales with men.

There must have been over a hundred Germans on the nearer vessel, though the way they crowded into the bow permitted only a rough estimate. Nearer to their enemies, nearer to slaughter and gory . . . Many of the warriors wore scraps of armor, a breastplate or helmet or even, in one case, a pair of bronze greaves which must once have guarded the shins of some gladiator. The glittering metal gave more the impression of gaudy decoration than it did a fear of wounds, however. The Germans' clothing was a similar melange. It ranged from skins worn flesh-side out, through the booty of civilization—tunics of linen and wool, and a flowing silk chlamys which must have draped a very wealthy lady indeed at formal gatherings—to more or less total nudity.

In a few cases, the nudity might have had a religious significance, but Perennius suspected that in general it was merely a response to the sun reflecting from the southern sea. Besides body armor, most of the Germans carried shields. These were either simple disks of wood or wicker, or heavier items captured from the imperial forces.

Axes, swords and daggers were common, but every man seemed to carry a spear in his right hand. As they neared their victim, the pirates began clashing the flats of their spear-blades against their shields while they howled. There was no attempt to shout in unison. The deliberate cacophony rasped over the waves. It had the nerve-wracking timbre of millstones grinding with no grain between to cushion their sound.

Gaius called from the fighting tower. Longidienus was trying to grab the agent's arm. "No time!" Perennius shouted as he swept past. The forward hatch was closed. Perennius wrenched it up with a bang. The galley was the area forward of the rowing chamber where the bows narrowed. As the hatch lifted, the boom of the coxswain's drum and the grunt of the oarsmen in unison hammered the agent's ears. Six faces stared up in terror—the cook and his assistant, and four slaves, probably brought aboard as officer's servants despite Perennius' orders to the contrary. Even in the present crisis, veins stood out in the agent's neck at proof that his will had been flouted.

Ignoring the companion ladder as usual, the stocky Illyrian jumped below. A slave squealed and rolled out of the path of the hobnails. The lower deck was a stinking Hell, its air saturated with the sweat of men rowing for their lives. The drum boomed its demands from the coxswain's seat in the stern. The coxswain's assistant paced nervously along the catwalk between the rowing benches, shrieking encouragement and flicking laggards with a long switch. The law did not permit the whipping of freemen, citizens of Rome, without trial; but the nearest magistrate was a dozen miles away, and there were two shiploads of Germans in between.

The galley was not intended for cooking while the *Eagle* was under way. The liburnian had no sleeping accommodations for the oarsmen, one for every foot of her hull length. Thus she virtually had to be docked or beached every night. The galley did provide a location for the cook to chop vegetables and grind meal for the next day's bread, however, and to cook under cover when conditions on shore were particularly bad. Men bore cold rain under a leather tarpaulin far better with a hot meal in their

bellies than they did without. The ship's ready stores
were kept in amphoras, pottery jars whose narrow bases
were sunk in a sand table to keep them upright while the
ship rolled.

And with the foodstuffs was another jar which held the
coals from which the oven and campfires would be kin-
dled when the ship made land. That had been a source of
unspoken fear to Perennius in the past days. He had seen
a warship burn in the harbor at Marseilles, the pitch and
sun-dried wood roaring into a blossom of flame with
awesome suddenness. Startled sailors had leaped into the
sea or to the stone docks with no chance to pick a landing
spot, some drowning, some smashing limbs. But at this
juncture, the danger of self-destruction was outweighed
by the certainty of what the pirates would do if the agent
did not accept the risk.

"Oil!" Perennius snapped to the cook who jumped back
as if the finger pointed at his face were a weapon.

"Which is the bloody oil jar?" the agent shouted. He
began opening the stores containers and flinging their
clay stoppers behind him in fury. Grain, grain . . . fish
sauce, half-full and pungent enough to make itself known
against the reek of the rowing chamber.

The cook's assistant, an Egyptian boy, had not cringed
away from Perennius' anger. He reached past the agent
and tapped an amphora with the nails of one smooth-
fingered hand.

Perennius grunted thanks and gripped the jar by its
ears. The amphora was of heavy earthenware with a clear
glaze to seal it to hold fluids. It was held so firmly by the
sand and the adjacent vessels that the agent's first tug did
not move it. With the set face of one who deals with a
problem one step at a time, Perrennius lifted again with a
twist. The oil jar came free with a scrunch of pottery,
allowing the jars beside it to shift inward. The cook stared
in amazement. He would not have tried to remove a jar
without knocking loose the wedge that squeezed all six
into a single unit.

"Longidienus!" the agent shouted to the open hatchway
as he swung with his burden. The watch-stander and a
majority of his Marine section were already staring into

the galley in preference to watching the oncoming pirates. "Take this and hand it up to Gaius in the tower!"

The Marine reached down and grunted. He had been unprepared for the amphora's weight by the ease with which it had been swung to him. Perennius ignored the oil jar as soon as it left his hand. What he needed now was the container with the fire. Its slotted clay stopper identified it with no doubt or frustration, with only a thrill of fear.

"Help the Legate with his jar!" Longidienus ordered the Marines as he shuffled toward the tower with his own load. His men looked in concern at one another. The Latin command was not one they had practiced during the voyage. In any case, Perennius had no intention of trusting the fire pot to any hands but his own at the moment. The earthenware was startlingly warm to the touch; not so hot that it could not be handled, but hot enough that the flesh cringed at first contact as it would from a spider leaping onto it unseen. Perennius locked the jar between his left forearm and his tunic as he climbed the ladder. It felt first like a warm puppy, then like the quiet beginnings of torture. On the main deck again, the agent paused and gripped his amphora by the ears, just as the ballista fired with a crack like a horse's thigh breaking.

Perennius and everyone else on the *Eagle*'s deck turned to mark the flight of the bolt. Its steel head and two bronze fins all glittered in the sun. Though the missile did not rotate, it quivered in the air on its long axis with a busy attraction that belied its purpose. The bolt's flat arc seemed to peak some two hundred and fifty paces away. It dropped into the sea at a much steeper angle than it had risen, still well short of the pirate vessel. The shot had been perfectly aligned, however, and there was a pause in the bellowed threats from the Germans.

You may win this, boys, thought the agent. But there'll be a few of you well and truly fucked before it's over.

CHAPTER THIRTEEN

The young courier and the two seamen he had coöpted as ballista crewmen were alone atop the fighting tower. While the sailors cranked furiously on opposite sides of the cocking windlass, Gaius was readjusting the second bolt by straightening a fin crimped in storage. He greeted with a glance and a curse the oil jar which Longidienus proffered him. "No, take it, Gaius!" Perennius called. "And take this too till I get up."

The younger Illyrian looked up again, frowning beneath the rim of his helmet. He did not retort to the voice he knew so well. Gaius bent to take the amphora, lifting it with greater ease than the Marine had but without the hysterical abandon of the agent. The jar was stoppered, but it was not sealed with wax. Yellowish, low-quality olive oil sloshed around the plug and seeped down the side of the jar like a slip on the glaze. "Set it on its side," the agent directed. "We don't need much, it can run if it likes. But don't let *this* bastard fall—" He handed up the pot with the fire.

The mechanism of the ballista clacked. One of the sailors cried, "It's ready, sir." The sailor's enthusiasm took Perennius aback as he scrambled up the short ladder to the tower. It was beyond the agent's comprehension how Gaius had managed to gain immediate obedience, much less cheerful cooperation, from the sailors in such dangerous, unfamiliar duty. The only sudden emotion Perennius had ever been able to instill in strangers was fear; and he was far too intelligent to think that fear was a basis for getting anything difficult done well. There was a great future opening for Gaius if he wanted it—and if anyone on the *Eagle* could measure his future in more than minutes.

Gaius shot a worried glance at the oncoming pirates, then looked back to his friend. "Aulus," he said as the agent swung a leg over the low parapet, "I need to load the ballis—"

Both Perennius' edged weapons lay on the deck in their scabbards. He gripped the hem of his linen tunic with both hands and tore it through in a single motion. Gaius stared in amazement as his protector ripped a circuit a hand's breadth wide from the bottom of his garment. "Iron won't stop enough of them, my friend," muttered the agent. "Like wasps—but we'll burn their fucking hive!"

Oil from the leaking jar pooled along the parapet. Perennius tossed the linen in the pool to soak. He took the other pot from Gaius, whose face was beginning to show comprehension in place of concern. "Cut that cloth," the agent directed as he flicked away the slotted lid. "Tie half around an arrow and give the rest to me."

The coals were a nest of hardwood banked carefully on a bed of sand. Perennius took the strip of oily linen from Gaius and dangled it into the pot so that one dripping corner blackened the ash it touched in the very center. The agent blew; a firm, even flow rather than a fierce pulse that would have sent cinders flying and cooled the flame it was meant to raise. His reward was the tongue of fire that ran up the edge of the cloth. The flame was yellow and smoky without the rush that naphtha or pitch could have offered; but it was what they had, and it would serve.

With the oily cloth afire within, Perennius set down the amphora without fear that the sand would shift and smother the coals. "Light that," he said, nodding to the bolt Gaius held with the linen knotted just behind the head, "and send it to the bastards." He tore more of his tunic's skirt away. Gaius obeyed, grinning like a fiend. The bolt thunked into the trough of the ballista. Its band of cloth now trailed smoke from a rind of flame. Gaius knelt, sighted between the vertical baulks of wood to either side of the trough, and loosed.

Because Perennius was behind the ballista, its bolt had little apparent motion to him. The missile lifted. It was a glitter against the pirates' sail and a black dot in the sky as it rose above the target. At the peak of its arc, the bolt blurred in a furious yaw, caused probably by the tail of linen tied to its shaft. A dot again after its momentary instability, the missile plunged. For a moment, the guttural bellowing from the pirate craft dissolved into less threatening sounds. A cheer broke out on the *Eagle's* deck.

A German had raised his shield to receive the missle. His face was a sunburned blur amid flowing blond beard and hair. The press of his fellows in the bow might have prevented him from ducking away even if he had been willing to show fear. The five-pound bolt, rather a short javelin than an arrow in weight, snapped through the wicker shield and the man who bore it before it crunched into the pelvis of a pirate in the second rank. The men crashed backwards, pinned together in a tangle of limbs flailing spasmodically like those of a spider on a knife point.

Perennius did not cheer with the others. The rag had been stripped on impact and lay as a black smear on the face of the wicker shield. That was not serious. Luck might send a later bolt into the more flammable target. But the agent had seen that the snap of the ballista's acceleration had snuffed the flame out even as the bolt sailed from its trough.

Gaius hooted with glee as he tied more linen around the shaft of the next missile. The fact of the whole plan's failure had been lost in the young man's delight at killing two of the enemy. "Half-cock on the next one, Gaius," the agent ordered as he opened his own pouch. "Don't draw the string all the way."

"Blazes, Aulus!" the courier cried. His normal deference to his protector was lost in the present rush of hormones. "It won't get there if we don't cock it!"

"God strike you for a fool!" Perennius roared back. "It

doesn't matter if it gets there if the bloody fire goes out in the air!"

Shocked back into the agent's reality, Gaius spun and passed the order to the seamen on the windlass.

The captain's strategy of getting past with both pirate vessels on the port side had clearly failed. The nearer of the pirates, now closing on the liburnian with a rush, had already worked to starboard. The *Eagle* was in theory caught between her opponents. In fact, however, the separation between one German vessel and the other had increased as they raced for their prey. The further pirate had not worked to windward with anything like the finesse of her consort. She was now the better part of a mile distant. That at least permitted the *Eagle* to engage the nearer opponent alone; though Perennius was under no illusions as to his ability to beat off a hundred heavily-armed Germans with the force at his disposal.

Now that the direction of the attack was more or less certain, Sestius led his half-section forward to join Longidienus and the other Marines. Perennius noticed two seamen wearing loin clouts and carrying pikes had joined the Marines. Most of the deck crew had disappeared below. Leonidas held his post in the stern. The captain had belted on a sword. A pair of his men still gripped the tiller behind them. The *Eagle* was as ready as she would ever be.

There was one more datum on the credit side. No short, cowled figure had appeared among the barbarians screaming on the pirates' deck. For now, the *Eagle* had only men to deal with. Bad as that might be, Perennius found it at least better than the alternative.

"Had a pair of these, mule-drawn, in our troop," said Gaius to the stock of the ballista as he crouched behind it. "Used them at Arlate, though we didn't engage ourselves. . . ." Perennius had not wondered at or even given thanks for his protégé's unexpected competence with the crew-served weapon. Time enough for that if they got out of what was coming.

After they got out of it.

The ballista was not simply a large bow mounted crosswise in a stock. The arms holding the string were separate, stiff billets of wood, each about thirty inches long. The butt of either arm was thrust into a skein made from the neck sinews of draft oxen. The skeins had been wrenched to the greatest torsion possible in their heavy frame. Only then were the arms drawn back against that stress by the cocking windlass. The bow string itself was of horsehair and an inch in diameter; nothing lighter could transfer the energy of even a rather small piece of torsion artillery to its missile.

With the trough elevated to 45° and the cord drawn only half the three feet of travel possible, Gaius sent a second flaming bolt into the sky. Its arc was clean and perfect from the point it leapt from the weapon to its hiss on plunging into a wave the length of a man short of the pirates' deck. Groans from the Marines mingled with raucous cheers from the Germans; but there was a pool of yellow flame, oil burning on the water, for an instant before the cutwater scattered it.

"Load another," the agent said in grim triumph. "We've got them now!" And he dropped a bullet into the cup of his own sling.

Several of the Germans were shooting arrows into the sea with self bows—bows which depended on the tension of a single staff of wood to power their missiles. The composite bows of the horse lords of Scythia and Mesopotamia were far more effective weapons. Perennius would not, however, have traded the sling he held for even one of those fine recurved bows and the skill to use it.

The sling was marvelously compact in comparison to any other missile weapon save a hand-flung rock. There was a short wooden grip, a leather pocket for the bullet, and two silken cords a yard long to provide leverage. Perennius used silk cords because they were strong and because they were not affected by the damp. In a downpour, leather stretched and the sinew and horn laminations of composite bows could separate from the wooden core. The silken sling was affected only to the extent that rain made its user uncomfortable; and that, for Aulus Perennius in a killing mood, was not at all.

Now the agent grinned, sighted, and snapped the sling

around his head in a single 360° arc. He released the free cord while still holding the wooden handgrip. The bullet slashed out over the ballista and the two startled seamen cocking it. Six hundred feet away, a German died as two ounces of lead crushed his skull. Perennius' mouth was still set in humorless curve of an axe-edge. He set another bullet in the pocket and resumed the business of slaughter.

The sling would throw anything within reason, including clay balls that would shatter and could not be thrown back. Pebbles would do in default of prepared ammunition. Perennius preferred almond-shaped bullets of lead. Their density carried them further through the air than bulkier missiles, and their double points could punch through the armor of cataphract horsemen at shorter ranges. The ammunition the agent had brought to his pouch had the word "Strike!" cast in the side of each bullet. At worst, the hope expressed by some armorer did not make the bullets less effective, for they struck like deadly hail as the vessels closed.

The ship-jarring thud of seventy-two oars striking their locks in attempted unison had been a part of existence since the pirates were sighted. Now the sound ceased. It was replaced by a continuing clatter and the hiss of the liburnian's hull cleaving the water on sail-power and momentum. Gaius cursed as his forehead bumped the ballista he was sighting. Perennius ignored the change except to shift his bracing foot as he shot, then shot again.

The agent's whole upper body, not just the strength of his arms, was behind the snap of each bullet. It was for that reason that Perennius could not wear armor, though he knew as well as anyone that he would be the target of every German archer when they realized what he was doing. A chieftain as gray and shaggy as his wolf-skin cape suddenly squawked and pitched forward, under the bows of his own ship. A bullet had broken his shin. A moment later, the man who had pushed into the vicim's place collapsed in turn. A lozenge-shaped fleck had appeared in the weathered surface of his shield. The German did not cry out as he died. The bullet had lodged in his diaphragm after punching through his lindenwood buckler.

Perennius had aiming points, but for now he was not really trying to choose his targets. The range and relative motion of the ships would have made it difficult to snipe at individuals—though it was a thing he would have managed, trust the gods and his own trained eye, if one of the chitinous Guardians had shown itself with the pirates. Now there was no need to be choosy. The Germans were clustered too thickly to miss. A round glanced from the bronze helm of one and into the throat of the fellow screeching just behind him. Both Germans fell in a confused tangle of limbs and weapons. One pirate was much the same as another, with the champions and bare-chested mad-men of the front rank more likely as more worthy victims.

An arrow with a barbed iron head thumped the parapet of the tower. An inch higher and it would have been in the agent's knee. The archer was a naked man who squatted amidships near the *beitass*, the pole which stiffened the forward leech of the sail. Perennius ignored him as he ignored the handful of other archers. Statistically, they were not a serious threat; and there was no way to get through the next minutes save by trusting Fortune and the best chances offered.

The short German bows were unlikely to disable any of the armored Marines if they hit, and accurate archery from shipboard was almost impossible anyway. Waves and fluctuations in the breeze kept moving vessels trembling up and down even in calm seas. That did not affect a slinger, since the bullet would hold the plane of its arc no matter what the ship did in the instant between aim and release. Perennius could not have called the gyroscopic effect by name, but he used its results like any good empiricist. A one-inch twitch in the arrowhead meant the shot missed by a man's height at a hundred feet—that was if it had been properly aimed in the first place. Perennius had the gravest regard for the rush of a hundred German swordsmen; but their archers, like thirst, were simply a factor that had to be ignored in battle.

It was something of the same problem that caused Gaius to overshoot his intended target. He had aimed for the pirate steersman, in the stern with two other men. A

swell threw the missile high, so that it should have cleared
them by thirty feet—but Fortune favors the bold. The
blazing arrow thudded through the sail and into the top
of the mast. The bolt and its result were lost to almost the
entire companies of both ships as they prepared to come
to grips.

At the coxswain's order, the *Eagle*'s rowers had stopped
stroking and had attempted to draw their oars in through
the ports. It was an operation the men performed every
night and during intervals of the day when their stroke
was not called for. In those cases, however, there was
leisure to pull one oar in at a time and to take care that
the handles cleared the men and benches across the rowing chamber. There was neither time nor calm now. The
men on deck feared the foaming, furious Germans. The
oarsmen were crowded together with no view but a flash
of sea through their ports, even that occluded by the
runnels of sweat in their eyes. Drowning, fire, missiles
rained down on them through the ventilators—every man
could feel his own terror approach through the swimming
blackness. When through the fog of adrenalin and fatigue
poisons they received the order to secure oars simultaneously, they obeyed; but they obeyed in anarchic panic.

The *Eagle* slowed as its oars ceased their stroke. In the
rowing chamber, men fell as oar-butts slammed their
temples. The ship itself resounded with the battering of
oars into benches; sometimes the same oar repeatedly, as
a terror-blinded seaman kept jerking against immovable
timber instead of angling his shaft an inch to one side or
the other to clear. There was no one on deck to drop the
yard and sail. Leonidas could only hope that the leverage
of the high-hung weight would not be enough to snap the
mast and bury the *Eagle*'s fighting complement in a tangle of sail and cordage. No one else aboard knew or
remembered to care.

The German steerman and the pair of men with him in
the stern were darker and more squat that the general
run of the pirates—Herulians among Goths. None of the
three were armed at the moment, though their spears and
shields were laid against the low gunwale beside them.

The man at the oar shouted. His two companions tugged at the windlass that raised and lowered their own sail.

Perennius sighted over the mass of Germans now almost below him. He shot the steersman in the chest.

The Herulian straightened with a cry. He fell forward, across one of the men who had just unblocked the windlass. The yard clattered down in a rush. The belly of the sail flapped, then crumpled flaccidly, as the wind had its will. The pirates had been making only a knot or two into the wind. Their mass and headway were too slight to keep their bow from swinging slightly as the wind took them aback. The closing impact was therefore the two knots driven by the *Eagle*'s sail alone. It was still awesome.

The liburnian displaced some eighty tons; the pirate vessel perhaps half that. The crews alone massed ten tons apiece. All of that kinetic energy had to be absorbed by the hulls as the ships ground together, starboard to starboard. In the *Eagle*'s rowing chamber, that meant death and maiming despite the best efforts of the coxswain and his assistant.

The oars could not be fully withdrawn, but with care all but the blade-tips could have been sheltered within the hull and outrigger. There had not been time for care. Now the pirates' cutwater slammed along the side of the liburnian, catching every oar that still projected. The oar-looms turned into flails within the rowing chamber. The ashen oars broke, but more limbs and bodies broke also. Men on deck heard a screaming like that of pigs in an abattoir. Twelve feet of oar-shaft flipped up, dislodging a ventilator grate.

It was small consolation to the victims that something similar was happening to the pirates.

The skill of the Herulian seamen was no more in doubt than was the courage of the Gothic berserkers pressing forward in the bow. The *Eagle* was probably the first oared warship the pirates had tackled, however, and that led to a misjudgment. No one on the pirate ship was prepared to see the oar-blades rise into a chest-high obstruction as the ships swept together. Men waiting to board either ducked or were struck down by blades and shafts splintered on the cutwater. Leonidas' exercise had been a protective one, intended to save his oars and rowers. Because the liburnian had twice the pirate vessel's height above the water, the half-effective defensive move proved to be a shattering offensive weapon.

Alone, it was not enough. A German with naked, tattooed limbs hurled the first grappling iron aboard even as an oar struck him down. There were three more irons clawing the *Eagle*'s foredeck and outrigger before the ships ground to a complete halt. Marines staggered as their deck lurched and the liburnian's sail thrust against the combined mass. Howling with glee, pirates began scrambling over writhing comrades and up the oars.

"Let's get the bastards!" Gaius shouted. He drew his long cavalry sword with a flourish. The young Illyrian leaped down from the tower. His waist-length dress cloak flared behind him like a crimson membrane. To Perennius' utter amazement, the two seamen snatched up ballista bolts and followed Gaius to the deck. If they had stayed where they were and thrown the bolts, they might have been of use. Charismatic leadership did not seem to confer tactical skills when it suppressed the instincts of naked men to run from armored attackers.

Well, Aulus Perennius might not be able to get a sailor to follow him into a whorehouse, much less a battle, but he didn't need anyone to teach him his present business either.

More than half the Marines surged forward to meet the Germans. Only one of the scratch force turned and jumped down the forehatch. It was a better percentage than the agent would have guessed. He had no time for the melee, because the Herulians in the stern had noticed the smoke puffing from the ends of their loose-folded sail.

The ballista bolt had been snatched from the mast by the weight of the yard and sail. Hidden but not suffocated, the oily rag had ignited the sail. Perennius had not expected his makeshift fire-arrows to do serious damage. He had hoped for a diversion which, had it occurred early enough, might have permitted the liburnian to run past the pirates as Leonidas had planned to do. Perennius had his diversion now, though it was probably too late.

One of the Herulians snatched up the bucket which lay

in the shallow bailing well aft. He turned and the sling bullet took him on the point of his hip. A trifle low, but the angle was tricky ... and it would serve for the time, as the man bled and screamed and tried with both hands to compress the shattered bone into unity.

A spear thrust at the agent over the tower parapet. Perennius skipped back, putting the frame of the ballista between himself and the German who wanted his life. The remaining Herulian amidships was the only one of the pirates who seemed to retain an interest in his own ship. He was short-gripping his spear to probe at the sail with the point in an attempt to find the source of the smoke.

"Fire, you donkey-fuckers!" Perennius shouted, hoping Germans from the Danube migrations could understand the dialect he had picked up on the Rhine. "Your ship's burning!" He shot the Herulian seaman through the center of his boiled-leather breast-plate, just as a Goth stabbed the agent from behind in the right thigh.

There had been a brief struggle as Marines on the cat-walk tried to throw back the pirates climbing aboard. The Germans were handicapped by their need to scramble up oar shafts with their shields slung and a hand for their spears. They had both numbers and fury, however. The angle gave them an unexpected advantage as well. The German spears tended to be longer than the eight-foot javelins issued to the Marines. When the pirates thrust up from their deck or a shifting perch among the oars, their points passed below the Roman shields. Three Marines crashed down with their calves pierced before the rest hopped back onto the deck proper. Germans leaped after them, pushing the defenders back further by sheer weight.

Perennius threw himself forward with a cry. The weapon that had pierced his leg was a poor grade of iron and not even particularly sharp. It had the strength of a hulking, two-hundred-and-fifty pound pirate behind it, however. Blood leaped after the black iron as the agent drew himself off the point. The pirate grunted and raised his weapon to finish the job.

Flat-footed on deck, the Goth was as tall as the fighting tower. To thrust over the parapet, he had to raise his spear overhead with both hands, but that awkwardness was slight protection to Perennius. The German wore silvered chain mail, but his head was bare. His blond hair was long. It was gathered on the left side by a knot close to the German's scalp, so that it streamed like a horse's tail past his shoulder.

The agent's sword lay somewhere on deck. His shield was packed in the cabin with his body armor. With a bullet in its cup, the sling would have been an effective flail even though the range was too short for normal use. And any thought of further retreat ended with the crunch of iron against the mechanism of the ballista behind him. The German who had driven Perennius to the back of the tower had not forgotten the slinger either.

If Perennius jumped forward, the Goth would spit him on the shaft of his rising spear—but the agent might get close enough to kick the bastard's brains out. Perennius tensed, and the Goth tensed, and the boat-pike Calvus swung like a flail dished in the side of the pirate's skull.

Sabellia and Calvus had appeared around the swollen belly of the sail. They held pikes from the rack on the mast. The Gallic woman was screeching as she thrust at another pirate around the corner of the tower. Her pike thumped his breast plate, leaving a bright streak on the bronze disks and a scar on the leather backing when it skidded off. The point did not penetrate.

The strength required to swing the full length of a fourteen-foot pike was amazing even by the standards Calvus had already demonstrated, but it was also an absurdly awkward way to use the thrusting weapon. The traveller must have been watching Sabellia even as he clubbed down the Goth. He shifted his grip. He was still holding the pike well behind its point of balance. The pirate Sabellia had struck now raised his shield and stepped forward again. The long, round-tipped sword in his right hand was poised for an overhand cut.

Perennius held the free end of his sling and flipped the handle-weighted length of it down to entangle the German's sword wrist. Calvus lunged, ramming his pike through the shield, the startled pirate, and an inch or more of the fighting tower beside. The crackle of wood and bones was as sharp as nearby lightning.

Perennius sprang down. His right leg collapsed as he had expected, but it held him again when he thrust himself back off the deck with both hands. The Goth pinned to the tower's planking was thrashing. His arms and legs hammered the wood as all his muscles retracted simultaneously, relaxed, and clamped again. The whites of his eyes had rotated up. His sword dropped beside him. The agent snatched the German-made weapon, careful to keep his right leg straight as he bent over.

Sestius and his Marines held a surprisingly solid line between the fighting tower and the mast. Gaius was still on his feet, the agent saw with relief. The young Illyrian stood in the center of the fight, everything a commander should be with his bright armor and his long, bloody sword. The pirates had so awkward a path to board that their numbers could not tell fully. Beyond that difficulty, it was clear that the strength and enthusiasm of the men who remained to board the liburnian was less than that of the individuals in the first wave.

The German leader, if he were still alive, had shown as little of generalship as had Perennius himself. Unlike the Imperial agent, the mixed force of Germans had no subordinate officers to make up for defects in command—the way Gaius, Sestius, and Leonidas on the poop had done. Only two Goths had circled the fighting tower instead of charging straight for the line of Marines. A serious attempt—and one aimed at the shieldless backs of the Marines instead of the galling slinger on the tower—would have ended all resistance on the liburnian's deck in a minute or less. Now the ignored path around the flank was Perennius' to exploit—as point man and not as commander, of course.

Sabellia was trying to turn and face the main German threat. Sestius himself held the tower end of the Marine line. The Gallic woman clearly wanted to be beside her lover. She was not large even for her sex, however. Her pike weighed over twenty pounds and was very clumsy besides. When Sabellia tried to raise the shaft and turn, the pike head fouled one of the forestays of the mast.

Calvus was trying to withdraw his own weapon. When he tugged backward, the point squealed out of the tower. The Goth remained hopelessly impaled. Clearing that pike was obviously a task for whoever survived the battle. To the agent's amazement, the traveller continued to jerk at the shaft as if he could somehow overcome the friction of perforated wood, bronze, and bone with nothing more than the corpse's mass to hold against his tugging.

"Blazes!" screamed the agent. "Take hers and come along with me!" For all that Calvus seemed genuinely dim-witted about practical things, his demonstrated strength was too obvious an asset now to be neglected. Sabellia's instincts and courage were all that Perennius could have hoped for at his back—but a man who could drive a pike like a ballista bolt was utterly beyond a soldier's hopes.

There was a splotch on the ragged edge of the agent's tunic. The wound oozed, however, with none of the fierce arterial spurting that would have meant the agent's death by now. It made him weaker and slower, but he was Aulus Perennius. When a black-bearded German faced him with a shout at the starboard side of the tower, Perennius cut him down. The blow would have decapitated the German if the sword-edge had been up to the job.

The confusion on the pirate vessel itself was suddenly more than raucous blood-lust. Genuine flames amidships were rolling clouds of smoke as white as steam out of the crumpled sail. Half the men still aboard the shallow vessel were either trying to fight the fire or were shouting at it in pointless terror instead of trying to board the *Eagle*.

Perennius saw a chance and took it. The two ships were rotating slowly about their common center. In a few minutes, the *Eagle* would be taken aback, her untended sail fluttering back against her mast as the combined momentum of the vessels torqued her into the wind. At the moment, however, the liburnian's canvas and bluff side were downwind of the pirates. If the ships had not

been linked by the grappling lines, they would already
have begun drifting apart.

And there were only two lines still fastened.

The axe-wielding Herulian who had been facing Sestius
danced back, aiming a cut and a curse at the Roman
agent who had just appeared on his right flank. Perennius
ducked his upper body away from the blow. He made no
attempt to parry the heavier weapon with his sword.
More surprisingly to anyone who had seen Perennius fight
before, the squat Illyrian did not exploit the German's
loss of balance. The fellow stood with his shield wide to
the left fronting Sestius. His axe pulled the right side of
his body around to follow his backhand blow.

The Herulian was not the most important target.
Perennius squatted and cut at the horsehair rope reeved
through the shaft of the nearest grapnel. His sword tore
chips from the edge of the runway which acted as his
chopping block. The wound in Perennius' thigh burned
and his leg threatened to buckle, but he could not have
reached the hawser without bending at the knees.

A Goth clung to the rope as his feet slid on the shaft of
the oar he was trying to climb. He screamed and tried to
thrust his spear at the agent left-handed. To the other
side, the Herulian with the axe cried out also. Sestius had
used the diversion to pin his opponent's knees together by
thrusting below the German's wicker shield. The Herulian
fell backward as the government-issue spear tore through
ligaments and the porous ends of the leg bones. The
Herulian might still have swung at Sestius' ankles while
the centurion drew his sword, but Sabellia slipped past
her lover with something bright in her hand. As Perennius
had suspected before, the finger-length blade of her knife
was long enough to let out all a man's blood through his
throat.

Oarsmen were fighting their way onto the deck by both
hatches and through the ventilator whose grating had
been lifted by the initial shock. If the sailors had been
armed and trained, their numbers would have been
decisive. As it was, their terror was likely to demoralize
the Marines who had been holding steadily despite their
losses. Flight was obvious suicide, but the instincts of

battle are housed far deeper in a man's brain than is the intellect which seeks to direct them. Perennius cursed and cut again. Both ends frayed into anemone-tufts of horsehair as the hawser sprang apart under tension. The Goth's despairing spear-thrust nocked the side of the *Eagle* as the man himself hit the water. He was dragged instantly to his death by his equipment and his inability to swim.

The agent levered himself to his feet, using the Gothic sword as a crutch. The blade bowed under his weight. It did not spring back when he lifted its point from the wood.

There was no way this side of Hell that Perennius could reach the remaining grappling line. It was fast in the outrigger, twenty feet aft of where he stood. Already fresh Germans boarding the *Eagle* were running toward the agent instead of joining the rank that faced the Marines.

The grapnel Perennius had cut free lay on the deck before him. The released tension of its line had sprung free the one of its three hooks which had been embedded in the liburnian's deck coaming. The agent thrust the point of his sword under a hook and flipped the iron up into his left hand. He could not afford to bend over. Perennius' right thigh was spasming even though he was trying to keep his weight off it. "Cut the other line!" he shouted in Greek. He brandished the grapnel, holding it by its eighteen-inch shaft as an explanation and a way to call attention to himself in the tumult.

Wailing, bloody oarsmen forced their way up from the chaos in the rowing chamber. Some of them were even throwing themselves over the port side, though they could be only a brief salvation even for those who could swim. "We've got to separate the ships!" shrieked Perennius in a hopeless attempt to be heard above their clamor.

The Goth who rushed Perennius along the outrigger's runway wore a helmet of silvered iron. Its fixed visor flared over his brow like the bill of a Celtic woman's bonnet. There was nothing feminine about his long sword or the strength with which he cut at the agent's torso with it.

Perennius interposed the grappling iron as if it were a

buckler. The claws were thumb-thick and forged from metal as good as that in the Goth's sword. Sparks flew from both objects. The shock to Perennius' left arm was severe, but the two feet of greater leverage almost tore the quivering sword from the Goth's hand.

The agent tried to thrust at his opponent. His bent blade and the weakness of the leg that should have carried him made the attack more of a stumble. The German skipped back anyway, disconcerted by his numb sword-hand. As the pirate did so, the deck lurched and he lost his footing. Screaming, he fell backward onto the oar-blades. Despite the desperate clutching of his hands, the Goth slipped off and went head-first into the sea.

Perennius went down also. The wind blew a pall of smoke from the other vessel. It reeked of leather and wet wool. Out of it came another German with his metal-shod shield raised and his spear poised to stab the kneeling agent.

There was nothing wrong with Perennius' right arm. He hurled his sword against the warrior's trousered shins. The weapon clanged and cut. The pirate gave a yelp and pitched headlong. His helmet fell off and he dropped his shield to scrabble at the deck coaming with his left hand.

Perennius hit him on the temple with the grappling iron. The German's legs relaxed, but there was still life in his arms until the agent struck twice more. The body slid sideways off the runway, as the other had done before it.

Blazes, there was open water between the ships!

A freak of the breeze sucked away the bitter smoke for the moment. The ships had lain parallel with their starboard bows interlocked. Now there was a broad V of water between the liburnian's bow and the cutwater of the pirate vessel. There was still a grappling line snubbed to the *Eagle*. Even as Perennius stared, the hooks of that iron tore free. They took with them a foot of the deck coaming. The *Eagle* lurched again. Without the drag of the smaller ship, the wind was already starting to swing her head to leeward.

The agent risked a glance over his shoulder. Behind him, Calvus was straightening. The tall man held the boat-pike near the butt as he twitched its head free of the pirate's hull planking.

The traveller had just pushed the two ships apart single-handedly.

The *Eagle*'s defenders could not see what had happened. The roar of despair on their own vessel was enough to cause the pirates who had boarded already to glance around. There were less than a dozen of them. The Marines' tight ranks and full armor had made them dangerous opponents when there was nowhere for them to run.

Perennius grabbed a fallen spear to replace the sword which had splashed over the side. He was still on his knees. "Get'em from behind with your pike!" he cried to Calvus, but when he looked around he saw that the tall man was stiff in his trance state.

The line of Germans broke from the flank nearest Perennius and his companion.

It was as sudden and progressive as cloth ripping under tension. A red-bearded pirate flung the spear with which he had been sparring with Sestius. It clanged on the centurion's shield boss. The German dropped his own shield and ran. He launched himself from the deck of the liburnian and into the waist of his own vessel despite the widening gap that separated them. Behind him came his companions.

The pirates broke so suddenly that the exhausted Marines had no time to pursue. Gaius alone followed them. The courier had a deep cut on his left shoulder and the light of battle in his eyes. Blood rippled into droplets from the point of his long sword as he brought it around in a final arc. A Herulian with a wolf-skin kirtle screamed as the Roman blade severed one heel even as he threw himself overboard. In the water, men drowned or splashed to hand-holds on the pirate ship's gunwale.

And there were no pirates alive on the *Eagle*.

CHAPTER FOURTEEN

Perennius was dizzy, sick with blood loss and reaction. He tried to rise but found that even holding himself on knees and knuckles required all his concentration until the moment of vertigo had passed. God of Morning, he thought with his eyes closed. Let your servant behold you once again. But it was now late in the afternoon, and the second pirate vessel was luffing toward them with men at her rail.

Hell, he was never very good at resting anyway, the agent thought. He rose carefully. Calvus' hands were at his shoulder and wounded thigh. Their dry warmth offered more comfort than the burden they took from Perennius' own muscles.

The *Eagle* was not entirely clear of the first pirate vessel, for that matter. The survivors of that smoldering craft seemed as disinterested in continuing the fight as were those standing in the carnage of the liburnian's deck. Neither ship was under control. Because the *Eagle*'s sail was set and her sides were higher than those of the pirate craft, she was drifting downwind faster than the Germans were. That was not going to be sufficient so long as the liburnian shared the sea with an undamaged shipful of pirates.

The captain, Leonidas, was obviously aware of that. He was shouting at the mate. That officer in turn was holding a pair of seamen and actually placing their hands on the shroud he wanted trimmed. Both sailors were blood-spattered and slack-faced. Perennius recognized one of them from the ballista crew. No wonder the mate was having difficulty raising him out of shock. A wonder that the man had survived at all, the way Gaius had rushed them into the melee.

Calvus was bandaging Perennius' thigh. The tall man was using a length of wool and a jeweled brooch that the agent had last seen fastening the cloak of a Goth he had killed. The wool provided absorption and a compress, all you could do while you waited to see whether the wound festered and killed you.... "Can you make the winds blow the way you want?" Perennius asked. He rotated the spear in his hand so that its iron ferule rapped the bloody deck.

The traveller straightened. "No," he said. He pointed at the bandage, partly visible beneath the torn edge of the agent's tunic. "It will hurt as it heals, and there'll be the usual stiffness," he said. "But no infection."

All over the deck, men were sorting themselves out. Leonidas had disappeared down the after hatch. Missing seamen were beginning to reappear on deck for their officers to put to work. Speaking harshly under the rein that kept him from rushing back to present needs himself, the agent demanded, "How did you separate us from the pirates?" He waved at the shallow, wallowing craft which was now well astern of the *Eagle*. "How?"

"You said we had to loose ourselves from them," the tall man said simply. "I could not have reached the line without being killed myself, but I could push the ships apart with my pike. Eventually the line would give or the hooks would pull out." Calvus' tongue touched his lips in a gesture of hesitation which Perennius did not remember the traveller showing in the past. "That meant that I could not help you fight, but ... you need little help in that."

Perennius closed his eyes, then opened them to snarl with a frustration directed against the world, "Could you lift this fucking ship? Could you do that?"

"No, Aulus Perennius," the traveller said.

The agent spun on his left heel. "Let's see what we've got left to kill the next hundred with," he said.

"Aulus!" shouted the courier when he noticed the agent,

"Gods above, we massacred them!" Gaius' enthusiasm was as natural as it was premature. He had not yet learned the lesson that it does not matter in war how well you fight, but only whether or not you win. The *Eagle* had fought very well indeed; but Perennius' mind, unlike his protégé's, was on the unscathed company of pirates rather than on those whose blood painted the liburnian's foredeck.

Gaius waved his sword with an abandon that showed he had forgotten it. Blood had dried on its point and edges and was streaked darkly across the flats of the blade as well. Perennius stepped to the younger man and grasped his sword wrist. "Clean your equipment, soldier!" he ordered harshly. Gaius' present euphoria was as incapacitating as the blubbering despair which would follow it if the agent did not shock him back to reality at once. They all needed the courier's demonstrated charisma if they were to survive.

The wound on Gaius' shoulder was not as serious as the agent had feared. The segmented body armor had sleeves and a skirt of studded leather straps. A blow had severed two of the straps, but the cut beneath the young man's bloody tunic was short and shallow. There was no grating of bone ends when Perennius probed it firmly.

"Yes sir!" Gaius said. He braced to attention despite the twinge as the squat agent tested his shoulder.

Perennius grinned like a shark as he turned to Sestius and the Marines. Gods! but the kid was good. Men would follow him to Hell!

Men had. The body immediately underfoot was that of the other ballista crewman. A spear had spilled several feet of intestines from his unprotected body.

Longidienus was dead. An arrow, of all things, through the throat. Sestius had been the real commander of the detachment ever since the first day on board, however. As expected, the centurion was readying his troops for the next fight with professional calm. If he did not demonstrate the verve that young Gaius had, it was because he knew as well as Perennius did how slight their chances of survival were.

Sestius broke off a discussion with the man whose calf he was bandaging when he saw the agent approaching.

"Sir," he said, the Cilician accent polished out of his voice by fifteen years of Army. "Four dead, four may as well be. . . ." He and Perennius glanced together at a gray-faced Marine with a broken spear-shaft showing just below the lower lip of his cuirass. "Three that'll be all right unless they get time for the wounds to stiffen up, which I don't guess they will." He squeezed the wrist of the man he was bandaging. "Next!"

"Perennius, are you all right?" Sabellia asked, rising from behind the centurion's armored bulk. She flipped to the deck the arrow she had just forced out of a sailor's biceps point-first so that the barbs would not tear the flesh even wider. The woman's arms were bloody to the elbows. Perennius knew that not all the gore resulted from the medical work she was doing at the moment.

"Huh?" the agent said. Sabellia was bent down again with a water-dripping compress before he remembered his wounded thigh. "Blazes, I'll live," he added with a certainty he could not have offered had he thought about the words. "Sestius, get the casualties stripped, arms and armor collected, and a seaman behind every goddam point or edge of this ship. If they're going to run up on deck screaming, they can damned well stay and soak up an arrow that might waste somebody useful otherwise."

The man whose arm Sabellia was binding looked up in horror. He was obviously one of the oarsmen who had leaped up on deck just in time to stop a missile.

"Go on, leave the wounded," Perennius growled to his centurion. "She can handle the rest." Sabellia lifted her eyes. They were large and dark, and they covered any emotion the woman might have felt the way straw can momentarily cover a fire it is flung on.

The *Eagle*'s sluggish wake bobbed with flotsam: bodies, stripped and flung over the side. They would float until their lungs filled or the gulls, wheeling and screaming above, pecked away enough of the soft parts that the rest sank for the bottom-feeding eels. Further off, beyond even the smudgy pall of the vessel they had fought, were the heads of men whose arms still splashed to stave off drowning. The ones still alive in the water would be those who had leaped in unburdened by equipment: oarsmen, driven to panic in the liburnian's belly, Germans who threw away their arms and chose water over fire as a route to Hell. They had no value either as fighters or as hostages. No one on either side would spare a thought for them until long after they had lost their hand-holds on the waves.

But the second pirate ship had sheered slightly from its attempt to close with the *Eagle*. Perhaps the fact that the liburnian suddenly got under way again was primarily responsible for the change. Now the German craft was wearing around to her disabled consort. As Perennius squinted to see past the *Eagle*'s high stern, blocks rattled and the pirates' sail dropped smoothly.

"Will they let us go now?" Calvus asked in his usual tone of unconcern.

"Can you make them let us go?" the agent asked.

The tall man dipped his head. "No," he said, "at this distance—" already a quarter mile separated the hunters from their prey—"I can't affect anyone except my own kind."

"Then they'll be back," Perennius said grimly. "They want to know what happened . . . maybe take aboard some of the able-bodied men, that's all they're doing. But they haven't forgotten us, and unless our rowers are in better shape than I think they are, they've got plenty of daylight to catch us in." He paused, looking at Calvus with an expression of rueful joy. "You know," he said, "they gave us an old cow . . . but she gored a few Germans, didn't she? I keep thinking that the Empire . . . Ah, screw it, let's find Leonidas and see if he's got any better ideas than I do."

From the sea astern came the squealing of a windlass. The Germans were raising their sails again. The mechanical sound formed a descant to the pirates' hoarse shouting.

The Tarantine captain rose from the aft ladder as Perennius approached. During brief glimpses caught while the fighting went on, the captain looked cool and aloof in his command chair. The agent had felt flashes of anger, irrational but real none the less when he was bathed with his own sweat and blood in the melee. Closer view provided a reassurance which Perennius needed emotionally if not on an intellectual level. Leonidas too was drenched in sweat, and there was a bubble of blood where he had bitten through his lip during the action. "Right?" he said sharply, turning to meet the agent.

Despite the fact that the battle was only half over, the anger which had flared earlier between the two men was gone. The tension which had fueled the earlier outbursts had burned away in the open fighting. Each of them was intelligent enough to have noted how the other handled his duties during the crisis. "We're doing what we can," the agent said simply. "The fire was a fluke. I doubt we'll fight them off a second time, even arming some of your seamen. What're the chances that you'll be able to run us clear?"

From below them came a human babble and the clash and rattle of wood. Injured men were coming up the hatchway. Some of them were slung like sides of meat if their own damaged limbs could not get them out of the way unaided.

"Fucking none," Leonidas said bleakly. "But we're trying, too. Getting the rowing chamber clear." There were splashes alongside as broken oars slid into the sea. There was no time to fit the replacements carried in the hold, but at least their burden and awkwardness could be disposed of. "Capenus'll have a stroke of some sort going any time now, but Fortune! That won't do more than add minutes, the shape the men and hardware is below. Fortune! But we tried."

"How will they approach us this time, Captain Leonidas?" asked Calvus as the two shorter men started to return glumly to tasks they viewed as hopeless.

The Tarantine's eyes glittered at what seemed now an interruption, but the question's own merit struck him. "Likely the same way. Our poop's high—" he rapped the bulkhead beside him with a palm as hard as a landsman's knuckles. "Can't board us by this. Their little boats aren't high enough to lay alongside, either. *That* they'll have learned from the first try." He grinned in fierce recollection. "Damned if the oars didn't lay out more of them than your lobsters on deck did—not to knock the way the Marines

fought, sir. . . . But they've got the legs to overhaul us, the
shape we're in below decks. If they're smart, and if they're
not too afraid of your ballista—" a nod to Perennius—
"they'll lay along the starboard bow again, where there's
the most length of hull without the oars to fend them
away."

Oar blades curled into the water on either side. It was a
ragged stroke with jolts like mallets knocking as shafts
fouled one another, but it brought a cheer from the men
on deck. Perennius could glimpse the second pirate ship
now. It was nosing past the rising curve of the *Eagle*'s
poop at a distance. The Germans were standing off wide
to starboard instead of closing directly on the stern of
their prey. Little more than half the liburnian's oars were
moving, given the damage to the oars and to the men who
should have worked them. Besides that, the rowers must
be exhausted from their earlier pull. Their second wind
could not last long.

"I'd better go help Gaius with the ballista," the agent
said abruptly. "We were lucky once." He turned.

"Wait," said Calvus, touching Perennius' arm. "Why
don't we ram them this time?" he went on. His dark eyes
held the Tarantine's.

Leonidas' rage was predictable and this time uncon-
trolled. "Listen, fishbrain, I told you why we don't ram!
We—" Calvus raised his index finger in query. The
captain's flowing recapitulation choked off, though Leonidas himself seemed puzzled at the fact.

"I understood what you said," the tall man agreed.
Leonidas' eyes bulged. The agent watched Calvus with a
care dictated by more than present words. "We will lose
our mast and sail, and our own hull may very well be
hopelessly damaged. While there were two pirate ships
pursuing us, those were valid arguments against ramming.
Are they now?"

"Dammit, I'm not going to sink my ship!" Leonidas
shouted.

"Blazes!" Perennius shouted back, aware that they were
drawing attention away from the pirates. "We'll sink
ourselves, when the bastards drop us overboard, won't
we? Do you think it's a joke, that they sacrifice prisoners

to their sea gods? Or do you think they'll just turn us all loose when they've stripped the ship?"

The Tarantine's face worked as if he were forced to chew tar. "Pollux," he muttered, "but we can't stand to be boarded again, I know that. . . ."

Calvus touched the captain's wrist. "You don't want to shatter a thing that is in your charge, a thing that's important to you," he said softly. "That's good. But there are times that we have to sacrifice things of greatest personal importance for the good of the race."

For the Empire, Perennius thought, though he was no longer certain that Calvus had the Empire in mind when he spoke. In any case, Leonidas licked at the blood on his lip and said, "All right, I'll do what I can." The captain smiled bitterly. "She's not much, you know," he said. "Wallows like a pig and maybe won't give us the angle we need as quick as we'll need it. But we'll do what we can. Fortune bless us."

This time Calvus did not intervene as Leonidas and the agent turned to their respective tasks.

"You didn't know anything about ships when you came aboard, did you?" Perennius asked quietly as he strode forward beside the tall man. "You didn't know a damned thing about fighting in that alley in Rome. Blazes, that's why I wanted you shut in the cabin, so you wouldn't get in the way. What's going on?"

Calvus smiled again. "Logic is the same, Aulus Perennius," he said, "whether the units are ships or game pieces. Or men, of course." It was a moment before he went on. The timbre of his voice was no longer quite the same. "The other, I think, concerns me more than it does you. The woman, Sabellia, said 'They'll never hold. Come on, there's spears at the mast,' . . . and I followed her. That shouldn't have happened. It wasn't what I was raised for." He looked down at the Illyrian. There was no frown on his calm face, but the agent was sure that the statement of concern was true.

"I'm glad you got involved. You saved my ass," Perennius said. He was trying to react to a problem which, as the traveller had suggested, he could not himself imagine. "All except my ass, I mean." The agent attempted a smile.

He was more nervous at the moment about a situation he did not understand than he was about the German pirates already drawing ahead of the *Eagle*. Perennius knew as well as any man *how* to deal with the Germans. The only question that remained was his ability to do so under the present circumstances. That would sort itself out very quickly.

"I'm glad for the results, my—companion," the tall man replied. "But when a tool begins to act in unexpected ways, one naturally becomes concerned that it may no longer be fit for the job for which it was forged."

"Tools!" the agent snorted as they joined the motley gang of armed men—and Bella, not to forget Bella—around the fighting tower.

"Aulus, the fucking ballista's out of action," Gaius said as he saw the agent. "Do we have a spare skein in one of the lockers? Fucking spear took three layers out of one of these!"

"All men are tools, Aulus Perennius," the traveller concluded softly. "The tools of Mankind."

"Sir, the coxswain won't give me any oarsmen," Sestius announced, "and I think he's grabbed everybody whole from the deck crew besides. I can arm some of his castoffs for show—" the centurion's glance swept the deck amidships where oarsmen sent up with broken limbs had congregated. They knew they would get no sympathy except from each other. "Or I can go below and show him that your orders are to be obeyed."

Perennius nodded. He was glad that Sestius appreciated that the situation might have changed since he got his orders. Battles had been lost by the determination of hard-bitten subordinates to carry out instructions despite the manifest absurdity of those instructions. "Right, use what you've got on deck," the agent said. "Looks like we need the rowers most at the moment, though blazes! I'd like those other sixty Marines."

The agent paused. He was glad to be back in the midst of bloody disaster, out of the metaphysical swamp into which Calvus kept leading him. "Gaius," he said, "let's look—" his wound chewed up all the nerves on the right side of his body as he stepped toward the fighting tower.

"Blazes! Well, I'll take your word for it, and it's maybe a good thing anyhow." Perennius recollected how the damage had probably occurred. "Anyhow, it kept a spear out of my back. Another spear. Take the ballista apart, look like you're working on it, and make sure those bastards see what's going on."

He waved toward the Germans. They were still more than a bowshot away and well up on the liburnian's forequarter. The German commander seemed to have enough influence with his men to keep them balanced across the deck of his ship for now. With luck, that discipline would break down as the pirates made their run in.

Gaius looked startled at his protector's orders. "But s-sir," he said, "we can bluff them with the ballista even if we can't fix it. If I dismantle the thing, they'll know they don't have to be afraid of fire." He peered at Perennius as if he were expecting to see evidence of a head wound in addition to the bandage on the agent's upper thigh.

"We're going to try something different," Perennius said. He did not care if Gaius knew they were planning to ram, but he was worried about the effect on the others. If the Marines suddenly ran sternward for fear that the deck would lift beneath them, it might give the plan away to the pirates. And it was, despite the danger, the only plan that Perennius could imagine having even a chance of success. "We want this crew to come in just the way the first ones did."

The eyes of the younger Illyrian narrowed, but he gave a curt nod of assent. He cursed as the latter gave him a reminder of his shoulder wound, but he got to work promptly and obviously with his wrenches.

Sestius was bullying and cajoling injured sailors to pick up weapons in their good hands. Some of the men were hunched over cracked ribs or were weaving from concussion. Most of them would be able to stand with a spear leaned against them and at least give the appearance of defense. The survivors of the original Marine contingent looked glumly from their reinforcements to the hundred or more Germans. The pirates shouted as they eased in with a brail or two furled in the canvas. Several

of the Marines seemed to be in no better condition than
the broken seamen who were joining them.

"Perennius, this is yours," Sabellia said quietly.

Her voice broke into what was less a reverie than a
waking nightmare, as the agent surveyed his troops. He
looked at the woman, then took from her the silken sling.
It ran through his fingers undamaged, slick and deadly
and quite useless to him now that it would tear him open to
use it. Just a tool, unnecessary now and easily to be replaced . . . but Perennius smiled and took the sling and
dropped it back into his pouch with the remainder of the
bullets. "Glad you found it," he said truthfully.

Sabellia's short hair was damp. She had taken the time
to wash the gore from it and her face before approaching
the agent. Julia had had black hair, but both of the women
were short and had the same non-Gallic—non-Aryan—
features. "What should the rest of us do now?" she asked,
and the voice was an echo both of the far past and of the
alley in Rome where—

Perennius felt his skin grow hot with a surmise for
which he had neither evidence nor time. He deliberately
lifted his right leg, pivoting it at the hip so that the icy
pain would sear away all thought of other times. "We
stand to arms, looking like we're preparing to be boarded,"
he heard his voice say as the world narrowed down to the
present again. He lowered his leg carefully. "Might help if
we looked like we were scared to death." He glanced past
Sabellia to the pirates. "That shouldn't be too difficult."

As Perennius spoke, the German seamen committed
their craft. The pirates had been bellying over the waves
some thousand feet from the liburnian—ahead and starboard on a parallel course. Their helmsman was a grizzled man whose hair and beard flared with milkweed
fluff from beneath his peaked iron helmet. He threw the
crossbar of his steering oar hard forward. The bow of his
ship swung to port. The beitass was already clamped in
place. As the port leech of the sail came up-wind, its two
divisions damped each other fluttering at the rigid pole.

The helmsman gave a raw-voiced command. Loin-clouted
Herulians snubbed or slacked the lines at which they
were stationed, whichever the need might be. The square,

leather-tightened sail swung on the mast to catch the wind at increasingly closer angles. As it did so, the sail's leverage rotated the vessel through the medium of the sailors straining at their lines. Gothic landsmen ducked or cursed as sheets snapped toward them.

Gaius jumped down from the tower, a perfect, boot-first arc controlled by his left palm on the wooden parapet. The tip of his scabbard rang on the deck as his knees flexed to absorb the shock. "A fine time to see how they'd swallow a ballista dart," the youth said with a toss of his head toward the pirates. He drew his long-bladed spatha. The nicks in its edge were obvious now that the steel had been rinsed of its coating of blood.

Perennius was returning to the state of mindless calm with which he generally entered battle. He was vaguely aware that Calvus stood beside him. The traveller was as still and erect as the pike in his hands. "Yes," the agent said. He imagined the chaos among the Germans if their seamen dropped their straining lines when a missile screamed down at them. Then he said, "Here they come."

The pirate craft had seemed to hover as it came about. Its starboard side, to leeward, had dipped and rolled a great swell in the direction of previous motion. Neither the keel nor the shallow draft of the German vessel were adequate to keep her from making leeway, sliding broadside over the sea. Because the *Eagle* was still plowing forward on the same course, however, the imperfection of the lighter vessel's sailing was disguised.

The pirates hung like a missile at the top of its arc. Then their ship began to slide toward the liburnian at a falling missile's deadly, increasing pace as well. Behind the agent, Leonidas was calling directions to his coxswain and steersmen alternately. Beside Perennius, Sestius repeated in stumbling Syriac the orders he had just given his men in Greek and Latin. "Keep your shields low. Duck beneath them but don't raise the shields or the bastards'll hock you sure from below."

Still slipping to starboard, but with enough way on to curl water around its bow, the pirate vessel bore down through bowshot to javelin-throw. The liburnian was moving at a fast walk. Cutting into the wind as she was, the

German craft could add no more than a knot to the closing speed. That the rush together of prey and slayer seemed so awesomely fast was an effect of the players' size. No beast carries forty tons above the surface, and the sail swelling over the pirates' deck at a sharp angle to starboard added bulk beyond its mass. A German archer, ordered sternward by men whose honor lay in their spears, managed to put an arrow through the forward leech of his own sail.

Perennius knew the men with him on deck were tensely listening for the sound of thole-pins being pulled and the oars themselves being shipped rattlingly as they had been during the first attack. Instead, the pattern of stroking remained the same, only one per four seconds, because the oarsmen were exhausted. The volume diminished, however, as for a stroke and another stroke the starboard oarsmen marked time with their blades lifted high and dripping back into the sea.

There was a hoarse cry from among the pirates. Even the Goths understood what was about to happen sooner than did the men on the liburnian's deck. The view of the men on the *Eagle* was blocked by the fighting tower and the overhang of the deck. The liburnian's bluff bow swung starboard half a point. The German craft a hundred, fifty, twenty feet away would have crunched along the starboard hull as her predecessor had done. Now the curling bowsprit and the jib for the unset boat-sail bisected the view of onrushing attackers.

As Perennius had anticipated, the pirates had shifted forward when the ships closed. Their weight lifted the stern and dissolved the last chance that the Herulian steersman would be able to prevent the Roman plan from succeeding. All the liburnian's oars stroked together once more. The pirates' sail was slatting down according to prearranged plan. It was unable to change their attitude at the last instant, and the steering oar only clipped the wavetops with the load of warriors forward.

The *Eagle* rode the Germans down with the merciless assurance of a landslide.

The liburnian had been designed to hole her opponents below the waterline when she rammed. Her projecting bronze beak had been removed when she was laid up, however, and it had not seemed either practical or necessary to the agent to have it refitted before they set out. As a result, it was the liburnian's up-curved stem-piece which made the first contact with the pirate craft. It rode over the Germans' gunwale just starboard of their cutwater.

The crash threw down everyone in both ships.

One of Sestius's Marines rolled over the edge, but his screams were lost in other sounds. For long seconds, mechanical noise was the only thing which the world permitted to exist. Though the pirate ship was smaller and lighter, it was built Northern fashion of rough-sawn oak. Its hull could not withstand the mass of the liburnian, but it resisted to the point of mutual destruction as the aged pine planking ground through it.

The *Eagle*'s mast snapped at the deck. The mast could be stepped or unstepped depending on whether the ship was being readied for cruising or war. The certainty that the larger vessel would be crippled if it rammed with its sail set had probably convinced the Herulian captain that nothing of the sort could be intended. Like Leonidas, he was too much a seaman to imagine another captain so wantonly destroying his own vessel. Perennius, living through the result the Tarantine had forseen, wondered whether the traveller's persuasion had been only verbal.

The mast partners, the great timbers that spread the thrust of the sail across six deck beams, held—forcing the mast itself to shear just above them. Tons of mast, spar, and canvas lurched forward, driven by its inertia and the breeze still trying to fill the collapsing sail. The mast itself struck the parapet of the fighting tower and continued driving forward. The rear wall of the tower smashed in and all the cleats pulled out of the deck. Even so, the tower saved the contingent standing forward to repel boarders. The top-hamper would otherwise have spread general death and maiming among them.

What was happening aboard the pirate craft defied belief.

The German warriors had been screaming insults and descriptions of their battle prowess as the two ships drew closer. When the pirates realized what was about to

happen, even the front rank of slaughter-maddened berserkers was shocked into a different—if no more sane—
state of mind. Men who had steeled themselves to face
swords and missiles realized that eighty tons of timber
would make no more of their courage than it made of the
water creaming to either side of the prow. Their surge
forward, shields raised, spears clanging, suddenly reversed
into a panicked flight toward the stern with all weapons
dropped or forgotten.

The attempt to escape was both useless and too late.
The gunwale splintered. The pirates' bow dipped under
with a rush. Panicked warriors were ground between pine
keel and oak decking like olives in a press. The wood
shrieked louder than the men.

The sea did not enter the pirate craft through a hole but
rather over the whole forward half of the ship. The stern
heaved up, throwing the furious steersman to meet the
oncoming *Eagle* with the broken tiller in his hands. The
sea churned up foam and blood and splinters as the
liburnian plowed on.

The low-decked pirate vessel squeezed sideways with
its port hull in the air. Its own mast did not break as the
liburnian's had: it ripped apart the keel into which it was
butted. As the ship went fully under water, it belched a
huge gulp of air which had been trapped by the suddenness of the disaster between the hull timbers and the
decking immediately over them. Then the pirate ship was
gone. With it went almost every one of the men who had
been screaming for blood less than a minute before.

CHAPTER FIFTEEN

The *Eagle* herself was proceeding only on inertia. The shock had thrown her oarsmen off their stroke and generally off their benches, though there was nothing like the number of serious injuries below that the first attack had caused. The previous impact had been transmitted through the oars and the men who had cushioned it with their bodies. This time, the liburnian's hull had no such cushion. What that meant was not long to be explored.

Perennius lay under a flapping edge of the sail. He tried to stand up but was surprised by the weight of the spray dampened linen. Calvus gripped a double handful of the canvas and lifted it for the agent and Sabellia. "It's just my damned leg," Perennius muttered in self-apology.

"Come on, come on," Sestius was demanding, "Get up, you don't want to roll overboard now, do you?" He rapped at the heels of Marines who still lay on the decks, using the vine-wood baton that served him both as rank insignia and a practical tool.

"Glad I wasn't on that," Gaius muttered as he surveyed the remains of the fighting tower. The thigh-thick mast lay across it.

The cry from below decks was wordless and riveting. It was a moment later before the screams, swelling sternward from the front of the rowing chamber, finally contained a message intelligible to those standing frozen above: "Water! We're sinking!"

The *Eagle* had drifted to a halt several hundred feet from where she ground the pirates under. There was some

159

flotsam off the stern to starboard, but none of it appeared to be living. There was nothing else on the sea for scale or reference except the liburnian's own shadow dimming the brighter highlights of the waves.

One of the Marines trembled, then jumped straight over the side. He must have sunk like a stone in his armor. Perennius had other things now to worry about.

The rush on deck this time led by the cook. His assistant and the slaves must have been set to oars for the final pull, because none of them were intermixed with the next score of seamen climbing through the hatchway. The grate had been displaced from the forward ventilator when the first pirate ship struck. Now the vent provided a long, wide passage for rowers who jumped up on their benches and clambered through. Astern, the after hatch was spewing up the rest of the oarsmen despite anything the officers could do. The coxswain's drum could be heard banging furiously over the shouts.

Gaius clutched the agent's wrist in a grip that made the older man wince. "Aulus!" the young courier cried, "what are they doing? We're all right! We're *not* sinking!"

Got a hundred seamen who'd argue with you, Perennius thought. He was not quite bitter enough at his friend's incipient hysteria to say that out loud, however. Everyone had his own terror. Gaius had hidden his own so well in the past that when it broke out, it was the most irritating, a trusted prybar that suddenly snapped.

Perennius' eyes wandered toward the heap of canvas. It covered the ballista and perhaps the shards and coals of the amphora which had held the fire. Unbanked, scattered, the coals must have gone out by now. Must have. "Whatever it is," the agent said in a voice that reserved judgment, "we'll deal with it." He used his free hand to release the other from his protégé's grip. There was nothing clearly useful to be doing. Even the sailors, once they had swarmed from the rowing chamber, only milled around on deck babbling prayers. "Blazes," Perennius muttered, and he climbed down the ladder that had just passed the rowers upward.

When the agent had jumped down to get the fire and oil, the belly of the ship had been full of men and sound.

Now the only men were two officers, the coxswain and Leonidas himself. They were stumbling forward, over the litter of broken benches and the oar handles which swung slowly as the waves levered at their blades. That flaccid creaking was not the only sound below, however. There was also the gurgling rush of water.

The *Eagle* was decked at about her normal full-load waterline, a little more than two feet above the keel and bottom-planking. There was no proper hold. The liburnian's only cargo was her rowing complement on its two-tiered benches. The bilges had filled within hours of the ship's return to the water, because her seams had opened during the years she was laid up. After the hull planking had swelled, that dangerous flow had subsided to a seepage that kept waste in the bilges wet enough to slosh and stink but which no longer threatened the life of the ship.

The oar deck stood in water forward. The flow was not only in sheets through started seams, but also in an angry geyser around the cook's stores. Part of the bow must have been staved in. The Germans whose flesh had greased the outer hull would shortly have their revenge.

"Pollux, captain!" moaned the coxswain, "we *are* sinking. Pollux, how *could* you ram us into them when you knew the hull was rotten as punk? Oh, Castor and Pollux, favor a seaman who—"

"Shut up!" snarled Leonidas. The Tarantine still wore his sword. Its sheath had worked around to his back like a shagreen tail. "We'll rig the sail over the bows to slow the leaking, then we'll pull for shore. Land can't be more than just over the horizon."

Water gurgled and curled at his insteps. It was well up on Perennius' shins. The agent could see that the bottom rung of the companion ladder was about to go under.

The coxswain broke. His sandals splashed, then squelched, as he ran toward the aft hatch along the upper tier of benches.

"Well, what *else* can we do, then?" Leonidas screamed at his retreating back. The captain turned, cursing in polyglot. Then he sprang past Perennius and up the ladder. The agent could see the tears in Leonidas' eyes.

Perennius climbed the ladder after the captain, but only

in a physical sense was he following Leonidas now. The agent recalled how blithely he had bounded up and down through the hatchway less than an hour before. Well, the almighty Sun knew the same two inches of iron could have stiffened more of him than one thigh.

Leonidas was giving loud orders and gesturing at the sail with his sword. He seemed to have drawn the weapon to cut entangling cordage, but the gestures became increasingly brusque as men ignored him. A deck crewman, then two others, moved to help. The bulk of the crowd now on deck was rowers. On duty, they had had too little contact with Leonidas to respond to him as an officer when they were shaken with panic.

Both Gaius and Calvus waited at the hatch for the agent. They bent together, each supporting Perennius beneath one elbow and lifting him back on deck smoothly. If you can't have two good legs, the agent thought wryly, be a cripple with friends. Blazes.

He put a hand on the waist of either man and shooed them ten feet down the deck where there was less congestion of men working or babbling in fear. "Sestius!" he called, knowing that when the centurion joined, Sabellia would come also. The agent did not want to use the Gallic woman's name, did not want to think about her—did not want her to become separated.

Sestius strode to them promptly. He had been lending a clumsy hand to Leonidas and his sailors. The centurion's face was flushed even darker than usual. "Sir," he said, "we're going to wrap the sail over the bow like a bandage. That'll stop the water coming in until we can make proper repairs on—"

"*At ease!*" Perennius said sharply. Blazes, they were all coming loose. Maybe he was himself and he just didn't realize it. Sabellia watched from beyond the centurion's shoulder. Her hand was tight on her knife hilt, another response to tension when its cause was unapproachable. "We're going to leave the ship, now," the agent said to the faces bending close to his. "We're going to use this grating—" he touched a boot to the wooden grate displaced from the forward ventilator—"as a float, and we're going to kick it and paddle it along all night if we have to until we reach land."

Both Gaius and Sestius started to speak. "Aulus, we can't—" blurted out with, "Sir, the sail will—"

Both reactions were expected. "At *ease!*" Perennius snarled. He glared at the two military men. By god, he might not be able to lead men or organize them, but he could damned well make a small group listen while he spoke! "We *can* do it, and we are *going* to do it," he said fiercely to the panic which did not quite rule Gaius' face. "Because the whole hull is cracking, and that sail isn't going to do a damned thing for the big hole in the bow anyway. Now, get your armor off and your boots. Move!"

The order gave both men what they needed, a raft of hope on which their minds could float. Only Perennius himself had to worry about their real chances of paddling a fucking grate the gods knew—

"Land seems to be about seven miles off, Aulus Perennius," the bald man said. "The currents are a question, of course, but I was raised for strength—" he smiled—"as you know."

"Blazes, we're going to get through this," the agent said. Gaius and the centurion were fumbling at buckles. Their fingers were swollen by the shock of recent battle. "I said we would, didn't I?" Gods, Calvus had learned to smile like a human; and he, Aulus Perennius, was making jokes about his own sense of duty. "What is the land?" he asked aloud. "Cyprus or the mainland? I haven't much cared in the past so long as the seamen were satisfied; and I don't think this is the time to ask."

Two of Leonidas' men had dropped over the side. They were clinging to the hawsers they would try to run beneath the keel. The stern of the *Eagle* swung in the breeze. It rose noticeably higher from the sea than did the bow, so that it caught more of the wind now that they were not under sail.

"I don't know either," the traveller said. He gestured westward again. "The—heat of the air currents rising shows that there *is* land, but I don't know which land. I have many abilities, Aulus Perennius, but not many skills. Strength doesn't make me a trained warrior, and seeing farther into the—seeing light when others cannot, let me put it that way—doesn't teach me geography.''

"Help me," called Sabellia.

Sestius and the agent reacted with equal cold-eyed promptitude. "Mine, by the Lord," muttered a seaman in Syriac. Perennius rabbit-punched him, spilling the man down on his side before he could snatch at the amphora Sabellia was trying to raise through the ventilator.

The crew was expected to buy their food each evening when the ship was beached. There was a quantity of emergency stores, however, grain and wine, for times when they made land after dark or a storm prevented proper foraging. Those stores were still stowed below between the benches. The fact had been forgotten by men to whom the rowing chamber had become a place of fear and rising water. While the men of her own party were preoccupied, Sabellia had slid down through the vent and had manhandled free an amphora of wine. Sheer determination did not, however, give her the strength to lift the awkward five-gallon container over her head unaided.

"Take the jar," Perennius said to the centurion. There was already a movement of men toward the container. Some crewmen started to slip below to get their own. Leonidas cried out in fury. The agent ignored him. He bent at the waist, offering his left hand to Sabellia when Sestius had snatched the amphora up by its ears. With her weight on his good leg, Perennius lifted her. He shouted, "More wine below! Enough for all of us!" Under his breath, he added to the man and woman, "Now, let's get the *hell* out of here."

The sea was growing darker now. The sky was still clear and seemingly bright, but the individuals of the *Eagle's* crew were losing definition even as the liburnian's bow slipped lower. "Wait," said Sabellia, knotting her sash around the neck of the amphora. The others stood in a watchful circle around their prize. They exuded a tense willingness to fight the increasingly raucous crowd of seamen if necessary. "We'll be all right without food," the woman said as she jerked the knot tight, "but the sun'll be our death if we're still out in the morning with nothing to drink."

"The Sun is life," Perennius said sharply as Sabellia's words tripped a childhood recollection of blasphemy. But he was beyond that now in his conscious mind; beyond trust in anything but himself and perhaps—"Let's get in the water," the agent said. He bent and lifted one end of the twenty-foot grating.

Perennius slid into the sea after the makeshift float. He made as little noise as possible. Sestius followed with a huge splash, as attention-getting as it was unnecessary. The port outrigger from which they were abandoning ship was only three feet above the water now. Sabellia knelt, tossed the free end of her sash to her lover, and lowered the amphora with the minimal commotion of a duck diving. The jar was heavier than water, but the sea buoyed it up enough that the wool sash was an adequate shackle. The woman's tunic billowed up away from her body as she slipped in feet-first.

The sea was ice encasing Perennius's battle-heated body. The salt was fire on his wound. The lips of the wound puckered. The agent gasped. It felt for a moment as if lava were being sucked into his marrow.

"Gaius, Calvus!" Perennius hissed "Get *in!*" He could not have shouted even if the situation permitted it, but the harsh fragment of voice which pain left him suited well the whispered imperatives needed at the moment.

Gaius stared at the float with the expression of a man startled by Medusa. Both his hands were locked on the hilt of the sword sheathed at his right side. The skin over his knuckles was as mottled as that of his face. The grating had begun to drift away from the liburnian, pushed lightly by the pressure of the three who had caught hold of it.

Without speaking or even appearing to see his comrades in the water, the young Illyrian turned back toward the tumult on deck. Perennius started to call Gaius' name again in furious despair. He was certain that he would have to climb aboard again and try to throw the courier bodily into the water—that or abandon him. Perennius was damned if he was going to abandon—but he need not have worried. He had forgotten Calvus.

The tall man stood in his attitude of concentration. The splash Sestius had made had drawn some attention but no anger, not yet. There was still wine to be looted. The sun bled through clouds on the horizon. The sight of people drifting off toward it still looked like an act of despair, not hope. Later, and not very much later from the speed with which the *Eagle*'s bow settled, Perennius expected a blast of rage directed at everything surrounding those who saw themselves condemned. The agent and his companions *had* to be well beyond missile range of the liburnian by the time that happened.

Gaius turned back and stepped off the side of the ship. He had the blank-eyed aplomb of a man who had forgotten there was a drop-off. He spluttered in the water. Perennius seized him by the neck of his tunic and dragged him to the float with an expression of relief and joy. Calvus, quiet but now mobile again, sat awkwardly on the catwalk and pushed himself into the sea. Even though his feet were already in the water, the tall man managed to make a considerable splash. The agent continued to grin as he reached out to grab Calvus' hand. The traveller was as clumsy as a hog on ice, but by the gods! he was good to have around in a tight place.

Blazes, they all were—all his companions. If the empire were kept by no one worse ... it would be kept, as it seemed probable it would not in reality.

"I think," said the agent, shaken by reaction and the rage which was the only way he knew to combat despair, "that if we all kick together—quietly!—we can get a few hundred feet away without attracting much attention. We'll worry then about navigating. For now, the important thing is not to catch javelins between our shoulder blades."

Suiting action to his words, the Illyrian scissored out a kick that did not break the surface of the water. It was excruciatingly painful to his right thigh. That was, in its way, a blessing. It took his mind away from the uselessness of his action and the mission beyond it to the only goal which had mattered to Aulus Perennius for twenty years: the stability of his world.

CHAPTER SIXTEEN

It became much worse after dark. While there was still a trace of light, it served as a goal toward which to kick. When even that trace had shrunk and vanished, the grating was alone with the sea and the moonless sky. Perennius trusted Calvus' sense of direction, though he did not understand the mechanism. The others seemed to trust Perennius, though the gods alone knew why. He should *never* have set sail without a full complement of Marines! When he got back, he'd find the bureaucrat responsible and—

It was hard to imagine getting back to Rome, when you were thrusting at the water which surrounded you without even a horizon to be seen.

Sabellia yelped. She began splashing at the water with an arm as well as her legs. Sestius, across from her at the "bow" end, shouted, "What is it? What is it?" as the float bobbed and yawed.

The commotion subsided as abruptly as it had begun. "It's all right," the woman gasped. She was clinging to the grate with both hands again. They had all stopped their desultory kicking for the moment. It was a good time for another break. "Something b-bit my toe. It was just a nibble, but . . ." Sabellia did not have to finish the sentence for the others to scan the surface around them. It was so dark that no fin could have been glimpsed against the waves anyway.

There had to be more small fish than sharks, of course. In Italy, still protected from the shambling terror of the

Germans, rich men raised mullets as pets as much as for food. The owners could sit on the lips of their ponds and call, while the water boiled with scaly bodies rushing to be the first to caress their master's fingers. That memory was now like a scene from Hell.

"Do you want a sword?" Perennius called forward to the woman. Gaius had kept his blade, lashing it to the grating between him and the agent. If it would offer Sabellia some security, that was better than having the salt etch it uselessly where it was now.

"No, it just startled me," the woman said. "I have my knife, if I needed ..." She reached over with one hand and stroked the clothes in a soggy packet between her and the centurion. All the castaways but Calvus, alone in the stern where his efforts equalled the combined efforts of the rest of them, had stripped off their clothing only minutes after they set out on the float. The cloth had dragged at their limbs, weighting and robbing of force all their attempts to distance themselves from the liburnian. Tied atop the grating, the garments did not interfere with movement, but they were still available against the morrow's sun. Sunburn could disable as thoroughly as blazing oil when its victims were spread-eagled on the sea for its attentions.

A rumbling sound clutched at their bodies in the water seconds before their ears heard it through the air.

"Aulus!" the courier cried. He heaved himself up on the float as if the shock waves were in fact tentacles squeezing and releasing and ready to squeeze again.

"It's just a whale calling," the agent said sharply. He had been momentarily frozen himself by the immersion in distant sound.

"No," said Calvus, his voice drifting with the breeze, "it was the ship. It just went down."

The cries could as well as not be those of gulls, wheeling against the stars in search of the white water that indicated fish shoaling. Indeed, the cries could be those of gulls even if the flesh that sparkled their thin commotion was not that of fish at all. The sound still told of men dying.

Perennius had seen it happen off Alexandria harbor, a

grain ship foundering within minutes of the help that would have saved at least the crew. The stern rose sharply, its great rudder flapping desperately for help. Then, swifter than a ship on the ways being launched, the vessel had plunged vertically. In its rush for the bottom, the ship sucked in and swept along the screaming crewmen who had flung themselves over the side at the last instant. Compartments crashed inward under the increasing pressure, belching up cargo and timbers and men, some of them still alive. The customs boat Perennius was aboard had saved three men and the ship's cat. It was more than anyone among the rescuers had thought probable.

The *Eagle* had died without even that hope. Might the merciful Sun take them to his bosom.

"Back to work," Perennius said aloud. "We've got a ways yet to go."

It was hours later that they heard the other ship.

Perhaps Calvus could have said just how many hours it had been. For the rest of them, the time since sunset had been a blur of fatigue punctuated with moments of terror or despair. They had been exhausted, physically and emotionally, when they entered the water. The sea's chill and the difference it provided from what they had been doing before at least colored the first brief span of time on the float.

The remainder of the experience was a white blotch as fatigue poisons leached away the attempts of minds to think along with the ability of muscles to move. When the castaways rested, they lay their heads on the pine grate and were drenched, eyes and noses and the mouths through which they tried to breathe, by seas. The salt water pulsed through the interstices of the grating. When they labored, they stretched at full length in that sea with only their hands on the wood to buoy them and remind them of the purpose for which they punished themselves.

It was during a pause that they realized, more or less together, that the squealing sound was not the breath in their lungs or an artifact of fatigue in their ears. Someone was stroking a ship closer. There was even an undercurrent of voices chanting as they kept the long sweeps creaking forward in unison.

"Herakles!" said Sestius in the tone of a man who watched an apotheosis. He tried to lift his torso onto the grating, but his arms would not support his weight. "Somebody's found us."

"It's a boat?" Gaius wheezed from behind the centurion.

"Wait, dammit, keep your voices down," Perennius insisted. For the first moment, he was speaking only from instincts of secretiveness burned into him during circumstances in which every human was an enemy. When his mind cleared enough for thought, however, his reaction was the same. He tilted his head, and tried to drain water out of his left ear canal by stretching it with a fingertip. That did not help clarity enough. "Calvus," he called over the waves' mild slapping, "can you tell who it is?"

"They're speaking German, Aulus Perennius," the traveller replied. "I think it may be—"

"Help us!" cried Gaius over the sound of oarlocks. "Help us for god's sake!"

The agent's first motion was toward his side and the sword he was not wearing there. "Gaius!" he snarled across the bundled clothes. "Shut up or—"

"Aulus, we're going to drown!" the younger man screamed. Everyone has his own fear. . . . "Help us! Help us!"

Perennius' mind had already planned the killing. He would go under the float, not over it. He would seize Gaius by the knees, jerk his head under water, and shift his grip to the younger man's throat to strangle him. But as the agent's hands poised to drive him under the narrow grating, his intellect reasserted itself over the murderous reflexes which had been his life for so many years. He relaxed. The tempo of the sweeps had already slowed. Moments later the squealing stopped entirely. It was replaced by a louder rumble of voices which Perennius himself could now tell were speaking German.

Blazes.

"All right," the agent said, loudly but in Latin. "Calvus is an envoy to Odenath, Bella's his wife, the rest of us are high staff officers accompanying him. We're worth money! And blazes! let me do the talking—understand?" As he spoke, Perennius was grubbing through folds of wet garments to reach the pouch containing the bullets he had not fired during the battle. He had forgotten to take the pouch off when he jumped into the sea, a lapse he would have called self-destructive madness if someone else had done the same thing. Now the agent opened the flap and spilled the leaden missiles out into the sea.

He hoped the sling itself would pass in the darkness and confusion. At any rate, he was not ready to abandon it just yet. But high, ransom-worthy Roman officers were not likely to be found carrying pouches of sling bullets.

The sweeps were creaking again, noticeably closer. Soon the castaways would be able to see their rescuers cresting a swell.

If they were the people Perennius suspected they were, they would have a very clear memory of bullets from his sling.

The ship, a darkness of sharp lines against the blur of the elements, loomed over the grating to starboard. It was almost close enough for Perennius to reach out and touch the nearest oar.

"Christ protect us!" said Sabellia in a voice that held little hope of that protection. "They're the ones we set afire and got away from."

And who else would have come upon us in these waters, thought the agent. He cried in German, "Wotan has blessed you, glorious warriors! Your arms will drip with gold from our ransom!"

It might have worked. Perennius was still not surprised that the pirates clubbed him unconscious as they dragged him over the gunwale of their ship.

CHAPTER SEVENTEEN

"You hit this one too hard," a voice was saying. The words buzzed and threw purple after-images across the surface of Perennius' mind.

"No, he's not dead," another voice replied. They were both speaking in German, but the dialect differed from that which Perennius had learned in his youth. The vowels were shorter and flatter than those of the South Rhineland. "Besides, what does it matter? We should have thrown them all back into the sea. Except for the women."

There were sounds besides the men speaking nearby. There was an indistinct murmur, more voices at greater distance . . . the crackle of a fire . . . occasional clapping and hoots of triumph.

There were also moans.

The agent's hands and arms were tied to a post behind his back. He opened his eyes a slit to watch through the hedge of lashes. The ship the *Eagle* had fought clear of that afternoon was now hauled up on a narrow beach. The cookfire close by laid gleams and shadows across the sun-bleached oak of the ship's planking. The hull was clinker built. Each row of planks overlapped the row beneath it instead of butting smoothly edge to edge as was the normal method here in the South. It gave the pirate vessel a ridged, implacable appearance like that of a crocodile digesting a child on a mud bank.

Across the fire from their ship, most of the pirates were

173

gang-raping two women. The nearer of the victims was Sabellia.

"Well, go ahead and cut his throat, then, Grim," the first voice was saying. "Biarni! Isn't that meat cooked yet?"

Perennius opened his eyes and raised his head to the post from which he had been sagging. He gave what was meant to be a smile of greeting. The agent's legs sprawled out in front of him. He had to remember to kick with the left one, though the numbness in the right was less than he would have—"Warriors!" he said aloud in his Schwabian dialect. "Our ransom will make all of you ring-givers! And I will sacrifice to my own gods in thanks at being overcome by heroes so great!"

"He's awake, Anulf," said the owner of the second voice. He looked uncertainly toward the other Goth who stood beside the bound agent.

Perennius was tied to one of the posts of what had been a fenced garden. The pirates had slashed gaps in the wattle fencing to use the posts for immobilizing their prisoners. Gaius was struggling with his bonds eight feet to the agent's left, and the huddled figure at the post beyond the courier was presumably Sestius. The farmhouse itself still burned sluggishly in the background. It must have been quite a display when its thatch blazed up. A moment's thought would have given the pirates the building for shelter; but they obviously spent few enough moments on thought.

Vicious little children, and nothing but a tottering Empire to keep the world from becoming *their* world.

Grim, the Goth who had drawn a single-edged knife to finish the agent, had no left arm below the elbow. He wore a green tunic with embroidered sleeves. The tunic was of good quality, but that was no indicator of rank among pirates who had had the opportunity to pick their choice of looted clothing. The obvious leader of the band was the man the other had called Anulf, a great, brown-bearded hulk of a fellow with a livid bruise on his forehead.

Perennius thought he recognized Anulf from the instant before their ships collided. The Gothic chieftain had been in the front rank then, wearing a gilded helmet crested with the image of a long-tusked boar. The pirate had gone down with a crash as an oar blade ended his fight before it began. He was not wearing the helmet now, nor the leather cuirass faced with large bronze disks which the agent remembered also from the battle. Anulf did carry his long sword, however, slung across his back from a baldric. The birds-head pommel waved over his shoulder like one of the Wotan's ravens.

Now Anulf looked at Perennius with the interest a shopper gives a carcass in the poulterer's shop: checking the hind feet to be sure of buying rabbit and not cat. "You're the leader of this lot?" the German asked. "The woman said you are."

"The woman?" Perennius repeated. Sabellia had broken? Of all of them, the agent would have guessed she would hold out the longest. . . .

But as Perennius turned his head to the right, a swarthy Herulian rose to his feet crying, "Five!" The German still wore a tunic of iron-buckled deerskin. It flapped back down over his thighs as he stood up. Two friends pounded his back in triumph. One of them was jiggling ale or looted wine from the jeweled cup he offered.

Sabellia's wrists were tied to another post. Early on, two of the cheering pirates had probably held the woman's ankles outstretched also. That was no longer necessary. Sabellia's face lolled toward the agent. The eyes were open with fully-dilated pupils, but there was no mind behind them. Her mouth was drooling. The pirates had carried out their business with no more than the requisite brutality. The bloody lip might very well have been self-inflicted. The scratches on Sabellia's breasts and flat ribcage were the results of individual warriors' teeth and harness, not deliberate whipping. Even the bruises already starting to appear were most likely the result of enthusiasm and the rocky soil.

Only once before had Perennius seen eyes that looked as Sabellia's did now. He had been with the detachment which crucified a slave who had murdered his master. At the last, the victim no longer had the strength to stand on the spike which had been driven through the instep of his feet, pinning them to the base of the cross. The man's knees sagged, drawing his wrists down against the nails that held them to the crossbar. In that position, the diaphragm could not inflate the lungs against the full weight of the torso pressing down on it. The eyes of that slave, beyond pain and fear of the suffocation which would kill him in a few minutes, were as empty as Sabellia's.

A huge, blond Goth wearing a mail shirt but no trousers lowered himself onto Sabellia. He was accompanied by the encouragement of several of his fellows. The attempt to equal the Herulian's feat looked doomed to limp failure, especially since the victim's labiae were swollen from the bruising.

"Yeah, the funny bald one," Anulf was saying. "I took her first myself. None of the others would have dared, but Anulf fears nothing!"

"Dare?" shouted the Herulian with the chalice. It spilled as he turned. He pointed at the Gothic chieftain's face. "What do you know about daring when you lie on your back all the fight?"

The wrists of the figure beyond Sabellia were tied to a post just as the Gallic woman's were. Perennius stared beyond the frustrated mumbling of the would-be rapist and the mewling woman beneath him. There was no one astride the second victim at the moment. She squirmed into a sitting position against the post. The motion implied either double-jointed shoulders or more slack than was to be expected in the straps that held her. She looked back at the agent. Her face was at first void. Then it quirked with the tiny smile that had become an expression increasingly common with her.

Perennius knew why "Lucius Cloelius Calvus" had always worn at least a tunic while in company. Of course the agent had never thought that "Calvus" was a real name.

The fire crackling beneath the pig halved lengthwise gave Anulf's beard a redder cast as he turned to the interruption. The Herulian had paused to take a slurping drink from his cup. No one else seemed to be paying much attention.

Calvus' chest was as flat as a man's, flatter than the agent's because Perennius' chest muscles bulged even at rest. Calvus' pectorals lay in sheets that belied their demonstrated strength. Her nipples were small and pale, even though the firelight emphasized contrasts. Her body for as far as Perennius could see was as hairless as her head. Presumably Calvus' genitals had determined her sex even to Germans who were taken aback by her appearance.

The story that Perennius had sketched out, that Calvus was an envoy and the rest of them were on "his" staff, had become absurd at the moment the pirates tore off the traveller's tunic. Well, the agent would come up with another story.

Even now, the most feminine thing about Calvus was the lack of a prominent Adam's apple in her slim throat. Perennius found it hard to believe that he had overlooked that feature for so long, but—a bald woman six feet four inches tall?

Anulf wore wooden-soled boots. They were cross-strapped up his calves. He flicked his head to the left, drawing the Herulian's eyes toward the cooking fire. Then Anulf kicked out fiercely, planting the sole of his right boot in the Herulian's groin.

The Goth's victim doubled up, spewing wine from his mouth and nostrils. Anulf was not finished. He snatched the knife from his one-armed companion. The Herulian had sunk to his knees wheezing and vomiting. Anulf stabbed him behind the shoulder blade, a pounding blow which he followed with a second. At the third stab, the Herulian who had just finished with Sabellia tried to grab the Goth's wrist. Anulf threw him back, but the hilt of the knife remained protruding from the wound this time.

The murder had made surprisingly little noise, but now every German Perennius could see was standing. Men were appearing from the darkness. There were not as many of them as the agent had feared; only a score or so out of an original complement of over a hundred. Some of the able-bodied pirates must have boarded the second ship and gone to the bottom with it. None of the men Perennius saw had serious wounds. The pirates' own casualties must have gone over the side with no more ceremony than so much spoiled fruit.

Anulf glared around his assembled band. "When I need advice on courage from a Herulian donkey-fucker," he roared, "I'll *ask* for it!"

The body of Anulf's victim was shuddering. The knife hilt danced in the firelight. The Herulian who had tried to intervene in the killing had stepped back. His own short sword was half drawn. The blond Goth who had taken his place on Sabellia now grabbed the Herulian's elbows from behind. Another Goth cuffed the Herulian hard enough that his knees sagged.

The Herulians had been a small minority of the band, just enough to provide the Goths with seamen to work their ships. The fighting, due in part to the agent's sling and marksmanship, had accounted for most of those. It was quite obvious to Perennius from the appearance and attitude of the pirates he saw that there were only three Herulians left in the band: two of them standing, surrounded by Goths, and the third on the ground twitching out his last few seconds of life.

With deliberation, a Goth wearing brass bracelets coiled the length of both forearms stepped forward. He planted a spear in the chest of the Herulian who had grappled with Anulf. The victim jerked backward. The Goth holding him from behind cursed as the point pricked him through the Herulian's body.

The last surviving Herulian had been edging away from the trouble. He was not wearing a weapon. When the spearhead thudded through his companion's jerkin, he turned to run. He tripped on Sabellia's outstretched legs and sprawled on the ground between the two women. Anulf himself stepped forward. He pinned the Herulian with the point of his long sword before the man could rise. The dying man's body arched like that of a fish on the gaff. He screamed, but the sound disintegrated into bubbling as Anulf leaned more weight onto his weapon. When the chieftain withdrew the sword with a sudden jerk, the Herulian was silent. Eight inches of the blade were stained with arterial blood as bright as the fire that illuminated it.

"Should've done this weeks ago," Anulf muttered. He wiped at the bloody sword with the edge of his tunic.

"Bastards wouldn't have run us right into those oars if I had."

Aulus Perennius had been in too many fights to concentrate on any one thing when his death might be in the hands of the man on the other side. But even while he watched men seizing weapons and tensing for murder, the agent kept one eye on Calvus. He recognized the traveller's fixed expression in the moments while Goths were deciding whether or not to let the incident pass. And Perennius recognized the expression that followed on Calvus' face, when Anulf's sword crunched free of the Herulian's ribs. That second expression perfectly reflected the joy Perennius himself felt at watching the German die between the rape victims.

"Biarni!" Anulf said as he turned from the body. He reached over his back with both hands to guide his sword into its sheath. His fingers were trembling. "Cut me some goddam meat! And where's the wine?"

The agent exchanged glances with Calvus. Between them, Sabellia had begun to snore heavily. The pirates were settling down to a meal of wine and pork. The meat was half-charred and half raw from the look of the slabs. Perennius would have time to come up with a story before anyone got around to questioning him again. And he would have time to come up with a plan to escape from these Goths, as well. After he had murdered every one of them.

Perennius looked at Sabellia. Every one. He was very sure of that.

CHAPTER EIGHTEEN

What irritated Perennius as much as anything the next morning was the pirates' vulnerability. The band was as disorganized as it was weak. The Germans had posted no guards. It would have taken more than a brief alarm to arouse most of them from the drunken stupor into which they had collapsed. If the burned-out householder had returned that night, he could have avenged his loss at no greater cost than an arm sore with throat-cutting.

But oh! the terrible Germans. Families for miles in every direction had probably run for the hills, tossing their money and plate down the well so as not to risk the time to bury it. The twenty pirates who had survived their brush with the *Eagle* had panicked the district as thoroughly as their original numbers could have done. Or for that matter, as thoroughly as the thousands of whom these were probably believed to be the outriders.

Well, there might be thousands more coming. That didn't mean you ran.

It was some hours after the Goths had begun stumbling around again that any of them took notice of their prisoners. Perennius had shivered uncontrollably during the whole night. That was the reaction not only to being stripped and exposed to the cold, wet air but also to the exhaustion of his long bout of kicking the float forward. They must have been very close to shore when Gaius brought the pirates down on them. . . .

"All praise the unconquered sun," Gaius murmured to

the ball that had now climbed over the treetops to the east of them.

In Latin, Perennius said to the younger man, "The story has changed. I'm chief and we're envoys to the Gothic kings of the Bosphorus. Gallienus is offering eight gold talents to the Goths if they'll raid the Aegean coasts to soften them up for his own attack on Odenath next year."

Gaius blinked. "What?"

The agent gave a disdainful shrug. "*They'll* believe it. For that matter, I don't know but what *I'd* believe it if the right man told me. The things that pass for diplomacy in this world aren't always the things they explain in staff training." Pitching his voice a little louder he added, "Sestius. Did you hear?"

Several pirates were returning from a foray into the woods. They were hallooing to their companions. The landing site was a cup out of the Taurus range which fringed the coast. It was an ideal place to beach a few ships in a fair degree of isolation. Off and on for millennia, the little bay had been a base for pirates. One of the ironies of the present situation was that the pirates now were outsiders instead of native Cilicians as generally in the past. The bawl of a frightened, angry cow gave evidence of at least part of the foragers' loot.

Sestius had been slumped against his post ever since the agent had awakened from his own knock on the head the night before. Now the centurion turned. He moved with a difficulty which did not appear to be primarily physical. Between him and Perennius, Gaius straightened so as not to block the view. It was not the agent to whom Sestius' attention was directed, however. "*Bella*," Sestius called desperately. "Are you all right?"

"Sestius, did you hear me?" the agent demanded. All the Goths were moving around now, and at least a few of them were bound to take an interest in what their captives were discussing.

"Bella!"

The Gallic woman still lay supine. Perennius could see that her eyes were open. From where the centurion sat, she might have been dead. At that, the woman lay as still as death save for the slow, controlled movements of her chest. She could not shift a great deal because of the way her wrists were tied above her head. Even so there was an eerie quality to her stillness. The blood had dried her scratches into a black webbing. The depth of the bruises on her thighs and torso was particularly shocking because her skin was dark enough naturally to hide much of the damage. Sabellia slowly turned her head in the direction of her male companions. Her eyes showed them that the worst damage of the previous night had not been physical at all. "I'm all right," the woman said. Her voice made a lie of the words, but there was no weakness in it.

Three Goths and a heifer burst out of the woods. "Biarni, get your goddam pot boiling," one of the foragers called. "I don't want my meat burned again today!"

Perennius wondered where the pirates had found the heifer. There was not enough land cleared in the immediate vicinity to pasture a cow. The household had kept pigs and chickens which foraged for themselves in the woods. The beasts had been turned loose when the pirates arrived, but the reek of hog manure was unmistakable. Aside from the kitchen garden to whose fence the prisoners were tied, there was no sign of cultivation around the little bay.

The Gothic chief noticed his captives. He walked toward them from the ship where he had been arguing with some of his men. The three Herulians lay where they had fallen. Their skins were turning gray. The muscles of the one between the women had tightened, drawing the corpse up into a fetal ball. From the look Anulf gave them, Perennius suspected the Goth was regretting some of his haste the night before.

"Greetings to you, King Anulf," the agent called. He did not know what rank the Goth's fellows would have granted him, but neither had he met a German who did not think of himself as a king somewhere in his secret heart. They were a people who prided themselves on freedom, which appeared on examination to amount to the right to lord over everyone else in the vicinity. "The gold-giving Emperor Gallienus sent me to you, his equal, and to your fellows, asking for alliance." Noting that Anulf's face still held an expression of glum concern, the agent added,

"Also, my friends and I know something about sailing ships." There was little enough truth to that statement, but it was a useful one. At that, they probably knew as much as any of the Goths themselves.

Anulf raised an eyebrow, but the discussion was interrupted by a startled bawl. One of the foragers had driven his spear deep enough to bury the socket over the heifer's shoulder. She kicked out with her forelegs, then her hind legs, and spun in a circle that tore the spear-shaft out of the Goth's hands. He and his fellows shouted and jumped away, dodging the cow. The heavy shaft whipped in ten-foot arcs as it projected from the cow's side. The heifer seemed to have made up its mind to charge into the sea when it collapsed, spraying blood from its nostrils. Several pirates leaped toward the carcass with their knives out.

Anulf's attention returned from the interruption to his captives. Perennius was about to resume his spiel. As his mouth opened, Sabellia forestalled him by saying in Border German no worse than the agent's own, "Cut me loose for an hour and I'll fix you a meal as fine as the ones I prepared for the Emperor before he sent me as a gift to the Kings of the Goths."

The chieftain looked at her, then looked away without particular interest. The concept of women as human beings was as foreign to most Germans as it had been to Greeks in their Golden Age. "Gallienus could have waited," the Goth boasted to Perennius. "Anulf will come and see him in Rome one of these days."

"If you want to eat real food and *fast*, you'll have me fix it for you," the Gallic woman called. Both Anulf and the agent frowned in irritation. Sabellia was not speaking to them, however. The trio of foragers were looking approvingly at her. Sabellia lay on her back smiling. Her left leg was straight, her right knee cocked slightly. Perennius had been sure that the woman would draw both knees up to her chest and lie huddled on her side as soon as she was alert enough to feel German eyes on her. Obviously, Sabellia was already alert in ways that the agent did not wholly fathom.

Biarni, the pirates' cook, was a grizzled man who would

have been short even without hunching over his withered hips. Perennius suspected the handicap was the result of an injury. A birth defect of that sort would have resulted in the infant being exposed on the kitchen midden for dogs to eat. Injured adults did not stand a great deal more of a chance among the free peoples of the North— the way the pirates had disposed of their wounded comrades, some of whom could have survived, was an example of that. But there were a few exceptions, like Biarni; and Biarni was no less jealous of his prerogatives for the fact that his fellows held him in obvious contempt.

Now the cook paused halfway to the cow. He was holding out the long knife with which he proposed to cut the beast's throat. "Hey!" he said angrily to the foragers. "I'm the cook here. Don't you listen to that—why, *I'll* shut the dog-turd up myself!" He stumped purposefully toward Sabellia with a wave of his knife.

One of the foraging Goths stuck the butt of his spear between the cook's crippled legs. Biarni flopped forward with a squawk. His knife flew out of his hand and bounced harmlessly from Anulf's trousered calf. Almost the whole band of pirates laughed at the cripple's discomfiture. The exception was Anulf. The chief kicked the fallen man furiously, shouting curses and following as his victim babbled and tried to roll away from the boots.

The Goth who had speared the heifer now slid the haft of an axe from his studded belt. The weapon was of moderate size, but it had double bits and the look of hard use to it. The pirate sauntered over to Sabellia, raising his weapon casually.

Perennius tensed. He would have to use his left foot and kick over his injured right leg. If he could catch the Goth at the back of the knee, the man might fall backwards and—and get up to kill them all, but—

"All right, we'll see what kind of cook you make," the Goth said. As the agent relaxed, the axe chopped the thong against the post to which it was anchored. The pirate pumped his axehead loose while Sabellia rolled off her buttocks to her feet. Her smile had changed to something very different when the Goth who freed her looked away.

"Frigg's balls, you scut!" Anulf roared as he saw what was happening behind him. "Who told you to let the bitch loose, Theudas?"

The other Goth had been wiping wood fibers from the nicks in the edge before he put his axe up. Now, gripping his weapon just below the head, he wheeled and demanded, "Who died and made you god, Anulf? I guess you'd let us all starve, wouldn't you?"

"Yeah," snarled another of the men who had brought back the heifer. He strode toward the chief from the other side. "Just what *have* you done besides get most of us killed on this raid?"

Anulf's one-armed companion was reaching furtively for a spear at the moment tension broke. Biarni had gotten up when Anulf's attention turned from him. The cook, trying to creep away while he still watched his chief, had immediately fallen again into the coals of last night's fire. His squeals of pain and terror brought another surge of laughter from the remaining Germans. Their anger melted at the hilarious spectacle of a cripple dancing in a cloud of ashes.

"Here," Sabellia said. She stepped to Theudas with her wrists, still bound, upraised. The Goth sawed through the knot with his axe. Theudas was nearly seven feet tall. He bent over Sabellia, concentrating on his awkward task like a tailor threading a fine needle. The picture of his care was frighteningly at variance with the agent's memory of the night before, the huge blond figure kneeling to rape the woman for the fifth time.

Anulf's companion tried to hand him the spear. The chieftain looked around to see why he was being prodded. The anger that had been directed first at the cook, then at Theudas, now flared up at the one-armed man. Anulf slapped the spear away with a curse. Then he aimed a kick which Grim dodged with the ease born of experience.

Sabellia was draping herself with a cloak of lustrous brown wool appropriated from another of the pirates. It hung down to her knees. The throat, meant for the neck of a big man, hung from her shoulders. She had pinned it up with the hems overlapping. Perennius noted that the woman, despite her present kittenishness, had not brushed at the grit and leaves clinging to her skin when she stood. "One of you take the loin out of that cow," she called.

A pirate immediately roared, "Biarni! Get out and get busy or I'll kick your useless butt back to the Bosphorus!"

With most of the Gothic pirates following her, Sabellia stepped into the kitchen garden. "All right, pick some of that," she began. "That's thyme and we'll need it. Now let's see, is there any mint?"

Perennius twisted around his fencepost to watch the woman and her entourage. He was certain that it was all a ruse. As soon as Sabellia got her hands on a knife, she would stab as many of the startled Goths as her fury could reach. The agent recognized the look he had seen in her eyes. Murder was a reasonable desire, but Sabellia would be cut down before she got more than one or two of her rapists. Worse, her action would eliminate any chance Perennius himself had of release.

Anulf was watching his men with a look as sour as the thoughts Perennius hid behind a bland expression. Calvus, smooth as an ivory finial, sat in her pose of rigid concentration. The agent could not imagine what the bound woman was trying to accomplish. He hoped that it might be an attempt to keep Sabellia from some suicidal gesture.

Though he knew it was dangerous, the agent said, "King Anulf, if you will release me, I can better discuss my Emperor's offer of gold to your Highness." If Perennius's hands weren't free when the woman cut loose, all of them and the mission were well and truly screwed.

"Hel take you!" Anulf snarled. He stalked off to the ship and the wine still aboard it. Behind him skipped the one-armed man.

After that, the agent had nothing better to do than to watch Sabellia act.

Surely it was an act . . . but gods! it was a good one. And Perennius did not really know her that well, just assumed—*felt*—her similarity to another Gallic woman of years before.

Well, he hadn't known Julia that well either, as it turned out.

"Eggs!" Sabellia called, snapping a finger against her

palm. "Come on, fellows, they kept chickens so there has to be eggs."

"Hoy!" called a Goth. He lifted a largish brown egg from within a bush which he had parted.

"Right, look for nests," the woman encouraged. "We need, oh, one apiece. You're a such big men." Reaching under her cloak, flashing and then hiding her body in a fashion more enticing than her battered nudity of minutes before, Sabellia squeezed the biceps of the men to either side of her. One of them was the towering Theudas, the other his companion who had held a Herulian from behind for slaughter. "Now, where's the fennel? In all this garden, there must be some fennel."

The entourage made an absurd progress of the whole garden. Burly pirates, the *Eagle*'s murderous opponents less than a day before, paced beside the short woman. They held eggs, sprigs of herbs, and vegetables. Sestius was sunk in somnolent gloom. Gaius sat bolt upright. His face held a fixed expression while he tried to wear through his bonds by tiny movements against the rough surface of the post.

"Onions, now. No, those are leeks—well, bring them anyway, sure, but there ought to be—there, by the fence, that's right."

Perennius had already determined to his satisfaction that he could lift his post out of the ground if he needed to. The sunken part had rotted enough to permit that. Once the post was out of the way, he could slip his bound wrists under his body. That would be more painful than he cared to think about, what with the spear hole in his thigh, but it was possible too. He did not waste effort on bonds that could not be abraded in useful time anyway. And he did not slip into the black despair that was always useless. Besides, she wasn't Perennius' woman, not this one, not even the other when it came down to cases. . . . Perennius watched, making the basic assumption that there was something to see besides a woman selling herself to the gang that had already raped her in concert for the right to pick and choose her partners the next time.

And even if it were that, sooner or later there would be an opening for Aulus Perennius to act.

"Ah, wild horseradish," Sabellia said. She pointed toward a juniper outside the cleared area. In the juniper's shade grew a moderate-sized plant topped by a spray of hooded yellow flowers. "That one," she directed, "the pretty yellow one. But only bring the root, it'll lie just beneath the surface."

A Goth sprang to obey. He drew his dagger for a make-shift trowel.

"And now, boys . . ." the Gallic woman went on. She paused to squeeze again the arms of her nearest consorts, both of them laden with greens. "Now, the beef!"

The band roared with enthusiasm. It began to tramp toward the bloody carcass.

The agent had not been as hungry as the labor he had done since he last ate would have justified. That was due in part to the chill, first of the sea and then of the night on his damp body. Nausea from the rap on the head had contributed also. The pirates had really not cared whether the folk they dragged from the water lived or died. Perennius suspected that Calvus, still locked in his—her! —trance state had something to do with the fact that the others had not been clubbed as hard as was Perennius himself. They could not have been. At least one would have died of a crushed skull by now if they had all been treated as the agent was.

Sight of the dripping loin brought Perennius' appetite back with a rush, however, though his taste ran more to seafood than to beef when there was an option. Biarni had hacked the muscle out with unexpected skill. Cooking among the barbarians tended to be a process of boiling gobbets of flesh. The originals could be cows, pigs, sheep—or horses, if you happened to be with a raiding party on the eastern steppes. When haste required something different, like grilling, the results was apt to be the sort of disaster the pirates had faced—and had gorged on nevertheless—the night before. The crippled cook had shown despite that a familiarity with the heifer's anatomy. He had even gone beyond his instructions and had skewered the loin on an iron rod from the ship's furniture.

That initiative was a mistake, as Sabellia was quick to

inform him. "No, no," she cried, "we're not going to burn *this* like last night, are we boys?"

There was a chorus of cheers. One pirate aimed a kick at Biarni on general principles. "We need a platter. A big platter or a table."

The platter that two Goths produced was obviously loot and not part of the normal shipboard gear. It was solid silver and over thirty inches in diameter. Sabellia directed it to the ground by pointing her finger. Then she had Biarni slap the meat onto it with a similarly imperious gesture. "Now," she said to the assembled pirates, "who has a knife? A really *sharp* knife."

Perennius shifted the post with his shoulder, then pulled it forward with his wrists. All eyes were on the woman. The agent thrust upward, wincing at the flexion of his wounded thigh. The post itself would make an adequate club in the chaos of bleeding men jumping away from—

Sabellia took the dagger the blond giant at her side was handing over. She smiled, knelt, and began chopping at the beef with quick, expert movements.

On the beached vessel, Anulf was rumbling drunken curses to himself below the level of the gunwale. Neither Sabellia nor the men around her paid any attention to the chief. Even Biarni seemed fascinated by the woman's skill with the knife. "Call this sharp?" she bantered, tossing the weapon back to its owner after a moment. "Come on, *really* sharp, I want to shave this, not gnaw it into hunks." Someone else passed her a knife in replacement.

Other pirates began drawing the short blades most of them were wearing. They tested the edges. One enterprising fellow began to sharpen his knife, using a block from the farmhouse's limestone foundation as a whetstone. Soon the smoldering ruin was ringing with Goths scraping at stones with their blades. Some of them were so inexpert that they were dulling such edge as years of neglect had left.

The blond Goth took rejection of his own dagger in good part. As a joke he offered Sabellia the axe with which he had cut her loose. Both of them laughed. The woman reached up and squeezed the pirate's calf while she muttered a response too low for Perennius to catch. The agent had the post ready to be withdrawn, but there was no point in doing so at the moment. He could not imagine what Sabellia was about—if it were not what it appeared to be.

Whatever the truth might be, the Gallic woman was assuredly a cook as she claimed. She was mincing the loin as fine as the blades she was offered would permit—and some of them were sharp indeed. Even so, the edges dulled as she cut across the grain of muscle fibers, and she continually passed back knives to be resharpened. As Sabellia worked, she tossed occasional pinches of the chopped loin into her mouth. When Goths tried to steal bits as well, she rapped their knuckles with the flat or back of whichever blade she was using at the time. Only Theudas beside her was allowed a taste. She offered it to him to lick off the point of the double-edged dagger she held. Other pirates hooted in glee at the sight.

When about half the eight-pound loin was chopped, Sabellia began calling for sprigs of herbs. She shaved each in turn with tiny movements that rang on the silver tray like rain on tin. As she kneaded in the condiments— tarragon, fenugreek, bits of the long yellow root she had called wild horseradish—she kept up a constant flow of banter and explanation. Her hands were marvelously quick. Though the chopping looked easy, Perennius could well appreciate the strength of the wrist that did it with such apparent effortlessness.

Sestius was crying. The centurion's bonds prevented him from even covering his face with his hands.

Sabellia blended the raw eggs into the meat with the flirtatious showmanship of a female conjuror. She used a broad-bladed knife as her spatula. The knife waved in wide arcs in turning over the mass. Pirates laughed and cursed as they hunted the eggs they had set down to watch the meat-chopping. Several eggs had been stepped on during the interim. That gave the Goths something more to crow about.

The whole process consumed hours. Only the Gallic woman's patter made it seem otherwise. Biarni had built up the cook-fire again. Water was already bubbling in the pot which he hung over the flame from a folding tripod. No one, not even the cook, paid much attention to the chunks of meat boiling there in normal fashion. Sabellia's skill and the show she put on were riveting.

"All *right!*" she said at last. She handed to its owner the knife which she had just swirled the final egg into the mass. Using both palms and her closed fingers, Sabellia spread the chopped loin and spices across the circular tray. Her steel blades had irreparably scarred the engraving on the softer silver. The damage had reduced the tray to no more than its value as metal. The German raiders had not cared. To them, the Mediterranean Basin was full of things of beauty to be stolen and smashed and replaced with further loot. The fact that the Gallic woman had destroyed the tray without a qualm implied a sense of ruthless purpose in her that Perennius could appreciate; but the agent still did not understand where it was leading.

When she had the loin spread evenly over the tray, Sabellia snapped her fingers and pointed to retrieve the broad-bladed knife. The surface of the meat varied from the wet gray of portions that had been open to the air for some time to the rich purple of the most freshly-chopped muscle. The well-mixed eggs bound the flesh and spices, giving the whole the texture more of a fruit dish than of meat.

"All right," Sabellia repeated. She began to divide the mass with the back of her knife. There was another cheer from her entourage. Pirates crowded closer, kicking sand toward the dish. The woman shouted and snatched it up. She gave the tray to the huge blond to hold as she finished separating the portions. "One apiece, damn you!" she called good-naturedly. She began handing out the spiced loin with her free hand and the knife blade.

Goths with sticky patties of meat in their hands tended to try to gulp them there at the tray. Their unfed fellows quickly jostled them aside. "Hey!" Sabellia called, "where's the captain?"

"Hel take Anulf!" cried someone from the press. "I'll eat his too!"

"Maybe Anulf's got his own raw meat in the boat!"

Theudas suggested loudly. "Maybe Grim's got three legs to make up for only one arm."

"Whew *gods* it's hot!" somebody added amid the laughter. "Where's the fucking wine?"

The movement of pirates toward the ship was more a saunter than a charge. It obviously boded ill for the chieftain none the less. The Goths had let out their frustrations the night before against the Herulians. Their situation was not the better in the morning. Theudas saw personal advantage to himself in directing the frustration this time toward the chief who had led them into the disastrous fight with the liburnian.

Anulf's one-armed companion stood and faced his fellows with an uncertain smile. A pirate reached over the gunwale and snatched Grim out of the ship by his leg. "Come on, Grim," he roared, "it's good and it'll grow hair on your stump!"

Grim was not a small man despite his handicap, but when three more of the pirates seized him, he covered his frown with a smile. "Sure, guys," he said. "I'm hungry." He scurried over to the small group still around Sabellia.

Anulf stood up with his sword drawn. His face in its fury was the same mottling of gray and purple as the platter of chopped loin. "Right," he said in a thick voice. "And who'll be the first to try stuffing that filth down *my* throat?"

Half a dozen of the pirates were close enough that they might have reacted immediately. Anulf was wearing his armor, however. The old scars on his face and forearm were a reminder of all of them of the truculence that had made him their leader in the first place. The gunwale was only three feet above the beach, low enough for any of the band to leap. Any of the band willing to lose both legs to a sword-stroke.

Theudas shifted almost imperceptibly, twenty feet away from his chief. Sabellia was now holding the tray and the remnant of the meat. The blond Goth's right arm moved slowly. Perennius could not see what Theudas was doing because the big man's body hid it; but the agent understood the signs very well.

"You, Respa?" the chieftain demanded. He jabbed in

the direction of the gray-bearded veteran nearest him. The pirate indicated by the long sword jumped back. He knew as well as Anulf did that the chieftain could not fight them all. He knew also that the first man to rush would be spitted on Anulf's sword.

When the chieftain's sword and eyes flicked toward Respa, Theudas acted. He brought his arm and the axe it held around in a fast overhead throw. Anulf saw the glitter out of the corner of his eye. He leaped back with a shout and a crash of equipment. The axe-helve spun in the arc it drew around the polished head. The bitt that caught Anulf on the forehead rotated another fraction of a turn as well, splitting the septum of the chieftain's nose before it and he smashed to stillness on the deck.

"Hail King Theudas!" Sabellia cried in a high voice.

Respa had drawn his own sword as he jumped away from Anulf's. Now he studied the bigger, blond man for a moment. Fragments of chopped meat still clung to Respa's grizzled beard. "Well, let's see we've finished the job," he said. He climbed over the gunwale with his sword out. After a moment, he reappeared brandishing Theudas' axe. Its head was smeared with blood and pinkish brains. "Hail Theudas!" he roared. The rest of the pirates echoed the shout as they crowded around their new chief.

It was almost inevitable that the Goths would jostle the tray from Sabellia's hands. Perennius noticed the fact only because he was trying to notice everything in hope that there would be something useful in the confusion. Sabellia herself reacted with the rage and horror of a housewife staring back at the rat in her flour bin. She cried out and tried to force away the nearest of the men. They ignored her. Germans trampled the meat into the dirt, each of them twice her weight and strength. Sabellia had guided the band of pirates with skill, but she could no more overpower them than she could halt an avalanche. The agent realized that he had been seeing a cruder example of the influencing technique that Calvus had described herself as using. An example both of the technique and of its limitations.

Several of the Goths tramped toward the ship to bring out the remaining wine. Theudas began to polish the head of the axe Respa had returned to him. The new chief basked in adulation, though he must have known that the grumbling against him would start at least as soon as the wine was exhausted. Sabellia took advantage of the space around Theudas for the moment to grasp the big man's arm. "Oh—oh King," she said her voice desperately trying to regain its girlishness. "You didn't get *your* portion. And after all, it was for you that I—"

Theudas shrugged the woman aside with as little rancor as effort. The big Goth had more on his mind than a woman now. "Get out of the way, bitch," he rumbled as he thrust the axe helve back through his belt, "or we'll make last night seem gentle." Theudas switched his attention to the men returning with the wine. Two of them offered him a silver-mounted cow horn, brim-full and dripping from having been immersed in an amphora.

Sabellia had fallen, though Theudas had not shown enough interest to strike her. Her bare legs splayed, then were hidden again as the woman drew them under the borrowed cloak. She continued to squat on the ground. Her red hair glowed in the sun. Perennius could not see Sabellia's eyes, but he was quite sure that it was on Theudas that they were fixed. He did see her right hand disappear beneath her cloak. The hand held the knife which, like her, the Goths had forgotten in their new excitement.

Calvus spoke. It was with shock that Perennius realized that he had not heard the traveller's voice since the rapists had displayed her sex. In fact, Calvus' voice was as empty of sexual character as it was of accent. Like her clothed body, the voice permitted the assumption of masculinity but it really offered no evidence on the subject.

The second shock was the language Calvus used. The traveller was speaking to Sabellia in Allobrogian Celtic. There was no chance that any of these South-Baltic Germans would speak the dialect, but it was very familiar to the agent himself. In his youth, Allobrogian had been his language of love, the language of *his* love. . . .

"Don't become overanxious," Calvus was saying. "You've done very well. Now it's time to wait and not attract attention."

A shudder went through the Gallic woman, showing that she had heard. Her head lowered from the fixed aim she had been holding like the trough of a ballista. Use of a dialect from her childhood had cut through her black reverie as well as hiding the advice from the pirates.

Sabellia turned. She eyed the line of her fellow captives. Her face was as lifeless as clay with reaction to the façades of moments before and the emotions underlying it. Biarni used a dagger to spear gobbets of boiled meat and toss them to his fellows. The cripple was not the center of attention, but at least he was no longer the fool of a foreign slut.

"Don't try anything now," the traveller continued. Calvus lowered her voice to make the fact that the prisoners were conferring less obvious to their carousing captors. "It's too early, and in broad daylight you'll be seen. Only act when you have to; the later the better."

Sabellia nodded. Her expression was tired and disinterested.

"And if you can free only one of us," continued the gentle whisper from the agent's past, "it should be Aulus Perennius."

At that instruction, Sabellia looked up. As if Perennius were not present—and she might not know that the dialect was more than nonsense syllables to an Illyrian like him—she said, "He's wounded. I thought Quintus or perhaps the young one. He handles a sword. . . ."

"Lady," said Perennius, "don't worry about my leg." Sabellia stared at him. Calvus was watching also. The tall woman's face wore its normal calm and a trace of the new smile. "If you get a chance to cut us loose," the agent continued, "one swordsman won't do a lot of good. I might. I just might."

"Hey, shut the fuck up!" Respa shouted. He threw a shoulder blade at the agent. The heavy bone bounced off the post as Perennius jerked his head aside. The missile left behind the smell of cooked flesh and a bubble of laughter from the Goths seated for toasts and boasting.

Calvus' advice, to wait and attract as little attention as possible, was good. Perennius had a great deal of experience in waiting. Let them get drunk or whatever the traveller had in mind. The agent quietly flexed his muscles against each other or against the post. His wounded thigh was far less knotted by the trauma than it should have been. He wondered if that had something to do with the tingling Calvus' fingers had left behind as they bandaged the wound.

Perennius kept his own smile inside. He had experience in doing that, also. When he let his emotions show on his face while he prepared, people shied away as if they had seen a shark grinning.

CHAPTER NINETEEN

Three hours later, the pirates were slurping the last of their wine. A Goth named Veduc was describing, victim by victim, the seventy Romans he had slain the day before. It was the sort of performance that followed each victory; and a night's drunken stupor had turned the disaster of the previous day into the triumph of the present. Veduc swept his arms outward and fell on his back with a crash. The shield with which he had been gesturing clipped Grim. The one-armed man leaped up, cursing and dabbing at his bloody ear. Veduc began to mumble and raise his legs as if he were trying to walk forward, straight up the sky.

There was laughter, but not the raucous gales that the drunkenness should have heightened. Several of the Goths seemed to have slumped on their sides. Perennius' eyes narrowed. Respa, the veteran who had first hailed Theudas, now leaned forward. He started to crawl toward the center of the circle on all fours. Respa kept scrabbling at the ground, turning over and over a pebble as he shuffled through the midst of his fellows.

"Whoo, Respa's past it!" crowed a black-haired Goth wearing a Roman helmet. The speaker's face changed abruptly. He doubled up and began to vomit. His hands pressed to his belly. In between the wracking tremors, he gave squeals of animal pain.

There were more men suddenly on their feet or trying to get there. Hulking pirates swayed, looking around in horror as if the landscape were a sea of flames around them. One of them dabbed at his face with both hands. At first he patted gently. After a moment he began giving himself brutal slaps that stained his moustache with his own blood. "It's not there!" he cried. His voice was slurred. "I can't feel my face and I can't feel my hands!" He began to cry. Again and again he squeezed his palms to his cheeks as his hands slipped away.

Theudas rose. The man standing beside him whimpered and laid a hand on the chieftain's shoulder. "Storar?" Theudas said, looking at the pirate who had grabbed at him. Storar screamed and clutched himself as if he were trying to hold in his slashed bowels. His sphincter muscles opened. A gush of half-digested waste poured down his pants legs. The stink of it had enough impact, even among the surrounding horror, that Theudas backed away with his nose wrinkling.

The circle of boasting, drinking heroes had scattered like a straw fence in a windstorm. Nearby, oblivious to them as they were to him, Biarni was clutching the cooking tripod to keep himself upright. Biarni's eyes were glazed. The iron leg must have been very hot, but the cook showed no sign of feeling the damage. One of his palms slipped. His twisted body fell in a cloud of ash that mounted on the column of hot air. The pot and tripod overset, clanging. Boiling water sloshed on the coarse soil. It did not touch the flames that Biarni's struggles were stirring in the heart of the fire.

That, Perennius thought, was the measure of the disaster which had struck the pirates. A cripple was being burned alive, and not one of the Germans around him was laughing.

Theudas backed away from his band. His big hands were clenching as if he hoped in an instant to grapple with the cause of the catastrophe. His boot rang on the fallen silver tray. The blond Goth looked down.

"Now, Sabellia," Perennius whispered to the woman. She was huddled against the post to which she had earlier been tied.

Flies had buzzed around the dish of chopped loin even while Sabellia was preparing it. They coated the remnants of the confection in the dirt. Many of the insects lay on their backs, quivering with bursts of furious motion but unable to fly or even to crawl. The ground was black besides with still forms which were beyond even that. Their systems had been destroyed as thoroughly as those of the Goths, by the aconite root which Sabellia had called "wild horseradish."

The Gallic woman moved swiftly to Perennius. She knelt behind the fence post as Theudas turned. The Goth's surmise became furious certainty. Sabellia cut the thongs at the agent's elbows, then those at his wrists, with quick passes of the knife. To its broad blade still clung smears of the poisoned meat which she had served with the weapon.

Perennius stood and took the knife. The woman tried to hand him her cloak as well, to wrap around his arm in place of a shield. "Get the hell out of the way!" the agent shouted. He braced his left hand against the top of the post. Perennius was stiff, but a bow is stiff also and it kills none the less. . . .

Theudas charged. He had drawn his axe even before his eyes lighted on Sabellia. The Goth was no berserker, but sight of the slender woman who had played him for a fool drove him momentarily over the edge. The glint of dark steel in Perennius' hand brought Theudas up again. The woman scampered nude into the trampled garden.

"Sure, try me first," the agent said with a smile. "You aren't afraid of me, are you? Just because your mother used to suck my cock when we were—"

Theudas leaped forward again with a swing of his axe.

Between the length of the axe helve and that of the arm which swung it, the glittering head covered an arc with a seven-foot radius. The blow skimmed short of Perennius. The agent could not take advantage of his opponent's imbalance because of the injured leg and a knife as his sole weapon. Instead, Perennius slid behind the post that had held him a moment before. A length of thong still dangled from the agent's right wrist. He laughed at Theudas.

If Perennius had a shield available, he would have carried it—though even that might have failed the test. The agent had a professional respect for Theudas' arm and the weight of the Goth's weapon. A cloak wrapped around the forearm was a good makeshift in some circumstances. It could envelope a sword-edge and cushion its blow in multiple layers of cloth. Against the Goth and his axe, the most a cloak would have done was to act as a ready compress for Perennius' severed arm. The agent could have flung the garment like a retiarius in the arena, but the cloak was not a weighted net. Theudas' long left arm would have swept it aside in the air. The agent might have gained a fraction of a second—which his right leg would not permit him to exploit. Instead he stuck to one simple thing: a post stuck in the ground which the Goth could not knock down even in the fury of his charge.

Theudas cursed and sidled around the obstacle to the left. The Goth held his axe in front of him with both hands. The bitts were level with his eyes and ready to chop or thrust.

Perennius duplicated the Goth's movements perfectly. The agent moved a little faster than his opponent because the threat of the axe kept him slightly further from the post than was their common center. In theory, Theudas could have reached him over the post with the axe. The fencepost would have blocked the Goth's lunge, however, and it would have left his wrists extended to Perennius' knife if the stroke had missed. The big man cursed and moved; and the Illyrian moved in concert, giving a rich, false laugh.

The warrior had an audience. Gaius was showing sense enough to hold as still as the post to which he was bound, thank the unconquered Sun. The courier might have made Theudas stumble, but the agent could not have exploited such a misstep. Any such reminder of the captives' presence would have brought a swift, downward blow from the frustrated Goth—which Perennius could have done nothing to prevent.

But there were Germans still alive, too. Lest Theudas should forget them, Sabellia crowed, "Say, mighty chieftain! Your boys don't seem to be helping you. Why don't you tell a few of them to crawl over and puke on the Roman's boots? He's so much bigger than you alone, after all!"

Despite himself, Theudas glanced back at his men. Storar, doubled up on the ground, stared at his chief with eyes glazed by pain and horror. Respa had followed his pebble on hands and knees into the side of the ship. He was still trying to crawl after the stone. Every time Respa lurched forward, he struck his head on the hull. Then he would pause and do the same thing again . . . and again. . . . The rest of the crew lay in various contorted poses like driftwood on the sand. Many of the Goths moaned or twitched, but a few were as still as logs already.

Theudas roared and slammed into the chest-high post as he swung at the agent.

Perennius threw himself beneath the horizontal arc of the blow instead of stepping back as he had before. It was a dangerous move, but the Illyrian knew the post would interfere with the Goth's ability to strike low. As the axe hissed above him, Perennius slashed upward with the speed of a weasel lunging. The agent's leg was stiff, but there was nothing wrong with his arms or his timing. The knife scored the bones of Theudas' left wrist. The axe-head's inertia pulled it through the rest of its arc while blood sprayed the ground.

The agent rolled to his feet and smiled. He held up the gory blade. "It was poisoned, you know," he said.

Theudas screamed and hurled his axe. Unlike Anulf, Perennius was expecting that.

The blond Goth had arms like a catapult's. The axe-blade would have sheared a metal-faced shield and the forearm beneath it if it had connected. The weapon's mass was also its drawback. When Theudas had committed his full strength to the throw, there was no way that even he could deflect it to follow the agent's sidestep. The axe was still spinning and airborne thirty feet beyond Perennius when it split a post across the garden.

Then it was the agent's turn.

Storar was the closest of the Goths to their chieftain. There was a sword belted to the poisoned man's shuddering body. Theudas would have bent to draw the weapon, but he saw Perennius out of the corner of his eye. The agent, half the Goth's bulk and shorter by fifteen inches, was charging.

Theudas roared and kicked out chest-high. Perennius was waiting for that, too. The agent twisted sideways and grabbed the big foot with his left hand. The maneuver put massive stress on the agent's own right leg, but all that mattered for the moment was that the leg hold him up for a half second. The pain did not matter, never mattered in a situation like that.... Perennius drew his knife through the soft leather and the Goth's Achilles tendon, hamstringing the big man.

Theudas jerked himself clear. His murderous roar had become a shout of surprise. He did not feel the pain as yet. The knife had been only a hot line, a twinge that could have come from bones twisting in the agent's grip. Then the huge Goth planted his foot firmly and it collapsed under him. He bellowed as he pitched sideways. Perennius was on him.

It is easy to kill with a knife. A single deep stab into the body cavity is as apt to do it as not ... but the death may be days later. The very sharpness of the point is a handicap, for the tissues clamp down on the metal that parts them and seal off the gushing fluids that would otherwise follow the blade's withdrawal. Sometimes blood seeps into the body cavity like water from a badly-packed valve. At other times, an oozing trail of waste from a punctured bowel permits an early semblance of recovery before fever finally carries the victim off.

To kill quickly with a knife, you must slash. That is not easy at all when your opponent is a warrior of Theudas's strength.

The Goth fell sideways, but despite his surprise he managed to twist so that he was facing Perennius. His hands were high. The agent threw himself across Theudas' upper chest. Perennius' left hand grabbed a swatch of the pirate's long blond hair. The big man's arms locked around Perennius' chest and squeezed. Snakes kill by keeping their victims' lungs from expanding, thus suffocating them as effectively as a noose around the throat. Theudas, on the other hand, was strong enough to splinter ribs and kill in a spray of blood from bone-torn organs. The Goth tightened his hold. Perennius stabbed hilt-deep, just above the chieftain's pubis bone. The agent let his own terror of constriction draw the edge up through Theudas' belly until it lodged in a rib.

The Goth screamed. Even now, the pain was buried under cushions of shock. Theudas' lower body felt as if it had been liquefied and was flowing from his bones in warm ripples. He flung Perennius away from him easily and sat up. The Goth stared at his wound with the amazement of an atheist viewing a miracle. The knife had parted sheets of muscle for ten inches up the long torso. The severed fibers contracted, pulling the wound open into an oval a hand's breadth wide in the middle. Blood and pink intestine coiled through the opening.

The chieftain's eyeballs rolled up. He collapsed. Physical shock was only partly responsible.

All the aches and injuries of the past two days caught up with Perennius when he no longer had the present struggle to sustain him. He knew he had to keep moving, however. His wounds would otherwise bind him as thoroughly as the pirates' thongs if he permitted them to cool. The agent rolled to his feet, wondering if Theudas had managed to crack a rib after all. Sabellia, holding a sword she had appropriated, was stepping toward Theudas.

"Don't," the agent said. "He's already dead."

"I know he's dead," said Sabellia. She began to probe carefully with the point of the sword. She was extending downward the tear in Theudas' tunic, exposing his genitals. The Gallic woman wore the cloak pinned about her again, though the gap showed she was bare beneath it. She stood stiffly, teasing the cloth apart at full arm's length and the sword's.

"Stop, dammit!" Perennius said. He strode to her, his aches forgotten. For an instant, there was a chance that she might turn the weapon on him. Then his hand gripped hers over the bronze hilt. He used only enough pressure to remind Sabellia that he was there beside her. "Don't," he repeated softly.

"Aulus!" Gaius called from behind them. "For god's sake, man, cut us free!"

Both of them ignored the courier. Sabellia glared at the agent and demanded. "Do you think I'll regret it tomorrow? Is that what you think?"

"No," Perennius said. "I think *I* would." He released her hand and stepped away.

Sabellia sobbed and flung down the sword. "If you knew," she whispered. "If you could only imagine what I dreamed . . ."

"You might go cut the others loose," the agent suggested mildly. "Get some food together for us. I'll finish up around here."

The knife he had used was still lodged in Theudas's body. Perennius worked it loose from the rib. He was always surprised at his strength during a battle. He would not have thought that he could have embedded the knife so deeply in bone with a straight pull.

Then he began to cut the throats of the poisoned Goths, starting with Respa because he was still moving.

Perennius had learned very long before that he should never kill humans. If you kill humans, you wake up screaming in the night. Their faces gape at you at meals or when you make love. . . . What you must kill are animals. Young animals, female animals—it doesn't matter to the sword, and it need not matter to the swordsman. Sabellia was thinking of Theudas as the man who had raped her, the man she had forced herself to cuddle against . . . the man whom she would mutilate so that everyone who saw him would blanch. And despite her certainty, the Goth's face would be in her dreams, its eyes wide and its mouth choking on bloody genitals.

Perennius had awakened too many times to the sight of a Frankish raider, a *man*, wheezing blood. The Frank's hands were always locked on the spear that a young Roman soldier had just rammed through his chest. It was not an experience Perennius wished to magnify for one he was beginning to think of as a friend.

You could separate naked, two-legged creatures quite easily into humans and things you must kill. The danger was that at some point your rage might expand the second category until it wholly engulfed the first.

After a few minutes, Gaius and Sestius joined the agent. Both of them used spears. It was business, necessary because they dared not chance the recovery of even one of the pirates while the five of them were nearby.

"Are we going to take their ship?" the younger Illyrian asked with a nod at the pirate vessel.

Perennius had found a long spear for himself as well. He withdrew it with a crunch. "Might," he said. "Sestius, do you know anything about sailing?"

The Cilician grunted. "A little," he said. "Enough to know the few of us wouldn't even be able to slide this one off the beach."

The agent glanced back at Calvus. The tall woman was wearing a tunic again. Perennius' own experience with the traveller's strength suggested that Sestius was probably wrong in detail. The basic opinion was valid, however. Main strength and awkwardness might get the ship launched, but it would not help them work it in a squall. "We can buy something to ride," he said aloud. His eye brushed over the silver tray, the jeweled sword by the Goth he had just finished. "Buy any kit we want, I suppose. The gods know, we aren't short of money right now."

Perennius turned, eyeing the forested foothills of the Taurus Mountains. "For choice," he went on, "we'd have the century of Marines we were supposed to. But we'll get by." He slammed his spear into the chest of another moaning pirate and the ground beneath. "We'll get by."

CHAPTER TWENTY

The gong cleft the pale air with a note as thin as a bird's cry.

"Say, what is that?" asked Sestius. He was leading while Gaius, the other healthy warrior among them, brought up the rear. The party was not straggling, however.

Perennius pointed full-armed past the centurion. A face of rock soft enough to have been weathered into a spindle overlooked the track by which the party proceeded. It was still about a quarter mile distant. The figure near the spire's tip was hidden against the pink-touched gray of its surface. Sunlight blinked rhythmically from the stick the figure swung against his gong.

Sestius paused. He switched the spear he carried to his left hand so that he could try the slip of his sword with his right.

"Watch that!" Perennius snapped. "Nothing hostile." The agent began waving his own spear, butt-upward, toward the watchman. "If we act like we're a bunch of pirates, they'll turn us into fertilizer as soon as we're in bowshot. And I wouldn't blame them."

A bell began to chime at a distance beyond the high cone of rock. The stick ceased to flash. A measurable moment later, the last gong-stroke rolled down to the agent and his party. "Well, we've been hoping to find a village, haven't we?" Gaius said aloud. The unusually high pitch of his voice showed that he too was aware that the first meeting was likely to be tense.

"It'll be all right," Perennius said. He knew as he spoke

that the words were as much sympathetic magic as a reasoned statement. "Let's get going."

As the party walked on, it was noticeable that they all were trying to proceed quietly, even though they were already discovered. "We'll be all right," Sabellia said aloud in unconscious echo of the agent. "Three armed men—four—" a nod toward Calvus who trudged fourth in the file—"they'll talk, not try fighting right away. And then they'll see we're peaceful." She did not sound convinced either.

Beyond the rock spire, the twisting defile by which the party proceeded broadened into a valley. It was planted in wheat. The only interruptions in the smooth, green pattern were the ragged lambda shapes where the soil was too wet for the crop to have taken hold. The stems and leaves of the wheat beyond the gaps were a darker color than the sunbleached heads which alone were visible elsewhere. There were no evident fences or even corner stones.

The huts of the village huddled against the valley's further slope. There were thirty or so of them. It was hard to tell for sure, because the dwellings overhung one another as they climbed the hill. Most seemed to be small one- or two-room units. Since their backs were cut into the hill, it was impossible to be sure from the outside. There was no town wall. That was not surprising even in the present unsettled times. An enemy who bothered to attack from further up the hillside would be higher than the top of any practicable wall facing him.

What was surprising was the church.

"Thank God, we're among Christians," Sabellia whispered.

That much was clear. The building itself was a spire shaped much like the natural outcropping which acted as a watchtower at the valley's head. At its peak, high enough at eighty feet to stand out against the sky, was a cross. The warning bell continued to ring from the small pergola by which the cross was supported. Beneath the belfry, the building stepped down to the ground in three levels of increasing diameter. The cylindrical walls were of native stone. The ashlars had been quarried recently enough to retain a pinkish yellow color which contrasted with the weathered gray of the slope beyond. The building had not been vaulted or even corbelled. Instead, the builders had used trusses and thatch for the three stepped roofs. That implied that each successive level of the spire was supported on vertical columns extending from the ground to the level's base. That was an incredibly awkward way to design a structure of the church's magnitude. It was also proof of the dedication of simple villagers who had executed so impressive a monument to their god without help from the outside.

At the moment, villagers were running toward the church from the common wheat field and from the garden plots terraced up the hillside. Black-faced sheep were blurs on the crest above, but the herdsmen must already have joined the general flow toward the tower.

The one exception was a man in a black robe which fluttered as he kicked his donkey toward the newcomers. As the villager approached, he tried to keep his left hand raised. The gold or gilded cross which he held wavered and jerked as the donkey beneath him trotted.

"A brave man," Gaius commented as he watched the envoy. The courier glanced up at the outcrop from which they had been spotted initially. The rock was behind them now and he, like Perennius, was wondering if the lookout was still hidden in their rear.

"Three years ago, friends of mine were burned alive for refusing to sacrifice," Sabellia said grimly. "Then the Lord chose to spare me for his future works, so I wasn't requested to sacrifice to idols when others were. Why do you think Christians would fear death by bandits when we go to our pyres singing hymns of praise?"

"At least they've got donkeys to sell," remarked Sestius, possibly to put a cap on the present discussion. "I'll be damned glad to get off my own feet. Especially with the load of metal we're carrying—not that I'm complaining."

"Yeah, well," said the agent. "No reason for any of us to talk about what we picked up from the pirates. I don't doubt these folk are religious—" he nodded to the Gallic woman, keeping his face still and his eyes serious—"but there's no advantage to our putting temptation in their way. We'll offer them fair prices and as much more as it takes to get the animals . . . but we don't need to tell them just how much bullion we're hauling around."

The agent was a little worried about Sabellia. Her faith had not been a secret before. Not from him, at least. He was used to the point of reflex to correlating data—expressions, gestures; the scraps of personal details that come out inevitably when a group of people live in each other's wallets for weeks at a time. If Perennius' mission had involved ferreting out Christians, he would . . . but the agent's mind shied away from that thought in which business conflicted with something more personal and less common to him. In any case, Perennius had little enough use for gods that he could not get concerned by the foibles of those people who felt differently. If Sabellia refused to sacrifice to the Emperor who served and represented the Empire—then Perennius also served and represented the Empire. The Gallic woman had saved his life, and that was already more of a benefit to the Emperor than a pinch of frankincense on a charcoal fire.

But they were all under stress, even the ice-calm Calvus. If being catapulted into a community of fellow-believers put Sabellia off on some unforeseeable religious tangent, it might cost the party her services. It might cost Perennius her presence . . . and Perennius looked away from her, toward the man on the donkey, to avoid the direction his thoughts were taking.

The rider reined up noisily, ten feet short of Perennius' party. The five of them had shifted instinctively into a ragged line abreast. All of them were looking determinedly non-violent. The agent had grounded his Gothic spear point-first in the soil. The shaft was taking much of his weight. His right thigh throbbed while he walked on it but when he stood still the feeling became agony if the limb had to support his body.

The man in the dark robe raised his cross. Most of his scalp had been shaven, though the hair surrounding the tonsure was black and bushy. "If you come in peace, travellers," he said, "the blessings of the Annointed and of Dioscholias his servant be upon you." Surprisingly, the man spoke in the local form of Syriac instead of the

Greek Perennius had expected even this far back in the hills.

Stumblingly, the agent answered in the same Cilician dialect. "We are peaceful travellers, sir. Traders who expect to pay well for the food and beasts of burden we hope to buy from you." Sestius *was* Cilician, and the Illyrian was fairly certain that Calvus could speak the language with the same facility that she had shown with every other tongue they had encountered. Perennius did not trust them to carry on the negotiations, however; and he had learned never to use an interpreter if there were any possibility of avoiding it. At best, an interpreter added a third personality to the discussion in hand.

The villager slid from his donkey and knelt. He folded both his hands in front of him over the stem of the crucifix and prayed. "Thanks be to Jesus the Anointed, font of all blessings, and to his servant Dioscholias who first brought his teachings to our valley." The man stood again and said in a more businesslike tone, "Strangers, I am Father Ramphion, a disciple of the blessed Dioscholias, and his successor when he was translated to the throne of God. The Lord has blessed us by sending you into our midst. Come, join us in the love feast that is being prepared in your honor and in God's." Ramphion gestured toward the huts.

"Father, we thank you," the agent replied. "I am Aulus Perennius, and these are the companions of my journey." He introduced the others, giving their real names—or in the case of Calvus, the false male name that was all Perennius knew her by. "We will be glad of your hospitality." He smiled. "I had expected your fellows were engaged in another sort of preparations, after the warning gong."

"Oh, here," Father Ramphion said, offering Perennius the donkey's reins. "You're injured. You should not be walking."

"Actually, I think it's better for the leg that I do use it," the agent said. "But perhaps Sabellia . . . ?"

The discussion degenerated at once into multiple refusals of the offer. The donkey, unconcerned, tugged from Ramphion's hand to the roadside to crop grass growing between the track and the wheat beyond. Abruptly, Sestius ended the nonsense by accepting the charity and mounting the beast. Perennius felt like an idiot for having wasted time and let matters get out of hand in such a ridiculous way. The agent never knew how to deal with generosity.

Perhaps he was fortunate that generosity was so rarely to be met with.

Father Ramphion had not forgotten the question Perennius had earlier implied, though. As the two men plodded after the mounted centurion, Ramphion said, "Of course, we're prepared to defend ourselves if needs be. To help God defend us, I should rather say." He gestured toward the church. There were unglazed windows in the second and third levels of the stepped tower. The agent could now see that the only openings in the twenty-foot high base cylinder were the front door and a circuit of arrow slits at shoulder height in the stone wall. A proper military force with artillery and battering rams could take the structure without serious difficulty. A band of raiders like those the *Eagle* had fallen among would have turned away after an abortive assault or two against the stone. The church would preserve the villagers and such movable property as they could get inside it.

"But that has not occurred as yet, thank the Lord." Ramphion continued. "All of those strangers who have come to the valley since Dioscholias brought God's teachings here have been like yourselves. Men of peace, wanderers . . . some poor souls displaced and brutalized by the scourges that wrack the sinful world beyond. May they all find peace in God."

The valley itself certainly appeared to have found peace. Stacks of hay still remained from the previous year's harvest, though there must have been fresh pasturage for the village's flocks for over a month now. The common sheepfold was extensive; a gray, freestone structure adjacent to the human habitations. Smoke drifted above the valley wall, but Perennius could not pinpoint its source against the blur of rock and dull green vegetation. The valley was the sort of place that Sestius had described as being his dream and prayer of finding in his native province.

With that thought in mind, Perennius asked the villager. "Ah, are you all Christians here? That is—the church looks as if it would have been an enormous task, even with everyone in the village concentrating on it."

Father Ramphion nodded. He appeared to be older than the agent had at first believed him to be, perhaps even in his mid-forties. His limbs were strong and his fringe of hair had a youthful luster. "Not quite all of us, no," he said. "There are two brothers in the village, Azon and Erzites, who follow the appalling idolatry of their father. The rest of us, yes, we are followers of the Anointed."

Ramphion raised his eyes toward the spire of the church. What must be most of the populace of the village was lining up in front of the structure, men to the right of the doorway and women to the left. "It was a marvelous work, barely completed when Dioscholias was translated to heaven five years ago. Only the Saved had a hand in the building, of course. Azon and Erzites are victims of a particularly foul error. They claim to be Christians also, but they worship the Anointed in the form of the Serpent of Eden."

"Ah, Ophitics," agreed the agent. "Yes, serpent-worship is more common on the Black Sea coast than it is this far in the south."

"It's more common yet in Hell," Ramphion asserted tartly. In a more moderate tone he added, "But Azon and Erzites have their place in the valley. They are on Earth to advance the purposes of the Lord, as is every creature which he placed here. Blessed by the Lord!"

As if Ramphion's words were a signal, the assembled villagers chorused, "Blessed by the Anointed and his servant Dioscholias!" They surged forward, draping Sestius and the others behind him with garlands of field-flowers.

The next hour and a half were a confused blur of hymns and offers of hospitality. The village had no bathhouse as a settlement a little larger would have. Instead, the villagers led Perennius and the others to a tub quarried from the living rock to take advantage of a warm spring. To the agent, the offer was as tempting as the thought of sex to a sailor. It was only at the last instant that Perennius thought to refuse—on the grounds that he and Calvus had vowed to Hermes that they would not bathe until they reached Tarsus. Otherwise, the tall woman would have been alone in refusing to disrobe. That would not have mattered to the agent—had not mattered or even been noticed in past months—were it not for his present awareness of Calvus' sex. Logically, Perennius could have accepted without concern a situation which had not caused problems while he was ignorant of it. Perennius—and humans in general, he suspected—were not built to feel that way, however.

Gaius and Sestius splashed and bellowed happily. Their voices were thrown across the valley by the concave rocks. Sabellia sat a few paces down from the tub and waited her turn in the water. Mixed bathing was the norm in large cities—or was at least a common option. Sabellia was a rural woman, however, with a rustic sense of propriety which cropped up unexpectedly. Perennius looked back at the red-haired woman, huddled beneath the bathing hollow. He could remember—he could not forget—her drooling beneath Theudas and the panting Herulian. Perennius' knuckles banded red and white with the pressure of his grip on his spear. The villagers leading him and Calvus to a hut twittered in sudden alarm at the agent's expression. Then the moment passed, and Aulus Perennius was again a peaceful traveller, to whom weapons were a necessary burden and no more.

The villagers' own attitude toward mixed bathing was a surprise to Perennius. They had obviously expected all five of their guests to share the big tub simultaneously. Christ cultists had something of a reputation for strait-laced behavior. There were scores of variant cults, however—the priest's mention of the two Ophitics living in the valley was an example. Certainly there was nothing about the villagers' demeanor to suggest that they thought of common bathing as anything more than an exercise in cleanliness. Prurience required a level of sophistication which seemed blissfully lacking in the valley.

"Here, sir," said one of the women who was guiding them. Father Ramphion was busy elsewhere, it seemed. The woman opened the door of a dwelling. She stepped aside quickly so that Perennius would not brush her as he

entered. The shutters were thrown back from the unglazed window. The front room's southern exposure
lighted it brightly. The room was not clean, exactly—
nothing with a dirt floor and a thatched roof could ever
be clean in an absolute sense—but it had been swept out
only minutes before. A haze of dust motes clung to the
air, and a heavy-set woman with a straw broom stood
panting outside the door. This was obviously an occupied
dwelling whose owners had been whisked away with all
their personalty to make room for the strangers.

Perennius ducked as he stepped inside. In general, the
roof was high enough for him—it would not be for Calvus—
but the thatching sloped down from the back where it
joined the hillside.

"Beds will be brought shortly, sirs," a villager said
through the open window. Its sill and the door jamb
showed that the walls were of stones a foot thick. They had
been squared ably with a pick or adze but without any
attempt at polishing. The craftsmanship impressed the
agent even before he stepped into the room adjoining to
the rear and realized that it had been entirely carven into
the rock of the hill.

"Look at this," Perennius murmured to Calvus as the
tall woman moved to his side. The agent ran his palm
down a wall that was plumb enough to suit a temple
architect. Its surface showed that it had been hacked from
living rock with a pick. The incredible labor involved had
not caused the job to be skimped, either. The ceiling of
the back room was high enough that Calvus could stand
upright.

The room was somewhat less dark than the agent would
have guessed. Some light entered from the front room.
There was no door separating the two rooms, only an
open archway cut in the wall. Besides that, there was a
slanting flue cut in the ceiling to exit from the hillside at
some point above the thatching of the front extension.
The flue was narrow, but it let in enough light to see by,
even this late in the evening. The back room had been
cleaned with the same thoroughness as the front. Its walls
were colored the soft, indelible black of soot from the
hearth sunk in the middle of the floor. Not only would the

inner room be warmer in the winter, the arrangement avoided the dangers implicit when thatched roofs covered open fires as they did in most rural areas.

"You may leave your burdens here," one of the villagers called from outside. "They will be safe." After a moment, she added, "They would be safe anywhere in the valley."

Perennius had insisted on carrying a pack as heavy as any of the others did—any of them besides Calvus. The suggestion made him feel suddenly as if the straps were trying to ram him into the soil like hammer blows on a tent peg. The process of shrugging off his load was more painful than the carrying of it had been. He had been suppressing the latter pain over many harsh miles of goat track.

"Do you ever feel like settling down yourself," he asked the bald woman in Latin. "Just saying the hell with it, I've done all the job one man can do, the rest can try fighting it for a while?"

Calvus set down her own pack. She was still a little awkward, so the load touched the stone floor with a clank. None of the villagers outside seemed to care or notice. "Sometimes I feel that way, Aulus Perennius," she said carefully. Her face was in shadow. It would probably not have betrayed her feelings to the agent anyway. "I suppose everyone with a duty feels that way on occasion." Calvus started to walk back through the archway again.

Perennius' hand stopped her. "Why don't you, then?" he demanded. Echoes from the rock deepened his voice and multiplied its urgency. "Why don't you just pitch it when there's places like this in the world?"

Most people would have replied, "Why don't you?" and it was perhaps that response for which the target was hoping. Instead, the tall woman backed a half step so that she could straighten to her full height again. "Because," she said, "I know that it isn't true. I'm luckier than many, I suppose, because I will know exactly when I've done everything possible to accomplish my duty." Perennius thought she might be smiling as she added, "Of course, I won't retire then, in the usual sense. But that doesn't matter."

Perennius muttered something unintelligible even to himself as he led his companion outside again.

CHAPTER TWENTY-ONE

As they followed their escort of villagers to the church, the agent fingered the garland of daisies and columbines which he had not removed with his pack. Another ragged procession was wending toward the hut, carrying the burdens of the three bathers. Those villagers were singing something more cheerful than any hymn had a right to be. The two soldiers and Sabellia, who must have been hurried through her own chance at a bath, were being led toward the church directly from the alcove. The Gallic woman wore her own garments, but the two men seemed to have accepted tunics of bleached wool in place of their own travel-stained garments.

Perennius had refused a similar offer of clothing because he would have had to give up more than his tunic. The agent had shed his spear and equipment belt in the hut—it would have been insultingly churlish to do otherwise—but he had found a tiny, ivory-hilted dagger in the pirates' loot. That knife now weighted the hem of his inner tunic, a comfort to his paranoia. Perennius's groundless fears irritated him, but he had learned that sometimes it was better to feed them discreetly instead of depending on his control to prevent embarrassment.

The bell had ceased its warning from the tower when Father Ramphion met the strangers. Now it pealed again, but with a joyous exuberance in contrast to the measured beats before. The black-clad priest bustled out the door of the church even as the streams bearing the outsid-

221

ers converged on it. Ramphion raised both hands and cried, "God's blessing on this day and its works!"

"God's blessing!" chorused the villagers, both without the building and, mutedly, within.

It occurred to Perennius with some embarrassment that he had in the past been treated with equal pomp—but only under a false persona. Odenath had feted the envoy from Postumus, not Aulus Perennius himself; and there had been similar occurrences before. The agent had spent too many years among lies to be fully comfortable with the present situation. When he reached Father Ramphion, beaming by the doorway, Perennius said in his halting Cilician, "Father, we needn't be a burden to you. Our needs are simple, and we're willing to pay."

The village priest bowed to him. "We regard strangers as God's gift to our valley, the opportunity he gives us to repay the agony of his sacrifice by which we all are saved. Enter, and join our feast of love." Father Ramphion's broad gesture within had a compulsion to it as real as if it had created a suction in the air by its passage. Bemused and still uncertain, Perennius obeyed.

The interior of the spire was lighted primarily by rush-candles—pithy reeds dipped in grease. There were good-sized windows in the building's upper levels. Because the sun was low, the windows could only throw rectangles on the curved surface of the wall across from them. The church was designed much the way Perennius had assumed from the exterior. Eight thick columns supported the second level; four separate columns reached up the full forty feet to the base of the third. The belfry which was perched on top of even that must have been constructed of wood, because there was no evidence of the additional bracing which that structure would have required if it were stone. Though the church looked massively large from the outside, the columns filled its interior and gave it a claustrophobic feeling despite its volume.

What Perennius had not expected—though it might have been the norm for Christian churches—was the fact that all the stonework inside had been brightly painted. The porous limestone provided a suitable matrix for the paint, and the rock's natural soft yellow color was used both for

backgrounds and for the flesh of the figures. Those figures
were painted in stiff, full-frontal poses which seemed to
reflect local taste as much as they did the crudity of the
efforts. While the paintings were not the work of trained
artists, their execution displayed some of the same raw
power that suffused the architecture of the church itself.
The bright colors and the depictions of calm-faced men
undergoing gruesome tortures affected Perennius as real
events were not always able to do. The agent kept remembering Calvus' face and the way it retained its surface
placidity during her multiple rape.

It was Calvus herself who shook the agent from his
grim imaginings. "How would they have gotten high
enough to do that painting?" the bald woman asked in
Latin. She gestured with a flick of her chin instead of
raising her hand.

"Ah, that?" the agent said. "Scaffolding." He had to
swallow the "of course" that his tongue had almost tacked
on. Calvus did not ask questions to which the answers
would have been obvious if she had thought. There were
surprising gaps in the traveller's experience, but her mental precision was as great as her physical strength. "Would
have needed it just to build the walls," the agent went on.
He wondered how on earth the tall woman had thought
the stones had been lifted into place. Perhaps there were
people—where—she came from who could make stones
fly. She had denied that she herself could move anything
of real size without touching it, but . . . "You're right,
they seem to have built this without so much as a staircase integral to it."

Perennius was thinking as a military man. Any tenden-
cies the architect—if that were not too formal a term—
had toward military design were exhausted when the
bottom level was pierced with arrow slits. A rope ladder
served as access to the belfry, adequate for religious ends
and as a watchtower. If there was no easy way to use the
height of the upper levels against putative assault, then
there seemed to be no reason to do so either. The thick
walls, with the modicum of offensive capacity which the
slits gave, would suffice against raiders. A real military
force would make short work of an isolated tower, how-

ever strong it was individually. The waste of capacity still prompted an inward sneer. The agent thought that perhaps it was that from which arose his growing sense of unease.

"Herakles, Legate," Sestius called cheerfully from behind him, "This isn't the sort of place I expected to find out in the sticks. Or the kind of spread I thought we'd be offered, neither. Hey, what do you suppose they've got for wine?"

"Quintus," the agent said. His voice was as flat as a bowstring. "Bag it. Pretend you're at a formal dinner given by the Emperor. We *need* the help of these people."

The centurion winked and clapped Perennius on the shoulder.

The thick columns had trefoil cross-sections which increased their resemblance to walls. Perennius had the impression that he was in a spacious maze. Ramphion himself guided the strangers to a table beneath the belfry. There was no aisle from the door to the other side of the circular building. Those entering the church had immediately to dodge one of the outer ring of pillars. There was another such pillar in alignment across the room. It might be barely possible to see from the outer wall at one point to the equivalent point across the building, but the focus of any mass services would have to be the center of the room rather than the side.

Villagers were entering and filling the long trestle tables set up between the two rings of columns. The movement was not quite formal enough to be a procession, but many of the local people were singing. The agent was not sure whether a number of separate hymns were being intoned at the same time, or whether the acoustics of the room were so terrible that they created muted cacophony from a single work. The drab, joyous villagers flitted among the brilliantly-painted stones like sparrows in a flower garden.

Perennius paused and waved on the other members of his party as they followed the village priest. Sabellia was at the end of the line. The agent fell in step beside her and asked in Celtic, "Where's the altar? You have one for sacrifice, don't you?"

"Not for sacrifice," the woman snapped. "*Christ* was the world's sacrifice." But her face promptly pursed into the look of uncertainty it had shown before the agent's gaffe. "It must be movable," Sabellia said. "The building isn't like any church I've been in. *Anything* I've been in."

"Sit down, guests," Father Ramphion said with a two-handed gesture. "Accept the thanks of this valley which your presence blesses."

The central table was, like those around it, a cloth-draped panel supported by two trestles. There was nothing of civilized formality about the meal, with guests reclining on couches around a small table filled with delicacies. At the other tables, villagers sat on benches. In the center, six stools surrounded the table. Father Ramphion had positioned himself at the end further from the hidden door. Perennius nodded and took the chair across from the local man. When the remainder of the party had seated themselves along the sides, the priest clapped his hands. The singing and shuffling of feet on stone floors ceased at once. Muffled echoes continued to rasp among the odd angles for long seconds thereafter.

Villagers joined hands with their neighbors to either side. Those who were standing moved into the gaps between tables and joined them so that the whole room was linked by a double ring of hands. Father Ramphion made a ritual gesture, crossing his torso. Then he lifted his eyes and his hands. "Almighty God," he prayed in a voice which the room made reedy, "we thank you for blessing us, your servants, by sending the Anointed and Dioscholias his apostle into our midst to make known your will. For thirty-three years we have kept your ordinances that the Anointed may return when the way has been made smooth for him. Continue to bless your servants, and bless these strangers to your use. Let it be so."

Sixty-odd feet above the table, the bell clanged twice. The dim air quivered among the heavy columns. The priest relaxed. "Welcome, strangers, to our feast of love," he said in a normal voice. When he sat down, the cheerful bustle resumed all around.

While the offered meal was not of urban refinement, neither was it a simple one. The skeleton of it was wheat

bread and chunks of lamb roasted on skewers. Both dishes
were marvelously fresh and delicious. Beside those staples of a rural feast, there were a score of different cheese,
egg, and vegetable courses, most of them offered cold.
The one most to Perennius' taste was a collation of cucum-
bers and cultured goat's milk touched with additional
herbs. The agent noted Sabellia's eyes open in surprise.
Her tongue spread the morsel she had taken carefully
around her mouth as she separated flavors and piquancies.
Her expression was appreciative.

There was no difference Perennius could see between
the servitors and the villagers eating at the other tables.
They all wore homespun and had the calluses and sunburn of people who worked outdoors. Those who carried
food and water among the diners did so with enthusiasm
if not the polished obsequiousness of men and women
whose whole lives were sent in ministering to others. As
the meal progressed, those who had first been doing the
serving sat down to eat. They were replaced by some who
had eaten already.

Sestius noticed the situation, too. He pointed with a
cheese-laden wedge of bread and remarked, "Father,
where's all the slaves? Don't tell me you *all* work your
plots alone out here." Sestius' Cilician was rusty, but it
was still more serviceable than the agent's own.

Ramphion smiled. "We have no slaves in this valley,
no. But then, we have no private plots of land, either. We
decided, our forefathers—" Someone came by with a bowl
of chives in yogurt. The priest dipped some out with his
index and middle fingers, licked the taste off, and waved
the dish down to the others at the table. Perennius noticed that each dish was offered first to Father Ramphion,
and that he always sampled it openly—even ostenta-
tiously—before the strangers were asked to try it.

"Everyone in the valley was touched with the fire of
truth when Dioscholias preached," Father Ramphion
resumed. "Slaves and free-holders, men and women
together." He gestured, crooking his elbow so that the
arc of his hand did not threaten the centurion or Calvus
who sat nearest to him. "It was a night whose like may
never again take place—until the return of the Anointed,

of course," the priest added quickly. "You who are not saved cannot possibly imagine."

Sabellia coughed and shot an offended glance at the local man. She had not, Perennius noticed, made any mention of the fact that she too was a Christian.

Father Ramphion took a skewer of meat from a tray, offered the skewer and then the tray itself to Sestius, and continued, "We could not continue a society in which man was the servant to man, once we knew that all men were the servants of God alone. That night we carried away the stones of fences which had stood between fields for as long as human memory survives. We plowed across the old boundaries. Since then we have lived in common, as the Anointed taught us through Dioscholias."

The grilled lamb was delicious, particularly as it was set off by the tartness of some of the vegetable side-dishes. Perennius swallowed a bite and said, "Including your Ophitics, Azon and Erzites? In the commonality, that is?"

Father Ramphion spilled water from the earthenware goblet at his lips. He lowered the vessel and patted himself hard on the breastbone until the fit let him speak again. "Yes and no," the priest said. He raised his eyes to the agent's. "Their father was a local man who returned here after he received his discharge from the Army." All three of the other men at the table nodded in understanding. "That was after Dioscholias had brought the fire of the Spirit to fall on the valley, however. There was discussion and prayer about the matter, of course. At last Dioscholias announced that the Lord would not have so arranged events except as evidence of his purpose. The father and his wife, and the sons of their marriage, have since shared fully in all the valley's wealth—save its greatest wealth, the faith by which we are saved. They are not our slaves or our servants, but they perform tasks which free the rest of us to worship together in full community."

Perennius nodded again and took more meat. He had wondered who stood guard while the whole village feasted. The symbiosis Ramphion had described made sense. The agent imagined that each party felt superior to those on the other side of the equation. The Christians could look down on the brothers damned to eternal Hell, while the brothers could sneer at the remainder of the village which labored in their behalf as surely as in its own. The present feast made the valley's wealth certain; and from their generosity to strangers, Perennius did not doubt that the Christians treated their local sectarians as well as Father Ramphion had suggested.

Perennius was no longer worried about Sabellia. Father Ramphion had made it clear if not overt that the village did not want proselytes. It was equally clear that to the locals, the only Christians were those who were present or descended from those present when Dioscholias converted the village. The apostle was probably a local man himself, given the introversion of the faith as practiced here. A convert returning home from Caesarea, Egypt— some center of the new sect—with his own slant on the faith to which he was devoting himself. The situation seemed to make Sabellia angry, probably because of the sense of kinship she had briefly expected. That thought— that the Gallic woman had hoped for a sodality from which her present companions were barred—was unexpectedly painful to the agent. He returned to his meal.

Not only was the food excellent in itself, it was not flawed as it would have been at a rich man's table by being eaten from metal dishes. The slightest astringence —pomegranate cells or a vinegar dressing—would bring with it an aftertaste of silver or even gold. Poor men who drank their wines from glazed earthenware tasted them with a purity denied to those who could afford the best—in jeweled metal. The water of the valley was all that thus far had been offered to accompany the food, however. It was clean and cool, complementing the meal without attempting to compete with it.

Eventually, even Gaius was full to repletion. The young courier swayed in a forgetful attempt to recline on a stool. The bulk of the meal had left Perennius logy. The headache with which he had tramped for a day and a half was gone. Even his wounded thigh could almost be ignored. The agent was wondering whether or not he could bathe now. It would make a perfect conclusion to the relaxing meal.

Father Ramphion rose. The building whispered slowly into a hush as before. At the priest's side stood another villager with a goblet. The vessel was of glass so clear and colorless that it might properly have graced an emperor's table. The wine within it was of a tawny hue accented by the flaring rush-lights.

Ramphion took the goblet and raised it. "May all those present be turned to the Lord's service," he said, "as Dioscholias taught." He drank noisily from the goblet, then handed it to Sestius. The level of the wine had dropped appreciably.

The centurion had asked for wine twice in the course of the meal. Now he took the goblet in surprise. The priest continued to stand. Sestius obviously wondered if he should stand up also, but Father Ramphion's eyes held no such encouragement. Sestius drank and passed the cup.

Sabellia's hesitation had come when the wine was offered to the centurion. When it came her turn, she gripped the slick glass surface without concern. Because the villagers had tacitly barred her from full membership in the circle of their faith, there was a bitter reaction in the Gallic woman to damn them all as heretics themselves. Like the wine, her red hair absorbed highlights from the blazing, grease-soaked rushes. The color was no bad suggestion of the anger within Sabellia. But with her temper came control, and a remembrance of the mission for which she and the others had suffered so much already. Sabellia drank quickly and handed the goblet to Perennius. She wiped her mouth with her shawl.

It was not a particularly good vintage, the agent thought. More tannin, it seemed, than was to be expected from a white wine. Though one got used to the resins and honey added to amphoras to preserve wines for hard travelling. There was none of that in this local vintage. Perennius passed the cup.

Gaius drank with the noisy assurances of a youth whom exhaustion and a full belly had robbed of such sophistication as he might otherwise have displayed. He slurped, belched, and then took another deep draft though the level in the wide-bellied goblet had already sunk near the bottom.

Perennius was trying to decide whether to negotiate for donkeys now or to wait for the morning. It was not a hard decision. He was tired. The feeling of sluggish tranquility that blotted away his aches and pains at the close of the meal would make him a less-effective bargainer. This valley community might well feel it needed its livestock more than it needed gold. Father Ramphion stood, his shaven pate gleaming in the lights above him. He looked as if he were one of the haloed figures painted on the walls. The agent's eyes focused but his head did not seem to want to turn away from the priest's fixed smile.

Calvus lowered the cup. The wine had been strained through cloth. Nothing clung to the inside surface of the glass but a film no yellower than the light itself. Fire wavered on the whorls which marked the goblet's colorless purity. There was a collective babbling from the surrounding tables. Villagers were standing up.

"Aulus Perennius," the tall woman said. She was speaking Schwabish. Sabellia and Sestius might understand her, but the less stable Gaius would not. "There was an alkaloid in the wine. It should not be fatal, but it will numb you all."

Perennius clenched his left hand on the table's edge. He stood up. It was as if he were a squat male caryatid trying to lift the roof of a temple. The agent's stool crashed to the stone floor behind him.

"Aulus," the bald woman said, "I don't think this is a good idea. If they meant to kill us, they would have used something else, surely. . . ."

Father Ramphion's deep-sunk eyes glared at the agent. Villagers who had been chattering with joy now noticed the Illyrian's struggle with himself. There was further commotion behind Perennius, toward the door of the church. He could not turn to see what it was. "I'm as much of a man as this bastard," the agent whispered. He stared back at Ramphion while his right hand tried to find the dagger in his hem. There was no feeling in the agent's fingers, in any of his limbs.

Sestius slid to the floor, Sabellia did not fall, but she

was obviously fighting as hard to stay upright as Perennius
had fought to stand. Gaius flopped forward. He was trying
to mouth the words of a song through lips too numb to
have formed sounds. Perennius' ears were buzzing. Over
that empty burr came Calvus' voice saying, "He has built
up an immunity to the drug, Aulus. This must be part of a
long practice for them. Let yourself go or they may—"

Someone kicked Perennius' feet sideways. The agent
crashed to the floor. He did not feel the impact, though he
could still see perfectly well. The two women toppled,
Calvus by choice with the appearance of collapse, Sabellia
when her stool was jerked away. Rough farmer's hands
gripped the table and the trestles supporting it, spilling
Gaius beside his would-be protector in happy somnolence.

Father Ramphion had been leaning much of his own
weight on the table. Villagers, one of them the young man
who had brought the goblet, stepped close to the priest as
the panel was removed. Ramphion straightened slowly.
He did not need the hands that hovered in nervous help-
fulness near his elbows. "Praise be to God," he said,
enunciating very distinctly.

"Praise be to God!" rattled the response of his congregation among the curves of the chamber.

No one bothered to move the drugged victims from
where they sprawled. The sound in Perennius's ears was
taking on the magnitude of the roaring surf. The scene
was becoming darker though no less sharply defined. Four
villagers, one of them a husky woman, were carrying a
naked, bawling stranger toward the pillar behind Father
Ramphion. Other villagers plucked the rush-candles from
sconces on the same pillar. A crucified man was painted
garishly against the double-lobed surface of the column.
The sconces, Perennius noticed now, were of heavy iron.
They were set into the wrists of the painted figure.

"Dear God," wailed the stranger in Greek. "I'm a
Christian! You *mustn't* do this!" His nude body was pale
and soft-looking. Folds in the skin of his abdomen suggested recent privation. Someone's house-slave, run away
from Tarsus or even further to a valley of fellow-believers?
Or perhaps a government official, making quiet inquiries
into the district's tax rolls? In any case, a man alone or in

a small group, charmed no doubt by the hospitality offered by these jovial sectarians. . . .

" 'This is my body, that is broken for you,' saith the Anointed," Father Ramphion recited. His voice was made squeaky either by the drug he had taken or by the dose now ringing like a carillon in Perennius' ears. "So must we break the bodies of the unbelievers who oppressed him, that the Anointed may return to rule on Earth. All praise be to God, and to Dioscholias who taught his commandments to us!"

"Praise to God!" trembled and blended with the screams of the man who was about to be sacrificed.

The villagers who held the man had no difficulty with either the victim's weight or his struggles. At the pillar, the pair holding his arms lifted them. Two more villagers, taller than the norm, seized the victim's wrists and began lashing them to the sconces. The step at the feet of the painted figure was not itself painted, but rather a brief curb jutting from the surface of the stone. A real victim could rest his feet and weight on the curb until fatigue dragged him off to die of suffocation.

Someone with Calvus' length of leg could stand flatfooted on the ground, the agent thought. Perhaps they would break her shins before they tied her up. . . .

The goblet which had held the drug had now been refilled with wine as red as blood. Father Ramphion raised it and began intoning a prayer to which his congregation shouted responses. The victim screamed, thumping his wrists against the stone and iron which held them. As the scene receded into blackness, Perennius was telling himself dizzily that this sort of behavior was a threat to the Empire.

CHAPTER TWENTY-TWO

"Hercules," Perennius muttered, though the process of coming around was no worse than that of being awakened from a sound sleep. His toes and fingers tingled, and there was still the buzzing somewhere in his head. There was no particular pain, however. In fact, the drugging seemed to have helped the agent's previous collection of aches and throbbing, including that of his spear wound.

Two hands steadied Perennius as he rose to a sitting position, Calvus on one side and Sabellia on the other. In the light creeping through the room's grated door, the agent could see the forms of Gaius and Sestius. They were slumped and snoring. All five of the party now wore simple belted tunics of local manufacture, like those the two soldiers had donned even before the feast. The agent wondered whether Calvus' sex had caused any surprise this time. The pirates, after all, had seemed to take the revelation in stride. Perennius shuddered and said, "Hercules!" again.

The light was dim, but the agent's eyes were fully dark-adapted. "Just like the room they gave us to store things," he said. "Except that one didn't have a barred door, did it?"

He stood. Sabellia murmured a warning. The Illyrian tried a step anyway and lurched, grabbing the door for support with a crash. The door was of welded iron bars with no interstices more than a hand's-breadth apart. Cross-bars braced the verticals, inside and out. Like the church, the door was of obviously local design and manufacture.

Equally like the church, the door looked more than solid enough for its intended purpose. As for the living rock that formed the ceiling, floor, and walls—

Perennius saw the shadow of the cudgel slashing at his knuckles just in time to jerk his hand away from the bars. The knobby length of root crashed against the iron. It filled the stone chamber with its vicious cacophony. "Next chappie to touch the door," said a harsh voice, "is the first to go when they need more meat down there." The speaker who had suddenly bulked against the light on the other side of the bars made a gesture with his thumb. "Make my life hard and I'll make yours a little shorter," he added with a chuckle. "And if the week or two's difference don't seem like much now, it will, chappies. Hear the voice of experience. It *will*."

"Sorry, friend," said the agent easily. "I just tripped. The gods know, I've got enough problems of my own right now. I'm not looking to make problems for anybody else." Perennius stood inches back from the grating. He was shifting his weight unobtrusively from one leg to the other to work the life back into the muscles.

Like the other hut, this one had two rooms. The outer one was built out from the hillside, while the inner one was set into the rock with only the doorway and a flue to connect it with the rest of the world. Judging from the patch of gray sky at the end of it, this flue was much like the other one: ten feet long and too narrow to pass a man's clenched fist. That left the iron-grated door which looked beyond affecting with bare hands even if there were no guard present. Since there was a guard, however, there were additional possibilities.

"Hey, don't worry," the big Cilician said with a laugh. "Your problems'll be over pretty quick now, won't they?" He walked back to a couch along one of the sidewalls.

"You'd be Azon, then, I guess," the agent said. The guard was slope-shouldered and covered from elbows to wrists with curling black hair. His appearance was striking enough that Perennius could be fairly certain that the fellow had not been in the church earlier. Besides, the man had a coarseness to him that set him apart from the other villagers. He looked like what the rest had proved themselves in fact to be: a red-handed murderer.

The guard turned to face Perennius again. The light from the single oil lamp on the floor opposite him fell slantingly across his face. "That's close," he said. His hand worked menacingly on his cudgel. "It's Erzites. And just what might you know about that, chappie?"

"Hey, friend," Perennius said. His raised his palms in a gesture of innocence though he knew the bars hid him from the guard more than the reverse. "Nothing meant at all. Life's too short, right? It's just that before I went under, I heard Ramphion say something about hauling us out to Azon, shits to a shit. I don't mean—"

The cudgel whipped out and slammed the door again. Erzites followed the blow with a kick that must have hurt even though he hit the iron with his sandaled heel instead of his toe. "Those goddam bastards say that?" he shouted. "Goddam, I think sometimes we ought to—" He caught himself, breathing heavily. "Well," he said, "they can say what they like. But I know who the *really* smart ones in this valley are."

A less experienced man might have pressed Erzites further, while his anger boiled and waited to be released at the nearest target. Perennius instead moved back from the door. Sabellia was massaging the limbs of her man and murmuring quietly. The bands of light which fell across her were too pale to bring out the colors of her skin and hair. With his mind on other things, the agent knelt beside Gaius and began working to arouse him also.

"Have you had a chance to look at the bars?" Perennius asked in low-voiced German.

"Yes, Aulus Perennius," Calvus responded where someone else might have added, "of course." She reached past Perennius and began kneading Gaius, under the tunic as if direct contact with his flesh were important. Perennius filed the fact with the way the woman's hands had drawn much of the fire from his thigh as she bandaged him. "The welds are all too solid for me to break them with my bare hands in these cramped quarters."

"Hey, you can't tell that by glancing at it in the dark!" Perennius objected. The courier was beginning to make conscious noises beneath the agent's hands—or more probably, beneath Calvus'. "Even if it's not dark to you," Perennius amended, reminded to his unease that there were facets of the tall woman which were closed to him. "There may be scale in the middle of the best-looking joint in the world. Put pressure on it and it'll snap like glass. It's not like you can see *through* iron, after all . . . is it?"

"Damn, what the hell's going on?" Gaius muttered. He tried to roll over so that he could look at the people touching him. His own hands did not quite have the degree of feeling which would permit them to support him.

"No, I wasn't raised to see through iron," the tall woman said. Perennius could not be sure whether or not there was humor in her voice. "When the guard struck the grating, though, it rattled as a unit—not as so many discrete bars. They must have been very careful in their work. If one bar could be loosened, I could use it to snap a hole in the remainder; but that doesn't seem to be the case."

"Yeah, bastards are careful, all right," the agent muttered. He lifted Gaius into a sitting posture, ignoring the younger man's repeated demands for information. "And you can tell that just by hearing a club hit it?"

"Yes, Aulus Perennius," the tall woman said patiently. She slid herself over to Sestius. The Gallic woman had been listening to the conversation as she continued to massage the centurion.

"All right," Perennius said. "Would the club be enough of a lever to get things started?"

Calvus paused and looked out into the other room. Erzites was invisible from where she knelt, but the cudgel leaning against his bed was in her line of sight. "Perhaps," she said. "Perhaps."

"Well, something better may turn up . . . and it may not," the agent muttered. "I figure we'll go with what we've got." He snorted under his breath. "What we're going to have if we get lucky." He stood up again and walked to the door. He was careful not to touch the metal.

Erzites noticed the motion. One large, hairy hand gripped the end of the cudgel, though the villager neither spoke nor moved further at the moment. Behind Perennius, Sestius was beginning to groan into wakefulness. The agent called in a mild voice, "How long's it going to be before they decide to kill us, Erzites?"

The cudgel head tapped the floor lightly while the villager made a decision as to how to react. At last he got up and walked toward the grating. Light reflected by the bars would make Perennius behind them little more than a voice and a blur. At last Erzites said, "When the Lord sends them a sacrifice—so they say—they spend as long in church, praying and singing, as it takes him to die. Him or her," the villager corrected himself.

Erzites fingered the coin he wore as a medallion. It hung by a thong reeved through a hole punched in its rim. It was a Termessian double obol, old enough to be real silver and so worn that the snakes intertwined on its obverse were only a pattern of shadows. "Fucking sick, I call it," the guard continued, "but it's their business. . . . Mostly it's one at a time or two. You lot were rare, getting that many who really wouldn't be missed. But who's to say you ever got clear of the pirates, Ramphion puts it to me when I wonder? And it's their business, my brother and me we just watch the larder."

Perennius nodded encouragingly. He was wondering whether he would have an opportunity to torture the guard before killing him.

"They won't come for any of you while the last one's still alive," Erzites went on. "That'll take, who knows? Maybe three days? Had one flat croak when they clamped him to the wall a couple years ago. . . ." The guard frowned and began counting with his left index finger against the fingers wrapped around the grip of his club. "Maybe it was four years ago?" he said in puzzlement. "But I figure you got a while yet. Way this last one bellered when they dragged him out, he ain't going to croak for a while."

Perennius noticed that while the villager was no longer showing any particular hostility toward his charges, neither was he coming incautiously close. Any attempt to grab Erzites through the bars would fail a foot short, even given the length of Calvus' slender arms.

"Why, they'd be lost without you and your brother, wouldn't they?" prompted the agent. He was careful to avoid any suggestion of treachery. It wasn't time for that yet, especially since Perennius had not yet figured out what sort of offer might be attractive to someone in Erzites' position.

"Too damn right!" the villager agreed with a series of vigorous nods. "Why, they'd go nuts trying to pick who'd watch the meat and who'd watch the road. Figure they'd be damned to bloody Hell if they missed the vigil, so they call it. Course it's damned hard lines for Azon and me when they get big eyes the way they did with you lot." He spat against the bars, but the anger behind the gesture was clearly directed at Ramphion and his sectaries rather than at their imprisoned victims. "Talk about freezing your butt off up there on the rock . . ." Erzites continued. "And it's no damn pleasure being stuck here with the meat, either, every damn hour I'm *not* up there." He jerked his cudgel, presumably toward the head of the valley. It was an angry, sexual gesture.

"Just like you weren't even human," Perennius sympathized. "Say, any chance of getting some wine? I know, I don't suppose we're meant to have it, but just a taste'd sure make—"

"Shit!" the guard said. "*You* get wine? *I* don't get wine, not a sip. It's a fucking sacrament, it's only for *them* when they're nailing somebody up, don't you know. Wine." He turned away from the door. As he walked back to his couch, he muttered, "I hear other places people just drink wine any time they feel like it." His couch squealed under his weight. "They don't have to steal a cupful and hide when they drink it. . . ."

"That's right, Erzites," the agent said. Perennius was irritated at the pleading note he seemed to hear in his own voice. That was bad form for a pitch like the one he was making. "And you know, smart men like you and your brother could make it big with help from—"

"Shut the hell up!" the guard shouted. "I don't want to hear about it, you know? Shut up!"

Perennius slipped back a step into the protective darkness of the cell. His companions watched him silently. All of them were now alert. The agent spread his arms, drawing the others' heads close to his by suggestion rather than by actual contact. The couch continued to creak in the other room as their guard settled his weight. "We need to get his attention," Perennius said softly, "and we need to get it on one of you. Now, I don't like the choices, but it seems to me the only thing we've got to offer is sex. . . ."

Sabellia's sudden tautness was no greater than the tension that had gripped Perennius' bowels for minutes, while his mind planned and his mouth had spoken friendly words. The agent continued to speak now as if he were ignorant of the effect he was having.

Because like it or not, they had no other choice.

CHAPTER TWENTY-THREE

"Hey, Erzites?" Sestius called in a husky whisper. There was no need for silence, but the tone seemed appropriate to the purpose.

The greatest problem had been to convince Sestius of what he must do. The centurion had foreseen Sabellia's role in the skit, but it had been a shock to him that he would have to act as her pimp. Sestius could see that Perennius had to remain as far out of focus as possible; and it was obvious that neither Galus nor Bella herself spoke enough Cilician to carry out the task. The centurion had still balked, with an increasing and unreasoning anger that came near explosion. That would have called Erzites' premature attention, so the possiblility had Perennius measuring Sestius for a rabbit punch.

It was only after Calvus laid long fingers on the centurion's cheek and throat that Sestius had grown calm again.

Even that had not ended the discussion—or rather, had not brought Sestius around to what the others regarded as reason. He had shuddered frequently while Perennius pressed his case. No one suggested that Calvus could do the talking. Though the woman had not spoken a word of Cilician in his hearing, the agent was sure of her fluency in that dialect. Her grotesque appearance—grotesque if one knew her real sex and did not know her as a person—made her a dangerous risk for the job, however.

The darkness had been enhanced by the fact that the prisoners were huddled in a back corner of the cell. The two large pots along the wall, for water and their wastes, screened them further. Sabellia had whispered abruptly, "Morals don't matter. You can do it easy, you *have* to do it if we're going to get out. You didn't watch them crucifying the fellow they brought in, you were gone by then. I don't want to be up on that wall next."

"Easy!" the centurion sneered. "Sure, I saw *you* prancing with those goddamned Germans, I *saw* you—"

"Did you see me before that, too?" the woman rasped back. Her right hand gripped Perennius' shoulder. He could feel her tremble like an arrow drawn to the head. "Did you watch them rape me, Quintus? Twenty-three times. I counted every one, I could only count. . . . Did you want that to go on every day until I—don't you turn your head away! Every day till I bled out! Is that what you wanted?"

"I'm sorry, Bella," the centurion had mumbled.

"Don't be sorry," she snapped back. "Act like a man and it won't happen again."

The Cilician had nodded. "All right," he said, "all right."

Now the guard turned to his charges. They had waited until he got up and tore off a piece of a loaf from the hamper of food near the lamp. Every moment's delay increased the risk that the current victim would die and the congregation would come out in force to choose another. The escape attempt would certainly fail, however, if Erzites were angry at being awakened. Even now there was a hostile rasp in the guard's voice as he replied, "You'll get food when I'm damned good and ready to feed you."

"Naw, not like that," Sestius said in a clumsy attempt to be ingratiating. Perennius was moving slowly to the grating by the centurion's side. "Look, you can't have much fun with these crazies, right?" Sestius continued. "I don't mean just wine. I mean sex. I'll bet you've never been laid, not the way a man as strong as you has a right to be."

The guard began to laugh unexpectedly. He walked toward the door, slapping his club against his palm. There was real humor in Erzites' laugh. The twitching cudgel was a motion and not a threat. "Say," he said, "I'll bet you're going to offer to get my ashes hauled, ain't you? Going to have one of the women do it, or do you figure I'd rather have the kid? *Sure*, I'm going to open the door for that. Or maybe you were going to say I could just stick my cock through the bars and let somebody get his teeth in it?" Erzites slammed the knotted head of his club against the iron in another burst of anger. "You think I haven't heard it?" he shouted. "You think I haven't heard it all?"

In Perennius' right hand was a shard from the waste jar. The two pottery vessels were the only source of solid weight in the cell. Calvus had broken the waste receptacle by the pressure of her fingers on the rim. There had been a popping sound like that of the tendons of a knee going out, but there was no sharp crash to bring the guard's attention. Erzites would not have taken any action—if the prisoners wanted to slide in their own slops, that was their business. But it would have made the guard curious and even more cautious than before.

"Look, I'm going to tell you," Erzites was saying. He was dangerously cheerful, in charge and aware of it. The Cilician had dropped the chunk of bread in his flash of anger. Now he picked it up, wiped it on his trousers, and took a bite. Erzites' teeth were as strong and yellow as a camel's. "The old man made do with what came in trade, sure, and that was damn all," the guard said through the wad of bread. "None of the others—" "others" tripped out so naturally as a term for the sectaries that it was obviously the one the brothers used between themselves— "would give him the time, of course, and the bastards wouldn't let him keep a pretty one around until the next lot came through. Not even after Ma died."

The villager walked back to the hamper and drew out a skin of water. He was obviously pleased to have an audience. Perennius suspected that Father Ramphion and his fellows circumscribed to the extent possible all intercourse, not just sexual, with the two Ophitics. Out of the guard's sight, behind the rock of the wall, the agent was carefully coiling again the sash tied around the potsherd. Perennius would have liked to double the length, but he was afraid that a knot in the middle of the line would throw off his cast.

"Well, the old man knew some field expedients from his army days," Erzites continued. He smirked. The guard was obviously relaxed, but the habit of caution was so well ingrained that even now he remained at a safe distance from the bars. "Brought me and my brother up on it, too. Donkeys." He pumped his cudgel up and down. "And I tell you, women don't compare to a stump-broke jenny. Nor boys, neither, though the others wouldn't let us use them since my brother wasted one." Erzites frowned at the memory. "Weren't his fault the brat bled out."

Perennius had not realized quite how much of reality he had saved Gaius from until then. The younger Illyrian began to gag in the background of the cell. Apparently he understood enough Cilician to get at least the drift of the description. Erzites laughed. Then he noticed that the agent was almost touching the bars. "Move back, damn you!" the guard ordered with a gesture of his club.

Not quite close enough.

"Calvus, can you make him come closer?" whispered the agent as he obeyed by a step.

Sabellia had been hovering behind the centurion. She was waiting for the moment she would strip for the guard's inspection. The grating was not wide enough for her to see past the torsos of the two men in front. Now Calvus eased the nervous Gaul aside. "Erzites," the bald woman called over Sestius from her greater height, "that sounds marvelous. Do the women here make love to donkeys also?"

Sestius looked back in shock. Perennius could imagine the slim-fingered hand gripping the centurion where Erzites could not see it. The soldier shifted out of the way.

The guard also was surprised, in part by the grammatically-correct Cilician coming from a prisoner whom he had never before heard speak. Calvus smiled at him and continued, "I've always wanted *real* satisfaction, you know, Erzites." She pressed close to the bars. "Tell me about the donkeys. Tell me about their—members." Her hands touched the lower hem of her tunic. Instead of lifting it, as even Perennius expected at that point, Calvus tore the tough homespun as if it had been gauze. She extended the tear upward at a deliberate pace as she straightened. Sestius muttered something behind her. Erzites' eyes were drawn, but it was under a frown of puzzlement. The guard was taken aback by more than Calvus' hairless groin. "Quit that," the villager muttered uneasily.

"Do you ever let the jacks mount you, Erzites?" Calvus asked, spreading the halved garment away from her body. The tall woman was thin, even by male standards. There was nothing conventionally attractive about her form. Perennius beside her felt himself oddly moved. The effect on Erzites was quite different—but the agent was sure it was *intended* to be different, despite the woman's phrasing. "I think that would be *really* satisfying," Calvus said. "I'd *die* for that, you know, a member so long and thick. . . ."

"Don't talk about that, woman!" the guard shouted as he took a step backward. "A donkey on *me?* That's—" He broke off because he could not think of an adequate word for the feeling which the concept engendered in him.

Calvus pressed her groin forward against one of the vertical bars. She rubbed up and down it. Her torso was thrown backward to emphasize the obscenity of what she was doing. "You know what I mean by satisfying, don't you, Erzites?" she said. Then she froze like a wax mannequin.

"Quit that!" Erzites screamed. He lunged, ramming his cudgel at the narrow pelvis kissing the iron. The rootwood smacked, just as Perennius flipped his weighted cord around the guard's neck.

Erzites jerked back and swung at Perennius. The head of the club rang on the grating. If the guard had instead unwrapped the single coil from around his neck, he might have been free before Sestius clutched wildly and caught his right ankle. Erzites shouted again. Perennius yanked hard at the sash. Because the other end was not knotted, it slid loose when the guard bent toward the pull. Erzites' club slammed down against Sestius' gripping arm. The centurion yelped and lost the hold he had just taken.

Calvus, recovering from the brutal blow, shot out a hand and caught Erzites' club wrist. There was no fumbling to hold the big villager, only a straight pull that hauled his arm back through the grating like a gaffed trout. The iron boomed at the soggy impact. Erzites' forehead hit a bar a millisecond after his shoulder made the first contact. That fractional delay and the force absorbed by his torso saved the guard's skull from crushing. He sagged unconscious. There was a line of blood across his forehead and cheek.

"Get back!" Perennius ordered as Gaius and Sabellia tried to grab handfuls of the guard. The agent sprawled over Sestius. The centurion was moaning and clutching his bruised arm to his chest with the good hand. Perennius wrapped the sash around Erzites' arm and one of the bars against which Calvus held it. Alone of the six people in the hut, the tall woman was not gasping for breath. The splotch of blood on her left hip was her own. The club had cut her flesh by smashing it against the wing of her pelvis.

Perennius snugged the loop against the guard's arm, then locked it with a square knot. The sash would not hold Erzites permanently, but neither would it have to. The agent straightened. "There, you bastard," he gasped. "Try and get loose from that and I'll break your arm besides."

Sabellia reached under the lowest crossbar and snaked the cudgel inside. She handed it silently to the agent. Then she cradled Sestius in her arms to help him slide back from the door where they were in the others' way.

Perennius was still breathing rapidly and through his mouth. He handed the knobbed, arm's-length club to Calvus. "You all right?" he asked.

"Here, let me try that," Gaius said. He was puzzled that the agent had given the lever to the woman instead of using it himself. If the older Illyrian was injured or exhausted, then the younger man was more than willing to show his own mettle.

Calvus and Perennius ignored him. Gaius' attempt to push past the woman and take the cudgel failed unremarked. Calvus carefully set the knobbed end of the stick so that a vertical bar provided a fulcrum with which to pop one weld of a crossbar. "I'll be all right," the tall

woman said. "I didn't care for it, but it was necessary."
The agent could not be sure whether her answer was
limited to the blow she had taken on the hip. As Calvus
now knelt, the tear in her tunic had fallen closed again.

Calvus began bearing down on the handle of the club.
Perennius gripped the same crossbar and a vertical. The
agent used all his strength in a vain attempt to push the
one away from the other. It gave him something to do
besides wait for the sound he expected, the splintering
crash as the grating held and the wooden lever did not.

The cudgel did not break. Instead it bent in a smooth,
creaking arc until the tip which Calvus held touched the
floor. The root-stock was tough and perfect for the purpose for which Erzites had chosen it. Its whippiness made
it a more effective weapon. That meant also that the
wood could not transmit the necessary force as a lever.

"Blazing Hell!" the agent shouted. He released his own
hold and dropped to the floor. His eyeballs had felt as if
they were springing from their sockets with the effort.

"Here, let me try," Gaius suggested again.

"Gaius, will you *please* wait for orders?" the agent
growled up at him. It should have been obvious that the
problem was in the tools rather than in the muscles behind them. Gaius was damned well old enough to avoid
the childish need to be a part of every activity.

"That was the weakest one," Calvus said. "If it holds,
the others will. Perhaps he—"she gestured toward Erzites
with a flick of her chin—"has a knife or the like on him.
If we could cut or even chip a weld, then perhaps the
lever . . . ?"

"Right," said the agent. It was a reasonable next step,
now that their only real chance of escape had disappeared with the club's flexing.

The grating made it difficult to strip the guard on the
other side of it. Calvus' slim hands and arms had advantages over Perennius' bunched muscles, but she herself
was so awkward that the agent wound up doing most of
the work himself. Erzites came around slowly. When they
began to pull his tunics off, he struggled with increasing
consciousness and vigor. There were seven of the garments.
The outside one was foul. The innermost had decayed to

stinking tatters that must have been close to the guard's own adult years. By that point, Erzites was cursing loudly and trying to fight them with his free hand.

Sabellia touched Calvus, then moved to the grating as the taller woman gave her room. The Gaul held another shard of the waste jar, a curving, hand's-length fragment of the rim. It came to a point that was as blunt as a fingertip except for the slight knife-edge extension of the glaze. "Hey!" Erzites shouted. He jerked his head back as far as the bonds would let him. The shard plowed across his cheekbone to his right eye.

"Move and it's gone," Sabellia said in a soft voice. The villager began to tremble. He squeezed the threatened eye shut. The other one stared out in terror. Perennius finished his task without obstruction.

Sestius was recovered enough to go through the garments as they were passed into the cell. His forearm was badly bruised. It had not been caught between the club and the stone, and neither bone was broken. "Not a damned thing," the centurion grumbled as he fingered the cloth. The light was too bad to search the tunics in any other fashion. "Lice. And if we could train up this stink, it ought to be able to cut iron. But nothing else."

"We need a knife, Erzites," Perennius said in a friendly voice. "It'd be best for you now if we did get away, you know. We'll let you go if we do, I promise that. But if we're still locked in this cell when somebody else comes . . . well, I'll use the time I've got. You'll be dead before we are, I promise you. If it looks like I'll have a while before they can really interfere . . . I know tricks that'll make being buggered by a donkey sound like the most fun in the world, chappie. . . ."

"Christ be my witness, there's *nothing!*" the naked man whimpered. "The club and the food, the bed's just a matteress on a stone ledge, that won't help. . . . The others'd kill us if we brought anything else here to watch the meat. Look, I'll go get a prybar, that's what I'll—" He stopped when the absurdity of what he was babbling penetrated even to him.

There was a crunching sound. Calvus had set the edge of a piece of pot against one of the welds. The hard-fired stoneware had crumbled beneath her fingers as if it had been terra cotta. As expected, the iron was unmarked. "I wonder if we could use his teeth as a saw?" the tall woman said. "Of course, it would be a problem disarticulating his jaws with no tools, but if we could slice through at one hinge with a piece of the jar...." No one could listen to Calvus' matter of fact tone and doubt that she was absolutely serious in her suggestion.

Sabellia had removed her claw of pottery when its threat had done the trick. Now Erzites bellowed again in terror and jerked repeatedly against his bonds. Perennius reached between the bars and caught the villager by the throat with one hand. It gave the agent a cold pleasure to squeeze in the knowledge that it was not his anger taking charge. The action was necessary to immobilize their prisoner so that he could not free himself in his struggles.... Erzites' hairy face became flushed. His screams and the bestial rasp of his breathing whispered to a pause. In the wavering lamplight, the whites of the guard's eyes began to turn up.

Perennius took a deep breath himself. He released his prisoner. "When they come with the keys," the agent said in a voice that was meant to be more calm than he could manage, "how many of them will there be?"

"Christ save me," Erzites wheezed. He had closed his eyes. Now he was massaging his throat with his free hand. His brief delay to recover ended even as the agent was reaching out again. "They'll come a lot of them," the villager said. He opened his eyes and jumped, but Perennius was relaxing. "They're careful, Ramphion and the others. They know fighting men, and there won't be less than a score of them with clubs to take you. They don't want you dead, but they've strung up folk unconscious before to croak without coming around. 'As the Lord wills,' they say."

Perennius sighed. "All right," he said matter of factly. "We'll go with the teeth."

"*Wait!*" screamed Erzites. "My brother! He's got a sword!"

"Well, what good does that do," asked Gaius as the others paused. "He's a mile away on look-out, right?"

Panting, tumbling his words over one another, the villager explained, "He'll be back at dawn. We trade, him and me, day and day when there's meat on the wall and nobody else in the valley to watch. I forgot, Christ strike me dead, I forgot he'd be back, I *swear* it!"

That was probably true, unlikely as it would have seemed to someone with less experience of interrogation under pressure than Perennius had. Even after your subject broke, you had no guarantee of the truth or completeness of what came babbling out. Erzites might well have been shocked into such a state that he forgot to volunteer a crucial detail. Certainly that was more probable than the notion that he had been deliberately concealing his brother's imminent reappearance.

"Well, I don't see it makes any difference," said Sestius reasonably. "Except we've got to work faster at cutting through the bars."

"No, no," Erzites pleaded. "Listen, I'll talk to Azon— *he'll* cut you free with his sword, sure he will, Azon'll do that for me, Christ *save* me! I'm his brother!"

"Shit," said the centurion, "he'd watch us pick you apart with tweezers, wouldn't he? Before he'd risk pissing off Ramphion and his lot."

"You know, I think Erzites here will be able to convince his brother," said the agent thoughtfully. "Of course, we can't leave him naked and tied to the bars like this. Sure."

Behind Perennius, Sestius and Sabellia exchanged glances of disbelief. Even Gaius was surprised. Calvus and the villager could see the agent's face. The woman's thin lips formed themselves in an answering smile. Erzites, watching them both through the bars, began to tremble.

CHAPTER TWENTY-FOUR

"Erzites!" demanded the voice from outside. "Lend a hand."

Erzites stood in the middle of the outer room. He ground the butt of his club into his left palm silently.

"Erzites!" called the voice again. "Where the hell are you?"

"Answer him!" hissed Perennius, giving a twitch to the rope of sashes knotted around the villager's throat. The agent did not hold the free end. Calvus had that duty. Any time the slim woman chose, she could break Erzites' neck with a single jerk on the tether.

"F-fuck off!" Erzites shouted back. "You're late!"

"Fuck yourself!" replied his brother angrily. "I had to gather the fucking eggs so we'd have something to eat, didn't I?" The hut darkened as Azon's big form, a near twin of his brother's, filled the doorway. He bent and entered. Father Ramphion or an earlier leader had decided that a gap of an hour or so in the manning of the look-out point was less dangerous than the chance of unattended prisoners somehow escaping in a similar period. Having tested the physical wards, Perennius was inclined to disagree; but the dearth of traffic past the valley really mooted the point anyway.

"Say," Azon went on, "I could hear 'em really going to it at the church. They'll be up for more meat any time, I'll bet you."

His brother hit him alongside the head with the cudgel. It was a nervously clumsy blow. The shaft instead of the knobbed end of the weapon struck Azon. He was too thick-boned a man to be laid out completely that way. Even so, Azon fell to his knees. He flung out his arms toward his brother in a gesture compounded of defense and supplication. Erzites grabbed him by the hair, screaming, and began to batter at him repeatedly with the club. The two men were locked so closely now that the weapon could not be used effectively. Erzites was mad with fear. He would not back off a step to finish the job properly.

The tip of Azon's sword, thrust sheathless under his belt, clanged on the floor when he fell. Azon made no attempt to draw the weapon against his brother's unexpected attack. His hands clutched wildly. Erzites' tunic, knotted over the shoulder where it had been torn for removal, now tore again. Suddenly tangled in his own garment, Erzites paused and cursed. His brother broke free.

The left side of Azon's head was a mass of blood. A chance poke from the butt of the cudgel had closed his left eye forever. Panic blinded the right eye also and the mind behind it. The big villager bolted forward and slammed into the door of the cell. He bit at the bars with the fury of a wolf in a trap. Sestius lunged forward in an attempt to grapple with him. The centurion jostled Perennius but did not prevent the agent from getting his own iron grip on Azon's throat.

Erzites wheeled. His tunic pooled at his ankles. He gripped his club with both hands, as if it were a threshing flail. It hissed through the air as the guard swung with all his strength. Azon's head deformed. The grating rang from the impact of the skull being driven into it. Erzites struck again. The body was jerking in Perennius' grip, but that was only the dying response of its autonomic nervous system. The cudgel made a liquid sound when its knob struck the second time. Matter splashed the metal and Perennius' forearm. The agent released Azon.

The third time, the club struck the door a foot above the slumping corpse and flew out of Erzites' grasp. The killer also collapsed on the floor, wheezing. In the last instants of the fight, the brothers had been almost equally mindless.

Perennius dragged the corpse closer by its belt. He reached across to draw the sword. It was a standard government-pattern short sword. Its blade was dull and very badly maintained. The hilt was of bronze in a fish-scale pattern which might once have been gilded. Chances were that the weapon had belonged to Azon and Erzites' father when he served with the imperial forces. The valley must have gathered a considerable armory in its decades of murdering travellers. The brothers' own lack of equipment underscored their separation from all communal aspects of village life. There was no need for it to be otherwise, of course.

Perennius gave the sword to Calvus, though the three other of his fellow prisoners were babbling and jostling forward. Erzites was still in a state of collapse. The agent tied off the villager's tether. The villager had just proven he was willing to do anything to save his skin. Perennius saw no point in risking the fellow's escape.

Calvus put the point of the sword at the joint between a vertical and a crossbar. She held the weapon almost point down. Perennius started to apologize for the fact that the sword was so dull and that the point had been rounded by improper sharpening. The tall woman rapped the oval pommel sharply with the heel of her right hand. Metal rang. The crossbar jumped as the sword inserted itself where the weld had been.

"Herakles!" Sestius blurted. Sabellia had more experience or at least more awareness of the other woman's capacities. The Gaul fell silent and drew the centurion back to give Calvus more room to work.

Perennius stopped himself with his mouth open. He had been about to say that if Azon had been correct, the five of them might be only minutes short of being trapped by villagers returning for a new victim. There was no reason to say what they all knew; and it was hard to imagine anyone working faster or more efficiently than Calvus, anyway.

The blade was of good steel. Its dull edge should have been a handicap. If so, the bare-handed blows with which Calvus struck the pommel were more than hard enough to overcome the defect in materials. The bald woman placed the point carefully, rapped the hilt, and shifted the sword to the next joint while it was still singing with the parting sound of the weld it had just cut. When Calvus reached the end, the crossbar dropped to the floor with a clank.

"Wait," said the agent as Calvus raised her sword to the next higher of the five crossbars. The agent set the freed bar into the grate much as they had attempted earlier with the wooden cudgel. In the outer room, Erzites was watching them. He was fingering his throat where the rope had rubbed it. He was not attempting to break free.

Perennius braced his left leg on the stone doorjamb and gripped the lever with both hands. Nothing moved. The agent's closed eyes sizzled with sheets of violet and magenta. He began to breathe out. The framework and his lever were rigid, and his muscles bunched like the surface of a sheet of water-glass. "By *god!*" Perennius shouted. Two welds popped like hearts breaking. Calvus slammed her sword through the third and top-most. The vertical bar banged away. With that and the one crossbar gone, there was now a gap through which even Sestius, the bulkiest of the prisoners, could squeeze.

The agent had fallen when the bars gave. Now, panting heavily, he allowed Gaius to help him to his feet again. Perennius felt a mingled pride and embarrassment. He knew that Calvus could have made a surer job of it if he had asked her to. But Perennius had succeeded . . . and it had been important to burn away in action some of the emotions raised by the bloody fight he had just finished.

Sabellia crawled through the opening without being told. Military discipline held back the other men until Perennius said, "Right, but don't go out of this hut." He nodded Calvus through with a rueful smile. She most of all of them must have recognized his doubtful judgment in using the prybar himself. Well, she'd seen him use worse judgment too, in that alley in Rome. Perennius was damned if he knew why she trusted him. . . .

The others were peering through the doorway. They made room for the agent when he joined them. Perennius lay flat and scanned as wide an arc as he could without actually sticking his head outside. The situation was about as he had expected. They were in one of the huts, differing in no external respect from the others to either side of it. Perennius had not checked the hinges on the iron door, but he suspected that they could be unpinned and the door removed at need. Even a careful search of the village would display nothing more than that the locals were Christians — illegal but common, and of no particular concern outside cities where they came into violent conflict with other communities.

From the circular tower of the church came the faint sound of singing. The door might open at any moment to a procession that would soon become the head of a hunting party.

Erzites screamed. The sound was so unexpected that Perennius dodged sideways before he even looked to check the cause. As he did so, Sestius struck the villager a second time with the sword.

"Hell and Darkness!" the agent shouted. He leaped up, grappling the centurion from behind and immobilizing the bloody sword. He was too late. Azon's weapon had done its work. Erzites still whimpered and clutched his neck, but there was no disguising the arterial pulses from between his fingers. Perennius shook the bigger man in fury until the sword dropped. "I told him he could live if he helped us!" the agent said as he pushed Sestius away.

"I didn't tell him that," Sestius said. His eyes were on the floor. He was rubbing his wrists.

Perennius swore again and returned to the door. He did not care about Erzites, whose bare heels were now thumping the floor. He cared very much for the principle of keeping faith with agents, however. It always mattered, because you always knew you had played false before; and in the uniquely personal relationship of intelligence principal and agent, more passed between the two than either intended.

So be it. There was other work waiting.

CHAPTER TWENTY-FIVE

Perennius pointed. He crooked his elbow to keep his hand inside the hut. "Calvus," he said, "do you see the wagon they were loading with hay down there? The half-full one."

"Yes, Aulus Perennius," the woman agreed. It was an ordinary, rugged farm cart with two wheels and a shaft to which a pair of donkeys could be harnessed. A saw-bladed hay knife projected from the stack from which the cart was being filled. The load was presumably intended to feed the draft animals in the stone corral. Work had been broken off when the strangers were announced.

"Can you move it to the church?" the agent asked. The haystack and the building were a quarter mile apart. There was no direct road, and the ground was only nominally level.

"Yes," said Calvus. The simplicity of her answer was disquieting, because it seemed inhuman. It was also the only thing simple about Calvus. . . .

"The hut our gear was stored in should be the third one over," Perennius continued. He gestured with his left thumb. "The rest of you go, take weapons—not armor— and some gold. Run for it till you get to the head of the valley. Don't take animals, that'll cause a stir and they'll slow you down. By the time you get there, you ought to know if it's safe to come back and load up properly. If it isn't, get to the nearest post and report this . . . hive. You're on your own from there."

"I'm coming with—" Gaius began.

Perennius jumped to his feet. "You're doing as I damned well say, boy!" he shouted. He shook his fist in the younger man's face. The anger Perennius had banked at Erzites' murder now blazed again from his eyes. "Now, *hop!*"

The fit passed as if it had never occurred, as so many outbursts had passed in previous years. Some day . . . Perennius handed to Calvus the bar he had used for a lever. He took Azon's sword himself. It was blunt but still bloodily serviceable. Sabellia looked at the agent, then darted through the doorway with the two soldiers behind her.

"Well, noble lady," Perennius said to his companion. "We're either going to create a diversion or do something that should have been done thirty-odd years ago. Let's see which." He paused to take along the oil lamp, still burning, before he led Calvus outside.

The two of them had not quite reached the haycart when Sabellia and the soldiers exited the storage hut. The two men carried spears and belted swords. Sabellia presumably had retrieved the long knife she had brought in preference to weapons whose size made them awkward in her hands. Perennius had half-expected at least one of the men to carry a packload of loot—which would not even make a good monument for them if the pursuit caught up. The woman waved. When Gaius paused behind her, she caught his hand and tugged him back toward the shortest line to the valley's head. The spike outcropping, now vacant, was their towering endpost.

Calvus looked over the cart, then gripped the shaft to lift it. "Wait," the agent said. The hay had an Autumn smell, an undertone called a "green odor" though it was a part of vegetation whether green or a year chopped, the way this hay was. Perennius held the lamp flame under the edge of the hay piled against the rear stakes of the cart. Only when the hay was burning with a popping, smoky flame did the agent dump the slight remnant of olive oil onto the cart. "Let's go," he said, bracing himself against the side of the cart. "We need to jam this into the door of the church."

As at other times, Calvus' initial clumsiness was almost a match for her strength. She more or less got the hang of pulling the cart after the second time she overbalanced. Both times the cart rocked onto the back of its bed with a crash and a shower of sparks. After a point, the center of gravity shifted when the pole went up. Holding the cart became a matter of weight rather than strength. Calvus could lift the cart level again from behind, despite the flames, but when she raised the pole too high from the front, she could not keep the load from flopping all the way over till it grounded.

Sparks flew harmlessly into the green wheat. They lodged in Perennius' hair and tunic, snapped at his palms like mice when he crushed them out. The smells of hair and of wool burning were similar and similarly nauseating. Perennius had blisters on the back of his neck where the skin had no protection but the sweat that streaked from his scalp in quick runnels. The load of hay was burning faster than he had expected. It had been densely compressed by a year in the stack, but the process of chopping and loading it on the cart had loosened the mass a great deal. Still, it was necessary to have a very good fire going before they reached their goal. They had that. The unconquered Sun could see!

The smoke, the crackling of the flames, and the way the cart jolted the agent's shoulder in bouncing over the uneven soil were all parts of the same blurred continuum. It ended when Perennius' downcast eyes saw the cartwheel bump onto the surface of the roadway proper. He looked up. They were twenty feet from the door of the church. The stone cylinders mounted up higher than he could see for the haze of smoke above him.

"We've got to turn it and back it to the door," the agent called. He thought Calvus could not have heard over the crackling of the fire which now involved the whole rear of the cart. Perennius stepped away from the side-stake he had been pushing against. The heat, more than a discomfort now, was driving him off anyway. Before he could touch Calvus' arm and repeat his command, the woman had slowed and begun to swing the shaft to reverse the vehicle.

"Blazes, be careful," the agent muttered in unconscious humor. He gripped the shaft also, ready to throw his weight across it if it started to lift. "This goes over and we won't tilt it back from behind." Sparks and the bitter, cutting smoke enveloped them as the pair thrust the cart backwards at increasing speed.

The squeal of the church door opening inward was even louder than the shouts which immediately followed.

"Now!" roared Perennius, a prayer in the form of an expressed hope. The cart smashed to a halt. It was caught by the stone doorjambs on either side. The blazing load shifted, caught its breath, and spewed up with redoubled fury.

"Get ready for them," the agent said to Calvus. He drew the dull, bloody sword from the hay where he had thrust it. "They'll use benches to shove it back, and you've *got* to hold."

From the cries within, some of the villagers had been burned when the vehicle jarred to a halt and the hay continued to slide. Perennius dropped to his hands and knees to peer under the tilting bottom of the cart. Orange fire swished and bloomed in the doorway. Villagers had begun to rake it back into the interior and out of their immediate way. Something heavy thumped against the framework of the cart. Calvus held her grip on the shaft without twitching a muscle of her limbs or her thin, still face.

There was a tattoo of orders from within. They were loud enough for Perennius to hear them over the roar, but the words were not intelligible. The agent was still bent over in a salamandrine crouch. A makeshift ram beat the flames and slammed into the cart. Charred wood collapsed. Perennius saw legs that capered in sparks and smoke while the owner screamed. Calvus held, the beginnings of a smile on her face. The assault dissolved and the legs disappeared again behind the bright-shot haze.

The hay and the cart itself were licking the stone with an orange tongue. At the edges, soot smeared the fresh-hewn yellow rock. At the center, in a scar tapering upward, the fire was hot enough to burn the stone on the outermost level of the church into quicklime. It was white but dreadful with the reflection. The tongue left whorls of soot across the face of the next cylinder also.

A man started to crawl under the cart. He held a spear and muffled his face with a cloak. Perennius heard singing behind the attacker. The villager was blinded by the cloth that kept the fire from his skin. Perhaps it protected him from what he knew he would see waiting. Perennius reached in and thrust at where he thought the villager's neck would be. The agent would have cut instead, but the wheel blocked a sidearm swing and the cart itself prevented a vertical chop. The sword's mutilated point met bone. Perennius shouted and threw his shoulder against the pommel. He remembered the way the blade had chiseled its way through iron with Calvus' strength behind it. The sword grated a hand's breadth inward.

Above the agent and his victim, the cart shuddered to another attempt to ram it out of the way. The vehicle rocked inches forward, toward Calvus. Then the woman slammed it back against the church harder than it had struck the first time. The axle broke. The left wheel spun lazily outward. The whole cart lurched toward Perennius. The agent rolled backwards in a cloud of sparks belched from the shifting hay. His sword was still gripped firmly by the villager's body, as firmly as that body was held by the weight of the cart above it. An arrow snapped from one of the slits. It missed by a hand's breadth the agent who until then had been in the dead zone hidden by the cart. The barbed point pinned his tunic to the hard soil.

The section of roof over the doorway collapsed into the interior of the church.

Gasping, Perennius worked the arrow out of the ground without haste. He knew there would be no more shooting. Edges of flame were cutting from the nearer arrow slits. They left their own stains of soot and caustic across the face of the church. Thatch and wooden beams roared inside, shaking the stones as hymns had never done.

"We'd best move away, Aulus Perennius," Calvus shouted over the voice of the fire.

The agent looked up at her. She extended a hand to lift him from his splay-legged seat on the ground. Perennius stared past the woman to the church. The outer cylinder had begun to act as a chimney, drawing air through the slits and the part-blocked door to feed the Hell within.

Everything must be ablaze by now. Not only roof members but clothing and furniture, paint from the walls and gases driven from corpses that were being reduced to calcined ash. There could be no screaming now, not that voices could have been heard over the roar.

"Right," Perennius said. He accepted the offered hand and rose slowly. As they walked away from the funnel of fire, he said, "I wonder if they drained the bath. I'd really like to get clean."

CHAPTER TWENTY-SIX

"All right, let's see your papers," demanded the commander of the detachment at the west gate of Tarsus. "*Dis*-mount, dammit."

"Hey, you're not checking them," said Gaius. He waved toward the stream of traffic into the city.

Sestius was already off his donkey. He grimaced, only partly at his stiffness from the ride. It was for Perennius to say, "Gaius, let me handle this." He walked over to the officer. The agent's hand was in his purse.

The ride on a donkey's narrow back had left Sestius with a limp. Perennius could imagine what similar punishment would have done to him. Instead of riding, the agent had walked, leading his donkey. The miles had left his wound afire, but they had also worked his thigh to suppleness again. It had been a punishing two days, but now the agent did not limp. Under other circumstances, he might have ridden anyway so as not to delay his companions. Because of Calvus, that question had not arisen.

Gaius rode splendidly and loved it. His only objection was that a donkey was not a fit mount for a cavalry decurion. Donkeys were what was available in the valley they had depopulated, however. The small-holdings they passed later had nothing better, so Gaius had made do. Sabellia, like Perennius himself when the agent was healthy, had no great affection for riding, but she did it adequately when the need arose. Sestius was scarcely adequate—he had fallen several times and under unexpected circumstances—but he was too much a soldier to put any weight on his own feet that could go on others'.

Calvus had been awkward the first few days on shipboard. Mounted, she was a disaster. When she made an effort to cling to the donkey with her knees, the animal stumbled and fell from the crushing grip. When Calvus attempted to mitigate that vise, she inevitably fell off. There could be no question of the traveller's strength, but she did not have the instinctive control needed for some very ordinary tasks until she had practiced them for days.

They did not have days to spend on this. Calvus walked.

"Yeah, sonny," said the guard commander, "it could be that we do let local people through without checking them. What's it to you?" He tapped his baton on his left palm as he walked toward Gaius.

The gateway thrust out from the wall. Pillars supported a groined vault over the intersection of the road that Perennius and his troupe were on and the north-south road along the outside of the city wall. The guards were a detachment of heavy infantry, Syrian Greeks by the look of them. Even an argument between their commander and a traveller left them disinterested.

"Of course you're right to question us, sir," Perennius said. "Gaius, get off that donkey! Sir, we're travelling in cotton. Other fabrics as well, but I'm told this is the time and place to make a market in Cilician cotton." The agent slipped his right hand palm-down over the commander's upturned left. The baton hesitated. "A terrible thing, this disruption," Perennius continued smoothly. "But of course that means profits for a man who's willing to take a few risks . . . and profits for men who do their duty as well. I trust our papers are in order? And *do* forgive my bodyguard, you know, he's young."

The fact of the coin did not surprise the officer of the guard. The light weight did, especially after he spread his own enfolding fingers and saw the sun wink on gold, not silver-washed bronze. The pirates' loot had more than made up for losing the bank drafts with the expedition's gear aboard the *Eagle*. "Hermes!" the commander muttered. He covered the aureus again as quickly as he had exposed it. "Yes sir," he said. "Well. I'm sure a gentleman of your experience can imagine how careful we need to be, what with the Games and all the talk of portents— dragons in the countryside! And they say the Borani have been raiding near Ephesus again."

Sestius started to say something, but he managed to restrain himself. It was very difficult not to make yourself a center of attention by blurting out facts that everyone nearby would want to hear. At the moment, however, Perennius needed to gather information rather than to give it out. And the gods knew, it did not matter in the least to these folk if they were about to be raided by Germans rather than by Scyths.

The agent nodded toward the stream of people still making their way into the city. Whole families were travelling together, but without the impedimenta that would suggest a panicked flight from the countryside. In families wealthy enough to have slaves, the latter preceded the father to clear the way. The children were strung out behind their father in descending order of age. Then came any older members of the extended family; and last, the wife and mother. Submissive womanhood was by no means a virtue universally accepted among the Cilicians. It was noticeable that in families which owned a single mule or donkey, the wife was as likely to be mounted as the husband was. The women wore their finery under travelling shawls. Coiled earrings dangled nearly to their shoulders. The jewelry was gold if they could afford it, silver or brass if they could not. Sabellia, aware of her own battered appearance, glared back at the bold-eyed women as they passed.

"All the traffic's for the Games, then?" Perennius said to the officer. "Who's giving them?"

"Our lord Odenath," the commander replied proudly. "Holding a day of supplication all over the province in thanks for his victory last year over the Persians. His *latest* victory. You know—" the men had not been speaking loudly, but now the officer bent closer to Perennius and dropped his voice to a conspiratorial whisper—"there's those who say a dragon appearing here means the same thing among princes. The one in Rome replaced by one from the East. I don't know about that . . . but between you, me, and the bedpost, I wouldn't mind if they were right." The officer straightened and swept his hand out. "Who's helped *us* while other folks loll around, screwing their way through all the titled sluts in Rome?"

The agent nodded in false agreement. Blazes, he'd heard worse. It was not Gallienus to whom Perennius' loyalty was given, whatever that current holder of the office might believe. Besides, the last gibe amused the agent. The Autarch of Palmyra had his virtues, to be sure; but there was nothing in the scores of beautiful women entering Odenath's seraglio to suggest that one of those virtues was chastity.

"You'll have Hell's own time finding lodgings today," the commander called after them as they entered the gate. Perennius waved back with a smile. He knew from experience that gold would get them food and lodging as quickly as it had gotten them entry to Tarsus. Money was never necessary. Its effective use, like that of violence, involved more subtleties than many folk realized. But money smoothed most paths if one were willing to use it.

Tarsus was an ancient foundation. It had grown under the direction of various peoples, all of whom found the Roman fascination with straight streets to be unaesthetic and dangerous. Why go out of your way to make the key points of your city accessible to an invader? Let every branching be a potential cul-de-sac to trap him under the fire of rooftops on three sides. Let his spears if leveled jam in narrow turnings and if vertical catch in the second-story overhangs. And besides, who ever saw a straight line in nature?

The maze did not concern Sestius, nor was it intended to do so. It was local knowledge of the convoluted streetscape which made the maze so useful. The centurion had not been in Tarsus for five years or more, but the pattern of alleys and "boulevards" scarcely wider might not have changed significantly in five millenia.

Because of the crowd, all five of the group had to lead their donkeys as Calvus and Perennius had done during the whole journey. Even with training, most animals will not try to force their way through a mass of humans, though they could do so easily. If the crowd parts for their bulk and sharp hooves, well and good. But infantry with shields locked and spear-points advanced is proof against the finest cavalry in the world—proof even against elephants, unless the beasts are already blind and maddened by previous wounds. Sestius, in the lead, made better time with his own shoulders and elbows than the keel-like breastbone of his donkey would have done if the centurion insisted on riding.

Sestius stopped at an archway. He began trying to pull his mount through the narrow opening into the side of a building. Perennius, further back by the donkey's length, had just passed a doorway into the same structure. The entrance was gorgeously tiled. The interior of the building exhaled echoes and steam. The agent dropped the reins of his animal. It had nowhere to wander to in the crowd anyway. The Illyrian squeezed forward to Sestius and asked, "A bath? We're staying in a bath?"

"The front of the building's an inn," the centurion said. He waved the hand which was not tugging at his recalcitrant donkey. "The Mottled Fleece. Run by a family from my district since, oh, well . . . forever."

Perennius nodded. There was a fleece hanging at the far corner of the building where the street they were following debouched into a broader one. There was no way of telling what color the wool had been originally. The lower portion of the fleece had been polished to the leather by the shoulders of every man and beast to turn the corner sharply. Even the upper part was black with the grime of ages. The fleece was mottled for the same reason that the family of the inn proprietors were countrymen of Sestius: historically, that had been the case.

Perennius' party had entered Tarsus through the Jewish quarter. It was a street of sailmakers who sat in their shops, whole families in order of age. They pushed their needles through heavy canvas while they chattered to one another in Hebrew. They would deal with customers in Common Greek, but the present holiday crowds were only objects and a hindrance to trade. Adjoining the Jewish quarter was apparently a quarter of native Cilicians. Elsewhere in the city there would be Greek communities, and Armenians, and a score of others: Kurds and Scyths and Italians. Some of the groups would be no more than a dozen or two souls, and yet they would still look to the welfare of their own national community before troubling about the welfare of the city. Even so, Tarsus ranked far higher in their minds than did an abstraction like "the Empire," though it was from that Empire that the peace and safety of them all depended.

It was daily realizations like that which drove Perennius to wild frustration or the narrow focus of a knife edge. The impending disaster itself was beginning to weld the disparate strands into a unity which no deliberate policy had been able to create. But that disaster would have to be delayed longer than the agent believed possible, or the Empire would run its course before the unifying process could.

For now, the knife edge. Perennius gave the centurion's mount a judicious kick in the ribs. The animal bolted through the archway. Perennius' own donkey followed, without urging and so abruptly that the agent had to jump out of the way. Perennius' fingers were touching the handle of the sling he had retrieved from the gear jumbled in the pirate camp.

The courtyard they had entered through the arch gave onto the inn's stables. The area was already crowded with beasts and men. An ostler saw the newcomers and began waving them back angrily. Someone should have barred the archway, but that had been neglected in the confusion. Sestius ignored the directions. Sabellia was leading her mount through the narrow opening with the other two behind her, so the centurion could not have left even if he had intended to do so. Sestius began talking to the ostler with a series of sweeping gestures. The other man's face cleared. He embraced Sestius, both of them gabbling in a conversation which seemed to consist primarily of proper names and relationships.

At last the centurion broke off. He waved his companions to a flight of stone steps into the three-story building. "In here," he cried. "Zenophanes'll take care of our animals and baggage."

Perennius let Sabellia precede him up the stairs. Gold

was a good general key, he thought, but the networks of families and nations which riddled the Empire were themselves a better entree for those who could tap in on them.

"My god, Quintus," a white-haired man was crying to Sestius in the hallway. "They quarter eight soldiers on us—Arabs, can you believe it?—and now you come home. What we'll do, I can't imagine, but we'll manage. But my boy—aren't you supposed to be lined up already for the parade? The others left hours ago!"

"Ah, I'm—" the centurion began. He caught Perennius' eye and went on, "I've been discharged, Cleiton. My friends and I have some business in the area, and then my wife and I'll be settling down."

"Oh, well, then you'll want to *watch* the parade," the innkeeper determined aloud. "Come on, quickly, up to the roof with you or you'll miss the start."

Sestius looked at the agent. Perennius in turn looked at Calvus and then shrugged. They obviously would not accomplish a great deal more in the present confusion. "Why not?" the Illyrian agreed. He began climbing the ladder that served as access to the inn's upper floors.

The roof already held a number of family members and other guests of the inn. There was a low parapet, less for safety than to collect rain water draining down the shallow, tiled incline toward the front of the building. Drains at either corner then sucked the water into cisterns. Roman administration had brought aqueducts and public water supplies to Tarsus; but the cisterns continued to work and to be used.

A blare of horns demonstrated that Cleiton was correct about the parade starting. The agent found a spot at the parapet and sat on his folded ankles. He forced his right leg to comply with the posture. The street below was so crowded with onlookers that the marchers had virtually to clear a path for themselves as they advanced.

Probably for that reason, the front ranks of the parade were infantry marching four files across. All the men wore dress armor. The feather plumes were fitted into their helmet slots. On the leather-faced shields were designs freshly picked out in gilt. Perennius catalogued the represented units reflexively. Elements of the Fifth, the

Twelfth . . . Imperial line formations, as befitted Odenath in his capacity of Restorer of the East. Hobnails clashed in unison on the cobblestones. Then the cornicines with their curved bronze horns and the trumpeters blew a salute. The crowd cheered. Some of the onlookers cheered Odenath as Emperor.

Two pairs of heavy cavalrymen followed, restricted by the narrow front. They were cataphracts: horses and men both were armored with great scales of bronze which had been polished for the occasion. Instead of combat headgear, the men wore helmets with anthropomorphic face-pieces of silvered bronze. The masks glared stiffly at the crowd. One thought of the mounted figures as statues until a head turned or nodded. The effect was one which Perennius had always found to be disconcerting. Now it reminded him of the stiff-carapaced Guardian he had killed unknowing . . . and the five more like it he had come so far to face. But the armor also made him think—

"Aulus!" Gaius whispered. He tugged on the agent's arm. "I heard people shouting—"

Perennius touched the younger man's lips to hush him gently. In the past, the agent's patience had extended only to the actions of enemies. Clumsy execution by an ally, ill-timed interruptions by friends, would set Perennius off in a blast of rage. He was changing, and he looked in puzzlement at Calvus on his other side before whispering, "I know what they're cheering, Gaius. We're not in that business right now, and this might not be a healthy place to suggest otherwise. Hey? Sit and watch the parade." The agent's hand moved from Gaius' face to his shoulder. He guided the young courier down to sit.

Calvus looked at the two men. Perennius wondered if she too had noted the change in his temper. Well, he always handled himself better when he was on assignment than when he viewed the world with only his own eyes.

The parade involved only token units from Odenath's forces. If the officer at the gate was correct, similar displays were going on all over Cilicia today, so the small scale was inevitable. The troops following the four cata-

phracts were also cavalry—of a sort. They were Arabs in
flowing robes and burnooses, carrying long lances and
mounted on dromedaries. Though the Palmyrene horses
ahead of them must have been used to camels, the odor
still made them skittish. Perennius could well imagine
the havoc in Persian columns when their cavalry boiled
away from the Palmyrene lancers. Now—snorting, aggres-
sive and hesitant by degrees—half a dozen of the big
animals straggled down the street. Their dark-skinned
riders studied the crowds without affection. The Arabs
fingered their weapons as they watched the packed city-
dwellers. The troopers managed to give the impression of
housewives, testing the edges of knives in a chickenyard.

Following the cavalry were more foot-soldiers escorting
wagons. The wagons carried a selection of loot from
Odenath's victories in past years, along with prisoners
and beasts intended for the Games which were to be a
part of the celebration. In a traditional Roman triumph,
the troops would have worn tunics and wreaths. This was
neither Rome nor a triumph. Odenath obviously felt that
his own propaganda purposes were better served by men
in full armor, their weapons glittering in a hedge about
the wagons. Persian prisoners were tied facing outward
from stakes in the center of the wagons carrying them.
Some of them might have been among the men who had
sacked Tarsus before Odenath's forces harried them back
across the frontier.

Suits of gilded chain mail. Tiny steel bucklers whose
surfaces were silvered or parcel gilt. Long curved swords
whose watermarked blades impressed Perennius more than
did the precious stones with which some of the hilts were
inlaid. Peaked, chain-veiled helmets . . . Two full wagons
of such military hardware. Then came loads of silk
garments, dyed crimson or purple and shot with gold
wire, to demonstrate that the Palmyrenes had captured
some of Shapur's personal baggage. That was a useful
datum to file mentally and to check against Odenath's
official account of his victories.

But Perennius was tired, and he was not really interested even in the paraphernalia of battle and victory. The
agent was almost dozing when the animals for the beast

show were rolled by next in their cages. A dozen gazelles leaped nervously and clacked their horns against the bars. Wild, straight-horned bulls followed. Each was tethered between a yoke of draft oxen which dragged the intended victims along despite their efforts to break loose and gore. Two russet, angry lions snarled past in iron cages. Their manes were torn short by the scrub of northern Mesopotamia where they had been captured. There was an elephant from the Mediterranean coast of Africa, smaller and more docile than the Asian species whose importation had been ended by the renewed power of Persia across the trade routes. Even so, the elephant was too valuable to slaughter in a local affair like this. The beast was fitted with a howdah in which four archers sat. The men showed more interest in overhanging buildings than they did in the cheering citizenry.

The last cage held a—

"What in blazes is that?" Perennius demanded aloud.

Cleiton had followed them onto the roof. He was sitting in the group around Sestius and—Sestius' woman, that's what she was—but he heard the question. Leaning toward the agent, the innkeeper said, "Now that's something isn't it? Not from Palmyra, either. Some shepherds caught it right here in Tarsus, not a mile from the wall. I figure it must be a dog, don't you? But a portent, like if it had been born with two heads instead of—" He waved.

The beast could almost have been a dog . . . and as the innkeeper had suggested, animals are born misshapen on occasion. Unlike human monsters, monstrous beasts became tokens of the gods instead of trash to be tossed on the midden while they still wailed with hunger. The creature looked more like a wolf than a dog, and a damned big wolf besides . . . though a wolf so close to a bustling city would itself have been cause for some surprise. . . .

Its head was not that of any dog or wolf the agent had ever seen. It was outsized, even on a creature with the bulk of a small lion. The jaws were huge, and the red tongue lolled over a serrated row of teeth as the beast paced its narrow cage.

"Killed everything in the cave they were using for a sheepfold," Cleiton continued. "Forty-three sheep and a boy, way I heard it. They rolled a wagon across the mouth to hold it till people got to them with nets. Mean bastard."

"It's a dire wolf," Calvus said. She was watching the animal with an interest which longer association with her permitted the agent to read beneath the calm. "It shouldn't be here, of course. *Now*. Like the tylosaurus."

"In Rome," Perennius said as he watched the great wolf, "I saw the head of a lion with fangs longer than my fingers. Did that come from the same place as these others?"

"In a way," the traveller agreed. "A sabretooth—" she looked at the agent. "It must have come the same way, the way I came and the result of my coming. Aulus Perennius, I was not sent to interfere with your world, but my coming has done so."

There were more horns and marching feet in the boulevard below, drawing cheers and echoes. Perennius glanced toward the parade. He jerked back to look at Calvus because of what he thought he had seen there. There was a tear at the corner of the tall woman's eye.

The agent's mind worked while his muscles paused. It was as if he had walked into a potential ambush, where the first move he made had to be right or it would be his last. Perennius did not curse or blurt sympathy. He had seen the traveller accept multiple rape without overt emotion. All the agent understood of the tear now was that it chilled him to see it on a face he had thought imperturbable.

Perennius reached out. Only someone who had experience of the agent's reflexes would have realized that there had even been a pause. He touched the traveller's wrist with his fingertips. Then he turned back to face the parade without removing his hand.

"I had four sisters," Calvus said in her cool, empty voice. "Like the fingers of your hand, Aulus Perennius, five parts and not five individuals. And now I am here alone in your age, and along the route I travel there are anomalies ... but not my sisters. Not ever my sisters." She squeezed the agent's hand with a wooden precision which bespoke care and the strength beneath her smooth skin.

The crowd gave a tremendous roar. Behind the infantry, a pair of fine horses pulled a chariot. The vehicle's surfaces were gilded and embossed. In the car stood two statues, probably of wood but again gilded and glittering and draped with flowers. The statue placed behind was of the Sun God, crowned with spiked rays and himself holding a laurel crown over the figure in front of him. Perennius did not need the signs being carried before the chariot to know that the leading figure represented Odenath. The statue stood taller than the agent remembered the Autarch to do in person; but that was to be expected, and the statue's expression of arrogant determination was real enough. Odenath's statue was draped in the gold and purple of triumphal regalia. Its left hand held a sceptre and its right a sheaf of wheat to symbolize the prosperity its victories had returned.

More cataphracts rode behind the chariot. The leader carried Odenath's war standard on a pole. A bronze dragon's head caught the breeze through snarling jaws. The crimson silk tube attached to the bronze neck swelled and filled. The gold-shot tail snapped in the air twelve feet behind the pole that supported it.

"The Dragon from the East!" people shouted in the street. "Hail the Dragon from the East!"

Perennius spoke because he was the man he was, and because he himself found concentration on the task in hand the best response to grief. It was with that motive, and not in the savage cruelty with which the words might have come from a less-directed speaker, that he said, "If you had four sisters, Calvus, then I wonder what we can expect to see besides the three we have."

In the street the mob boomed, "Hail the Dragon from the East!"

CHAPTER TWENTY-SEVEN

"What I don't understand . . ." said Perennius. He dipped his bread into the pot of lamb stew which had been brought up to the roof for Gaius, Calvus, and himself— ". . . is why they sent a woman. Your—government, I mean."

Gaius nodded vigorously around his own dripping mouthful of stew. The group's baggage was stacked around them, along with straw-filled leather mattresses. The agent had suggested the roof, despite its ten degrees of slope, in preference to being crammed into one of the common rooms. The family's own apartments were more crowded still, because the members had doubled up in order to devote half the space to paying guests in the present glut. The roof gave the party a measure of privacy and protection from thieves that they would not have had inside under the present circumstances. They would be better off under a tree if the weather broke, of course; but at the moment, it was a pleasant evening.

"That wasn't really a matter of choice," Calvus said. "We—my sisters and I . . ." She paused for a moment, but her eyes showed nothing until she continued, "We are female for the same reason that workers ants are female, or bees."

"They are?" the younger Illyrian asked. He felt the thought which Perennius did not express even by a glance. Mumbling an apology for the interruption, Gaius took some celery from the condiment tray and began to concentrate on it.

The traveller nodded placidly and took more stew herself. Calvus ate with a quiet neatness that suggested boredom with the process. "Sterile females, myself and my sibs. With a . . . common lineage."

Calvus paused again. "I don't have all the words I need to explain," she said, spreading her hands. "But I don't mean only a common parentage, or that we five are as close as twins from the same egg. We are *one*. The thoughts I think, my sibs think—all of us." The tears suddenly brightened the tall woman's eyes again. "We were one. We were one."

Perennius ate. He refused to look at Calvus beside him. If she wanted to steer a practical question into emotional waters, it was her doing alone. Tarsus climbed a few steps out of the sea behind him, so that there were façades facing the agent against the further background of the Taurus Mountains. Higher yet, clouds covered the sky like etchings on silver. Every shade of gray and brightness was represented in swatches which blended imperceptibly with one another. Like life, like the Empire . . . and sunset was near.

"One effect of sisterhoods like mine," Calvus continued in a dry voice, "is that the birth group is more important to the individual than her self. The species as a whole is worthy of the sacrifice of the self; and this by nature without any necessity of training. You will have seen ants react when their nests are broken open with a stick."

"Some run," the agent said softly to the sky.

"Some run," the traveller agreed, "to assess and repair damage, and to carry the young of the nest to places of greater safety. Because they were raised so that their natures would cause them to do so for the good of the nest. And some bite the stick, or swarm up it to bite the hand wielding the stick. . . . We were not all raised to patch walls and carry babies, Aulus Perennius."

"If we had some time," Perennius said, "I'd teach you to use a sword—if I thought I could find one that would hold up. I'm not complaining, Lucius Calvus. I just wondered."

A slave popped up the ladder with a mixing bowl of wine held in both hands. He switched it without comment for the bowl which the three diners had almost emptied already. From below, where Sestius and Sabellia shared dinner with the innkeeper's family, came a burst of laughter and an order which the house slave appeared to understand. He grumbled a curse in Phrygian. Holding the bowl, he disappeared through the trap door again with his body vertical and his back to the ladder.

Perennius gazed after the slave with amusement. "Nice to meet somebody who's good at his job," the agent said.

"Well, that still doesn't explain why you pretend to be a man when you're really a woman," Gaius said. His tone and the frown on his face suggested that the tall woman's words had not explained very much else to him either.

"When I'm really neither, you mean?" Calvus asked, and she had to know that the courier had not meant anything of the sort. "Think of me as a mule, Decurion. What the pirates did mattered as little to me as it would have to a board with a knothole."

Perennius turned. Calvus would not meet his eyes. He touched her cheek and guided her face around until she was looking at him. "They're all dead," the agent said. "Every one of them. Now, do you want to tell the boy why you passed yourself off for a man, or shall I?"

The face that Perennius could not have forced to turn now softened into a smile. "You tell him, Aulus," the woman said, "if you can."

"Blazes, what do you think I spend most of my life doing?" the agent grumbled. "Chopping weeds?" He patted his protégé lightly on the knee to return the discussion to him. "Look, Gaius," the agent said, "how many six foot four bald women have you met in embassies to the Emperor?"

"Well, he could have worn a wig," the courier mumbled through his wine. He was startled enough to have continued to use a masculine pronoun.

"Fine, how many six foot four women whose wigs slip in a breeze or a scuffle—have you forgotten what we went through *before* we met the Goths? Blazes, friend—" Perennius had to catch himself every time so as not to address Gaius as "boy"—"who takes a woman seriously? Oh, I know—Odenath's tough, but his wife Zenobia could eat him for breakfast. And sure, there's been some at Rome, too. But not openly, not at Rome. Queens are for wogs, and lady ambassadors would be an insult, however—" he looked at Calvus—"persuasive she might be. There are limits." Perennius' voice lost its light tone as he repeated, "There are limits." In the agent's mind, Germans knelt and laughed and grunted. "But those things can be worked out too," he concluded.

With a barking laugh and a return to banter as he looked at Calvus, Perennius added, "Damned if I yet know how you managed it, though. Manage it."

"I was raised to have control of my muscles—and bodily functions," the tall woman said. The agent was beginning to understand that "raised" was a euphemism for "bred" when the woman applied it to herself. "And as you know, I can be persuasive. There are many things for sailors to look at at night beside details of who's squatting at the rail." Calvus laughed. It was the first time Perennius had heard her do so. She twitched her outer tunic. "Full garments help too, of course."

There was again a bustle at the trap door. This time Cleiton himself climbed through ahead of Sestius. Sabellia followed the two men. Her red hair was beginning to curl into ringlets as it grew out.

"Quintus has told me where you were planning to go," the innkeeper said, gesturing as soon as he no longer needed his arms to haul him onto the roof. "This is impossible now. Besides, Typhon's Cavern has a bad reputation at the best of times. I'm not superstitious, but . . ."

The centurion broke in on the sentence whose thought, at least, had been completed. "Cleiton says the story is that there's a dragon in the area around the gorge, now. Some people are saying it's Typhon himself, released from Hell."

The agent grimaced. Sestius had been told to get information, and the soldier could not help the sort of nonsense he was told. Perennius thought he had heard an undercurrent of belief in the myth Sestius was retailing, however. That sort of crap, like tales of hostile armies a million men strong, buried reality and made a hard job harder.

Cleiton saw and understood the agent's expression. The innkeeper straightened. His voice regained for him whatever dignity he might have lost through the gravy stains on his tunic and his wispy beard. "These are not stories, honored guest," Cleiton said stiffly. "Kamilides, the son of Sossias, sister of my wife's uncle, manages a villa on the edge of the gorge, Typhon's Cavern. Something began raiding their flocks over a month ago. Kamilides organized a hunt with dogs and nets, thinking a lion must have crossed the mountains. What they found was a dragon as big as—"

The innkeeper paused. The best recommendation for his truthfulness was the fact that he rejected as preposterous the simile he had probably heard from his informant. Instead Cleiton went on, "Very big, hugely big. It was a dragon with legs, and when it chased them it ran faster than the horses of those who were mounted. Three of the men were killed. The rest were saved only because they scattered in all directions and the beast could follow only a few. They left the villa just as it was. Kamilides says if the owner wants his sheep, he can come up from Antioch and look for them himself. The monster is worse than the Persians, because everybody at least knew there *were* Persians."

Perennius stood up so that he could bow. "Gracious host," he said, "I apologize for my discourtesy."

Not that the fact Cleiton believed the story made it more likely to be true. Still, the agent had once seen a crocodile arise from its mudbank and chase the horsemen who were trying to collect it with lassoes for the arena. Mud had slopped house-high, and it was only the horsemen's initial lead that saved them from the reptile's brief rush. Perhaps, perhaps . . . and there was that thing in the sea before.

But there was no choice. They were going to Typhon's Cavern, myth and the Guardians be damned.

CHAPTER TWENTY-EIGHT

CHAPTER TWENTY-EIGHT

The sun was not directly as grim a punishment as was the dust which rose from the road's seared surface. Perennius swirled the mouthful of water repeatedly before spitting it out. The dark stain on the road dried even as he watched.

"I don't know anything about Typhon," Calvus said. Her outstretched legs were long enough that her toes were lighted by the sun over the wall against which the party sat. Her feet were slim. The big toes seemed abnormally pronounced by comparison with the other toes "Tell me about him."

One result of the dragon scare was that Perennius had not been able to hire drivers to take charge of the baggage animals. Sabellia was an effective drover. The rest of them had proven they were not, at considerable cost in temper and bruises. You cannot expect to hit a donkey with your hand and hurt the beast nearly as much as the blow will hurt you. "Blazes, what would I know?" Perennius said. "*I* haven't had the advantages of a rhetorical education."

"Well, *I* didn't ask you for it, did I?" said Gaius in a hurt voice. He sprawled against the wall to the other side of the older Illyrian. Gaius leaned forward from the wall so that he could look directly at Calvus. "Typhon," he continued in the declamatory sing-song that was indeed the mark of the education Perennius had procured for him, "was the son of Tartaros and Gaia, Hell and Earth. Typhon is the Hundred-Headed Serpent, the Hundred-

Voiced, who strove against the gods. He was cast down from the very threshold of Olympus by the thunderbolt of Zeus—or, as others have it, by the blazing arrows of the unconquered Sun in his guise as Apollo by which the Greeks know him."

Only Perennius' exhaustion had spoken in his gibe about rhetorical educations, but that was not an excuse he would have accepted from anybody else. The advantages Perennius had had as a boy were intelligence and the willingness to be as ruthless as a task required. The agent saw very quickly that flowery prose and the ability to argue points of grammar by citing minor poets dead a thousand years were the only routes to preferment in the civil service.

They were routes open to the talented poor as well as to the rich, since the Empire itself and many individual communities provided schooling by accomplished rhetoricians. Perennius could have fought his way alone to a position as a high-placed jurist, the way the poet Lucian had. Or he might have accepted the private tutoring that Navigatus had offered to pay for early in their association. Perennius had been handicapped; but the Goth, Theudas, had started as the agent's apparent superior also.

The system of choosing administrators for the Empire was fair enough, to the extent that anything in life is fair. Perennius refused to become involved with it simply because he saw the process as the greatest and most ineluctable threat which the Empire faced.

There had been threats to the borders ever since Rome was a hilltop settlement of bandits. The Germans, the Moors, the glittering host of the Persians . . . all could be turned back or slaughtered by the Imperial forces—if the latter were intelligently marshalled, competently led, and supplied in accordance with their needs and the Empire's abilities. Venal officials were a problem as old as government. The damage they did was inevitable; and, like that of caterpillars in a fruit tree, was supportable under all but the most extreme situations.

What was far more dangerous than graft was the increasing number of administrative documents which were unintelligible even to the men who drafted them. Archaic words; neologisms; technical terms borrowed for effect from other disciplines and then misused in a number of different fashions—all of these horrors were becoming staples of the tax laws and the criminal code, of reports on barley production and the extent of flood-damage on the Pyramos. Civil servants were affecting Tacitean variation without the brevity Tacitus had prized equally; fullness beyond that of Cicero without Cicero's precision.

And not a damned one of them could add his own household accounts, much less figure the income of a province. Slaves did both, and both badly.

But Perennius' mind that saw the Empire talking itself in declining circles toward destruction was by that the more fiercely determined that Gaius would succeed. The darker the shadows over the general future, the greater Perennius' need to emphasize his closest approximation to personal continuance. Thus the tutors he had not suggested but rather forced on his protégé. Even now, listening to a series of glosses on Homer and Hesiod which were as impressive as they were pointless, the agent could not wish that Gaius had been apprenticed to a mule driver.

The younger Illyrian paused. Sestius, in the shade further along the wall, said, "Around here, we always said Typhon came out of the earth in Cilicia." When Calvus turned, the centurion made a languid east-west gesture. "All along the Taurus here, there's straight-walled valleys, hundreds of feet deep . . . and sometimes a mile across."

The tall woman nodded in understanding. "Sinkholes," she said. "Your rocks are limestone. When the water eats them away under the surface, there's enough volcanic activity to collapse the shell covering the holes."

Sestius shrugged. Beside him, Sabellia appeared to be more interested in the sounds their hobbled donkeys made foraging on the other side of the wall. All members of the party were too tired to act animated. "Whatever," the centurion said. "Anyway, some of the gorges have caves at one end. The one that's called Typhon's Cavern, the one you need to go to—" Sestius had not been told the full purpose of their mission, but he had seen the tentacled thing from the balcony and must have had suspicions—"is

. . . well, nobody knows how far that cave goes. There's a path into the gorge along one of the walls. I mean, the place is big, there's trees and sometimes they pasture sheep down in it. And you can get into the cave itself easy, it's got a mouth like a funnel and it just keeps going down, getting a little tighter and a little slicker each step of the way."

The Cilician paused and shrugged again. "Some people think it leads all the way to Hell, sure. There's a chapel built at the throat of it, of stone and real old. And I suppose some people even believe that Typhon crawled up out of the cave. But though the place has never had a good reputation, this latest stuff about a dragon is new. And it isn't a myth."

"Your Guardians?" Perennius asked with his eyes closed against the shimmering road.

"I doubt it," Calvus replied. Her voice drifted out of the tawny blur. "More likely it's another result of my arrival. We hadn't any experience with the process before my sibs and I were sent here. The side effects of the process—" the catch in the tall woman's voice might have resulted from nothing more than a dry throat—"were not things that had been foreseen. At least, not things that we were warned to expect."

"Would you have come anyway?" the agent asked the world beyond his eyelids.

"Yes." The word seemed too flat to convey a loss of siblings which was more traumatic than a multiple amputation. "But I'm not sure they knew that we would come. I'm not sure the technicians realized how well they had raised us."

"Well, if we've got dragons as well as Guardians to deal with," Perennius said, "we'll deal with them. At least the bastards don't seem to be able to track you down while we're moving."

The appearance of another variable did not distress the agent. Rather the contrary, and Perennius knew himself well enough to guess why. The agent was practical and experienced enough to make all the preparations possible under the circumstances. He could never be comfortable risking failure because of his own laziness. That would have been as unthinkable as refusing to take a useful action because it might involve his own injury or death.

But when it was impossible to plan, when Aulus Perennius had to react to what the moment brought . . . when success or failure balanced on his wits and a sword's edge—that was when life became worthwhile for its own sake. If the mission were entering the mists of chance more deeply as they approached their goal, then so be it. They would deal with what came. *He* would deal with what came.

"Time we got moving again," the agent said aloud. "According to the itinerary, there's an inn some five miles farther on."

"It may be abandoned," the centurion suggested. "Cleiton said there isn't any traffic past the gorge any more."

"There'll be somebody there to serve us," Perennius said unconcernedly, "or we'll make do with what they left behind." The agent began to stand. He used his hands in the chinks of the wall behind him to support his weight until he was willing to ease it back onto his legs. The spear wound was warm to the touch, but it seemed to have caused less swelling than even a bruise usually would. Again he wondered whether Calvus could influence muscles as well as minds.

"And tonight," the agent went on, "we'll talk about what we're going to do when we get there. When we get to Typhon's Cavern."

CHAPTER TWENTY-NINE

"Well, there's *some*body home," Perennius commented as he watched the thread of smoke. Because the inn was half-way down the slope to the ford, the party had a view of the stables within the far sidewall of the courtyard. There were no immediate signs of activity there, but three of the stable doors were closed as if they were occupied. The smoke was from a flue of the vaulted common room to the rear. The structure could easily sleep a hundred men on straw pallets, but the evidence of the single fire suggested the handful whose beasts might be in the stable.

"Part of the estate," Sestius said. There was a low tower on one corner of the common room. The bath and the gatehouse, on opposite sides of the gate in the front wall, looked as if they were adapted for defense also. The centurion added morosely, "They may have got a care-taker to stay on when Kamilides and his crew lit out."

Gaius had bent to tie his donkey's reins to a bush. He straightened with a puzzled expression. There was a piece of bone in his hand. "Aulus, look at this," he said, step-ping closer to the older man.

Perennius glanced at the bone. "Part of an ox thigh," he remarked. "What about it?"

"Camel, I'd guess," said Sestius, peering at the courier's find. "Ox would be—"

Gaius ignored the technical discussion. "Not *what* it is, but look at it," he said. "Here, at the break."

The thigh had been worried by dogs or jackals, then nibbled by rodents who had hollowed out the narrow cavity completely. There was deeper scarring on the dense bone than either of those causes could account for. "Chisels," the agent said with a frown. He rotated the bone. "Somebody cracked it with pointed chisels to get the marrow out." At the broken end, among the jagged points left when the bone snapped, were cleanly-sheared surfaces reaching over an inch into the bone from either side.

Sabellia had noticed something which the men had not. As they talked, the Gallic woman picked up an object a foot or two from where the thigh-bone had lain. Perennius glanced over at her and saw what she held. He swore softly.

"Here," she said, handing the object to the agent. "I think it'll fit."

The object was a triangular tooth three inches long. Both its cutting edges were lightly serrated. The tooth fit the "chisel marks" in the thigh bone perfectly. Perennius tossed the bone away. He handed the tooth back to Sabellia. "I think," he said as he unhitched his donkey's reins, "that I'd as soon be inside walls for a while—" he nodded down toward the inn—"until we learn a little more about what in blazes is going on in these hills."

Perennius clucked to his donkey. The animal obeyed without the usual struggle. The five of them kept close together on the fork leading from the main road to the inn three hundred feet from stream-crossing. They all, even Calvus, spent far more effort watching their general surroundings than they did in watching the road or the inn which spelled safety at the end of that road.

The inn was built around a courtyard. The gatehouse in one front corner doubled as accommodations for the manager and special guests. The common room across the rear was for drovers and others without the wealth or prestige needed for one of the private apartments in the gatehouse. Both sides of the courtyard were lined with stalls which could also be used to store merchandise. The corner tower in the back, and the arrow slits in all four walls, were not merely decoration. The building had been designed with an eye to more than the casual banditry.

As the party neared the inn, Gaius kicked up his donkey

to reach the gates before the others did. Still mounted, the courier pushed at the center of the double leaves. When they did not budge, he began to hammer on them while he shouted, "Gate! Gate, damn you, we want to get inside!"

Nothing happened before the others had joined him. "I don't suppose they're expecting guests, whoever they are," Perennius said dryly. "One of us can go around to the back and try shouting into the common room, I suppose. It'd probably be simpler to shinny over the wall here, though, and—"

The sound that broke over the agent's comments came from back along the road the way they had come. It was not a bugling or a roar in any normal sense. The sound it most reminded Perennius of was that of a cat vomiting. It was a hollow, chugging noise, followed by a horrid rattling. The sound was so loud that, like a waterfall, it provided an ambiance rather than an individual noise.

The inn wall was eight feet high. Perennius' face went blank. "Lucia," he said to the tall woman, "give me a leg up like you did before." It was the first time he had used the feminine form of her assumed name, as if she were a woman of his acquaintance.

As if he were acquainted with her as a woman.

Calvus cupped her hands in a stirrup. "Yes, Aulus," she said. Her donkey brayed and turned in a tight circle when she dropped his reins. Sestius' beast was restive also, though the other three donkeys seemed to be rather calmer than their human owners.

The centurion hammered on the gate with his spear-butt. "Hey!" he shouted. "Herakles! Open the fucking gate, will you?"

Perennius knew this time to expect the lift which the woman gave him when she straightened. The agent swung over and down into the courtyard in a single arc, his right hand pivoting on the top of the wall to swing him past. It might have been smarter to pause for an instant and make sure that the wall was not faced with spikes or sharpened flints. At this juncture, the agent thought he could better afford the injury than the loss of time. He hit the ground upright with his knees flexed against the shock.

There was some motion across the courtyard, but he ignored it as he ran to the heavy bar of the gate. The—call it a roar—was sounding again. It was noticeably louder, even through the thick timbers of the gate.

"Legate! Perennius!" Sestius screamed. Gaius and Sabellia were shouting something too. "Legate!"

Perennius put his shoulder under the bar and used his knees to lift. The bar was of iron-bound oak. It was not really meant to be worked by a single man. In his present state of directedness, the agent could have lifted it with one hand.

The leaves of the door knocked Perennius backward. They were driven by Sabellia's donkey, bolting through the first hint of an opening despite anything the rider could do. Perennius' own donkey and Calvus', the latter streaming the tags of broken reins, slammed in after the Gallic woman. Gaius followed. He was actually controlling the donkey he rode. He had drawn his spatha in his right hand and was looking back over his shoulder.

The dragon that was charging them drew Perennius' stare also. The agent threw his weight against a gate leaf even before Sestius and Calvus had run inside. The mass of the panels meant a delay before even Perennius' strength could start them swinging closed again. That alone was more delay than he liked to think about.

More hands joined Perennius, those of his party and a tall, fair man the agent had never seen before. The leaves slammed against the stop carved in the inner face of the stone lintel. The stranger was screaming in Latin, "The bar! The bar!" It was Perennius who first spun to grip the bar where it had fallen, but Calvus plucked it from his hands and banged it home in the slots. The dragon hit the gate from the other side.

The really terrifying thing about the dragon was that it looked over the wall at them.

The creature had stridden down the hillside on its two hind legs. Now its forelimbs snatched at the humans scattering back from the gate. The hooked claws left deep triple scratches in the gate panels and the stone. The beast's eyes glittered like polished jet. Its scales were black and red—the latter not rusty mottling but the angry crimson of a cock's wattles.

Perennius opened his mouth to shout orders, everyone to hide in the gatehouse, lest the creature leap the wall or batter through with its elephantine mass. The dragon's jaws opened also, wide enough to engulf most of a man's torso. The beast gave its hunting cry. The sound was felt in its paralyzing intensity by everything in the echoing courtyard. One of the donkeys threw itself on its back and began kicking the air while its burden scattered. Other hooves battered at the reinforced doors of the stables. The dragon's breath stank like the air of a well-sealed tomb.

The open door of the common room sucked the humans out of the courtyard like water through a tap. The agent was not sure which of them had led the rush. Perhaps the idea had struck them all at the same time. Running the length of the courtyard was like charging through the zone beaten by hostile artillery, but that hundred foot distance was a necessary insulation. The gatehouse was simply too close to the monster.

The creature was forty feet long and as vicious, ounce for ounce, as a shrew. Even Gaius went scrambling at the roar. He had dismounted—landed on his feet, at any rate—and brandished his sword in the dragon's face. The courage involved in the action was both pointless and insane, so the sound that shook the youth to his senses did at least a little good. The six of them, Perennius' party and the stranger, bolted within the common room and closed the door. The dragon had begun chewing on the top of the wall.

It was close to pitch dark inside to eyes that had been under an open sky. The two men facing the newcomers were only figures in silhouette against the glow of the cookfire in a wall niche. The agent did not need the details he would get when his eyes adjusted, however, to read the others' stance as that of archers with their bows drawn.

"What in blazes *is* that thing?" Perennius asked. He threw his back to the door in a disarming pantomime of terror at the dragon outside. At the moment, the agent's greatest concern was for the arrow pointed at his midriff. It would not advance the situation to admit that, however.

"If it gets in, you bastards," said the man who had joined them at the gate, "it's your fault. Jupiter preserve us if it gets the horses. We'll *never* get clear of here on foot!"

"Where do you come from?" demanded one of the bowmen. Like the other speaker, his Latin had a pronounced Gallic accent. The head of his arrow was beginning to wobble with the strain of holding the bow fully drawn. The man relaxed slightly, a good sign but dangerous in case his fingers slipped while the weapon was still pointed as it was.

"Well, from Tarsus," the agent said. His companions were extending to either side of him along the wall of the room. The Gaul who had first spoken was sidling to join the archers. It was clear that if the stand-off exploded into violence, the three of them were dead even if the arrows hit home. "They talked about Typhon and dragons, but blazes! I had a wool contract and I don't make my living by listening to bumpf from silly women. But . . ." Perennius gestured back with his thumb, then added ingenuously, "You fellows part of a garrison from hereabouts?"

That the three of them were soldiers was as obvious as their Gallic background. Their professional bearing, bowstrings drawn to their cheeks; their issue boots; the youthful similarity of the men themselves—all bespoke army. The question was, whose army? And Perennius was beginning to have a shrewd notion of the answer to that one, too. The alleyway in Rome and the Gallic voices closing the end of it whispered through his memory.

"Slack 'em, dammit," grunted the first speaker. As the archers obeyed, he added, "Yeah, we were, ah, going on leave and this thing . . ." Then, "Magnus, Celestus—I'm going to check this goddam thing from the tower."

The arched doorway in a back corner led to the crenelated tower above the roof proper. Perennius stepped forward to join the Gallic—non-com was more likely than officer. "Gaius," the agent said, "you others—be ready to get the donkeys in if that thing moves away, right? Don't take chances, but we need to get them closed up or they'll draw him back themselves."

Perennius was off before either of the archers could decide to stop him. The agent's boots made precisely the same echoing clatter on the stairs as did those of the man in front of him. The meeting could not be pure coincidence, but the agent strongly hoped that it was not as—somcone, some *thing*, had planncd either.

The dragon was hissing into the courtyard at the donkeys. The sound was like that of flames in ripe wheat. The creature did not appear to notice the men rising behind the battlements of the tower, but something else invisible to them made it turn abruptly. "Have you tried shooting it?" the agent asked.

The Gaul snorted. "Do I look crazy?" he demanded. "This is how it acts when it's *not* pissed off!"

The dragon's turn was complicated by the length of the rigid tail which balanced the body. It did not spin as a man would have done. Instead, the creature backed as it rotated like a swimmer reversing at the end of a pool. The new object of its attentions veered into sight also. It was a donkey, the one Sestius had ridden. By now it had shed its saddle and all accoutrements. Instead of bolting into the courtyard with the remainder of the party, it had broken away and run around the building in panic.

The donkey might have been as safe behind the common room as it would be within the courtyard, but the madness to which the dragon's bellows had driven it did not permit the beast to halt there. When it galloped past the bath house at the south front corner of the complex, both donkey and dragon realized what had happened. The former vectored off braying, back up toward the main road. The dragon strode after it. As Perennius had found its power and savagery stunning when the creature roared and clawed at the wall, so its speed was a horrible augury for the agent's chances of being able to leave the inn and complete his mission.

The dragon moved its legs with the deliberation of a robin picking its way across a lawn. Distance and the absurdity of a biped on that scale permitted the strides to seem dainty, but each one thrust the body forward another ten feet. There was a serpentine grace to the movements. The neck and tail swung sideways in unison toward the leg lifting for each stride. When the clawed feet struck the ground, dirt and gravel blasted away in a volume that mocked the cloud raised by the donkey's frantic hooves.

The dragon reached its prey well short of the hilltop. It strode in parallel with the donkey for a moment, like a greyhound with the rabbit it is coursing. Then the great head dipped lower than balance alone would have required. The jaws hung open. The slam of their closing was like the sound of a marble statue hitting the ground. The donkey responded with a screech that had no semblance to the noises that living things make.

Inertia carried the dragon a further two steps. It tossed its head, spraying the air and its belly with a vast quantity of blood. The donkey was silent and flopping limp by now. The tossing did not tear loose the gobbet encircled by the great jaws.

The dragon stopped. It raised its head again and threw it from side to side while it gripped the carcass with its front claws. The forelimbs were powerful, but the size of the great hind legs made them look small by comparison. Muscles, tendons, and bone gave way with a ripping sound. The donkey, missing part of its pelvic girdle and hams, thudded to the ground.

The dragon's jaws unhinged like those of a great snake. Its head cocked skyward while the tongue and throat muscles combined to force the huge mouthful down the esophagus. The beast's nostrils made sucking sounds until the lump disappeared further downward and the jaws fitted themselves once more into their sockets. The dragon bent forward for another bite.

It was a shocking demonstration, but the Gaul looked more sickened than afraid. He felt the agent's eyes on him and read their expression. Gruffly, the Gaul explained, "There was four of us. Marcellus was late getting mounted like always. We'd hoped he might be joining us anyhow. Mithra!"

On the hill fronting the inn, a third of the full-grown donkey had already disappeared down the slayer's maw.

The Gaul ran a hand through his short, under-helmet haircut and went on, "Now this on top of that other. I swear, I don't know. . . ." He turned, eyeing Perennius more carefully while his fingers drummed the cross-guards of his spatha. "I'm Ursinus," he said. "Like you figure, we're soldiers." He did not mention his post or unit.

The agent nodded. "I'm Perennius," he said. "I've been other things, but I'm a wool buyer now." He frowned toward the dragon before adding in corroboration, "It can't have eaten *all* the sheep, but I don't suppose there's been much shearing going on lately. You been here long?"

"A day." Put like that, Perennius' question had not aroused suspicion. "Thought we could outrun it, even without remounts, if we travelled light. Mithra. Lay-over here, then ride on in the morning. Only it jumped us when we were watering the horses, and we beat 'em so hard for the next mile that hell, I don't know when I'll want to chance going out again. Plenty of food and fodder here, but not a soul. Not a goddam soul."

The dragon had finished its meal. It was a sloppy eater. Behind on the blood-splashed ground lay the donkey's head and left forequarters. The latter, at least, was meatier than some of the chunks the creature had bolted. The dragon wandered back up the hill with its tail swinging, as if the beast had forgotten the inn and those trapped there. Perennius was far from sure that was the case.

Judging from his expression, Ursinus was equally doubtful. "We thought it might leave us be if we kept hidden a couple days," the Gaul said. Then he added, echoing the statement an archer had thrown out in anger, "I hope by the Bull that your lot didn't convince it to stick around longer."

"It's fed now," the agent suggested mildly. He walked toward the spiral staircase again as if oblivious to the way the Gaul's fingers were toying again with his sword hilt. There was not enough room on the narrow stairs to draw the long spatha quickly. "Might be a good time for a break if your horses have had a day to rest."

Ursinus snorted as he fell in behind the agent. Their boots clicked and scuffled again on the stone treads. The Gaul's hand was relaxed again. "Right, with it south of the ford for sure we're supposed to ride past it. Not fucking likely, bud. And don't think one donkey's going to fill that bastard up, no. . . ."

The mortar had been less discolored than the stones by soot from the poorly-vented fires. The walls of the common room, curving upward to groins, were a latticework of pale on dark to Perennius as he stepped out of the stairwell again. He was in time to hear Gaius asking, "Say, you fellows were in Rome about a month ago, weren't you?"

The younger man had seen Perennius work. In the youth's ignorance, he thought he was duplicating the agent's subtlety. He should never have done that on his own hook, and even he should have realized that the question identified the asker as surely as the answer could have done the Gauls.

"It's them!" shouted one of the archers, out of Perennius' sight beyond a pillar.

Somebody else would have to handle that, the agent thought. Behind him he heard the rattle and curse of Ursinus trying to clear his spatha and jarring his elbow on stone. It was Perennius' own damned fault. He knew that Gaius was smart enough to connect these Gauls with the earlier ambush . . . and he should have known that Gaius was too inexperienced to keep from blurting the connection in his pride.

Ursinus was good. Reflex had tangled his arms with a sword half-drawn in the strait stairway, but the Gaul met Perennius' lunge with a kick. The agent had not delayed to draw a weapon of his own. He had thought he would be on Ursinus before the Gaul could respond effectively. Now Perennius did the best he could, grabbing the bigger man's foot even as Ursinus tried to hop back around the core of the helical staircase.

Perennius had underestimated the Gaul once. Now it was Ursinus' turn to think he could surprise his opponent by leaping toward him instead of trying to pull away. Perennius had the advantage of being at the base of the stairs with all the room he needed to maneuver the flying Gaul. The agent stepped back and kept Ursinus' right leg rising. The Gaul hit the floor on his shoulders and left hand, unwilling to release his sword to take some of the shock with his right arm too. The crash did not stun Ursinus, but it left him open for Perennius' hob-nailed kick to the head.

The agent drew his own sword and dagger. He put the sword into Ursinus' chest with a swift lunge that ended when the point jarred against the stone beneath the Gaul. The killing was a judgment call that Perennius did not especially care to make . . . but the fight was not over, and Ursinus had proven himself too damned good to be put out of it by a quick boot. Perennius tugged the blade free without examining the damage. He was running toward the sounds of fighting from the far end of the big room.

One of the Gauls was crumpled in the central bay over an arrow nocked too late to be used. The agent did not have to guess who had cut the man's throat so deeply that only the spine and the cartilaginous windpipe kept the lolling head attached to the body. Gaius and Sestius crouched to either side of a pillar. Their swords angled up, threatening the archways that opened into the final bay. Fanned back from the pillar which hid the remaining Gaul were Sabellia and Calvus. Sabellia held her bloody knife advanced. Her legs were splayed, her knees cocked to launch her toward the Gaul if he showed himself. Calvus held a spear awkwardly. The tall woman eyed Sabellia as if hoping to gain pointers from the red-head.

"Hold it!" Perennius shouted as he burst into the central bay.

"Now!" cried Sestius. He and Gaius rushed the hidden Gaul from either side.

Perennius heard the bow-string snap. He did not hear the arrow strike, and he knew what that meant. If the arrow had missed—and men do miss point-blank shots when no prize but life itself is at stake—the iron head would have smashed and sparked clearly on the rock walls. There had been no need of risk. The isolated Gaul could have been talked out, waited out; at worst, charged by men wearing the armor packed on the donkeys outside. Anything would have been more sensible than the present melange of shouts and swords glittering in overarm cuts.

The pillar still hid the sword-wielders and their victim from Perennius as he ran to the slaughter.

The Gaul was sprawled on his face. He had dropped his bow. Apparently he had tried to cover his head with his arms instead of drawing his sword. Sestius slashed a final time at the man. The centurion's heavy blade thunked deep enough into the skull to stick when he tried to remove it. Gaius was still thrusting into the Gaul's abdomen.

Sestius straightened and turned, leaving his sword where it was. The fletching and half an arrow's length protruded from his chest, well-centered and between the second and third ribs. Only a drop or two of blood had seeped onto the centurion's tunic around the shaft. When he opened his mouth to speak or gasp for breath, the blood spewed out. It splashed the stone floor an instant before Sestius' body fell to cover the splotch. The scream the centurion could not voice for choking burst from Sabellia's lips instead.

Perennius caught Gaius by the wrist. "You're all right?" the older man demanded. Gaius' eyes were glazed, but he bore no obvious signs of injury. He did not answer Perennius. Instead, he leaned on his sword as if it were a cane.

Sabellia was weeping and mopping at the blood on Sestius' face. She was probably unharmed. It wasn't the time to check that, anyway. Calvus anticipated the agent's question, nodding as soon as the agent's eyes fell on her. "Nothing touched me," she said. Then she added, "They were part of the group that attacked us in Rome."

"I guess everybody's figured that out," said the agent bitterly. He turned back toward the younger Illyrian. "If Gaius'd kept his mouth shut, we might even've learned why. Well, maybe we can. . . ."

Ursinus was not dead. He had rolled over, but he had been unable to summon enough strength to rise to his hands and knees. He saw Perennius coming, trailed by the tall woman. The Gaul made another attempt to rise. It too failed. His lips blew a froth of blood. The hole in his chest was making liquid, sucking sounds as Ursinus tried to breathe. He spat, drooling a line of blood and saliva down his chin.

"It's over, Ursinus," the agent said. "We're going to help you now."

"Bastard," the Gaul whispered. "Don't you think *I* know it's over?" But he relaxed none the less, letting the tension go out of arms that had trembled as they failed to lift him.

"Get some wine," Perennius hissed in an aside to Calvus. To the dying man, the agent said, "Were you supposed to ambush us here, then?"

Ursinus coughed red-shot phlegm that the agent wiped away with the hem of his own tunic. "Mithra," the Gaul said. He forced a smile. "We were running away. One of the things what was giving us orders had its mask slip. Hell if I was going to stick around after that, dragon be damned. Not if God offered to come down and wash me in blood." It was an unfortunate expression and brought on another fit of coughing.

"Gray?" Perennius asked. Calvus was back with a skin of wine. The agent held the open end to Ursinus' lips, letting the Gaul suck greedily at it while the agent squeezed the skin for him. "A band around it and a hole the size of a cow's bung near the top?"

"Oh . . ." the Gaul moaned as he took his mouth away from the flask. His eyes were closed. "You think you're going to join them, then?"

"We're here to kill them, Ursinus," the agent said in a level voice. He daubed at the Gaul's face again. "How many of them are there?"

Ursinus ignored the question if he even heard it. "More guts than I've got, then," the Gaul murmured. "Just wanted to get the fuck away, way from dragons and crinkly monsters that talk. . . . Mithra." His eyes opened. "Sacrovir stayed," he said. "Didn't care what it was, he wanted the guy who'd killed his mother. We followed him here after it all went sour in Rome, but . . . I said—" The Gaul's eyes bulged as if he were straining to swallow some object so great that it was choking him.

"Easy, easy," the agent said.

It was too late for ease, too late for Ursinus entirely.

The Gaul's arms and legs began to flail on the stone as he gagged. The movements swelled into a mad, unsynchronized fury as Ursinus' eyes went blank. His back strained into the arc of his last convulsions.

Perennius swore. He stood up. The agent had seen enough people die. He did not need to watch another.

Gaius caught the older man's arm. "Blazes, Aulus," he said. "Q-quintus is gone. It was so quick, one minute and then . . ." Gaius too had seen his share of dying, but this time it was a peer and a man he had come to know well. The youth was aware also that Fortune had made the archer left-handed. Otherwise the shaft would have been past the other side of the pillar and through Gaius' pulmonary arteries instead of those of the centurion.

Perennius gripped the shoulder of the younger man— the boy, in this persona. The agent shouted, "Sure he's gone! And it's your big mouth that killed him, isn't it?"

Even the sputtering fire could only suggest color on Gaius' cheeks. "I didn't—" he said. He tried to jerk his shoulder away and found he could not, no more than he could have pulled free a decade before. Perennius' red, shouting rage was only a suggestion of the murder that already strained to supplant it.

"You didn't think!" the agent shouted. He shook the tall youth to the harsh rhythms of the words. "You shot off your mouth, handed them who we were on a platter— what *else* was going to happen when they learned that? We could've *all* been greased in a rat-fuck like that! Couldn't we? Couldn't we? And now there's Sestius lying there—"

The rigid expression of Gaius' face, anger and horror molded on an armature of innocence, gave way. The young Illyrian's free arm had been rising as if to strike a blow or fend one off. The arm encircled Perennius' waist as Gaius fell sobbing to his knees. "Oh god, Aulus!" he cried, "I did kill him. Oh god, oh god!"

Perennius staggered. His skin was as clammy as if he had been douched with melt water. The great vaulted room sprang into entire focus again. "Blazes," the agent whispered. Then he said, "I'm going. . . ."

Gaius was not holding him tightly. Perennius stepped

away from the other's kneeling figure, the motion bringing only redoubled sobs. Perennius walked to the door to
the courtyard. He was tottering with reaction. He stepped
outside; and he was standing there, breathing deeply with
his back to the wall, when Calvus joined him a moment
later.

"I told you to keep out of my mind," Perennius whispered. His eyes were closed. "Saw you standing there like
a statue . . . Might've killed him, Calvus. *Me.* Might've
killed him except for you."

"In some ways he's very young," the woman said.
"Younger than his age."

"It's the pretending it just . . . 'happens,' " the agent
went on. He was looking at the empty courtyard now.
"They didn't do it. Sure, we all screw up . . . and this is a
business that you screw up, maybe somebody gets dead.
But if you pretend you didn't do it, the arrow was Fate or
Fortune or any damn thing but a kid talking . . . I thought
he was going to say it wasn't his fault. And then I might've
killed him."

"Don't confuse what men say with what they mean,
Aulus Perennius," Calvus said.

"I don't—" the agent rasped back.

"No, you don't," the tall woman responded more sharply
than Perennius had ever heard her speak before. "You
take those lies as a personal slur on your intelligence. And
you know they aren't! They're the prayer of somebody
human that the world not tell him something he already
knows. You've watched Gaius. Do you think he *really*
doubts he was responsible for what happened?"

"He shouldn't lie to me," Perennius muttered.

"He didn't," Calvus said, "and he didn't lie to himself."

The agent looked at her. "Yeah," he said. He took Calvus'
hand loosely in his own. "Ah. Thanks."

Calvus smiled at him. Her expression was still untrained
but now real. "Aulus Perennius," she said, "I didn't touch
your mind. I promised you. Even if I thought you were
wrong, I wouldn't have gone back on that promise. To
you. I don't trust my instincts that far, you see."

"Blazes, *you* don't have to lie," Perennius said with a

David Drake

return of his earlier anger. "Look, I *saw* you, you did what you had to, and I want to for*get* it."

"He felt guilty," the woman said. "He wanted to admit it, but he was young. Pride and embarrassment, you can understand. But he wanted so desperately to ask forgiveness that it didn't take much of a, well, nudge." Calvus was still smiling.

"The hell you say," Perennius said mildly. "Well. Not that it mattered." He cleared his throat. "Besides the Guardians, we've got that dragon to take care of now, don't we? And one man."

"An allosaurus," Calvus agreed. They were both looking across the courtyard. The fresh scarring near the gate was evident even in twilight. "The dragon is an allosaurus, that is."

"Umm," the agent grunted, accepting the datum. Hydra, chimaira, allosaurus . . . it didn't much matter. After a moment he said, "Blazes, I wonder if there's some truth in the old stories after all. Hercules and women turning into trees and everything? Well, we'll handle it, however things shape up."

The door swung open again. Both faced around quickly. The agent took a half step to see past Calvus. Sabellia stepped out. Her eyes were reddened but dry. "Our gear's in with the animals," she said, nodding to the block of stables. Four more doors were barred shut than had been when the party looked in from the hillside. "I'll get a meal together. Those—others were just boiling porridge."

"Right, I'll give you a hand," said the agent. He looked away from Sabellia as he spoke. "Need to see to the horses, too, it seems." They began walking toward the stables in parallel, though they were not precisely in concert.

"I was raised to believe in an ordered, understandable universe, Aulus Perennius," Calvus called after the agent. "I think that I am coming to believe in heroes as well."

CHAPTER THIRTY

"Blazes, this is going to be awkward," said Gaius as he held up the mesh gauntlet. Even with the fireplace niche stoked high, the lighting of the common room was more an occasional absence of shadow than good working illumination. The room's volume and blackened stone saw to that.

"I'm coming too," said Sabellia. She did not raise her head or her voice.

"Awkward, but the only thing I see working with that many of them, Guardians, and the way the land lies," Perennius said with a shrug. He lifted the facemask from one of the sets of parade armor.

"Listen, there's three horses!" the red-haired woman said loudly. "You're not going to leave me here!"

"You stay here, like you've been told," Perennius said. Sabellia's mouth opened for a retort. The agent overrode it, shouting, "There aren't three bloody sets of armor, are there? Just what the hell good do you figure to do getting wasted the first time they shoot? You didn't *see* what that does to a man. Believe me, it's quick and it's final, just as final as it comes."

The woman's set look gave way to dejection though not despair. "Oh, I know, Aulus," she said softly. "It's just . . . there's another of the gang there, you say, the ones who killed Quintus. I—I'd like that one. God, I wish you'd brought another suit of this. God I do."

"You don't know what it took to get just these," the agent remarked. He held the mask to his face where it

303

covered his judicious expression. The difficulty had been less the intrinsic value of the parade armor than the question of how the prefect would report the loss of the armor to his superiors. The masks were cast of bronze to a pattern of plump-featured male beauty, then silvered for dazzling effect. The back-piece laced to each mask covered the rest of the wearer's head. Because the back-pieces were of brass rather than bronze, they could be polished to a sheen that the sun would turn golden.

For present purposes, the look of the armor was not as significant as the fact that the ensemble cased the whole head of the person wearing it. There were two tiny holes for the pupils of the eyes, and an air passage replacing the nostrils and septum of the large, hooked nose. Calvus had said that the mask might work, but at no point should metal touch the wearer's skin.

"Here, give me that," Sabellia said. She had already trimmed backing pads for one set of greaves. Now she whet her knife, using spittle and the stone that was a part of Perennius' baggage even when he was travelling light. The greaves were silvered also. The low-relief figures of Mars and Goddess Rome on them were parcel gilt to set them off. The prefect had parted with them and the helmets only for an equal weight of solid silver from the pirates' loot. Perennius did not know whether the man planned to use part of the massive bribe to square his superiors in Palmyra, or whether he simply intended to desert and keep the whole amount for himself.

Sabellia began cutting deftly at the piece of hide. The agent's own attempt had been too small to cover the interior of the mask. The blank Perennius had cut did not allow enough overage to fill the mask's face-following concavity. Sabellia trimmed with only an occasional glance at the arrogant metal visage turned up beside her.

It struck Perennius how unusual the group was in its attitude toward the valuables to which they had fallen heir on the bloody strand. The agent had promptly appropriated the wealth to the purposes of the mission. It had not even occurred to him to do otherwise. Gaius had accepted that without comment, both because his protector had so decided and because his own longings were toward a sort of heroic glory which had little to do with wealth.

Sestius had been after the security which grew from land and family. The centurion would not have been averse to abandoning the mission and dividing the bullion, but he was too good a soldier to press for that; and anyway, wealth was not his first priority. Sestius had gotten another kind of security, but that had been awaiting him in any event—on his farm or wherever his choices took him. Sabellia's hopes might have been directed prosaically on her man, or at some higher spiritual plane on the religion which she had emphasized only when they entered the valley of cultists. Perennius was inclined to doubt that the woman was as simple as either of those focuses would imply; but whatever was in her secret heart, it was not a love of wealth for itself.

And Calvus. In this at least, Perennius thought he saw himself in the tall woman. Objects and occurrences were good or bad depending on how they affected the success of the mission.

But as surely as Perennius recognized that, he recognized that a more human side was developing in the woman's character. Just as he knew it was appearing in his own. "Blazes," he muttered. His three companions looked at him. Calvus was smiling.

The footsteps up the stairs were quiet, but they would have awakened Perennius even if he had been able to get to sleep. They paused.

"Come on up," the agent called. He did not turn his head.

"I thought you must be asleep," Sabellia said as she walked out onto the top floor of the watch tower.

Perennius was wrapped in his cloak with his back to one wall of the parapet. The high curtain of clouds had thinned enough that the moon was a noticeable glow in the heavens. There were no stars. The agent shook back his cowl when Sabellia settled carefully on the dewy stones beside him.

"Thought it might be a good place to get some sleep tonight," Perennius said. He looked at the woman, then motioned around the tower with his eyes. "Reminds me too much of back when I was a kid on guard duty, though. I just dozed, waiting for Franks to hit the palisade."

The cloak Sabellia wore was the one a pirate had given her while she gathered herbs and poison. The brown wool was the same soft shade as her hair, since the light was too faint to show colors. "It's going to be dangerous tomorrow," the woman said. Her sandals peeked out beneath the hem of the cloak. Her hands kept the garment tight about the rest of her body.

Perennius shrugged. "It's always dangerous," he said. He met her eyes and added, "I'm sorry about Quintus. I—wouldn't have had it happen that way if I'd planned a little better."

"I think he wanted to do something himself," the woman said, letting her eyes drift up toward the empty sky. "He was jealous, you know."

"Listen," the agent said. The statement had touched a sore point. "I may not be the best damned leader going, but I *am* in charge. I don't expect a lot of crap from centurions under me!"

"I don't mean that, Aulus Perennius," Sabellia said.

"Oh," Perennius said. He looked away, feeling foolish. "Well. I never gave him cause, I think."

"Maybe I did, then," Sabellia said. Her bare arm reached out to Perennius. He twisted clumsily to meet her. He was trapped by his own weight on the folds of his cloak. Sabellia's garment opened as her arms released the front hems. She wore nothing beneath the soft wool.

When Perennius cupped her breast, the woman shuddered. He cursed and jerked back, ashamed of his awkwardness and of forgetting the bruises and cuts that laced her torso.

"No, no, darling," Sabellia whispered. One of her arms drew his head down while the other caught his hand and pressed it back to the breast. "Not pain, no." Her flesh was firmer than he expected, and the nipple was already rising to meet his tongue.

Perennius had time to wonder whether Sestius had been given a similar send-off the night before. But that really did not matter.

CHAPTER THIRTY-ONE

"If this doesn't work," Perennius said, "the best I can suggest is you gather up people in Tarsus, archers, slingers. Artillery for the dragon. It'll take somebody as persuasive as you are, but it's better than trying it alone if we don't make it back." The agent was aware that the bronze facemask muffled his voice to those outside while it made the words echo in his own ears. His voice was hollow, as hollow as he felt the words themselves to be.

Perennius' headgear was hot, heavy, and almost blinding. He bent over at the waist, directing his eyeholes like weapons at Calvus as she lifted up the bar of the gate. Perennius could not see what her expression was as she said calmly, "They'll probably use area weapons, despite the traces that would leave for the future to find. They wouldn't do that in Rome or even Tarsus, because there'd be too many surviving witnesses to pique the curiosity of a later age. Out here ... if they think they know where I am, they'll risk a few acres of glazed earth so long as it's an anomaly in the wilderness rather than a disaster more riveting than Pompeii." The gate began to creak open as Calvus pulled at it.

"Still clear," called Sabellia from the roof of the gate house. The dragon, the allosaurus, patrolled a broad territory. The best way Perennius had come up with to deal with the monster was to avoid it. Riding north while the beast was still to the south of the inn was a good way to achieve that end. Perennius wasn't a hero. Heroes gained fame and medals for the chances they took. Aulus Perennius had instead a reputation for getting the job done. If he had any regret about that fact, it was that the job he wished to do more than anything else was to save the Empire. That was beyond him as it was beyond every man. And perhaps beyond all men, the agent thought in the gloom of his nightmares.

"Blazes, we'll be back," Perennius said. He pressed his horse with his heels. "Don't guess there'll be a better time," he called to Gaius. "Let's do it."

The younger man obviously did not hear the instruction. Neither did he see that Perennius had ridden off until the agent was a length ahead. Then Gaius kicked his own mount forward with a clatter, pulling abreast of Perennius in the easy canter the agent had chosen until external influences forced their pace. Gaius rejoined just as Perennius realized that they had been separated.

The masks made vision just as difficult as they did hearing. Perennius had bought gorgets and shirts of leather-padded chain mail, standard heavy-cavalry issue, at the same time he acquired the parade greaves and helmets. The gorget in particular made it very uncomfortable to swivel his head the way the narrow field of view required. "I know this's got problems, these masks," he said to Gaius in the raised voice they needed to hear one another, "but I'm more afraid of the Guardians than I am the lizard. The rigs take so damn long to lace together. . . ."

"Oh, I . . ." the courier said. "I didn't—I mean, I wasn't thinking of taking it off or anything."

Gaius had almost added "sir." Perennius could hear it in the abject tone. That hurt worse than a blow would have. It hurt the more so because it was a reaction which the agent had over the years tried to stamp into just about everyone else he had known. "Look," he began. He realized his voice was an inaudible murmur and went on louder, "Look, Gaius, all my life I've been telling myself it's all right to lose my temper. It's not all right. I know it's not. I apologize, and I swear by—by the Goddess Rome that I'll never do it again, at least with you."

Gaius twisted to face the agent as squarely as the four-pommeled military saddle would allow. The silvered bronze hid his face, but the courier's surprise was evident in his

stance. He knew that Perennius had as little belief in the
formal gods of the State as he did in any of the Oriental
cults that had been appealing to the more superstitious of
Rome for the past five centuries. Gaius knew also that
Perennius would willingly die before he trivialized Roma,
the personification of the Empire. "I, I deserved it, Aulus,"
the youth said awkwardly. "I did what you said. I killed
him."

Perennius felt cooler and more supple than he had in
months. The merely physical discomfort of the gear he
wore was forgotten. "Gaius," he said, "when you screw
up as often as I've done and as bad as I've done, then
maybe I'll have a right to shout at you. As for what
happened, well . . . we needed these horses—" he patted
the shoulder of his mount—"so it was going to come to
that. I figure we got off about as cheap as we were going
to. Those Gauls were pros. You and Quintus were damned
fools to rush the last one that way, but Quintus was a big
boy. Only thing I care about is that you learn from what
happened so the next time you screw up some new way."
The agent smiled, forgetting that the other man could not
see his face. "The way I do."

Gaius nodded vigorously, causing his equipment to jingle.
"Aulus," he said, "I will. I swear I'll make you proud of
me. I swear by—" and he had sense enough to swallow
the next thought without voicing it.

"Blazes, friend, you have made me proud," said Perennius. And he was quite serious.

They paused at the crest. "Wouldn't hurt to water the
horses," Gaius said as he noticed the rivulet they would
have to ford at the bottom of the hill. "I wonder if we
dare take a sip or two ourselves?"

The question was hesitant. A drink would require them
to unlace the masks. It would have been possible to cut
and hinge the face-covering so that the wearers *could*
drink—as the sun and their constricting gear made almost imperative—but Perennius had not thought of that.
Perhaps one of the others had, but the agent had made
the plan so intensely his own that no one else had—or
had dared—offer significant suggestions.

That was one of the things Perennius was kicking himself about. There were others. "Good idea," the agent said
after a moment's consideration. "I'd been sort of hoping
they'd have an outpost or the like short of the hole.
Try these out." He slapped his body armor with his chain-
gauntleted hand. "With one or two of them, I mean. If it's
going to be all five at once, I think we'd better chance—
getting undressed for not being parched when we hit
them." The agent made a quick sweep of the horizon. He
turned his body to the right, then to the left as far as the
saddle permitted.

Gaius clucked his own horse forward, down the trail.
Perennius recalled something Ursinus had said while they
watched the donkey being killed. "It jumped us when we
were watering the horses. . . ." Instead of following his
companion, the agent tugged his horse's head around. By
turning the animal, he had a full view of their back-trail
despite the constricting gear. "Fucking whoreson," Perennius muttered.

Half a mile behind them, hunching over the previous
ridge as if following a scent trail, was the black and
crimson figure of the allosaurus.

Perennius' horse saw the great hunter at the same time
its rider did. The horse froze momentarily. The agent's
quick tug at the reins became a vicious yank as he felt
himself balked. "Ride!" he shouted as he spurred the horse.
"Bastard's after us!"

Gaius had not had time to react to the warning before
the dragon's savage cry echoed around them both.

The road was wide enough for two horses abreast under
normal circumstances. At their present headlong gallop,
Perennius thought it better to follow Gaius than to attempt to close on him. The call of their pursuer was a
better spur than anything on a rider's heels, but the cry
was driving the horses to the limits of their footing. They
were following a country track hacked along hillsides,
rather than a well-laid military road. Perennius was a
competent rider but not a brilliant one. Now he braced
himself with one hand on a fore-pommel to keep from
sliding onto the horse's neck as they pounded downhill.

Ahead of them, Gaius' mount leaped the narrow creek

without slacking or wetting its hooves. Perennius knew the limits of his own ability too well to risk prodding his own horse into a similar jump. A trick that was simple if executed with proper timing would be skidding disaster if that timing were off. As it was, one of the horse's unshod hooves did turn on a smooth stone. There was an explosion of spray and a heart-stopping moment for the rider. Only Perennius' iron grip on the saddle kept him from high-siding. That would have left him stunned in the creek as the monster bore down. The agent swayed drunkenly. As his horse bolted up the rise, he was forced to drop the reins and clutch the pommels with both armored hands.

The men would not have had the opportunity to check on their pursuer even had they not been encumbered by the metal they wore. The beast's gurgling roar burst over them redoubled as the horses were only starting to gallop up from the creek. The dragon had crested the rise from which they had first seen it. That meant that it was covering at least three feet of ground to every two of theirs. Perennius had assumed that nothing as huge as the allosaurus could keep up a high rate of speed for more than a short spurt. The truth was a draining surprise.

Ursinus had been wrong. He and his two companions had not escaped because they outrode their pursuer. They had been saved by the sacrifice of the fourth member of their party. It was as brutally simple as that. And with the same horses burdened by men in full armor, there could be no question at all of how the present race would end unless the riders found a haven which their speed could not vouchsafe them.

Gaius charged over the rise, by now three lengths ahead of the agent. The younger man tried to wheel his horse to face the monster. Perennius, half-blind from sweat and frustration, almost rode into him. Gaius was drawing his spatha. "*Ride you idiot!*" the agent screamed. He was aware that Gaius must be speaking also and that both of them were barely able to hear their own voices over the cry of the allosaurus.

Perennius' mount had checked no more than required to veer around its fellow. They were on a rolling pasture of brush and sheep-cropped grass. Four hundred feet ahead of them was the near rim of a sinkhole, the mouth of Typhon's Cavern. A quarter mile beyond, with the rose and saffron of its rocks standing out against the dusty vegetation above it, was the far rim of the gorge.

The great gap in the earth stretched half a mile to either side. The eastern end was blocked from sight by a range of knobby outcrops, while the road wound around the western end of the rim. There was a separate track worn more by sheep's hooves than human deliberation. It plunged straight toward the gorge's south rim. Perennius lashed his horse in that direction instead of trying to skirt the cavity. The agent had Sestius' description of the site to guide him. The horse was too wild with fear to know or care that it was being driven toward a gulf.

The situation was out of control. Perennius knew he did not even rule the horse he rode. The agent's input was tolerated because the animal was not consciously aware that it was being driven forward instead of to the left. The agent had hoped that they would be able to deal with the Guardians in scattered pickets along the way. If that did not occur, then he had intended to reconnoitre the gorge at leisure, seeking a path to its floor besides the one switching back and forth along the south wall. Sestius had claimed there was no other path because the lips of the cavity overhung the floor elsewhere around the edge. Perennius had still hoped that care and the long rope lashed to each man's saddle would provide access in secrecy.

Right at the moment, Perennius' greatest hope was that the allosaurus would not be able to turn sharply enough when it blundered through the screening brush and confronted the sinkhole. The agent was quite certain that his own mount would plunge over the side. And Perennius was more than doubtful that he would be able to leap clear himself.

A figure rose from the cover of a ragged succulent. It wore a hooded cloak of blue so dark as to be black. Though the figure was little more than a shadow in a blur of sweat and dust to Perennius, the object it held and aimed glittered.

The world went red. Perennius' skin had crawled with

prickly heat. Now his whole body contracted with what its surface told it was a bath of ice. The agent's ears rang at a frequency high enough to be a perception rather than a sound. The ringing filled his head so completely that even the call of the dragon only strides away was swept into nothingness. All over Perennius' body, hair sprang up against his clothing with a violence that moved the iron-sheathed leather.

The agent was not shot off his mount. The horse, goaded by the crash and glare above it, hurled itself in an insane caracol. Even if Perennius had been fully aware, he was not horseman enough to have kept his seat amid that fury. Battered, his senses stunned by the ride and the discharge that turned him into a momentary flare, the agent sailed off when his mount shifted from beneath him. Perennius was unwitting of the fact until he hit the ground in a spray of dust and clangor.

The air stank of ozone and charred leather. The thongs that held the mask to the back of Perennius' helmet burned through when the mask took the point of the Guardian's blast. A rosette was seared across the silver facing. At the tips of the rosette, the brass back-piece and the iron gorget still shimmered as they cooled. Perennius' eyelashes had been burned away. At the moment, the agent was not sure that he was alive at all. His vision had tumbled dizzyingly from the mask's near blindness, through a red flare that was a result of direct nerve stimulation rather than sight, to the unmasked dazzle of a bright Cilician day. Nothing quite registered yet in his mind.

Gaius leaped his horse over Perennius' prostrate body. The beast was a white-bellied blur above the fallen man as the Guardian fired again. The air sizzled with the corona enfolding the young rider. His out-thrust sword roared with the cascade of sparks pouring from its point and double edges. Gaius lost neither his seat nor control of his mount. The horse gathered itself and sprang again as its rider's heels demanded. The Guardian made a high, keening sound nothing like the syllables which had come from the vocalizer of the thing in Rome.

The tip of Gaius' spatha split the cowled head as the horseman charged on by.

Reflex raised Perennius to join the battle his intellect was still too disoriented to comprehend. As the agent's shoulders lifted from the ground, the long-taloned leg of the striding allosaurus brushed him aside. Gaius' mount was skidding over the edge of the chasm. The monster's jaws slammed so close behind the horse that a fluff of long tail-hairs scattered from the edge of the carnivore's jaws. Dust, gravel, and the dragon followed the young Illyrian over the side.

Perennius wore over eighty pounds of armor and equipment. His thigh wound pinched him even at rest. The agent had been enervated by fear and the ride, then stunned by the shot he had taken and his fall. When he saw Gaius ride into the gorge with the dragon following, Perennius rolled to his feet. There is a limit to how long a man can live on his nerves. Aulus Perennius would reach that limit when he died on his feet.

The rim of the sinkhole had been undercut by the hungry ground waters. One of the earth-slips to which Cilicia is prone had shaken down much of the south wall into a jumble on the chasm's floor. The slope that resulted was steep, but at least it had some outward batter. Perennius ran to the edge without pausing for the tentacled thing that sprawled in his path. The edge of Gaius' sword had volatized with the energy it had sprayed back into the atmosphere. The weapon struck the Guardian as a blunt, glowing bar. It had the weight of a horse and armored rider behind it. The creature's conical head was not sheared but caved in. Shards of gray chitin were trapped in a magenta gelatine.

There were three more Guardians toiling up the trail toward the rim. They wore no masks or disguises, only their gray exoskeletons and a shimmering array of tools. The alarm that summoned them had been a little too late. It was unlikely that they were prepared for what came sliding down the slope toward them.

The trail itself slanted broadly to the right for several hundred feet before it cut back in the other direction. Gaius, whooping and still astride his horse, ignored the trail. He blasted gravel straight downslope toward the pair of Guardians a level below him. The gradient was one to one, too steep for real control given the gallop that had taken man and mount onto it. It was not quite abrupt enough to make the descent a fall rather than a ride.

Horse and horseman bathed in a roaring dazzle. The Guardians had neither the desire nor the ability to direct their bolts at the man alone as their shattered fellow had done on the chasm's edge. The mane and tail of the horse flared out and burned. The powerful neck and shoulders withered as if they were at the core of a furnace. Shattered bone ends protruded from the carcase which was otherwise charred too black and dense to be seen as from an animal. It plummeted between the two leading Guardians, taking brush and a hail of limestone with it as it rolled toward the chasm's floor.

Gaius' long iron shirt flashed brighter and whiter than the sun in the instant the alien bolts gnashed at it. The spatha folded back on itself as if its blade were wax and not steel. Gaius flew forward, separating from the horse whose forequarters had been devoured beneath him. His armor glowed red and then red on black as air quenched the thousands of spot-welded wires which comprised the mail. Stiff as a statue and surely as unknowing, Gaius skidded until he hit a trio of mulberry trees, eighty feet below the rim.

No one, not even Perennius, was watching Gaius. The dragon was on top of the leading pair of Guardians.

For something that weighed as much as a yoke of oxen, the beast had incredible agility. It could not avoid the abrupt descent, but even as inertia carried its leading right foot over the side, its tail was swinging around. That long, cartilage-stiffened member was the lever by which the allosaurus pivoted its mass. As the beast slid into the chasm, it was already twisting broadside, cat-quick, to scrape itself to a halt in the shortest possible time. The allosaurus was not intelligent, but its nervous system housed bundles of reflexes as finely honed as ever an assassin's razor. The pair of gray, chitinous things on the ledge where its claws slashed for purchase were no more of an incident than the creosote bushes shredded in the same instant.

Perennius made his own reflexive judgment. He leaped

over the side himself. The price of being wrong was death, but that was nothing new.

The dragon came to a skidding halt on the trail, facing the third Guardian at a distance of twenty feet. One of the beast's three-clawed forelegs was extended up-hill. It clutched an outcrop at the end of a triple furrow in the thin sod. The jaws which had crushed their way through the bones and tough muscle of the donkey were open. The allosaurus had just begun its terrible, gulping cry when the Guardian's shot tore its head off.

The crackling discharge blew apart the beast's calvarium in an explosion of shrinking bone and expanding, gaseous nerve tissue. Its teeth shattered like glass as dentine responded to the induced heat. The dragon reacted like a beheaded chicken. Its hind legs thrust it forward in an uncoordinated lunge that spilled it off the trail and past the Guardian. The great beast began to roll sideways down the slope. It gathered speed as the angle steepened. The tail and neck flailed wildly, but the massive torso merely rotated faster and faster. The cream belly-scales alternated with the red-shot black of sides and back. Fifty feet above the floor of the chasm, an outcrop gave the huge carcass impetus enough to hurl it away from the wall. Limbs spasming with momentum and death reflexes, the dragon smashed down on the quake-strewn boulders which had preceded it into Typhon's Cavern.

The Guardian rotated on what might be a ball joint above its tripodal legs. It was raising to meet Perennius the weapon which had just ripped the allosaurus. The agent was skidding on his armor-protected left hip and shoulder. He kicked the creature off the trail and grappled with it as they rolled together after the dragon.

Perennius gripped with both his hands the tentacle holding the weapon. He squeezed and pulled as if he were disjointing a lobster to get at the meat in the claws. The rock and brush through which they careened meant nothing to him, would have meant nothing even if the iron and leather encasing him did not absorb much of the punishment. Rock gouted in a spray of splinters and quicklime as the weapon fired into the ground. Then Perennius held the creature in his left hand. His right hand flung away the weapon and the separated fragment of tentacle that still wrapped the glittering object.

Both combatants were brought up by a clump of holly. The bush had been flattened by the tons of dragon, but the stems had sprung up again in time to stop Perennius and his victim short of fifty sheer feet neither of them would have survived. The greave had been pulled from Perennius' right shin. His bare forehead was bleeding from a gash he could not remember getting. The Guardian's own flexible exoskeleton was dusty and abraded. Pores and the joint of head and segmented carapace were oozing a pink, waxy substance with an odor like that of bergamot. The creature had not made any sound, even when Perennius pulled it apart.

One of its remaining arms snatched a globular object that clung to its chitin like steel to a lodestone. Perennius watched the trebly-opposed fingers rotate the object toward his head while he tried to interpose his own arm. The agent's flesh moved far slower than the images of disaster which flickered through his brain. He saw his carcass burned or sawn apart, perhaps simply vanishing. . . .

The object struck his blood-matted hair and recoiled. The blow was no worse than a child could have delivered, scarcely noticeable to Perennius in his adrenalin-heightened state. The Guardian had no weapon beyond that hurled into the brush with its dripping limb attached. It was using in desperation some piece of gear as a hard object to arm its blows. That showed a courage that Perennius could have appreciated if he had been more nearly human at the time. As a response to what he was about to do, the blow was on a par with spitting in his face.

The agent stood up. He lifted the Guardian easily. The creature weighed some eighty pounds. The blows with which it pummeled him were light even in reference to its size. The exoskeleton that smoothly covered the alien's limbs had no room in it for muscles like those which bulged Perennius' arms. The agent knelt with his weight on his right knee and left foot. He lifted the creature over his head, holding it by one leg and the stump of the arm he had severed. Then, shouting in a bestial triumph, Perennius brought the alien down across the armored shelf of his braced left thigh as if he were breaking a bundle of reeds. The Guardian's thorax crackled in minuscule echo of the crashing discharge of its weapon seconds before. Fluids leaked and coated Perennius' knee stickily as he raised the creature for a second blow. Its legs and arms had gone limp. In a fit of revulsion, the agent instead flung the alien away from him. He watched it bounce down the wall of the chasm.

CHAPTER THIRTY-TWO

The sound that Perennius heard as the Guardian's corpse disappeared was the patter of a pebble against the rocks above him. The agent turned and looked up. The stone, no larger than a walnut, pinged on his mailed shoulder as it followed the earlier corpses into the sinkhole. No one was visible to Perennius at the rim above. He drew the short sword which still hung at his right hip despite the scrambling to which the agent had subjected his gear.

"Aulus?" called Sabellia's voice from the brink. "Where are you, Aulus?"

"Watch out," Perennius croaked. The sword in his hand felt heavier than it should, because of the ring mail clinging to and weighting his sword arm. The agent thought of stripping the armored gauntlets from his hands. "There's another one coming. I think it's human."

The figure striding up the trail was clearly human. There could have been no question had not so many other questions stalked into the agent's life so recently. The newcomer walked at a swinging pace despite his burden of armor and a long, six-sided shield. He did not attempt to run or to clamber up between switchbacks. The man was obviously smart enough to make sure that he was fresh when he reached the agent.

"You're alone, boy," Perennius called to the figure. The man was now only a hundred double-paces from the agent. The portion of trail between them was narrow, picked out by sheep for their convenience. Perennius was considering whether it would be to his advantage to retreat to a wider section of trail with more room for maneuver. "Let's talk about this."

"Sure, let's talk," the other man said. He had a spear but he dropped it to draw instead his long sword from its shoulder-belted scabbard. He continued to walk forward. "How do you like Rome, old man? Are you one of Gallienus' pimps? Maybe that's why he trusted you all this way out here."

Gallic accent, of course. Ursinus had called him Sacrovir, it must be the same one. "Hey, I've never been to Rome," the agent called. Blazes, his legs were too weak for fancy footwork. Even if the kid didn't know his business, Perennius was out of his depth now. The agent drew his dagger. He held the blade thumb-side for thrusting rather than heel-side to stab. "I was with a Fifth Legion patrol from Melitene. You helping these *monsters?*"

"I saw my mother after what you did to her," the young man said. He wore a mail vest whose waist and short sleeves were trimmed with leather in a zig-zag pattern. The shield had an iron boss and rim, but there was no insignia. The agent suspected the shield had been purchased somewhere nearby instead of being packed the length of Europe to get here. "Burned her alive when she wouldn't tell you what you wanted to know. When I got here, they told me you'd be coming."

The young Gaul was almost close enough to take Perennius out in a rush if the agent looked around. At least the bastard wasn't an archer, like the pair back at the inn. . . . "Who's 'they' who've been handing you such a load of crap?" Perennius demanded. He took a short step forward, then another. If he gave his attacker all the physical initiative, the younger man's charge would be overwhelming. Perennius' own scalp crawled as he glanced at the Gaul's shining helmet, bronze sheet stock stiffened with a frame of iron tubes beneath. Perennius' outfit had been chosen for protection, not for fighting. Certainly not for fighting humans. "You take the word of monsters?"

"By the gods, I *saw* my mother!" the young man shouted, and Sabellia came down the rocky slope at him naked but for her tunic. It failed as an attack because Sacrovir was too skillful, and it failed as a diversion because the agent was too sluggish to take advantage of it.

The young man pivoted. His shield rose to deflect the rain of pebbles that had warned him, then jolted up another inch to slam aside Sabellia with similar ease. The woman's knife sprang into the gorge. Sabellia took the initial shock on her chest and the arm outstretched to snatch at the youth's neck. Then her impetus brought her head and the pivoting shield-rim into contact. Her body spilled limply to the side of the trail. Dust and pebbles she had dislodged continued to fall as Sacrovir swung toward the agent in a loping rush.

The younger man covered the twenty feet between them in four strides. Perennius had a moment to wonder if the Guardians could somehow affect minds the way Calvus did. Though that was needless. Humans had been leaping to absurd conclusions for ages without needing outside influences.

Perennius blocked with his sword, not his dagger, the youth's first overarm slash. The agent wanted to try his opponent's strength before he trusted the lighter weapon in the place of the shield he lacked. The shock of the swords meeting made the agent stumble. His right side burned the way his whole torso had when the Guardian's bolt sizzled on his armor. Because Perennius was off balance, his dagger-stroke at the Gaul's knee would probably have missed even if the long shield had not buffeted the agent like a ram as he jabbed. Sacrovir knew how to use that shield.

The agent staggered backward. His opponent—younger, taller, fresher—cut at him sideways, holding his spatha waist high. Perennius stepped inside the blow. Perennius chopped at the Gaul's instep as the other man's wrist struck the agent's side. Perennius' sword gouged the shield when the other dropped it to interpose.

The sword-cut was a feint. Perennius' left hand and the dagger swung over the Gaul's outstretched sword arm. Sacrovir looked a good deal like Gaius, the agent thought, as his armed fist slammed against the base of the other's right ear.

It was not until the instant of jarring contact and the

brown eyes rolling upward that Perennius realized that
he had not killed the man who toppled away from him.
Perennius had struck with the knobbed pommel of his
dagger, not the point that would have grated lethally
through brain and blood vessels across the younger man's
skull.

It had happened very quickly, as it had to happen when
both opponents were so skilled and so determined. It had
happened too fast for conscious decisions. Perennius had
not killed, though it would have been as easy to do so.

The agent knelt at the feet of his sprawling opponent.
Sacrovir's left arm hung off the trail. The weight of his
shield was threatening to tug the supine body with it
further into the chasm. Perennius laid down his sword to
lift the iron-and-plywood shield. He laid it across the
torso of the youth it had been unable to protect.

A slab of stone that must have weighed six talents
hurtled to the valley floor. It was safely outward of the
trail and of the agent. Perennius looked up. Calvus,
her hands freed of the missile she had not thrown at the
Gaul, was descending the wall with ease. The woman's
awkwardness did not matter when each handhold locked
her as firmly as an iron piton to the limestone. Calvus
stepped down beside the agent while he was bending over
Sabellia. At full stretch, Calvus' limbs gave her the look of
a gibbon from one of the islands beyond Taprobane.

While Perennius struggled with his gauntlets, Calvus
ran a slim finger from the point of Sabellia's jaw, up the
reddening bruise, to the bloody patch on the Gallic
woman's cheekbone. "Nothing broken," the traveller said
softly. "Minor concussion, perhaps. Nothing too serious."
Then she said, "You did recognize him then? I didn't
think you would. Could. He'll be all right, too."

Perennius back-trailed her eyes from his own face to that
of the supine Gaul at whom she had glanced before
speaking. Sacrovir was snoring. There was a smear of
mucus with no sign of blood in it over the Gaul's moustache. "Him?" the agent said. He was puzzled, but the
matter was not important enough to spend time on now.

Perennius began to stand up. He was angry that the
motion required him to put down his left hand for support.

"From Rome, you mean? No, I didn't see any of them. He must be the Sacrovir that Ursinus talked about. When he died." In the same flat voice, the agent said, "I'm going to see Gaius now. The Sun has received the soul of a brave man."

"It'll be faster," said Calvus as the agent began to stumble down the trail, "if I lower you." She extended an arm and nodded downwards.

Perennius swallowed, then angrily stripped off his gauntlets. He flung them to the ground. The remainder of his padded armor was hellishly hot and confining, but it would take longer than the agent cared to spend to remove it. He looked at his protégé fifty feet below. Gaius moved only when the wind blew the trees against which he rested. "Calvus," he said. He extended his hand, stubby and tendon-roped and strong. "Swear to me that what we're doing is going to save the Empire if we succeed. Swear that."

Calvus took the agent's hand in her own, slim and stronger yet than that of the agent. She knelt and found a hold in the roots of an olive tree. Perennius swung out, dangling over the slope in her grasp. "That isn't true, Aulus Perennius," she said. "I can't—"

"Easy, I've got a foothold," Perennius said.

Calvus released the agent's hand with the same care with which she chose her words. "The Empire is doomed, gone," she said. "We have a chance to save humanity from these—others. But not in your day, Aulus Perennius. Not for fifteen thousand years."

Perennius made a sound in his throat. His face was deep in the tilted crevice which now supported him. Calvus could not see his expression. When Perennius looked back up at the woman, it was only to say, "All right, I can hold your foot till you've got a hold. Come down."

Calvus scrambled to obey. The agent said, "That isn't good enough, you know? I can't care about hum—there, sure, put your weight on it. I can't care about humanity. That's the pirates who raped Bella, that's a kid from Gaul who fights for gray things with arms like worms. That's not worth dying for, Calvus. That's not worth me bringing Gaius to be killed."

"Do you need my hand here?" Calvus asked. The lower end of the crevice was ten feet above the next switchback.

"No, I—" Perennius said. His hand gripped a spike-leafed shrub. The stem crackled when he put his weight on it. The agent felt Calvus' fingers link around his ankle, ready to support him if he started to slide. "That's all right," he said. Stiffly but under control, Perennius descended half the distance. When his hobnails missed their bite, he skidded the remainder of the way. Calvus was with him in a series of quick, spider-like clutchings.

"You weren't supposed to follow me," the agent said. He was breathing hard as he eyed the last stage down to the trail. They would be a hundred feet west of Gaius, where he lay in the track the allosaurus had flailed in the vegetation. "You could've gotten killed." The agent looked at Calvus. His face was still but not calm. "Could've gotten Bella killed."

The tall woman nodded. "The allosaurus crossed the ford and picked up your track an hour after you had ridden out. Sabellia said we could either draw it away from you . . . or if it ignored us, we were safe anyway. She rode, I walked." Calvus attempted a smile. "The last distance, I ran, Aulus Perennius. And then I couldn't find any way to help you."

"I need a hand," the agent said. As he crawled vertically down the rock face, he added, "Do you expect to be able to get people to die for nothing, Lucius Calvus? Is that what you expect?"

"Not for nothing," the woman said. She extended herself so that her right hand alone supported her weight and the agent's. "Aulus, this is the most important thing on Earth since life appeared."

Perennius twisted his face upward. He shouted, "Not to me! Not to Gaius and Sestius and the people *we*'ve killed!" He looked down at the trail over which he dangled. In a neutral voice he directed, "All right, let me go."

The agent hit with a clang of ironmongery. He staggered. The armored shirt and apron were even more awkward than usual. The lacework of rings had been welded into streaky patterns. They gave the garments the effect of a stiff girdle in addition to their weight.

"Aulus," Calvus said. She touched Perennius' shoulder as he would have stamped down the short interval seperating him from Gaius' remains. The agent turned, not quite willingly, to face her. Calvus' touch was no more than that; but when Perennius had shifted his weight to stride forward, his shoulder did not move nor the fingers from it. Calvus said, "Even if I were to intervene, nothing goes on forever. Not your Empire, not humanity as you know it . . . or even as I know it."

"We shouldn't intervene, then? We should let things go?" Perennius demanded harshly. "Where's the bigger joke in that, Calvus? You saying it or me listening?"

Her calm voice, her ivory face, could not express troubled emotions. Perennius felt them as surely as the hand on his shoulder as Calvus said, "Aulus, if your Empire should survive another two centuries, as it might, the cost—" She broke off to wipe sweat or a tear from the corner of one brown eye. "In my day, nothing, no difference. Events open and close, according to their magnitude. Even what I was sent to do will mean nothing when the sun swells to swallow this world."

"Praise the Sun for the life he offers," whispered the agent, an undertone and not an interpolation.

"In *my* day," the traveller repeated with emphasis. "In between, the Christian religion would become a theocracy that would last a thousand years beyond this rump of an Empire. I can't offer more than a few centuries, Aulus. It's time is *over*. *Please* understand that."

"Well then, give me the rump!" Perennius shouted. "And don't be too sure that there won't be a way out then, my friend. Or—" and his angry voice dropped into a tone of cold ruthlessness—"do you think you can force me to help finish the job? Finish *your* job. Is that what you think?"

"I think," said the woman, "that we have grown too good of friends since we met for me ever to try to force you to act. And I think we know each other too well for me ever to think I had to force you to do your duty."

"Shit," the agent said dismally. He reached out to clasp the hand still tighter against his armored shoulder.

Perennius was looking away, toward the crags across the gorge.

Still clasping his taller companion, the agent began to walk to where Gaius lay. "I don't want a thousand years of Father Ramphions, no. But I'd take that if I could give *my* world a time, a stability like that of the past. And if . . ." Perennius' voice trailed off. He took his hand from his shoulder to place his arm around the woman's waist. The play of muscles as she walked was as finely tuned as that of a dog—or a tigress. "I'd give the whole game to those fucking gray monsters if I thought it'd bring Gaius back. I almost would."

"Aulus, that won't be necessary," the traveller said.

The catch in the tall woman's voice turned the attempt at lightness into something very close to open emotion. "Gaius will live." Calvus knelt beside the fallen youth. The laces closing his helmet had not burned through the way Perennius' had. They popped audibly at a tug. Gaius' face was sallow, bloodless beneath the weathered tan of shipboard and the road. "And so will your Empire, Legate," the woman added softly. She stripped away the gorget and began breaking the tack-welded hooks and eyes that closed the mail shirt.

Gaius breathed. There was even a flutter from his eyelids each time the woman's fingers brushed his flesh. Perennius drew off the younger man's gauntlets. He said, "So that I'll go in the cave with you?"

"No, my friend," the traveller said, concentrating on the injured man before her. "Because you'd do that anyway. We thought—they thought—" and she looked at Perennius while her hands continued their gentle work of massaging Gaius' temples—"that they were sending a machine back to root out those others. . . . And perhaps they were right, perhaps it was a machine they sent back. But I'm not a machine now, Aulus. I'll do the job, because it *is* my job and my pleasure. But I'll do it my way. Now, I'm going to leave you for a moment."

Perennius nodded. He expected the woman to stand up. After a moment's surprise, he realized his mistake. Calvus was gone from him, all right, but she had retreated not into physical distance but rather into her trance state.

The agent felt a twinge of fear, as if he were walking in front of a cocked and loaded catapult. He stood up. Whatever was happening was not directed at him.

Soon enough, though, they would—he would—have to deal with the remaining Guardian and whatever lay beyond. Perennius gave a harsh laugh. He spat away the ball of phlegm that choked him. No water now to drink when his mouth was clear, and no rest for the weary. No rest for the wicked. The agent bent down to examine Gaius' prostrate form. Calvus crouched over Gaius like a mantis awaiting a victim . . . but Perennius could not save the youth, and he could not despite his habits bring himself to doubt the traveller's good faith. You did have to trust somebody else, or you would fail and everything would fail.

Aulus Perennius had no use for failure.

Calvus straightened slightly. Beneath her hand, the injured courier sighed like a child relaxing in his sleep. Gaius was still unconscious, but his normal color had returned.

"I'll need to get his armor off," Perennius said. His voice broke. Looking away, he blinked repeatedly to clear his eyes of the tears. "I've got an idea for the shirt, and I need his helmet, and greave besides."

"Take my hands, Aulus Perennius," said the tall woman. She extended them. Her fingertips were cool on the agent's palms. Even as Perennius opened his mouth to note the need for haste, the pictures began to form in his mind.

At the first, Perennius was not aware of what was happening, because the spires lit by richly-colored discharges were unlike any buildings he had seen. The agent's mind accepted the images as signs of shock or madness. He felt the same horrified detachment that would have accompanied knowledge that the ground had fallen away beneath him and he was dropping toward certain death. Then details of awesome clarity penetrated. Perennius realized that he was seeing—or being shown—something by Calvus in a medium at which the traveller had never hinted.

Gray, segmented creatures used huge machines to bathe the spires in light. In form the creatures were the Guardians that Perennius had seen and slain, but now there were myriads of them covering the ground like shrubs on wasteland and directing machinery of a scale that dwarfed them. Ripples of livid flame dissolved swathes of the creatures, but still more of them crawled out of the cracking, heaving soil. One of the spires settled like a waterfall descending. The structure's walls crumbled in sheets, spilling the figures within as bloody froth in the crystalline shards. The figures were tall, mostly quite hairless; they were as human and as inhuman as Calvus herself. The alien creatures swarmed and died and swarmed in greater numbers. Another spire began to collapse as the scene segued into—

something else in its way as alien. Men and women of proportions which the agent found normal sat one per small, eight-sided room. Perennius saw—visualized—simultaneously the individual units and the ranks and files and stacks of units comprising a whole larger than any construct he had seen, the Pyramids included. The humans had body hair and wore clothing, as did only the hirsute minority of those dying in the crystal spires of the previous scene. But though every detail of this folk's activities was evident to Perennius, he comprehended none of it. The square shafts filling the interstices between alternate facets of the octagons were in some cases filled with conduits. Many shafts provided instead vertical passage for capsules which sailed up and down without visible mechanisms. None of the humans moved more than to reach or glance toward one of the eight shimmering walls of the units which held them. Suddenly, called by an unseen signal, everyone in the structure stood and fed themselves into upward-streaming shafts. They moved with the ordered precision of cogs engaging in a watermill. And the scene blurred, shifting by increments too minute for separate comprehension to—

figures in a great barn, framed by metal webbing. Down the long bay were hauled spidery constructs. They bulked out by accreting parts attached by the lines of humans to either side of the growing machines. Everything was glare and motion. Overhead pulleys spun belts which in turn drove tools at the direction of the workmen. The noise was unheard but obvious from the way everything trembled, from motes of dust in the air to the greasy windows in the roof. It all danced in the abnormal clarity of the agent's vision. The crudity and raw-edged power was at contrast to the slickness of the scene immediately previous—and even more at contrast to the sterile perfection underlying the chaos of the initial set of images. It was evident to Perennius that he was seeing a regression, despite the unfamiliarity of the concept to a mind attuned to stasis rather than to change. The regression was evident, even before the workmen—all men—downed tools together and the vision shimmered to—

a kaleidoscope, a montage of discrete images. Imperial troops advanced across a field while their opponents fled. The wrack the defeated left behind included the standards of units the agent knew to be stationed in Britain; the paraphernalia of the barbarian mercenaries fighting at their side; and their dying leader. The sullen rain washed blood from the usurper's gaping belly and the sword onto which he had fallen.

Elsewhere—perhaps a thousand elsewheres—identical proclamations were tacked to the notice-boards of municipal buildings. Perennius recognized a few of the cities. He could have identified other settings at least by province. As many more scenes and the races of those who read the proclamation were beyond the experience of even the agent's broad travels.

And at the center, at the core, though it was no more a physical center than the melange of images was actually viewed by the agent's eyes—there, connected to all the rest by cords of documents and bureaucracy, sat a man enthroned in a vaulted hall. He ruled in state, wearing the splendid trappings which no Roman leader had been permitted save during a military procession, the diadem and gold-shot purple robes.

And the Emperor's face registered as he signed a document with a vermilion brush—

GAIUS AURELIUS VALERIUS DIOCLETIANUS

Perennius knelt on a narrow trail, holding a woman's cool hands and staring at his unconscious protégé and friend. "Almighty Sun," the agent whispered. His mind was fusing the youthful face before him with the same face on the throne marked by thirty years more of age and power. "Gaius . . ."

"I had to change him, Aulus Perennius," the tall woman said. "The shock made massive repair necessary and . . . he could not have brought the revival I promised you if he remained the Gaius you knew. I'm sorry, Aulus, there was no other tool available . . . and my time is short."

"Almighty Sun," the agent repeated. He drew a shuddering breath. "Always wanted him to be a leader," Perennius went on. He leaned forward to stroke the younger man's stubbled cheek. "Always did want that, he could be a good one." The agent's eyes met Calvus'. "Not like me. I can't lead and I won't follow. Wouldn't be room for me where you come from, would there, Lucia. That's what you were showing me."

"I was showing you a progression toward order and stability in human affairs, Aulus," the woman said. Only Perennius of all living humans could hear the smile behind her flat delivery. "The realization of the goal to which you have devoted your life."

Perennius began to laugh. He could not remember an equal outpouring of gusty humor in the past twenty years. Welds in his armor broke as he hooted and bent over despite the stiffness of his casing. Objectively, the agent realized the literal madness of the scene. At a deeper level, he felt that for the first time in his adult life, his vision was clear enough to be called sane.

"Blazes!" he gasped with his palms clasped to his diaphragm. "Blazes! Well, by the time it comes, I won't be around to get in the way, will I?"

"There's still danger," Calvus said. "One of the Guardians remains."

The agent shrugged. "It going to have any hardware beyond what the other ones did?" he asked. He had resumed his task of stripping Gaius of his armor.

"It won't use area weapons that would threaten the brood it guards," said the woman cautiously. "But Aulus, the—thunderbolts—can kill despite your armor."

Perennius blew a rude sound between dry lips. "I could

be run down by a hay cart, too," he said. "And it'd serve me right if I let something like that happen."

Perennius rose to draw off the mail shirt by the sleeves. The right sleeve showed great gaps burned in the rings by the energy channeled up the out-thrust sword. The leather insulation beneath was seared, but the vaporizing iron had protected Gaius even as it burned away. "Sure," the agent said. He was puffing a little with exertion magnified by his heavy garb. "You just keep back where you won't get hurt. In a few minutes, this'll all be over and we can both start thinking about the future."

Perennius did not notice the expression that flashed across Calvus' face as she listened to him.

The first thing Perennius used his short sword on that day was a sapling from a clump of dogwoods. The blade hacked through the base of the soft trunk and pruned the lesser limbs away with single blows. There were three larger branches splaying up to form the crown, bright with shiny leaves. The agent set each branch separately on the stump. Using the stump as a chopping block, he lopped off those upper limbs a foot above their common fork. When that task was completed, Perennius had a straight, sap-globbed pole eight feet long from its base to its triple peak.

The agent wiped his sword. That only smeared the sap further over the blade's dull sheen. He swore without heat. Too much of Perennius' being was concentrated on greater problems for him really to care about a glitch which did not impair function. "Lucia," he said, "if it's not down there—the, the Guardian—it's going to be up here. Best if you—" and he looked away as he choked back the words that wanted to come, "stayed with Gaius and Bella"; but that would endanger the mission—"got back over the rim where there's some room to move. Safe enough with the dragon gone." Perennius paused. "You're cold meat for those thunderbolts, and the armor we got wouldn't fit you well enough to help."

"It'll be down there," Calvus said, "somewhere. They're raised—engineered, Aulus—never to leave the brood without an adult until the hatching. There's only one left. That's where it will be."

"That's not the best way to protect what they've got," the agent said as he draped the extra suit of mail over the forked end of his pole. "I don't like counting on the other guy to be stupid. It's a good way to get your butt reamed."

Calvus lifted her chin in disagreement. "It isn't a matter of choice," she said, "any more than it was your choice that your right hand be dominant."

"I can do a pretty fair job with my left, too," the agent said, accepting the metaphor as a judgment.

"All right, than it's choice that you don't see with your ears!" the woman snapped. She paused as she heard herself. An expression of beatific wonder spread across her face. "Aulus," she said, "I shouldn't have been able to do that. To become angry."

"Everybody gets mad," Perennius said. This time the misinterpretation was deliberate. The agent was begging the implied question of the tall woman's humanity, because he cared enough about the answer that he was not willing to hear the wrong one. Not about a friend. Blazes, he *did* have friends, now. "Well, we'll assume you're right till we learn different," Perennius went on. He thumbed toward the rim of the gorge. "I still want you the hell out of the way."

Calvus smiled. "You'll need light when you get into the cave."

"Listen, you wander around holding a light and you're *dead*," the agent said. His anger did not flare as it normally would have, because he knew the traveller was not stupid—nor even naïve enough to be saying what he seemed to have heard. "He'll just shoot past me, won't he?"

Calvus made a globe of her hands. There was a glimmering through the chinks. The flesh of her fingers themselves became translucent. She opened her hands and a glowing ball swelled out of the hollow to spin away from the woman at a walking pace. The ball continued to expand as it rolled through the air toward the far wall of the chasm. Its smooth outlines were still visible in the daylight as it blurred into the rock a quarter mile away.

Calvus quivered and came out of her trance. "A little effort involved in that," she said, slowly turning her palms to Perennius. The skin was unmarked by the cold light, as his conscious mind had known it would be. His subconscious still could not accept the fact. "But practical at a safe distance. And you'll need the light, my—Aulus."

Perennius noted the hesitation. Sliding his own sword home in its scabbard, he said, "You were going to say 'weapon'?"

"I was going to say 'friend,'" Calvus replied.

"Well, let's go kill things," the agent said. The last word was muffled by the bronze mask. He closed it over his face and waited for Calvus to lace it shut.

CHAPTER THIRTY-THREE

Donning the face shield again was itself like entering the passageway to Hell. Perennius paced down the trail steadily, but with the caution required by the drop-off to the side. He could see very little of his surroundings in general and nothing at all of his feet. The mask eliminated normal downward vision. The way it locked to protect his throat kept him from bending his neck sharply enough to repair the deficiency. The abandon with which the agent had flung himself into the chasm initially had been required by the circumstances. It would have been out of place now. Winning in battle requires a willingness to die; but the combatant who seeks death is almost certain to find death without victory. Perennius was determined that when he got the chop, it would be because the other bastards were better—not because he himself played the fool.

Gaius' mail swayed before the agent like a banner slung from the dogwood staff. Unlike a normal banner, its shifting weight seriously interfered with balance. Every step became a doubled effort—first a motion, then a stiffening to damp the rustling iron. When the trail sloped eastward, Perennius held the shirt before him. When the trail switched back to the west, as it did twice before turning finally toward his goal, he slung the pole over his shoulder and allowed the armor to swing behind him. It was not a perfect shield, even against the first blast; but the extra armor was one more factor to concern the Guardian. From previous experience, the agent judged that the chitinous monsters did not react well to the unexpected. The fact of his own survival, however, had not made Perennius contemptuous of the thunderbolts.

The mouth of Typhon's Cavern flared upward like the wide-spread jaws of a snake. The open sky was now almost three hundred feet above the agent. As Perennius plodded forward, what remained of the dome arched overhead. The rock under his feet was smooth. Acidic ground water percolating through the limestone had dissolved away a great bubble until the roofing layer grew too thin to support its own weight. At the bottom of the cavity, the water had polished and widened the fissure through which it had drained toward the bowels of the Earth. It had formed this cave, this track to a mythical Hell . . . and to a real horror quite as fearful as the imaginary one, if Calvus were to be believed.

Perennius continued to descend carefully. Already he was beneath the level of the gorge proper, though there was no sense yet of being within a cave. It was more as if night were falling around him, darkening his surroundings without physically enclosing him. Still further beneath the agent, at the point at which the cavern did narrow significantly, was a pillared, rectangular shrine. It had no roof. The natural curve of the wall protected the chapel interior perfectly, even though that curve was fifty feet above the transom.

Perennius approached cautiously. He did not draw his sword because it took both hands to control the weight of the pole-slung armor. The shrine was leveled by a low base. The pillars were short, square, and thick. They could easily have hidden a tentacled gray form, ready to blast the agent from behind if he stalked past without examining the building.

Perennius leaned the curtaining armor against the low transom. He drew his dagger but not his sword, so that his gauntleted right fist was free. Panting with tension and effort, the agent swung between close-set pillars and into the cramped nave. His mail clashed as it brushed the stone. The sound of his heart was loud in the bronze helmet encasing his head.

There was nothing in the roofless interior, no altar or

cult objects . . . and surely no tripedal horror with glittering destruction in its grasp. The rasp of the agent's breath
resumed, covering the thump of his pulse again. Perennius
sheathed his dagger, guiding its point with his free hand
into the slot which he could not see. Almighty Sun, he
thought. The stone was dim around him and the further
descent was black as the bowels of a corpse.

So be it. The agent slipped back outside and retrieved
the dangling mail. He skirted the chapel, pausing before
he went on to glance back and see that nothing had
played hide and seek with him around the pillars. The
smoothly-curving slope continued, and Perennius followed
it.

Even in the darkness, the walls were now close enough
that he could be sure that nothing could skitter around
him unnoticed. As Perennius walked, a ball of cold saffron
light the size of his head drifted past to precede him
down the cavern. It was as if he were walking down a
giant worm-track. The cave shrank only gradually, and
none of its twists or falls were dangerously abrupt. It
continued to descend. There were dried, straw-matted
sheep droppings frequently underfoot for the first quarter
mile. After that there were none.

At the base of a slippery drop of ten feet or so, Perennius
passed a goat skull from which the horns had been gnawed,
along with most of the associated skeleton. The animal
had come further than some herdsman had been willing
to seek a member of his flock. With the light before him,
the scramble down the cavern was less dangerous for
Perennius than had been the track along the cliffside. The
pale glow drove even the cave's miniature fauna, the mice
and insects, to cover in the fissures of the walls. Without
a light which did not flicker, without the certainty that
the footing was awkward rather than dangerous, hedged
about with the myths which the light dispelled . . . It was
not surprising that few other humans appeared to have
penetrated so far into the cave.

The air wheezed. Perennius was wrapped so tightly in
his armor that his skin could not feel the brief current. It
pulsed against his pupils, however, through the tiny eye-

holes of his mask. A door had closed or opened near ahead.

Perennius was not alone in the cave; and not all hobgoblins were things of myth.

The agent had been able to walk upright to that point. Now the rock constricted again and the cave took a twist to the right. Perennius swore very softly and drew his dagger. He knelt, then thrust the slung armor ahead of him around the bend. Nothing happened. Light from the hovering globe spewed through the interstices of the armor, dappling Perennius and the walls around him.

The agent slid forward on his greaves. The eight-foot pole bound against the rock. Perennius shifted the knife to his right hand. He slammed his left shoulder against the pole. The dogwood flexed and sprang free. Perennius lunged around the corner himself as if the extra suit of mail were dragging him forward. The tip of the pole thudded into the seamless door which closed the passage. It could have been rock itself, save for the regular patterning which the ball of light disclosed. Whorls of shadow spun from the center. The background had no color but that of the yellowish light illuminating it.

And then the light slid forward, merged with the barrier, and disappeared.

The first thing Perennius did was to wedge his pole so that the armor hung across the face of the portal. He could not assume that what was a barrier to him barred also the Guardian and its weapons. Calvus had projected the agent into a world whose uncertainties went much deeper than questions of provincial governors and border security. It was easier to doubt whether or not a wall was solid than to worry about a line of defense a thousand miles away. In the case of the wall, there were precautions Perennius himself could take. If the question made the task more involuted, well, solving problems was the greatest merit in life.

The air had begun to smell stale at the instant the light was sucked away.

Perennius did not know what had happened to Calvus or the light, but he restrained his initial impulse to scramble back through the darkness. "Some effort" the tall woman had said. Perhaps it had grown too great, forcing her to pause for a moment like a porter leaning his burden against a wall. The glow might resume any time. If Perennius were running back, it would show him as a fool and a coward—after he had insisted that he was willing to go down with no light at all.

The agent picked carefully at the barrier with the point of his dagger. The surface had the slight roughness of the limestone with which it merged at the edges. Whereas the soft rock crumbled when he scraped at it, the steel had no effect whatever on the material of the barrier. Given time, Perennius could cut away the plug intact, like a miner who encounters a huge nugget of native copper in a deep mine. Given time. Even in close quarters, even blind and encased in armor whose leather padding was slimy with sweat . . .

And perhaps Calvus was a cinder blasted by the creature which now crept to eliminate the last threat. To eliminate Perennius, pinned hopelessly against the closed entrance to its lair.

The agent felt through his knees the whisper behind him which his ears could not hear for the din of blood in them.

Perennius turned. He did not shift his curtain of mail. Remembering how Gaius' spatha had caught and channeled blasts away from him, Perennius drew his own sword and advanced it toward the darkness. Sap softly resisted the steel's leaving its sheath. The blade stirred the muggy air with the odor of fresh-cut vegetation. The agent wondered if the first bolt would catapult him backwards, stunned and ready to be finished at leisure. He focused all his will down into the point of the dagger in his right hand. By the gods, he would lunge against the blue-white bolt like a boar on the spear that spitted it, determined to rend its slayer.

"Aulus," Calvus called from just around the last turning, "I needed to be closer to manipulate the barrier. I apologize for leaving you in the dark this way."

"No problem," the agent lied. "Glad you've got an answer to this wall. I sure didn't." Perennius could not find the mouth of his scabbard. His sword scraped twice on his thigh armor, then dropped to the ground so that Calvus could clutch the agent's empty hand. Her touch was firm and cooling, even through the gauntlet.

The tall woman slipped past Perennius in the narrow way. Far more awkwardly, the agent also turned. He could hear the rustle of the draped armor as Calvus reached beneath it to finger the barrier directly. "Yes . . ." she murmured. Then she slid back past the agent, a whisper in the darkness. Her fingers rested at the nape of Perennius' neck, where the gorget buckled beneath the brass of the headpiece. "Be ready, Aulus Perennius," she said.

The door pivoted inward in a hundred or more narrow wedges from its circumference. The fact and the motion were limned by the glaucous light on the other side of the portal. The door's suction pulled a draft past the agent, the reverse of the pistoning thump at his approach when it had closed. A thunderbolt lashed the sudden opening and blew a gap of white fire in the heart of the ring-mail curtain.

The end of the dogwood pole had ravelled to a tangle of fibers. They were a ball of orange flame through which Perennius leaped. His optic nerves were patterned with the white lacework of blazing iron.

Within, the ground curved away in a slope. The cavity was large and spherical and as unnatural as the bilious light which pervaded it. Packed about the interior of the chamber were translucent globules the size of clenched fists. The globules were held against the rock by swathes and tendrils of material with the same neutral consistency as that of the door itself. A narrow aisle crossed the chamber, dipping and rising with the curve to an opening in the far wall. Beyond was a glimpse of another cavity, a bead on a string and certainly not the last.

Perennius cleared the threshold in the air. He missed his expected landing because of the concavity of the floor. Globules smashed between the stone and his own solid mass of flesh and iron. Ten feet from the skidding agent, the Guardian pointed its weapon and screamed. The sound was a chitinous burring with the bone-wrenching amplitude of a saw cutting stone. The creature's weapon did not fire. The alien stood frozen as its fellow had done on the balcony in Rome. This time there was no bravo to stun Calvus and release the energy the woman's mind blocked in the weapon.

Perennius rolled to his feet. Frosty gelatine from the eggs he had crushed slurped away from his left leg and forearm. The agent had poised his dagger to throw despite the poor visibility and his constricted limbs. There was no need for him to take that risk. Two sliding steps brought him to the alien. It did not move, save that the band of cilia beneath its head quivered with its rasping scream. Perennius brought down his armored fist as if he were driving a nail with the pommel of the dagger he held. The conical head shattered. The Guardian's long waist tentacles spasmed. The energy weapon flickered out of the creature's grasp. It clattered into the layer of eggs and stuck there. The creature's braced legs did not give way, and the throat cilia continued to vibrate.

Perennius struck again. His fist was slippery and he lost the dagger at the shock. The agent could no longer see for sweat and the emotions raised by the chitinous scream. Both of his arms began to flail down into the stumpy creature. Bits of exoskeleton prodded back at the iron as the pulpy material within spattered the chamber. Perennius did not know when the screaming stopped. His next awareness was the touch of Calvus' hand on his shoulder and the way the whole world focused down to a point as his muscles gave way.

CHAPTER THIRTY-FOUR

The air in the chamber felt cool beyond the fact that Perennius breathed it without the mask's constriction. Reaction from his berserk rage could only have left him unconscious for seconds. The tall woman had already stripped Perennius of his helmet, gauntlets, and greaves.

"You have to get out of here quickly," Calvus said. She rolled the agent over on his belly unceremoniously to get at the catches closing his mail shirt. "I'm taking your armor off because it will save time over all."

"What do you mean?" the agent demanded of the floor of the aisle. He did not twist against the woman's manipulations. He accepted her good faith; and in any case, Perennius could not have resisted her if she were as serious as she appeared to be. "We're not done till we smash all the—" Calvus flopped him over again and began drawing both sleeves over his arms simultaneously—"eggs, are we?" Perennius gestured with the right hand that was cleared in that instant.

"Aulus," the woman said, "please run. I won't be able to give you light, and I want to be sure you get clear." The chamber was distinctly colder, though the frosty glow with which it had been suffused was being supplanted by a warmer hue.

"Lucia, what's going on?" Perennius pleaded. He stood up. Reflexively he wiped at ichor that had splashed his left wrist, but he did not move toward the doorway.

"I was the only kind of hardware they—we—could send back," Calvus said. She took one of the agent's hands in each of hers. Her flesh was warmer than human. "There aren't any choices now for me, Aulus. I wasn't raised for there to be any choices once I reached the brood chambers."

The tall woman swallowed, holding the agent's stricken eyes with her own. She continued, "I have no gods to pray by, my friend. But my greatest hope is that when you leave here, you will remember that you *do* have choices. I—I have enjoyed working with you, Aulus Perennius. I respect you as a tool; and I think you know me well enough by now to hear that as the praise it is. But I respect you as a man as well . . . and I have been close enough to humanity in the time I've spent with you that I—wish you the chance of happiness that tools don't have."

She bent over and kissed Perennius. Her lips were hot. The chamber swam in a rosy, saturated light like that of iron being forged.

"Goodbye, Lucia," the agent said. His sense of direction saved him as he turned and bolted for the exit. Even in the lighted brood chamber, Perennius was blinded by tears that turned images into faceted jewels.

On the scramble back through the darkness, Perennius functioned by giving himself utterly to the task at hand. It was the way he had always functioned. It worked no worse this time for the fact he had found a willingness to live in other ways. There were no side branchings. The passage was a single artery to Hell. There were stretches in which the slope jogged into what would have been rapids when rainwater foamed down the cavern. They were difficult but not impossible, even without light. Perennius had scrambled through dark buildings and light-less camps in the past, trusting the senses which remained. Those senses had preserved him from the blades of those intent on his life. The agent was exhausted, but leaving behind the sweaty burden of his armor had freed his spirit . . . and the muscles would do as the spirit demanded, as they always had.

Calvus' touch was still a memory in his flesh—but not in his mind; Perennius could not afford her in his mind until he had carried out her last injunction.

The cavern was lighted for him long before eyes which had not adapted to total blackness would have seen even a glow. Light bounced into the gorge and threw a hazy grayness down the funneled throat of the cavern. Some of it seeped further down the twisting stone pathway. Even to Perennius' retinas, the amount of light was too little to see by. But it was a brightening goal, a proof of the success he had never permitted himself to doubt.

Where the cave flared around the last major turning, the smooth stone grew light enough to have a visible pattern. Perennius threw his head up. The little chapel was in black contrast to the sky which streamed light through the open roof and past the interstices of the pillared wall. Beside the building, haloed by her back-lit red hair, Sabellia was scrambling down the path into the cave. The head of the spear she carried winked.

"Back, Bella, *back!*" Perennius called in horror. His intended roar was a gasp. His legs for the first time quivered noticeably with fatigue.

"Aulus?" the woman called. "Aulus?" Her eyes saw only a tremble of motion from the cave. Sabellia slid down a dangerous shelf of rock rather than take the path which wound around it.

"*Wait!*" cried Perennius. Unconquered Sun, Creator and Sustainer of life, give me now the strength I need. The agent lowered his head and began to run up the zig-zag path. It was easy to believe that the Sun is a god when one stumbled out of Hell. And it is easy to believe in gods when there is no longer help in oneself for one's beloved.

Sabellia could see the agent now. She paused. She had heard his command, but there was more to her hesitation than that. Something in the air was wrong. The woman switched from hand to hand the spear she had found near Sacrovir when she herself regained consciousness.

Perennius had not permitted himself to look up the slope again. It would have thrown him off-stride, and he knew full well that a stumble might be the end. "Please run, darling," he wheezed. "Please run."

Sabellia threw her hand out to grasp the agent's in welcoming and fear. She obeyed as the agent had earlier obeyed Calvus. It was a time when trust had to replace understanding. Sabellia's weapon dropped and rolled clanging toward the cave from which Perennius had come. She took the agent's hand in her own, not to hold him but to add her own fresher strength to his as they pounded up the final leg of pathway.

The air their lungs dragged in had a searing dryness to it. Perennius, to whom every breath had been fiery with exertion, did not notice the change. Sabellia's grip on his hand tensed. The base and pillars of the chapel had taken on a rosy glow from the light they reflected. The light behind the couple cast their shadows on the stone.

"*Aulus!*" Sabellia shouted.

The agent threw her and himself sideways on the ground, shielded by the squat building as a glare like that of molten steel raved from the throat of Typhon's Cavern.

Sunlight past the pillars in the other direction had been a cool white. The light which seared from the cavern now was white also, but white of a palpable intensity that made the air scream. It calcined the stone it touched. Perennius remembered Calvus' eyes and the scenes he had watched through them, the blasts ripping rock and the crawling aliens. He understood now the weapons Calvus' folk had chosen to replace the mechanical ones which had failed them against the aliens.

The gout of fire shifted from white through yellow to red, so suddenly that the intermediate step was an impression rather than a sight. The rosy glow lingered somewhat longer. It was diluted by the radiance of the cave walls themselves until they cooled. There seemed to be no sound at all until Sabellia whispered, "Aulus? Is it over?"

Perennius was carefully spreading his bare hands. Part of his mind found it amazing that the play of muscles and tendons beneath the skin proceeded in normal fashion. "Sure, it's over," he said. He did not look at his companion. "She wouldn't have failed, would she?"

"Then we can—" the woman began. She started to grasp one of the agent's hands again, but the motion stopped as her voice had when she saw his face. After a moment Sabellia resumed, "Aulus, your job is over too, then. We could . . . you know. Quintus was going to retire with me, after this mission was completed. . . ." She stared at her own fingertips, afraid of what she might see elsewhere.

Perennius laughed. He put an arm around Sabellia's shoulders. "Retire?" he said. "My, you'd make an administrator, wouldn't you?" The agent quelled the trembling of his arm by squeezing Sabellia the tighter. "I'll make a pretty good administrator too, I think. Time I got out of the field." He glanced at the burnt stone overhead and out toward the sunlit gorge in which a dragon and other things lay. They would be beginning to rot. "I'm getting too old for this nonsense."

Sabellia touched the hand on her right shoulder. "You didn't think," she said, switching deliberately from Latin to the Allobrogian dialect she shared with the agent's youth, "that you could survive the frustrations of a bureau."

Perennius laughed again. "That," he said, "was when we were losing." He stood up with the clumsiness demanded by muscles cramped in his legs and torso. "The job's still got to be done. It doesn't have to be a religion, now that I know we're going to win."

The woman took his offered hand. She was careful not to put any weight on the battered agent as she rose herself. "We?" she repeated. "You and Gallienus?"

"Civilization," Perennius said, "as I guess I was raised to mean it." He used Calvus' term "raised" in pity and in homage. The image of Gaius in imperial regalia rippled beneath memory of the traveller's calm face.

"Need to convince that Gallic kid," Perennius said as he and the woman began climbing the path, "that I didn't kill his mother. Blazes! With the things I've done, people don't need to imagine reasons to hate me."

"I thought I was coming to kill him myself," Sabellia said, looking at her hand and the agent's. "But he was lying there, so young, and I . . . If you left him alive, Aulus, I would."

The agent paused and turned the woman gently to face him. A spray of dogwood overhung the trail edge. It brushed Sabellia's hair with white flowers. "I've been making an assumption," Perennius said. "I've been assuming that you'd want to come with me. As my wife."

"Oh, thank God," Sabellia said. She stepped closer, hugging Perennius with a fierce joy.

Perennius nuzzled her red hair. When he closed his eyes, he thought he could feel Calvus watching them with a smile.

DAVID DRAKE

☐ 53616-9 BRIDGEHEAD

$3.50
Canada $3.95

☐ 53614 2 CROSS THE STARS

$2.95
Canada $3.50

☐ 53605-3 THE DRAGON LORD

$3.95
Canada $4.50

☐ 53622-3 THE FORLORN HOPE

$3.50
Canada $4.50

☐ 53620-7 FORTRESS

$3.95
Canada $4.95

☐ 53618-5 SKYRIPPER

$3.50
Canada $3.95

BESTSELLING BOOKS FROM TOR

THE BEST IN PSYCHOLOGICAL SUSPENSE

FRED SABERHAGEN